# A SWIFT *and* SAVAGE TIDE

*A Captain Kit Brightling Novel*

# CHLOE NEILL

Berkley

*New York*

BERKLEY
An imprint of Penguin Random House LLC
penguinrandomhouse.com

Copyright © 2021 by Chloe Neill
Excerpt from *Wild Hunger* copyright © 2018 by Chloe Neill
Penguin Random House supports copyright. Copyright fuels creativity,
encourages diverse voices, promotes free speech, and creates a vibrant culture.
Thank you for buying an authorized edition of this book and for complying with
copyright laws by not reproducing, scanning, or distributing any part of it
in any form without permission. You are supporting writers and allowing
Penguin Random House to continue to publish books for every reader.

BERKLEY and the BERKLEY & B colophon are
registered trademarks of Penguin Random House LLC.

Library of Congress Cataloging-in-Publication Data

Names: Neill, Chloe, author.
Title: A swift and savage tide / Chloe Neill.
Description: First edition. | New York : Berkley, 2021. |
Series: A Captain Kit Brightling novel ; 2
Identifiers: LCCN 2021022750 (print) | LCCN 2021022751 (ebook) |
ISBN 9781984806703 (trade paperback) |
ISBN 9781984806710 (ebook)
Subjects: GSAFD: Fantasy fiction. | Sea stories.
Classification: LCC PS3614.E4432 S95 2021 (print) |
LCC PS3614.E4432 (ebook) |
DDC 813/.6—dc23
LC record available at https://lccn.loc.gov/2021022750
LC ebook record available at https://lccn.loc.gov/2021022751

First Edition: November 2021

Printed in the United States of America
1st Printing

Map illustration by Cortney Skinner
Book design by Elke Sigal

I wish to have no connection
with any ship that does not sail fast,
for I intend to go in harm's way.

—JOHN PAUL JONES

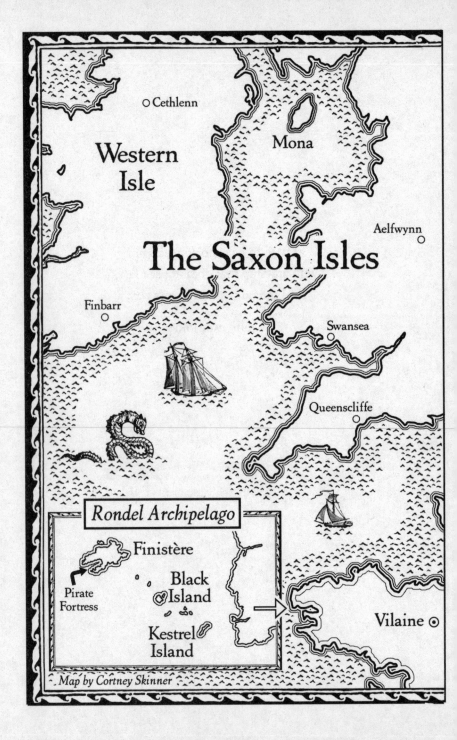

Cethlenn

Western
Isle

Mona

Aelfwynn

# The Saxon Isles

Finbarr

Swansea

Queenscliffe

## Rondel Archipelago

Finistère

Pirate
Fortress

Black
Island

Kestrel
Island

Vilaine

Map by Cortney Skinner

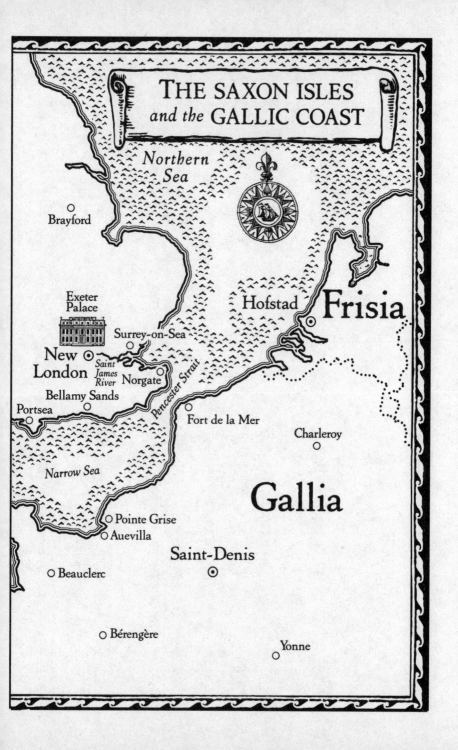

# THE SAXON ISLES
## *and the* GALLIC COAST

*Northern Sea*

Brayford

Exeter Palace

New London

Saint James River

Surrey-on-Sea

Norgate

Bellamy Sands

Portsea

*Dencester Strait*

Fort de la Mer

*Narrow Sea*

Hofstad

**Frisia**

Charleroy

**Gallia**

Pointe Grise

Auevilla

Saint-Denis

Beauclerc

Bérengère

Yonne

# PROLOGUE

War was a nasty business, but a necessary one. Or so believed the man who would much prefer to rule an empire than an island.

Gerard Rousseau had had an empire once. After nearly a decade of war against the Continent, after he'd led his armies through their villages and cities, their mountain respites and waterlogged ports, most countries had offered him obeisance.

His offer was a simple one: fealty or death.

Some chose fealty immediately; some needed to see death first. All eventually succumbed . . . until that interminable winter in Kievan Rus. If hell was real, it was not built of eternal fire, of basalt and brimstone. Hell was cold—a world frozen solid from endless gray sky to aching bone. Every breath a splinter, every small task made impossibly difficult.

And add that to damnable incompetence. He'd been refused the supplies he needed, his commanders refused to provide the necessary discipline, and the troops provided him had been too weak—or simply not clever enough—to deal with cold. He'd lost ground, men, and time.

Magic should have been his weapon and his prize—used by his Aligned soldiers to ensure victory, and gained as each victory brought more territory within his control. Magic was power, and weren't humans on the cusp of learning to command it? But his soldiers had failed him, disappointed him. He was the better commander, the better strategist, than any other on the Continent or in the Saxon Isles. But even he couldn't win a war alone.

Then it was treaties and submission and exile to the island, that insulting speck of rock and stone—and no current to speak of. For nearly a year he'd been denied what he was owed, and what any man of his will would demand.

Power. Fealty. Tribute.

A smile thinned his lips, broadened his round face. He'd made his escape right under their noses. A year of planning, of patience, of persistence, so he now stood on the deck of a ship that would carry him home. He understood his previous mistake—allowing others to get in the way of his ambition. But there would be no more hesitation, no more solicitude. The old ways of warfare would be tossed away. He would take what he wished, regardless of the cost, and rebuild a world beneath his benefaction.

Magic would be his weapon. The current—whether aetheric, ley line, or remnant of old worlds and old gods—would be his fife, his drum, his rifle, his cannon.

He closed his eyes and tipped his face to the sun, smiled at its responding warmth, which felt like sanctification.

He was emperor. And before the moon had turned, they would know it, too.

# ONE

S he despised aristocrats, save one: the damned viscount.

    Colonel Rian Grant, Viscount Queenscliffe, looked more soldier than member of New London's Beau Monde and was as honorable a man as she'd ever met.

She was no simpering miss herself, of course. Captain Kit Brightling was a member of the Queen's Own Guards and—with Grant—a new inductee into the Order of Saint James. Joining the order was both honor—appreciation for their work on behalf of their home, the Saxon Isles—and obligation—assignment to the council of the queen's closest advisers.

She and Grant had had one adventure together, uncovering a plot by Gerard to employ a magical warship. That adventure had featured one very good, and very dangerous, kiss. She hadn't expected to see him again, which was fine. Kit had no need of a viscount.

But then she'd seen his face across the palace's ballroom—just after they'd been inducted into the order—and her heart had stuttered like she'd put a hand directly into a current of magic. Broad shoulders, immaculate beneath his black tailcoat, and gleaming Hessians. He looked not unlike the roguish heroes in the penny novels she loved—the straight nose, the strong brow over eyes the color of a southern sea.

He'd strode toward her, the crowd parting around him like the sea, and offered his hand. He was taller than her, forcing her to lift her gaze. "Captain."

She thought she'd worn her uniform but, when she glanced down, found she was wearing long white gloves and a dress of pale blue-gray taffeta dotted with ivory, the sleeves capped and waist-high, as was the style. "Are we to dance?"

On cue, the players began their tune, and a waltz streamed through the ballroom.

"Only if you're brave enough," Grant said with a grin.

"I'm no coward," Kit said, and put her hand atop Grant's, even as her heart pounded. His other hand went to her waist, hers to his shoulder, and they began to move. One-two-three. One-two-three. His steps were strong and precise, his body warming the mere whisper of space between them. The fingers that skimmed her hip were hot enough to brand, as if they might sear the memory, or the connection, into her.

They couldn't have been the only ones dancing, but Kit kept her gaze on his face, on the promise in his eyes, the determination in the set of his jaw.

"You waltz tolerably," Grant said, amusement lighting his eyes.

"I waltz magnificently," she said. "A ship at sea has the same rhythm." But the sea's music was different—a thrum she felt in her bones. Kit was Aligned to it, could feel the particular magic that flowed through the waters surrounding the Saxon Isles. The magic that crisscrossed the earth, through soil and stone and under-water, deep and powerful currents that humans were trying to harness, sometimes with disastrous results.

"I wasn't sure you'd agree to a dance," Grant said as they turned a corner, Kit's skirts rustling with the motion.

She shouldn't have. She had no interest in members of the Beau Monde, with their haughtiness and pretentions. But then she'd kissed him, and that kiss had been potent as any current of magic, and it had pulled at her like the tide.

A bell struck, the sound golden and insistent.

"Is that a ship's bell?" Kit asked, as the sound—and what it signified—clawed at her attention.

"I don't hear anything," Grant said, but his voice sounded far away now, and his hands felt less substantial.

"The bell is ringing," she said, raising her voice, but the words barely audible over the din. *"I need to check on the crew!"*

But the floor undulated beneath her like the deck of a swaying ship. Water had begun to seep beneath the ballroom's closed doors, flowing toward them across the wooden floors.

"I think I should . . ." she began to say, and looked back at Grant. But he'd begun to disappear, his image beside her fading as water lapped at their feet, staining her satin slippers.

"Obligations . . ." he began, but his voice diminished to a whisper. "You must . . ."

Then the trickle was a swell, cold and dark, and covered them both.

She jolted awake, chest heaving and damp with sweat, and braced a hand on the swaying hull of the ship.

She wasn't in New London, nor in the palace. She was on her ship, the *Diana*. On the water, somewhere in the Narrow Sea.

"Bloody hell," she said, and pushed her short, dark hair from her face.

She actually had seen Grant across the ballroom after the induction ceremony. But she hadn't danced with him. The queen had called them both into her anteroom, where she and her spymaster, Chandler, had delivered the news: Gerard Rousseau, the self-proclaimed emperor who'd waged war against the entire Continent, had escaped his "prison" via fishing schooner. And, they'd come to learn, had rendezvoused with the Gallic flagship the Continental powers had allowed him to keep—the *Fidelity*.

No one doubted Gerard would return to Gallia, make his way across the country to its capital of Saint-Denis, and attempt to retake his throne. Otherwise, why leave Montgraf, the island to which he'd been exiled, and the comforts he'd been afforded there? It might have been a smaller kingdom than he was accustomed to, but it was still a kingdom.

"Search the waters for him," the queen had ordered Kit, "for the *Fidelity* and the magic he may be using. Find him before he breaks the world again. We are clever fools, Captain, and Gerard has played us all. The tide is turning, and it will turn swift and savage. We must stand before him and turn back his charge. The world depends on it."

The queen had ordered Grant to the Continent, to resume his prior work as an observation officer, and the *Diana* had been provisioned. That had been two weeks ago, and she hadn't seen New London—or Grant—since.

At twenty-four, Kit understood the ways of romance, and she wasn't one to pine over a man. Certainly not a viscount. But the fire ignited by seeing him across the ballroom—the unexpected shock of it, the exhilaration of it, and the discovery that she needed to see him again—hadn't diminished in the intervening weeks. It had left her feeling hollow in some deep inner corner of her heart that had never been opened before.

Etchings of Gerard's warship had been shown to the crew as the *Diana* flew across the Narrow Sea between Gallia and the Saxon Isles, a predator seeking its prey. They'd skimmed the coast within the blockade set by larger Isles ships, searching for Gerard . . . and waiting for war to begin.

The dreams, stark and disturbing, had begun when they'd sailed into the Narrow Sea, which separated the Saxon Isles from the Continent. Its magic—which had once flowed steady and true—now fluctuated, as if the current of power was whipping about in the depths of the water.

Kit thought she knew why: Gerard's loyalists had built a new kind of warship at Forstadt, on the shore of the Northern Sea, and in doing so they'd nearly destroyed the Northern Sea's current. The *Diana* hadn't sailed so far north this time, so either the Narrow Sea's magic was seeping north to fill the void, or Gerard's people had done more damage to the current in the interim. Kit didn't know. But there was little doubt now that human activity was behind it.

Whatever the reason, the twisted magic—and the dreams wrought by it—had wrapped around her apparent desire for Grant like the tentacles of a kraken. They'd become a leviathan that stalked her sleep.

The bell stopped ringing, but a fist on the door of her cabin replaced the cacophony of noise.

"A moment!" she called out, willing herself awake to face gods knew what awaited her outside.

Kit closed her eyes—shutting out the sight of her cabin and

the sea beyond—and reached down for the current. Past dark, cold water, the glimmer of light fading as she felt, deeper yet, for the silver cord of magic that surged through the water.

Some called the currents ley lines; others believed they were remnants of the old gods, spots where they'd touched the earth and left behind the fingerprints of their great and terrible power. Whatever their origin, they were tributaries of power, spread unevenly across the world and ever moving, ever swaying, like anemones in the tide.

The current may have been thin here, less a cord of magic than a shadow of it. But it was, at least, a connection to the sea, to her magic, to whatever in her birth had linked her soul to this place. That comforted her, gave her energy enough to throw her legs over the side of her bunk, pull on her thin night rail, and stride across wooden planks to the door.

She opened it, had to lift her gaze to the dark eyes of the tall, lean man who looked down at her with humor. Jin Takamura was her second-in-command. An officer by commission, but a thief by aptitude. Behind him, sailors scurried through the passageway. The watch bell had signaled the change of shift.

Jin's expression was mild; it wasn't the first time he had woken her. "Captain."

"Commander. What's happened?"

He cocked his head at her, a smile in his eyes. "What will happen if I suggest you look like you've been dragged by sea dragons for a few hundred fathoms?"

That he'd asked the question signaled there was no immediate threat to her crew, so she let herself breathe.

Kit grunted, pulled the thin night rail tighter. The briny air that blew down the companionway from the deck was bracingly chilly. "I will suggest you are perilously close to insubordination."

"Fortunately, I can walk a very narrow line." As if to prove his point, he lifted a foot and balanced on a single plank of decking.

"Hilarity." She paused. "I had another dream."

His brow furrowed. "The rising sea?"

Kit nodded. The plot of the dreams varied, but that was a common theme. "Report, please."

"It pains me to say this," he began, looking slightly mortified, "but we believe we've spotted the *Fidelity* in port."

"Port?" Kit asked. "Where are we?"

"Four miles offshore from Auevilla, to the west of the Touques and the docks."

Kit lifted her brows at the speed. The *Diana* didn't stop sailing—and the crew didn't stop working—just because she slept. She was sailed without pause, through changing shifts of sailors and officers. But she hadn't expected them to make such progress along the Gallic coast overnight.

"Steady wind," Jin offered, apparently reading her surprise. "And your very good crew, of course."

"Of course," Kit said, and recalled what she knew of the landscape here. The Touques flowed to the Narrow Sea just east of Auevilla, and the village's docks were located in that conjunction.

"What would Gerard be doing in Auevilla?" she asked. It was a Gallic town of gambling, turf races, fine cuisine, and seaside strolling—not military offices or barracks. The Beau Monde had adored it before the war and had returned when the conflict was over. "I'd enjoy a stroll in Auevilla," she muttered.

"So say we all. And we don't know if he's still there, only that there's a ship."

"Who found it?"

Now Jin paused. "Mr. Wells."

Kit rolled her eyes. "This is the eighth time he's spotted the *Fidelity* since we left New London. The last two weren't even ships."

"In fairness," Jin said with a smile, "one was a ship-shaped island. And, if I was the type to speak freely, I'd suggest the captain ought not have offered a piece of gold for the sailor who finds it. It tends to encourage . . . hopefulness."

Kit just looked at him. "But you'd never speak freely to your captain without leave."

There was a damned twinkle in his eye. "Of course not. I have a wife and children at home, and they'd prefer I not be forced to walk into the sea."

Kit sighed again. "I'd rather be bothered with an error than miss the ship. I'll dress. Hold us steady."

"Always," Jin said, and she closed the door again.

# TWO

K it cleaned and dressed herself as well as she could in the watery light of dawn. Her uniform nearly matched Jin's: fitted navy tailcoat over buff trousers; dark and gleaming boots; and the sabre. But there were epaulets on her shoulders, and the fading bit of ribbon pinned inside her coat. It was a pale blue silk with gold embroidery, and the only physical memento that existed of her foundling past, before Hetta Brightling had brought her into the Brightling House for Foundlings and given her a family.

She'd considered adding the small diamond pin of the Order of Saint James but thought the diamonds a bit much for the *Diana*.

She pulled a brush through her chin-length hair, pinched her pale cheeks to add color against her gray eyes. She wasn't vain, or no more than an average woman of four-and-twenty, but she had her own role to play. The deck was her stage, and better that she didn't look like she'd been dragged unwillingly from a dream.

When she opened the door again, she nearly ran into Cook—

name and occupation—who stood outside it with a delicate cup and saucer and a dour expression.

"To break your fast, sir," he said, and made a very poor curtsy.

"Early in the morning for sass, is it not?" But she was comforted by Cook's reliability—and the tea. Hetta had instilled ten Principles of Self-Sufficiency into her adopted daughters. Number Six was, perhaps, the most important: There is always time for tea. It wasn't really about the tea, of course—although every self-respecting Islesian appreciated a good cup—but the ritual.

So she took the cup and saucer with a smile and climbed the narrow stairs that led to the deck. The remaining wisps of her mental fog were cleared by the crisp breeze and pink glow of sunrise.

Kit looked up into the forest of lines, wood, and rigging that made up the *Diana*'s engines. She was a topsail schooner: 129 feet of oak and tar, with square sails on the foremost of her two masts. Everything looked trim and tidy.

Jin waited at the helm beside the ship's large wheel with the *Diana*'s navigator, Simon Pettigrew. The latter, who had dark brown skin and shorn dark hair, wiped a smudge from his round spectacles with an immaculate handkerchief. They were forever getting spotted by seawater.

"Mr. Pettigrew," Kit said, and sipped her tea. It was perfect, which was one of the primary reasons she allowed Cook, with his expansive use of sass, to continue to feed the *Diana*. That, and his liberal use of spices and herbs. The food she'd grown up with, while nutritious, hadn't been nearly as flavorful. The Brightlings' housekeeper, Mrs. Eaves, "didn't take with flavor."

"Do let us know when you're ready, Captain."

She sipped again, watched Simon over the rim of her cup, and drained it. She put the cup and saucer on the steering cabinet behind the wheel, atop the maps Simon had spread there, and straightened her jacket. "If you've been taking career advice from Jin, you ought to reconsider that decision."

Simon grinned at her. "I'd consider no such mutiny," he said, and pointed to a spot on the map. "Our position."

Kit confirmed, nodded. "Let's hear about the ship."

They strode down the *Diana*'s deck, the ship now heavier with the bulk of the two eight-pound cannons installed at the gunwales before they'd left New London. A clutch of sailors stood near the foremast, including Tamlin McCreary, the *Diana*'s watch captain, the curls of her long red hair waving around her pale and delicate face. She nodded at Kit, whistled a shanty as the ship's bosun, Mr. Jones, pulled off his well-worn cap with suntanned hands.

"Apologies, Captain," Jones said. It was his job to oversee the work of the seamen. "Wells here believes he's found the *Fidelity*."

Kit looked at the young sailor, who she recalled had just reached sixteen years and hadn't yet lost the knobby knees of childhood. There was sheepishness in his expression, an amulet for luck around his neck, and determination in his eyes. "What did you see, Mr. Wells?"

"Go on then, lad," Jones said, nudging him with an elbow. "Tell the cap'n."

"There's a big blue ship among the brigs at dock, sir. Three masts."

There were groans from the assembled crew.

"Every Jack knows the *Fidelity* is white as a Western whale," another sailor called out. There were murmurs of agreement.

Gerard might have ordered the ship repainted to avoid easy identification. The admirals, the queen had thought, believed Gerard was too arrogant to alter his flagship. But it wasn't the first time Kit had disagreed with the admirals.

Kit looked back at Mr. Wells. "Why do you think you've seen the *Fidelity*?"

"It's got—" He paused, obviously uncomfortable, and looked at Jones, cleared his throat. "Well, Captain, sir, the thing is . . . It's got a very wide arse."

The deck erupted with laughter.

Jones bumped him hard with a shoulder. "Stern, boy. A wide stern. Apologies, Captain."

"No apologies necessary," Kit said. "And there's nothing wrong with having a wide . . . stern."

Kit extended a hand. Without a word, Simon pressed a brass spyglass into her hand. She extended it, sunlight gleaming against metal, and held it to her eye, swinging the lens across the beach to the docks. Then she scanned the forest of masts and rigging of the ships anchored there until she settled on the wide blue boat.

"On the end there?" Kit asked.

"That's it, Captain," Wells said with enthusiasm. "That's the one."

The harbor curved, and the ships were docked at an angle, so even at this distance she had a decent look at the ship's lay. "Brig," Kit said. "Three masts, square-rigged. I can't count the guns, but more than a dozen. It's decidedly the wrong color. And there's no lion on the bow." The *Fidelity* was known for its roaring-lion figurehead; this ship had none at all, which was unusual for a vessel of its size. And the lack made the bow look, well, wrong.

Gerard had a thing for lions and symbols, but it wasn't difficult to imagine him directing it to be removed to enhance the illusion.

She surveyed the ship thrice over while the crew waited in silence, anticipation building and putting a nervous energy in the air. When that review was done, she lowered the glass, offered it to Jin. "The stern," she told him.

Her sailors remained silent, only the creak of wood and hemp cutting through the thick of it. After a moment, Jin looked at her, nodded. And there was a spark in his dark eyes.

"How many coppers have exchanged hands?" Kit asked, and sailors made busy—whistling, tightening lines, spit-buffing brass.

"Good," she said, "as betting is expressly forbidden by the Isles' Articles of War." But she reached into her coat, fingers brushing the ribbon pinned there, and pulled out a gold coin. "Who said it wasn't the *Fidelity*?"

After a clearing of throats, most hands were raised.

"In that case, I believe this goes . . ." She felt the building anticipation, and let it build. Much of sailing involved monotony, cold and damp, and staring at the empty horizon and willing something—anything—to appear. ". . . to Mr. Wells."

There was a moment of utter shock, and then yells of victory rang out across the deck. Wells's eyes were wide as Kit offered him the gold coin.

"We can't be absolutely certain until we're closer, and we can't guarantee Gerard is still in port. But I've seen the *Fidelity*, and there's no mistaking its . . . stern. Well done."

"Thank you, sir. Just—thank you!" Before Kit could react, he grabbed her hand, pumped it. "Thank you."

"You're welcome." She turned her gaze back to the port. "Let's go find him."

Kit was impatient, and she knew she wasn't the only one. Every sailor in the Crown Command wanted to find Gerard before he brought more death and destruction. But she knew finding the *Fidelity* was only the first step. With more than two weeks of lead time, Gerard might have abandoned the ship and could be hundreds of miles away. She forced herself to think slowly, methodically, and not rush to judgment or action.

They sailed in closer, staying west of the port to reduce the odds of their being seen—or considered a threat—by the Gallians undoubtedly watching the coastline. But that was still close enough for Kit to feel the shift of magic as it roped toward the shore. She stood at the bow now, eyes closed and hair flying about her chin, the salt of sea air joined by the scents of green things that signaled proximity to land.

She felt nothing different in the current here than she had a few miles out, nothing that suggested some magical experiment on the *Fidelity* or in the boats at the harbor. Of course, that didn't preclude illegal activity onshore. Use of the current had been banned in Gallia, just as in the Isles, but the taboo was only as strong as the community mandated.

She wasn't Aligned to land, but she'd see how far she could stretch her connection. She clenched her hands into fists, forced herself to follow the line of current through the water and into the liminal space where sea and shore battled for control. It was fainter here, and she had to concentrate to distinguish it from her own heartbeat. But it was there—not stripped away by some malignancy of Gerard's—and didn't seem obviously perturbed.

She opened her eyes again, nearly jumped when she found Tamlin standing beside her. "Good gods, woman. Have a care."

"I was watching you," Tamlin said. "You're very entertaining. Your face scrunches up when you listen for the magic. How runs the sea?"

Kit often thought Tamlin's mind was too nimble for her own good. "Thin, but even. Not bothered by Gerard." Yet, she silently added.

Tamlin nodded, turned her face into the breeze. She was said to be Aligned to the wind, but Tamlin also seemed to experience the world differently than others. Whatever its origin, Tamlin knew the wind and the knowledge it carried better than any other sailor in Kit's acquaintance.

"Anything in the wind?"

"Motes of something."

"'Motes of something'?"

Tamlin wiggled her fingers. "Motes. Like bubbles in the current's path, aye?"

"Someone is touching the current?"

"No, that's not nearly enough. I can't feel any change when you do that. Using the current for something." She looked toward the coast. "There, on land. Not great magic. Not Contra Costa," she said quietly. "Just enough to make it flex a bit."

"On land?" Kit repeated. "So much for the ban." Who was playing with that particular fire, Kit wondered, and at what cost for the rest of them?

"Best way to ensure a person does something is to tell them not to do it," Tamlin said.

Unfortunately, she wasn't wrong.

Kit returned to the helm, told them about the magic.

"We could sail back to Portsea or to the blockade line," Jin suggested. "Signal we've found the *Fidelity* and need more ships."

Portsea was an Islish harbor town almost directly north of Auevilla; it was the primary port of the Crown Command's naval forces. Dozens of ships were berthed there, protected from high seas by Wihtwara, an island to its immediate south.

Kit wished they had time to wait for more sailors, soldiers, cannons, but it simply wasn't possible. "We cannot risk it," she said. "If Gerard is gone, the firepower is unnecessary. If he's still there, he'll certainly run when the armada is sighted, and we'll lose him. We have a chance now to find him, and we have to take it."

"And if we find him?" Phillips asked.

"He has violated the terms of his release. We take him to Portsea."

"Not New London?" Phillips asked.

"The captain doesn't want Gerard any closer to the queen than necessary," Jin explained.

Kit nodded her agreement. "We'll begin at the docks. If he's still on the ship, just as well. If he's not, sailors will know more than anyone about where he's gone. Since they'll be speaking Gallic, so must we." Kit, being a child of Hetta Brightling, was nearly fluent.

Jin's smile fell away, and Kit knew the long-suffering sigh and parental expression. "I will not be leading the landing party," he surmised. He didn't speak Gallic.

Kit knew Jin preferred she stay safely aboard, minding the ship, while others faced the danger. But these were uncertain times, and she wouldn't force others to take that risk. More, she trusted Jin more than anyone with the *Diana*.

In response, Kit reached out, squeezed his arm. "I need you here. *She* needs you." She—the *Diana*, both ship and crew.

Then she turned her gaze back to the crew. "Who speaks Gallic?"

No hands were raised until Midshipman Cooper lifted hers. "I do, sir. Or enough to know what I'm about."

"But does anyone else know what you're about?" Lieutenant Sampson asked, and laughter rolled across the deck.

Cooper cocked her head at him. "At least, unlike you, they won't smell me coming."

More laughter and groans, and a friendly handshake between them. Cooper was new to the crew but was coming along nicely, Kit thought.

"I'm not interviewing a governess," she reminded them, "but a sailor. Passable will do, as long as you can swear." An essential skill for any sailor, to Kit's mind.

Cooper's smile was broad. "Oh, aye, Captain. That I can." She threw out a curse that involved a man, a burlap sack, and a very dirty goat.

"Inventive," Kit said with approval. "Fancy a trip onshore?"

⌣⌢

Kit abandoned her uniform tailcoat for a shabbier version made by Georgina, one of her younger sisters. Kit had paid in contraband sweets usually barred from Brightling House, or at least the ones that hadn't already been pilfered by her other sisters. Even Louisa, the newest Brightling and a former stowaway on the *Diana*, had been instructed in the art of chocolate thievery.

As for the coat, one never knew when a change of attire—or a costume—might be needed. The trousers would still be unusual— most women chose to wear the high-waisted dresses currently in fashion—but less so than her captain's uniform.

She'd left her cabin door open while she changed jackets, was pulling off her waistcoat when Jin stepped into the doorway.

"May I?" he asked.

"Of course," Kit said.

Jin came in, closed the door. She hung her waistcoat on a wall peg beside the tailcoat, then looked back at him—and saw the concern in his eyes.

"What's wrong?" Kit pulled on the jacket, rolled her shoulders. The fit was awkward, as it should have been for a poorly made garment, but she could still move.

"This is dangerous."

"It's just a jacket, Commander."

But that didn't make him smile as she'd intended.

"I know," Kit said, tone kinder now as she transferred her ribbon to the interior of this jacket's lapel. "I don't know what we'll find, Jin. I don't know if we'll find Gerard, or his lieutenants, or an army amassing outside the city wall. But I'm the only member of this crew with the authority to do something about it."

"Finistère was nearly a tragedy."

She went still, looked up at him. She'd gone ashore in Finistère, too, that time with Watson, Sampson, and Grant, to rescue a heroic Islish spy being held by the pirate cabal known as the Five.

"If you'll recall, we rescued Marcus Dunwood from Finistère," she said. "I'd do nothing different if I had to do it over again." Except find him faster, she silently added. Remove him from the pirate fortress and its filthy, waterlogged dungeon quickly enough that his illness could be effectively treated, so they wouldn't have been forced to give his body to the sea. But there was nothing to be gained in dwelling on it.

"Aye," Jin said. "But—"

She cut him off. "How many languages do you speak?"

He blinked. "Seven."

"And how many of those languages are Gallic?"

"None," he said after a moment, as if he'd had to pry loose the admission.

"And that's why I must do this myself. If we don't want to be labeled as spies, we must speak the part. I can speak Gallic—and act it, if Hetta's teachings are to be believed—and that's the best chance we have to find him. Needs must, Jin." She cocked her head at him. "You're terribly impertinent today."

He brushed back his long, dark hair. "I miss my girls. It's only been a few weeks, I know. But the time and distance feel longer now. We're on the cusp of something, and it feels as if even true north has been realigned."

"I know," Kit said. "I feel it, too."

He sighed. "And, if I'm being honest, I was truly hoping for some good Gallic wine."

Kit's lips curved. "I suspect I can help with the wine. And I'm going to do my best to prevent the war and keep us on the right side of that cusp."

"You'll need a story if you're to play strangers jaunting around a Gallic town."

"I doubt we'll be jaunting, but I was planning on 'sailors on shore leave.' It's simple and elegant, and we can both prove our sailing knowledge if necessary."

"Not in those boots."

Kit looked down. "These are Crown Command boots. The queen's boots."

"They're impeccable. Which is rather the problem." He narrowed his eyes. "Which, of course, you already know."

"I am the captain," she said, and opened her trunk, pulled out a pair of worn and marked leather boots.

"Been mucking stalls, have you?"

"Not recently," she said, and sat down to switch them out. "But Georgina may have. She found them for me." Possibly from the stables at the edge of Moreham Park, which stretched across Francis Street in front of Brightling House. Unlike Kit, Georgina Brightling had an affinity with horses.

Kit had a war.

"Twelve hours," Jin said as she changed her footwear, "and I'm sending in someone to find you."

Even without a segue, Kit understood the grim concern beneath his pronouncement: how long they ought to wait before assuming the away crew had been captured or killed.

"Forty-eight," Kit said. "We may need time to make the necessary contacts."

He just looked at her.

"Thirty-six," Kit said. "But don't send in a team. Sail back to the line and alert the fleet. Let them come."

"Twenty-four," Jin said.

"Fine."

"And wine," he said again. "As many casks as the boat will

carry. And bread, if you can manage it. The Gallians do make a fine loaf."

Kit made a little bow. "Shall we also bring cassoulet and petit fours to finish the meal?"

"Needs must," Jin said, echoing what she'd told him. Then he offered a hand, pulled her to her feet. "I'm impertinent because I care."

"I don't report your insubordination because I know it." She put a hand on his shoulder. "I'll be careful, as will you, because that's who we are. And if the mainmast has so much as a scratch upon its well-tarred surface when I return, you'll be reviewing the receipts for the next five voyages."

He shivered. "Cruel, Captain. Very cruel."

"Never forget it. Let's away."

They lowered the jolly boat, a small vessel stowed on the *Diana*'s deck. Kit assigned Mr. Sampson, easily the strongest member of the crew, to captain the boat. His eyes lit when Kit selected him.

"There will be no coin," she said, and that smile went bashful.

"A sailor never knows," he said philosophically. "Found a bit at the pirate fortress, didn't I? Sorry, Captain," he added, probably seeing the grim look on her face.

"It's no matter," Kit said. When the jolly boat touched the water, she pulled a gold coin from her coat, pressed it to her lips. "*Dastes*," she said, offering a thanks to the sea in the old language, and tossed it overboard. Gold found; gold returned to the deep and whatever gods still lived there.

And, gods willing, luck in exchange.

# THREE

They went ashore as far from the dock as they could manage, landing on the sandy beach where gentlemen and ladies strolled in gleaming boots and fine frocks, the ladies with angled caps or feathers bobbing in their hair. They'd move toward the docks on foot.

"Those are awfully nice gowns to douse in saltwater," Cooper said, when she and Kit had jumped into knee-deep water, grabbed ropes to haul the jolly boat into the dun-colored sand.

"I suspect the women who can afford those fabrics aren't obliged to clean them," Kit said.

The sand sucked at their boots when they reached the water's edge, and Kit had to pause as the world shifted. She'd been on board, on the water, for two weeks.

"Alignment?" Cooper asked beside her.

Kit nodded. "I'll be fine. Just takes a moment for the world to settle again." For Kit to accustom herself to the vacuum created by the loss of her connection to the sea, to the absence of the whisper that was her near-constant companion on board. It was as if total silence had fallen over a boisterous crowd.

After a moment, she looked at her sailor. "You're Aligned, aren't you, Cooper?"

She nodded. "To the land, sir, but it's particular to the Isles." She looked toward the shore, disappointment on her face. "I don't feel anything here."

"Alignments are particular," Kit said, "and each in its own way." She looked back at Sampson. "Be careful and be smart."

"Always, Captain. *Tiva koss*," he said. It was literally "gods' kiss" in the old language, and a hope that you'd be protected by the gods as you faced your enemies.

"*Tiva koss*," Kit said, turning toward the town and rolling her shoulders against the jacket's thick seams; Georgina hadn't spared Kit the experience of wearing a poorly fitting garment.

"Let's go," she told Cooper. "From here on, we speak only Gallic. But stay quiet unless I signal you."

"*Oui*," Cooper said.

They made their way through shifting sand toward the town's frontage, which lay a hundred yards away from shore. If the strollers found anything odd about the sight of them, they made no sign of it.

There were small cottages on this bit of sea, bathing houses where women could enjoy the water—as long as they remained swathed in voluminous bathing dresses. Being a sailor, thanks to the gods, gave Kit an excuse to swim in much less constricting attire. If she opted for attire at all.

When they reached a main road, they turned toward the river. Buildings lined the road, each grander than the last and painted in brilliant pastel shades. The shops were small but lively. Doors were open, with merchants doing brisk business. People filled the roads, gathering necessities or foods for dinner. Auevilla hadn't been spared during the war, but you couldn't tell it here. Kit deemed it a pretty, pleasant sort of town and, with its options for gaming and horses, could understand the appeal.

The sounds and colors changed when they reached the dock. Every quay was different, but the sounds and smells and activities were similar regardless of the location. Creaking rope and calls for crew and larks seeking customers. The air smelled of tar and wood and bodies at work and whatever foodstuffs the nation's sailors preferred. Here, the yeasty scent of bread was a lusty note beneath the others.

Kit pulled a silver coin from her coat. "Buy us some bread," she said in Gallic, and gestured toward the man who sold demi-baguettes from a basket under his arm.

"Sir?" Cooper asked, and took the coin.

"We're merely a pair of hungry sailors, walking the dock as we wait for our ship." The aroma was too tempting to pass up. But it would also add to their disguises, which might prove necessary given the burly guards who moved among the workers. They weren't in uniform, but their roving eyes and careful movements—avoiding the weapons tucked into trousers and boots—signaled their military connections. So there were soldiers in Auevilla, Kit thought, and kept a wary eye on them. Enemies, she knew, until proven otherwise.

Cooper strode to the bread man, did just enough haggling to come back with a pair of loaves. She handed one to Kit, tore a chunk off the other, and began chewing.

"Don't bother waiting for me," Kit said with a smile.

Cooper grinned over her mouthful. "When food's at issue, sir, I rarely wait.

"It's very . . . chewy," she decided.

Kit took a bite, smiled with pleasure. "That's part of its charm."

They walked down the wooden dock toward the *Fidelity*'s berth, passing a dozen ships with sterns both narrow and wide. There were smaller ships that probably fished the coastline, and wider vessels with deeper drafts that hauled cargo across the Narrow Sea—or would have, before the blockade.

A man with a copper chit pinned to his threadbare coat, his license for begging, sat against the wooden planking that held up the road behind the boardwalk. He had one leg, the empty trouser leg folded over. Maybe a veteran of the war, Kit thought. And given the rope-calloused hands, likely a sailor. The war had been unkind to so many, and in the year since, the treaty had only perpetrated its violences. Soldiers and sailors alike bore scars both physical and emotional.

"Hungry?" she asked in Gallic, and pulled away half the loaf.

He nodded wordlessly, took it, and ate with a speed that had sadness and fury battling in her gut. She pulled a silver coin from her pocket, put it in the tin cup at his feet.

"For your next meal," Kit said. "From one sailor to another."

The man's eyes widened. He nodded. "*Dastes*," he said, using the old language instead of Gallic, and slid the coin from cup to pocket.

They walked on, both nibbling their baguettes as they dodged sailors.

"Captain," Cooper said, and Kit followed the direction of her gaze.

Hanging over the doorways of buildings along the road were

narrow linen banners bearing the image of a golden lion circled by stars. This was the symbol of Gerard's rule—a symbol the king had banned from Gallia after Gerard had been exiled.

"He's been here," Cooper said.

"Or word has spread that he's escaped, and there are supporters in town." She knew he wouldn't get the same greeting in every village—not the ones where boys had died in droves, farms had burned, and the king had repaired what could be fixed. But any such animosity had apparently faded here.

How much of the town's business, Kit wondered, was because of Gerard? Because the possibility of war, or the preparations for it, had brought coin back into the village?

They reached the area of the dock where larger ships were berthed, found a half dozen at anchor. Among them was a gorgeous ship of ivory with SIMONE in gold across her stern. She was being loaded for departure, either to deliver goods up the Gallic coast or in the hope of running the Isles blockade. More likely the latter, as the possible return on the risk would be significantly higher. Smuggling simply paid better.

"A handsome ship," Kit said to a man who looked to be supervising the loading. "Good captain?"

"You'll not find another captain so good," the man said. "You!" he called out to one of the workers. "Lift that line, you lazy mongrel!"

"Is there work for those who aren't lazy mongrels?" Kit asked.

"Aye," the man said, and looked them over. "We're to attempt the blockade and make a run to Akranes. Captain's in the inn. He wants to speak to all personally. Mention you talked to me; it will smooth the way."

Kit pulled out a copper, offered it. "Thank you."

The man took the copper, slipped it into his pocket.

Having reinforced their cover story, they resumed their journey down the dock to the final berth and the wide-arsed ship that filled it.

She was undoubtedly the *Fidelity*. With multiple decks and gilding that no one had dared paint over, she was big, bold, and brash enough for a former emperor.

Kit's heart thudded with the thrill of success, and she had to work to keep her expression bland. She made a point of chewing as she looked it over, just as a sailor might have done, considering the size, the cannons, the enormous span of windows across what was likely the captain's cabin—probably four times as large as hers—and the awkward bow.

"The figurehead was definitely removed," Cooper said, tossing up a crumb of bread to a jackgull. "If you look at an angle, you can see where the brackets were. The holes were filled, but not very well."

Kit took a closer look, nodded. "Good eye, Midshipman." And those in charge of the renovation, such as it was, had failed to remove the long, horizontal lines of molding that ran just below the ship's gunwale. It had been painted, of course, but there was a story behind those lines that even color could not erase.

Kit spotted two guards near the ship, which wasn't nearly the number she'd have expected if Gerard was still on board.

One of the guards called out, approached them. "If you don't have business here," he said in Gallic, "be on your way."

"We're just taking a stroll until our ship departs, aye?" Kit said, and chewed. "This is a big lass. Don't recall seeing her before."

"New, ain't it? Been in port two days."

So recently, Kit thought. What had the ship been doing in the meantime? Or, more important, where had it been?

Kit made a point of looking at the *Fidelity*, seeming impressed by its size. "Helmed by a fancy sort, aye? With coin to spare?"

"None of my business, is it?" His eyes narrowed at her. "What damned business is it of yours?"

Kit settled her face into surprise. "Touchy, aren't you?" She held out what remained of her half of the baguette. "You need a bit to eat?"

"No, I don't want your damned bread," he said.

She gave him a level stare. "Not especially friendly in Auevilla, are they?"

"No," Cooper said. "Rather antagonistic."

"A woman's got a right to look at a good ship and inquire if there's coin to be had."

"There's no coin, and no berths, for nosy women," he said. "Get on with you."

Something more here, Kit thought. Keeping her gaze on him, she bit off another strip of bread. "You're my mum, now? Giving me orders?"

He turned fully toward them, hand at his belt and the dagger tucked there. "I'm the man's in charge of this dock. Move off, or you'll be moved."

"Not friendly at all," Kit muttered. "Come on, Yvette. Let's 'move off.'" She rolled her eyes dramatically.

"Where to?" Cooper asked. "I've some coin to spend."

"Looks like there's an inn just there," Kit said, pointing toward the main road and speaking loud enough for the guard to hear her. "Let's get what food we can before we board. Gods know we'll be eating hardtack soon enough."

She tossed the final bit of bread into the air. A jackgull dropped, snatched it midair before circling toward the masts again. All apparent ease, Kit dusted the crumbs from her hands. But she knew they'd drawn attention to themselves and were running out of time. They climbed up toward the main road in silence, and Kit worked very hard to ignore the itch in her shoulder blades and not glance behind her to see if they were being followed.

When they reached the main road, the scents of saltwater and working bodies gave way to horses—Kit never had met a horse she could abide, damn their evil souls—and the rank smells of humans living in close proximity. Two officers stood together at a corner, bodies close enough that Kit surmised they were sharing information they preferred to keep secret from others. Then the taller man turned, giving Kit a clear view of his face.

Kit stopped—and felt cold settle into her bones.

A complex web of scars marked the right side of his face, but there was no mistaking the hard line of his jaw or the malice in his deep-set eyes. Only a few feet away stood the only man who scared her more than Gerard Rousseau. The only man who, to her mind, was more dangerous. A man who was supposed to be dead.

"La Boucher," she murmured.

The Butcher.

His given name was Alain Doucette. He wasn't just an enemy, one of the thousands who'd tried to seize the Continent for their own glory, but a soldier with a powerful Alignment. A man who could access the current, and had done so to hurt others.

Doucette was a former Gallic army officer, and his unit of Aligned soldiers had helped him do the unthinkable, the seemingly impossible. At Contra Costa, a town in Hispania, they'd dragged the current to the surface, where Doucette hoped he could use it—the magic itself—as a weapon. But he'd been unable to control it, and thousands of soldiers had died in the resulting inferno, including Doucette.

Or so the Isles believed.

She'd only seen him once, years before Contra Costa, across the deck of the Gallic ship attempting to breach the Isles' defenses and make a landing at Faulkney. She'd watched as he'd whipped a boy who hadn't been fast enough with a spark. The sailor had barely been out of leading strings, and there'd been a sickening satisfaction in Doucette's eyes. He'd escaped capture that night, and every other time the Isles had tried to end his reign of terror.

Contra Costa had only been the last of his atrocities. Or so Kit had thought, as here he was in Auevilla and not rotting in hell as he ought to have been, his scars the only visible mark of what he'd done. He wore gloves, and she wondered if his hands bore the same marks.

The gloves matched his ivory uniform, which marked him as one of Gerard's imperial guards—a significant promotion over the position he'd held during the war. The jacket bore enough braid and medals to add half a stone to his weight. Both were a damned insult to every sailor and soldier in uniform, and one that she took very personally.

Brave of him to wear the uniform of a dethroned emperor, wasn't it? And a direct insult and threat to the reigning king. Kit guessed the pennants meant he had some protection against the obvious treason. Saint-Denis was, after all, very far away.

Was he the source of the magic Tamlin had felt? Kit tried to feel for the current threading the ground below them, but could sense nothing but a dull echo through rock and stone.

"Captain?" Cooper whispered. "Are you quite all right?"

"I'm fine," Kit snapped, and forced herself to fake a smile, to point up at the jackgulls circling and not stare at Doucette's damned face. "Do you feel anything unusual?" she whispered. "Magically?"

Cooper gave the tiniest shake of her head. "No, sir."

"Those are birds," Kit said without segue, before they were overheard.

"Yes," Cooper said, playing along. "Decidedly birds."

Kit turned to lean against the seawall so she could keep the man at the edge of her vision. "What do you know of Contra Costa?"

Cooper's eyes grew wide. "As much as there is to know for a sailor who wasn't there. I hadn't yet entered service, but I read the sheets and announcements. My brother was in the infantry."

Kit nodded. "A unit of Gallic soldiers, led by an Aligned commander named Alain Doucette, had been unable to dig Islish and Hispanian soldiers out of a cantonment near the village. He tried to bring the current of magic to the surface, use it as a weapon. He and his soldiers created an inferno that killed thousands, including Doucette and others in the unit. They posthumously named him 'La Boucher.'"

"La Boucher," Cooper said quietly, as if testing the sound of the words. "Not so posthumous, if he's the man with the scars."

"He is," Kit said, her voice grim with determination. "And it appears he's been promoted. This visit is no longer just about the *Fidelity*."

"We're going to follow him," Cooper guessed.

Kit didn't want to follow Doucette, didn't want to be any closer than necessary. Would have preferred never to have seen him, to be ignorant of his survival for the rest of her life, and for the Isles and Continent to be equally unaware. His actions during the war had been abhorrent, his loyalty to Gerard unfathomable. And beyond that, there was something almost physically repellent about him that had instinct demanding she put as much space between them as possible.

But that didn't matter. She'd follow him regardless, because she understood how lucky she'd been—how lucky the Isles had been—to have come ashore at the right moment, to have been in town at the right moment, and to have seen him. Now they knew he was here. Now they could defend against him.

"We need to find out what he's about. What he's doing here—and why." And what Gerard had planned for him. Because there was undoubtedly a plan.

She looked at Cooper. "If I tell you to wait here?"

"I won't," Cooper said. "So better you don't ask."

Loyalty had a keen edge, and it cut both ways. "Behind me then," Kit said. "Make no noise, attract no attention, and do exactly as I say. If anything goes wrong, run and find a place to secret until you can make it back to the boat and report what we've seen."

"Aye," Cooper whispered.

After finishing his conversation, Doucette strolled with purpose away from the sea and deeper into town. Kit let him get thirty feet ahead before she and Cooper slipped behind, strolling in the rolling gait that marked them as sailors to anyone who might be paying attention.

He had an uneven gait, Kit realized, favoring his right side. Perhaps the scarring extended down his body, or he'd been thrown in the explosion he'd helped trigger.

They paused at a corner, peering around it to see Doucette knock at a slender building with a gold knocker that glinted in the sunlight. The building bore no numbers, no name. The façade was nearly covered by an overgrown yew bursting up from a small patch of ground that fronted it. Might have been nice to see SECRETS OF INTERNATIONAL WARFARE EXCHANGED HERE in gilded letters on the door, but one couldn't have everything one desired.

The door was opened. Doucette glanced around, ensuring he was alone, and walked inside.

Kit and Cooper waited for a minute, then two, then five. It took all Kit's strength not to pace down the sidewalk, back again. She didn't care for waiting.

"He's going to be a bit," Kit said. "And we need something to do in the meantime lest the neighbors decide we're malingerers."

"I'm not sure I'd know how to malinger if I tried."

Kit snorted, glanced around. A teller of fortunes was seated at the nearest corner, a scarf-covered table in front of her, complete with tin cup for coins and stack of cards atop a bit of royal blue silk.

"There," Kit said, pointing to the woman. "I'll handle the transaction. You keep a wary eye."

"Aye," Cooper said, and they ambled across the road.

"A diviner of futures?" Kit asked with a smile, elbowing Cooper a bit. "That could be worth some coin."

The woman who looked up at them had green eyes, which

contrasted against her light brown skin. Her dark hair was wrapped in a scarf, and another ensconced her shoulders.

"I am Madame Mouret," the woman said. "And you need no divination from me. Your future is wind and water, sailor."

Kit's brows lifted. "Sailor?"

The look Mouret returned was, to put it mildly, withering. And, if she was being entirely honest, Kit felt a bit withered.

"You move like a sailor," Mouret said. "You've salt stains on your coat, and freckles across your nose that you've not bothered to powder. You've been in the sun and water but don't much care who knows it." She surveyed Kit again.

"Not just a sailor," she added. "But an officer, at that."

"Oh?" Kit asked, now interested. Fortune-teller or no, Madame Mouret had a very good eye for detail.

"You stand with authority, as if you expect others to obey."

Maybe she wasn't as good an actress as she thought, Kit mused, more withered.

Mouret held out a hand. "For the right coin, perhaps we can be a bit more specific."

Kit pulled out a silver coin, presuming that offering the woman a copper would result in Kit being dissolved on the spot.

Mouret dropped the coin into the cup, then picked up the stack of cards. One by one, she spread them across the silk. The first in the center, then four surrounding it at each cardinal direction. They were playing cards—worn at the edges—but not like any Kit had seen before. Instead of suits and royals, there were illustrations in red, blue, and yellow. A nobleman pulling a chariot with two horses. A man hanging from his foot. And, in the center, a skeletal man rowing a boat.

Goose bumps pebbled her skin. "La Morte?" Kit asked in

Gallic, pointing to the card—which was helpfully named in black script—but not touching it. That seemed unwise, and she was as superstitious as any smart sailor ought to be.

"Perhaps," the woman answered, placing the remaining cards aside. "Or perhaps the end of a journey, or the beginning of a new one." She pointed to the card with the hanging man. "But that journey will not be smooth, and will require sacrifice." She pointed to the chariot. "You will meet power with power. And the outcome is uncertain."

Mouret placed three more cards in a column beside the cross she'd made. A queen on a throne. A soldier on a horse with a golden staff. A man in torn clothes named "Le Mat." The hermit, Kit translated.

"And what do these portend?" Kit asked.

Mouret studied the cards. "Again, a journey. Not just physical—across land or sea—but . . . of the mind?" She asked it as a question, as if even she was unsure of the answer. "No, of the heart. Of the . . . spirit." She nodded. "Yes. And that will be a great battle, too. It remains unseen what will be found as you emerge."

It was all generalized nonsense, Kit thought. She knew there were some fortune-tellers who were Aligned, and who leveraged their access to the currents for divination. But there was no magic here.

"You've been to Saint-Étienne?"

Kit blinked back at Mouret. "What?"

She dropped her gaze to Kit's jacket. Kit looked down, realizing her ribbon was visible in the turned edge of her lapel.

"The pattern is traditional of Saint-Étienne, so I presumed you'd purchased it there."

For a moment, Kit simply stared at her. In all her years, no one had suggested an origin for the ribbon, not even the milliners she'd asked in New London.

"No," Kit said finally, covering the ribbon again and hoping her voice didn't shake. "I've never been."

"Ah." Mouret made a very Gallic shrug. "It is no matter."

"Movement," Cooper said quietly.

Kit forced herself to concentrate. She made a show of knocking a bauble from the table—not hard to fake, since her hands were now shaking—and managed a glance back as she crouched to pick it up. Doucette had come out of the building and stood twenty feet to their left. He patted the front of his jacket, as if reassuring himself that something was safely tucked away, then began walking again.

"Thank you for your time," Kit said, replacing the bauble. Without looking back, she began following Doucette, expecting Cooper would follow.

"You're welcome," Mouret called out behind them. And Kit thought she heard the woman murmur, *"Be careful."*

"He has something," Kit whispered, as Cooper fell into step beside her. "Something he didn't have before, now in his front pocket."

"How do you know?" Cooper asked, surprise in her voice.

"He touched his jacket there," Kit said. Hadn't she done the same thing to her coat—to the spot where her ribbon lay—innumerable times before? "And it hangs differently than it did when he went in."

Something heavy, Kit thought. Not just a note or letter. A collection of them? A weapon?

"Let's begin our great battle," she murmured, eyes narrowed on Doucette's back.

"Do you believe the fortune-teller?" Cooper asked collegially.

"Of course," Kit said.

She kept her eyes on the street but could feel Cooper's surprise. "You're quite serious? A teller of fortunes?"

"She said we'll have a journey, it won't be smooth, and the outcome is uncertain. Those are always the fortunes of sailors. It takes little talent to tell that particular truth."

But the ribbon's supposed origin—that was something she hadn't heard before, and she still wasn't sure how to make it out. But there was no time for the personal now.

Doucette led them farther into town—and farther from the shore and the *Diana*—and through narrow passages that moved like canyons through the town's buildings. It was quieter here, and every footfall seemed to echo like thunder in the silence. Kit didn't care for the squeeze of brick and stone around her, but she had no choice but to follow. The information she might obtain from or about Doucette was too great an opportunity to pass up.

The road spilled them out into a perpendicular lane and park across from it, bounded by a low fence of wrought iron. Kit waited in the arched entry of a building fifteen feet behind, pulling Cooper into the small space behind her.

Doucette stood alone. Some minutes later, they heard the sound of boots scratching on the crushed stone road. A man appeared. Also in uniform, with dark hair that swooped a good two inches above his narrow head.

"Sedley," Doucette said by way of greeting.

"Marshal," Sedley said with a small and obsequious bow. "Congratulations on your promotion," he said in crisp Gallic. "The Imperial Battalion will be unstoppable under your command."

So Doucette wasn't just part of the battalion, Kit thought with a curse, but the damned commander of it.

"Thank you," Doucette said.

"His Highness?"

"Safe. And plans are proceeding apace."

Doucette looked around, then slipped something red from his interior coat pocket. It was long as a sheet of foolscap, perhaps half as wide. A document portfolio, she guessed, that he'd retrieved from the building.

Doucette glanced about, then opened it like a trifolded letter, pulled out a folded bit of paper. Kit was too far away to guess its contents, but she could see areas of blues and greens.

"A map," Cooper whispered beside her.

"Aye," Kit said, gravity in the word. And an important one, given its case and its apparent secrecy. She watched the men's faces carefully, as if she might be able to read its contents in their gazes, their expressions.

She saw surprise in Sedley's eyes. Doucette's just looked . . . dead. Empty and cold, as if he was devoid of humanity. Had he lost it at Contra Costa, or had it never been there?

"He is certain?" Sedley asked.

"He is rarely otherwise," Doucette said, and tucked the paper and portfolio away again. "Your forces are in place?"

"As much as possible, but—"

Doucette held up a hand. "The course is set and the way is determined. If you cannot make the necessary arrangements, he'll find someone who will."

The tone was flat, but the threat behind the words was clear enough to Sedley, who blanched. "Of course, Marshal. I was not questioning the order. Merely . . . clarifying."

"In that case, as the situation has been clarified, you know how to proceed. And watch your step. There are enemy eyes about."

Sedley nodded and, having been dismissed, turned on his heel and strode down the street, a bit more deflated, and his step a bit quicker, than when he'd arrived.

Kit didn't consider herself a particularly covetous or greedy person, but that was before she'd seen the damned portfolio and the hint of its contents. If she hadn't been in Gallia and literally surrounded by enemies, she might have run forward and snatched it out of his hand. But she knew both men could outpace her in the maze of narrow streets, and she and Cooper wouldn't survive the race. That meant no intelligence would return to the *Diana*, to the Crown Command, to the queen. And that, now, was her singular mission.

"It's time to go," Kit said. "And quickly as we can."

She ignored the tangled knot of lanes behind them, intending instead to head down this straighter main road in the direction of the sea.

They rounded the corner . . . and walked straight into three men in uniform: buff pantaloons, black boots, red jackets, and tricorn hats. Each bore a rifle and bayonet, and they were pointed at Kit and Cooper. They were led by the bruiser from the dock, the one who'd threatened them when they'd asked questions about the *Fidelity*.

Damnation, she thought, and hoped against hope the men were simply out on a neighborhood stroll, taking in the village sights. But when the man from the docks pointed at Kit and Cooper, she knew they were sunk.

"*There they are!*" the dock man shouted in angry Gallic.

"Cooper."

"Sir?"

"*Run.*"

She couldn't lead them back to the *Diana*; she needed to lose them in and among the stone and mock-Islish buildings of Auevilla. She wished she'd had bread crumbs for a trail, presuming the ubiquitous jackgulls wouldn't have simply plucked them up. The sun, thankfully, gave Kit enough of a compass to let her roughly gauge her direction. So she veered southwest and led Cooper back through the winding streets at the fastest pace she could manage, pausing at corners to listen for the waves that would confirm their position.

They ran beneath a woman hanging linens from a balcony, could hear her shouting at the gendarmes behind them. *"They're here! They're here!"*

She'd usually given civilian Gallians the benefit of the doubt, until now. She didn't like Gallians or Gallia, Kit decided, bread be damned.

She heard a grunt behind her and glanced back, found Cooper on her knees. Fear was a shot through her heart, but Cooper climbed to her feet again.

"Tripped," Cooper said, and hobbled to her feet. Her mouth was grim and set, her eyes determined. But hobbling was hobbling.

Footsteps echoed behind them. Kit dashed back, took Cooper by the arm. Then she looked around, found a narrow passageway between two stone buildings, and led them into the shadows there.

Footsteps—running now—stopped only feet from where Kit and Cooper had pressed themselves against the shadowed wall.

"Which way?" one of the gendarmes asked, feet shuffling as he searched the road outside.

"Split up," another decided. "You two continue toward the

harbor; they might try to board a ship. We'll go back in case they turned a corner."

Kit held her breath until the road was silent again, waited another minute for luck, and looked out. The road was empty, the only sounds the flap of Gerard pennants in the breeze and the distant beat of wave against shore.

She glanced back at Cooper. "Can you run?"

Cooper nodded.

"To the *Diana*," Kit said. "And don't stop."

Quietly as they could manage, they crept out of their passageway, began to run in the direction of the beach and shore, keeping as close as they could to the buildings that lined the cobblestone road.

They followed a curve in the road, and both stopped short when they found the dock guard, huffing more than a little bit, standing with a gendarme in the middle of the street. More footsteps, and Kit glanced behind them, found two more.

All of them raised rifles.

"*Damnation*," Kit murmured.

Jin was going to be *livid*.

# FOUR

The gendarmes led Kit and Cooper at bayonet point back through town in relative silence, only occasionally murmuring things to each other that Kit couldn't hear, but which resulted in curious glances at the women.

At least the bayonets were rusty. New guns would have been a different kind of threat to Kit, Cooper, and the Isles. Proof of funds and a supply line equipping Gerard's army with new weapons. Instead, they'd only worry of lockjaw.

"Right into the sea," Kit muttered.

"What was that?" the guard asked.

"I said, you'll make us miss our ship." Kit threw up her hands. "We've done nothing but spend coins while waiting to sail. Ungrateful curs," she muttered, and managed to look angry instead of afraid.

But they made no response, which made Kit more nervous than if they'd made retorts about nosy women. Silence meant they were serious—and controlled. That would make them harder to fool.

"I'm sorry, sir," Cooper whispered. "It was the damned cobble-stones."

"I know," Kit said. "Are you hurt?"

"Only a sore knee, and that's nothing. More a bit embar-rassed."

"No need for embarrassment or guilt. What's done is done. We've survived this far, and we'll keep doing it."

They were pushed toward a central square and toward a long building of pale stone with small, high windows. A gaol, she guessed, given the uniformed gendarmes hanging about outside it. At least it wasn't a prison ship, which was exactly as described: old and unseaworthy hulks anchored just offshore to hold pris-oners too dangerous to keep on land, or because those prisons were already overfull. She'd anchored at a Gallic prison ship before—escorting diplomats who'd sought the release of Islish sailors during the war. She hadn't been inside, but her impression from the *Diana* had been more than enough. The hull was pock-marked and covered with barnacles and algae, and the entire thing stank of humans, waste, and fetid water. Calling them "ships" was an injustice to every other vessel that floated. They were misery made physical.

Two great wooden doors at the entrance were pushed open, scratched and squeaking. Kit and Cooper walked in behind their captors.

"Left," one of the guards said, and another old door was opened. Kit and Cooper were shoved through it.

This room was large, with plank floors that were pale with age and want of oiling, except where they were stained with gods only knew what. The walls were pale stone in the same con-dition, and two dozen prisoners, most presenting as males, sat or squatted on the floor or leaned against the walls in clumps of two or three.

If she admitted they were Islish officers, they might be handled more carefully. Separated from the other prisoners, held in private homes rather than gaol. Or they'd be immediately executed as spies. Gerard had never been one for diplomacy; little cause for it when you'd named yourself the emperor.

"It's not so bad," Cooper whispered in Gallic, careful enough not to forget her character. "I've never been in gaol before."

The guard snickered. "This isn't the gaol. This is just temporary barracks until you're removed to the ship."

Kit cursed again.

"The ship?" Cooper asked.

The guard's smile was wide and poorly maintained. With a bit of what appeared to be spinach for decoration. "Prison ship up the coast. It's anchored there 'cause of the . . . smell."

But they weren't there yet. They weren't wholly without hope. Just more or less so.

The guard closed the door behind them, engaged the bolt. Several of the men on the floor rose; those on the walls pushed off, moved closer. Maybe a bit less hope now.

"No worries," Kit whispered to Cooper. "Show no fear."

"I'm not afraid, sir."

Kit glanced at her, saw the gleam in her eyes, watched as she rolled up her sleeves. Her knuckles, Kit belatedly realized, were bruised.

"You're a bit terrifying, Cooper," Kit said, with no small approval.

Cooper tried for a grin. "I enjoy a bit of sparring now and again," she said, and looked over the crowd. A few of the prisoners looked interested in a bout. Others took their seats again. Most looked lean and a little on the hungry side, but their shirts and trousers of homespun were worn but clean. Definitely not as bad as a prison hulk.

"Over there," Kit said, and they moved to a sidewall beneath a window, kept the wall at their backs. Cooper cracked her knuckles.

They needed a way out, Kit thought, and considered the windows opposite, the door, the floor. All of them seemed secure, so they'd need assistance from the outside. Jin would send help. At least when their time was up. They just had to stay off the hulk until then.

Since they were stuck here for now, she might as well discover what they knew.

"La Boucher," Kit said, and continued in Gallic. "Who can give us information?"

That question was met with curses that put Cooper's bit about the goat to shame. Kit pulled a copper from the slot in the lining of her coat.

"Best information gets a coin," she said, and the avarice in their eyes all but lit up the room. A copper wouldn't be enough to buy the prisoners' freedom, she suspected, but might get them a cup of wine.

"He's a conjurer," one shouted out. "Not just Aligned, but touched by the gods."

"He has the blood of the old gods in him," another agreed. "Can work spells, can't he?"

"Let's start at the beginning," Kit redirected. "He didn't die at Contra Costa."

"No." A man on the floor, legs crossed and pale feet bare,

shook his head. "Only injured. But took him a year to recover, so they say. He crawled out of the debris and wandered away from the battlefield, broken and burned. Story goes, he lived with a farmer five miles away."

"No," said a man with light brown skin who stood nearby. He hobbled toward them, using a cane to cross the floor. "Was with a local clerk. I've a sister who worked as a maid near the village he stumbled into. He didn't remember a thing of the battle for months."

"Was a year," said the man on the floor. "And another yet before he could walk again."

And then found his way back into the arms of the loyalists, Kit surmised, who were undoubtedly thrilled to find him alive. Contra Costa had occurred in 1812; Gerard abdicated in April 1814.

Kit tossed them both coins. "How long has he been here?"

The man with the cane held out his hand, but Kit was done with negotiation.

"You'll all get your pay if the information's correct," she said. "How long?"

"Saw him first about a fortnight ago," he said.

So longer than the *Fidelity*. Kit would bet a handful of coppers the ship had landed here because of Doucette's presence, or he'd come here specifically to meet the ship. There'd be no co-incidence. "Have you seen the emperor?"

The curses that followed the question shouldn't have surprised her; she was in a gaol, after all, and it was a good bet they weren't wealthy Gerard loyalists able to buy or cajole their way out of shackles.

"'The emperor,'" said the man on the floor, "'ain't shown his face here.'"

Given the sneer, she expected he was no loyalist, and was telling the truth. She pulled out another copper, tossed it to the man who'd answered the question.

Before she could ask anything else, a *crack* split the air, and the building itself shuddered. Cooper jumped, and Kit held out her arms to keep her balance, but the vibration stopped as quickly as it had started.

Kit felt a new kind of unease. She'd experienced an earth-shock before, and this wasn't that. It was magic, irritated enough that even she—Aligned to the sea—could feel it roiling beneath the surface, as if angered to have been disturbed. And when she realized none of the other prisoners so much as flinched at the sound, her discomfort increased.

"You want to see how he uses his power?" the man with the cane asked, and gestured to the window. "Look there."

Kit looked back at the window that had been cut into the stone behind them, set-in with small iron bars. She stood on tiptoes, craning upward to see, and could just make out a man standing in a courtyard of scrubby grass that lay between the prison and the building behind it.

It was Doucette. And he wasn't alone. A man stood some yards away. Another officer, perhaps, although he wore no waistcoat or tailcoat. His linen was untucked, his dark hair unkempt. And his skin looked pale as death, his eyes hard-set and grim, as if he knew what was coming.

Another *crack*, another shock hard enough to rattle the door on its hinges, and it appeared. A glow of blue, like the phosphorescence that sometimes rode ocean waves, a cloud of faint green that glowed as the *Diana* moved through it. But while that color was beautiful, diffuse and soft, there was something sharper here, as if the magic had physical form.

This was the bright edge of the current, she thought with horror, pulled from the rock below to the surface it should never see.

Hard edges or no, it was . . . beautiful, with swirls of darker colors intermingling with lighter, and shocks of brightness at the edges, like lightning in miniature. She'd never really *seen* the current; her perception of it was altogether different. Her Alignment was more like a sixth sense. Probably a good thing, because its beauty, its dance, was hypnotic . . .

Kit shook her head to snap herself out of her thrall. This wasn't a pretty sunset or a well-hewn figurehead. It wasn't something to be admired, and she shouldn't be seeing it at all. No human should be able to effect so much power, to manipulate something so dangerous, without apocalyptic results. Manipulating the current was banned for a reason.

As if to prove he didn't care a whit for law or morality, Doucette reached out a hand toward his quarry, palm raised. His glove was gone now, but she saw no scars, at least from this distance. His chin firmed as he concentrated on his task, arm shaking with apparent effort.

Before Kit could blink, the current snapped forward like a whip and struck the man in the chest with a *crack* loud enough to vibrate the walls of the cell.

The man fell to the ground, body jerking, bowing, from the shock of the power unleashed against him. He made no sound, no scream, but his fingers dug into the soft earth, grasping for purchase or weapon or . . . release.

Kit grabbed the window's bars, trying in vain to pull them free—and apparently thinking she might fly toward the man and shield him from the current, take some of it herself, add to the scars on her palms. And then the man stopped moving. One final jerk, and his body went loose. His head lolled to face her, eyes wide but unseeing.

He was dead.

Her belly went cold with fear.

Doucette had used the current to kill a man. He'd pulled it from the ground and aimed it, just as he might a musket or rifle. And he'd taken a life.

Kit gripped the bars harder, heart pounding. She'd seen death before, had caused it herself. War was the ugliest business of humanity, after all. But this was different, even as it pained her to admit it. She had no power that could match this. No knowledge or ability that would allow her to fight it. And she didn't know anyone in the world who could.

Doucette's arm dropped, his shoulders slumping, as he released his grip on the current. The earth trembled again as the current slipped back into place, out of sight of human eyes.

Despite what he'd done, Doucette didn't look pained or injured and bore no scars other than those already visible. There was no inferno or splitting of the ground; no indication at all but for the initial sound and shudder—perhaps the shock of magic breaching the earth—that he'd done anything.

Was there no cost he must bear? she thought with frustration.

Suddenly, he turned and looked toward the gaol. And for an instant, with death and the lingering haze of magic between them, their eyes met.

He'd been literally scarred by his experience at Contra Costa, by what he'd done. But his suffering—and the suffering of countless others—hadn't dissuaded him from magic. Far from it—he hadn't been able to do this at Contra Costa. He must have spent some portion of the interim learning how to do more. How to kill in a manner that required no matériel—no shot, no powder, no flame. It would have taken time, dedication, and possibly more scars than she could see.

But his eyes remained empty and hard. Devoid of emotion.

Kit dropped back from the window, repelled by the possibility that he'd seen her face. And loath as she was to admit it . . . afraid. If he could do this at will and without consequence or apparent conscience, what could he *not* do? How could the Isles— how could *anyone*—stand against this?

"Captain," Cooper said quietly.

Kit merely shook her head, working to control that creeping fear and, more, to shield her subordinate from it. That, at least, was something within her control.

So she squared her shoulders, looked back at the others in the room. "You've seen him kill before."

More than half of them nodded.

"How many?" she asked, fear transmuting into fury.

"A dozen, maybe," said the man with the cane. "A guard who brought an extra ration. A soldier he sailed with failed to find the number of horses he wanted, another his quota of shot."

"It's how he gets information," said the man on the floor.

Kit lifted her brows. "What information is he seeking?"

The men looked at each other.

"Loyalties," the man on the floor continued. "Magic."

Something here, Kit thought. Something she needed to dig out. "What about magic? Is he looking for more like him? More Aligned? Or something related to technique?"

"All," the man said, the word punctuated by the rattle of the door that held them inside, and the jangling of metal.

Coming for her and Cooper, Kit expected. Fear was a bright star rising again, but Kit ignored it. She pulled a few more coins from her pocket, tossed them to the prisoners.

"If you have an opportunity," she told Cooper in the resulting scramble, "take it. Get out and get back to the *Diana*."

Cooper's cheeks were a bit wan, but her voice was steady. "All due respect, sir, bollocks to that."

Kit was beginning to wonder if any of her crew understood what *obedience* meant. "When we were on the street, you said you'd go back to the ship."

"I did, sir. I assumed you meant to go with me. Do you remember what I told you on Forstadt?"

That was the island where Gerard's Frisian supporters had been building a warship in his name; the ship he'd intended to use magic to fuel, and which had damaged the magical ecosystem of the Northern Sea.

"You said several things, I recall," Kit said, bracing herself as the door was pushed open.

"That I did, Captain. And at no little risk to myself, given my former captain was, pardon my Islish, a horse's ass. I'm not about to go cowardly now."

"'War doesn't need heroes,'" Kit quoted. "'It needs good sailors.'"

Cooper grinned unabashedly. *"Cox's Seamanship.* I'm not one to disagree with the sailor's bible, but I think the Isles deserve a bit of both."

"Are you always cheerful?" Kit asked, as the door was shoved open and the guard walked inside.

Cooper seemed to actually consider it. "Fairly often, sir."

"You there," the guard said, pointing at Kit. "Let's go."

Kit slipped a gold coin into Cooper's hand. "If all else fails, buy your safety." And then she was led away.

Her wrists were tied with rough hemp rope, and she was pushed down a corridor toward the back of the building, then outside to the courtyard where the man had been executed mere minutes ago.

His body had already been removed, but there was a sharp scent in the air, as if the current had singed it.

Cold sweat dripped down her spine, but she forced herself to stay calm, to think, even while looking as baffled and afraid as an innocent might. She was relieved when they made it to the edge of the courtyard but uneasy again when they reached a small, grimy shed with a single fogged window.

The door was opened. Dirt floor, rutted plaster walls, spiderwebs in the corners of the ceiling. And in the middle, an aged wooden chair.

She was marched to it, pushed down, and the door was closed again.

There were three men in the room: two of the gendarmes who'd chased her, and the man from the dock. Doucette wasn't among them.

She had to stop her breath from hitching, but she played her part again. "Oh, good," she said. "More fancy men to ask more rude questions."

"I am Marcel Beauvoir," said one of the gendarmes in Gallic. He had tidy hair and a small mustache. "What is your name?"

"Clémentine Lafaille," Kit said. It had been the name of her sister's favorite childhood doll. Hetta had obtained it in Gallia for Jane during one of her own visits on behalf of the Isles' former king, and Jane had given it the very grand name. And she'd kept that name until Jane decided Clémentine was interested in science. And then Clémentine, spirited as she was, got too close to a flame Jane hadn't, at that age, been allowed to light. That was the end of Clémentine, who was treated to a very solemn funeral in the garden.

Kit held tight to that memory, used it as a shield against her fear.

"And where are you from?" Dock Man asked.

"Beaulieu-sur-Mer." It was on the southern coast, beautiful and warm, and she'd have been happy to call it home. Again, but for the Gallians.

"What's your business here?" Beauvoir asked.

"As I've already told this one," she said, using a shoulder to gesture to Dock Man, "we're to sail on the *Simone*. I'm a sailmaker."

Dock Man's expression didn't change. "The *Simone* lifted anchor an hour ago."

Kit cursed. Not quite as inventively as Cooper, but as bitterly as she could manage. And threw in a bit about a goat. And when she raised her gaze to him, let her jaw shake a bit in anger.

"I was to sail on the *Simone*," she said again, insult clear in her voice. "Have you any idea how much coin they pay? I have obligations."

"Debts?" Beauvoir asked, moving closer. He smelled like garlic.

Kit worked up a faint blush. "Obligations," she said again. "I needed the pay."

"You were asking questions about a boat."

She made her expression exceedingly dry. "I'm a sailor, aye? Of course I was."

"A particular boat," Beauvoir said. "Anchored at the dock."

"The *Simone*?" Kit asked, brow knit.

"They call it the *Intrepid*," Dock Man said. "The blue ship."

"Ah," Kit said with a snort. "The ship with the wide arse."

Kit saw the blow coming and braced herself, but Dock Man's backhand was harder than she'd anticipated. Pain surged across her face, her cheekbone throbbing from the impact of his signet ring. She tasted blood, bright and coppery, but a poke with her tongue said none of her teeth were loose. That was some victory, at least.

She mustered her courage, looked him in the eye. "Ow," she said mildly, and spat blood on the floor. And the pain in her jaw was faintly eased by imagining the look of horror Mrs. Eaves, the Brightlings' very stuffy housekeeper, might have worn if she'd seen Kit do that.

"The ship," Beauvoir prompted, while glaring at Dock Man.

"It's an ugly bastard, but big and fancy. I thought, if the captain was hiring on, might be more coin in it."

"We know there are spies from the Isles in Gallia. You say you are Gallic, but no one knows you here."

"Why would they?" Kit asked. "I'm from the south. And I'm no more from the Isles than you are."

"You have the look of an Islishwoman about you."

"Do I?" she asked blandly, swiveling in her chair and using her bound hands to make a very Gallic gesture that questioned his parentage.

Dock Man came forward, bared his teeth. "Talk, you little bitch." He reached out a hand, and she braced for the second blow. But the gendarme stepped forward, grabbed his wrist.

"No," he said. "You do not have authority for this. And we dare not overstep—not when he is in town."

Kit wondered which "he" they meant—Gerard or Doucette?— and which scared them more.

"Are we done then?" Kit asked, relieved they'd asked only about the ship. They apparently hadn't realized she and Cooper had followed Doucette through town, or heard of his plans. All the better.

Beauvoir looked back at her, and the chill in his eyes had her swallowing hard. "Oh, you'll talk, one way or the other. Send for Fouché," he said. "He'll find out what there is to know."

Silence fell across the space, heavy and cold, as the other gendarme, apparently of lower rank, looked at Beauvoir. "You are certain?"

He might have faked the hesitation in his voice, but it sounded earnest to Kit. Which had her pulling at her wrists, trying to loosen the knots tied there.

"Go ahead and struggle," said the man from the dock, and kicked a leg of her chair. "You'll get yours soon enough."

⁓

Kit sat in the shed for what she thought was an hour, based on the shifting shadows on the far wall. One guard had been stationed outside, but otherwise she'd been left alone.

She had to get out—and she had to get Cooper out—before this turned any uglier. And not just because Jin would have her hide. Although that was a consideration.

She continued to work the ropes, trying to pick at the hemp with her fingernails. She'd already torn two to the quick, and for little enough progress. But the pain kept her from worrying over who this Fouché was and what he might do.

As she worked the rope, she strained to hear any developments outside—movement toward the shed, discussions by the guards. It wasn't until the hour waned that footsteps approached. Two men, by the sound of it, coming from different directions. The glass in the sole window was dirty enough that she could only see their shadows.

"Where is Fouché?" Beauvoir asked in Gallic, his frustration clear.

"Respectfully," said the other man, "he cannot simply appear at your command, Beauvoir. He has his own obligations to the governor. He asked that I come first to consider the . . . quarry."

When the door opened, she braced for whatever would come next.

Sunlight streamed into the room, putting the man who walked in in silhouette. Broad shoulders in tailcoat and strong legs in boots, his hair dark brown with streaks of sunlight.

He turned to her, and she stared at the face she hadn't seen in weeks.

The man who'd come to interrogate her . . . was Rian Grant.

# FIVE

Rian Grant was standing here, in this dank building in Auevilla, staring back at her. For a moment she was back in the queen's ballroom with the water rising at their feet, and she felt the world sway a bit. He looked even better than he had in her dreams, if such a thing was possible. Tall and strong and eminently capable.

She could see the echoing surprise in his eyes, before he schooled them into an impressively haughty expression and looked her over with a sneer fit for a member of the Beau Monde. His gaze settled on her cheek, probably already swelling, and went hard with anger.

"This is your spy?" Grant asked, in immaculate Gallic and a condescending tone. "This bit of fluff?"

"A spy," Beauvoir said again. "Caught sneaking around the docks."

Grant sniffed disdainfully. "I prefer to believe the Isles employs more substantial agents than this slip of a girl. What's your name, girl?" He'd switched to Islish for the question, but the disdain hadn't changed.

Kit rolled her eyes. "I am Gallic," she said in the language. "As I've already said, my name is Clémentine Lafaille, and I am from Beaulieu-sur-Mer."

"What's your business here?"

She made a frustrated curse. "We were to sail on the *Simone*. We came off the boat for some damned food. We walked the dock—and a citizen's got a right to do so, hasn't she?—and were accosted by these filthy goats. Now he says we've missed our damn ship. Are you going to pay for my wages now? And my comrade's?"

She saw the glint of pride in his eyes, but he gripped her chin as if frustrated. His fingers were gentle against her skin, but his arm shook, as if with barely controlled violence. "Stubborn chit," Grant said. "We know you're a spy. So you might as well speak the Islish of your birth."

She didn't know his game yet, but she read the urging in his eyes, and switched to Islish.

"They don't speak Islish?" she whispered through her sneer.

"Not as far as I can tell," Grant said softly, the words barely more than a breath.

"Get your filthy hands off me," Kit said in Islish.

"You?" he said in the same language. "Calling me filthy?" A mirthless laugh, and he released her chin. "I'd be careful of your tone," he said, every syllable crisp with condescension.

"Voice sounds like you're a rich Islish gent. And yet here you are, helping these damned Gallians."

"My business in Auevilla is none of yours. Your business, on the other hand, is very much mine. You will tell me why you're here, or I will show you why they called me to convince you."

Grant put his arms on her chair, leaned over it. And she nearly lost her composure at the scent of his cologne—bay rum—and the warmth of his body. So she thought of the Isles and gritted her teeth.

"You're injured," he whispered.

"I'm fine."

"Alone?"

"Cooper," she answered. "The Butcher is here. He killed a man outside the prison. They know there are Islish spies in town." Her hands were still shaking from it.

She could see Grant wanted to argue, to contradict. But he was controlled enough—and believed her truthful enough—that he only sneered with disdain.

"Liar," he said, through gritted teeth. "Make this look convincing," he added in a whisper, and cracked his hand across her face.

Or so it seemed. He'd surreptitiously slapped his other hand, and she whipped her head to the side to strengthen the effect. Given Beauvoir's smile, the effort had been successful.

"Bastard," she muttered as he walked away, shaking his hand as if it smarted from the slap. "You damned bastard." She rubbed her cheek against her shoulder to add a bit of color.

Beauvoir moved in, looked at Kit, Grant. "Be careful that you don't break her jaw," he said in Gallic. "Makes it more difficult to talk."

Grant gestured toward Kit. "If you believe I cannot handle an Islish chit, you're welcome to take over. I've other ways to spend my time . . . as does Fouché."

It was obvious bait, but Beauvoir took it. "Apologies," he said mildly, which earned him a nod from Grant.

He turned back to Kit. "Why are you here? If I have to ask you again, the price won't be nearly as easy."

She worked venom into her gaze, said through clenched teeth, "I was to sail on the damned *Simone*."

"They can verify?"

"I don't see how, as they've sailed away without me."

"Convenient. What information did you hope to obtain for the Isles?"

"The location of lying gentry," she said. "So go bugger yourself."

He gave a dignified huff. "Your mouth is filthy as your clothing. The truth, or your comrade still in the brig will be next in that chair. And I won't be inclined to be so patient with her." Again his eyes urged her to follow his lead.

Kit gritted her teeth. "Stay away from her."

"Tell me what I want to know." His gaze shifted to her cheeks. "Or a slap will be the least of her concerns."

Kit swore. "We want to know what Gerard plans on the Continent." That was accurate, but general enough that it would be no surprise to anyone in the hemisphere. It also saved her from admitting they'd found the *Fidelity*.

Grant's eyes narrowed even as his smile widened. And she understood, for a moment, how formidable he'd have been as a soldier—and yet how different his eyes were from Doucette's.

The remembrance came heavy; even bound, she squeezed her hands into fists to keep them from shaking.

Grant moved to the door, opened it. "Good work, Beauvoir. She has admitted to being Islish, and seeking information regarding the emperor and his strategy. Fouché will see you richly rewarded for this. I took the liberty of arranging the wagon before I arrived, as I presumed you wouldn't send for Fouché without reason. I'll have them taken to his town house. I've one of his horses."

Grant made the statement quickly, allowing no time for question or objection.

"Taken to his town house," Beauvoir said with uncertainty. "We cannot release a prisoner—"

"You can," Grant said, pulling gloves from the pocket of his tailcoat and slipping them on. "And you will. Otherwise Fouché will be obliged to communicate his displeasure to the governor. In that case, his attention would be directed solely"—Grant looked up, his eyes all aristocratic displeasure—"at you."

"Of course," Beauvoir said. He didn't look entirely convinced, but he didn't appear eager to wage this battle now. He offered a little bow, waved in Dock Man and the gendarmes.

They came in, and one of the gendarmes pulled Kit up from the chair. She kicked him in the shin.

"Traitor!" she screamed at Grant, as the Gallians grabbed her arms. "This is treason, and you'll pay for it. The queen will hear about this!"

For she was but an actress and the world a stage.

"Go ahead," Grant said with a chuckle. "Scream for your spoiled queen, girl. There's no one here that gives a damn."

She was dragged to the road, tried twice to bite the unlucky gendarmes who'd been given the assignment. "You cannot make me go," she screamed. "I am a citizen! I have rights!"

But the gendarmes seemed bored with her antics now, presumably because they were being robbed of their fun.

Cooper awaited her in an open wagon hitched to two angry-looking horses with fuzzy hooves, steam rising from their nostrils in the brisk air. Kit was shoved into the back, then to her knees, and she was grateful for the layer of mostly clean straw that cushioned the blow at least a little.

"You can stop screaming," the footman whispered in perfect Islish. "But do continue to look fearful and perturbed."

"*J'accuse!*" she screamed out, just for good measure, and then offered more Gallic gestures to the men who watched, narrow-eyed, from the side of the road.

The footman snapped the reins and the carriage jerked forward, humping over the cobblestone road.

"You're well, Cooper?" Kit whispered, when the gaol was out of sight. "They didn't hurt you?"

"I'm in tiptop shape, sir. They didn't move me until Mr. Cragwell came for me." Cooper held up her hands, which weren't bound. "Didn't even bother to tie me. I could hear you screaming across the courtyard. I thought they might have nipped off your fingers. And I saw Grant. I must admit to some confusion."

"You are not the only one," Kit said. The wagon jostled as they hit a rut in the road, and Kit pitched forward, gripped the side of the wagon with her bound wrists to keep from falling over. "Damnable horses," she muttered.

"Sir?"

"Never mind. Grant is playing messenger to someone named Fouché, who apparently has the ear of the provincial governor. I've no idea who Fouché is, but Grant will have a plan. But damned if I know what that is, either." And she was cautious enough not to speculate aloud in the middle of town. Whatever Grant had managed here, he'd managed it deeply enough to have Gallic officers trusting him within only a few weeks.

They passed shops and tradespeople, including a shop with a portrait of Gerard hanging in a great glass window. The painting was ... generous ... to the former emperor. Gerard wasn't a tall man, or a particularly nice-looking one. His cheeks were pallid, his dark hair short, his mouth seeming to always bear a pout. But he looked strong here, standing in a crisp ivory uniform bedecked with medals, topped by an ermine-trimmed cloak of scarlet velvet, his blue eyes lifted toward the sky—and the imperial future he envisioned.

"I still don't know what they saw in him," Cooper said quietly. "I've always thought he looked so ... plain."

"That's why they loved him," Kit said, "and love him still, or at least some of them. He was a student who became a general; a general who became an emperor. He is a man of infinite ambition, who succeeded, or nearly, at his aims. Everyone wants to succeed."

"You sound as if you admire him," Cooper said.

"I don't admire him. I admire his talents. He has a nimble mind and a strong will. And if he'd used them to help his people, rather than himself, the world might be a very different place. Since he didn't, he, like Doucette, can rot in hell."

The wagon came to a jolting stop outside a white building, its façade crisscrossed with dark beams in the old Islish style, the tall roof pitched to a narrow point.

"Be ready," Kit whispered. "And stay in character."

⁓

Grant jumped down from a tall dark stallion that gave Kit a bit of the evil eye and ordered them taken inside as a footman took the horse's reins. Another footman pulled them from the wagon, shoved them both into the building, where they were taken from a wide foyer into a pleasant-looking parlor.

Grant, who remained in the foyer, put a finger to his lips, requesting their silence.

Kit glanced about the room. The home they now found themselves in was pretty, if slightly shabby. Comfortable but worn chairs, candlesticks in need of polishing, a fireplace that needed scrubbing. And despite the sunshine outside, the heavy drapes were drawn, candles lit.

After a moment Grant walked in, Cragwell behind him. Grant carried a small knife, blade gleaming.

Cooper edged toward Kit, as if to protect her. Kit offered her a smile. "No concern, Cooper. Grant would prefer to battle with his fists, not a blade." Kit held out her wrists.

He put a hand beneath, his fingers warm and gentle, and gazed down at her with eyes that seemed impossibly blue, began sawing at the ropes. "The *Diana*?" he asked casually, as if his skin wasn't burning from the contact. Hers certainly was.

"Just offshore," Kit said. "Southwest of the pier. Sampson's in the jolly boat not far from the bathing houses."

Grant nodded. "We'll be getting Midshipman Cooper to the boat then." He made a final saw through the hemp, then tossed the split ropes away and looked down at her red and abraded wrists, still resting on his free hand.

"We could perhaps find some salve?" Cragwell offered behind them, and Kit nearly blushed. She'd almost forgotten they weren't alone.

"Not necessary," Kit said, pulling her hands back. She rubbed away the coarse and gritty remnants of rope. Her wrists were chafed, but she'd heal.

"But thank you," she added. "And by what means do you intend to get her to the boat?"

"By the safest means," Grant said with amusement, then glanced at Cooper. "Can you play dead, Midshipman?"

She looked at Kit, then Grant. "Er, probably?"

Grant nodded. "Then I'll be frank, as we're all of us sailors and soldiers. You'll be carried out to the wagon—as if killed here by Fouché for your illegal activities—for transport to a pauper's graveyard. They expect to see punishment from Fouché's abode. We are obliged to give them the show they request."

Kit looked from Grant, whom she trusted, to Cragwell, whom she didn't know. And after Grant's comment and a quick inspection, sized him up as a soldier.

"Rank," she demanded, thinking of Grant's New London majordomo, who'd previously served.

Cragwell bit back a smile. "Sergeant in the Sixtieth Foot."

A regiment that had seen action in Hispania during the Continental War. "All right," Kit said, and nodded at Cooper.

Cragwell gestured toward Cooper. "Ma'am? If you'll just come this way?"

Cooper looked at Kit with uncertainty. "Pardon the expression, but I don't like the idea of returning to the boat alone, sir. Jin will have my hide if anything happens to you."

"That makes three of us," Grant said, "including the captain."

Kit nodded. "Go, Cooper. Whatever happens here, you can get back to the *Diana* and give Jin a report about what and who we saw. I trust these men to help me get back aboard safely. And when I'm there, we'll need to sail quickly." Seeing the hesitation in her eyes, Kit put a hand on her arm. "I don't want to order you, Midshipman. But I will, if it helps."

That was enough to put the resolve back in her shoulders. No midshipman worth her salt wanted to refuse a captain's request.

"No, sir. I'll go, and report to the commander. And may the gods have mercy on my soul," she murmured, before following Cragwell into another room.

Kit blew out a breath. "That's one bit less for worry then." She looked at Grant. "Thank you."

"You're welcome," he said, and the words seemed to echo in the room. "We'll do the same for you when the wagon returns." For the first time in hours, she felt a bit of relief. And promised herself Jin would have the next turn at shore duty.

There was true silence around her for the first time in hours, and she realized they were alone, or mostly so. She looked back at him, found his eyes on her. And the air seemed to sparkle and crack in the space between them.

Gratefully, all thoughts of the gaol and Gerard and Doucette—and the fear and anger they prompted—simply fell away, which was its own miracle. Even if she only had a moment before she had to tell him what she'd seen.

"Captain," he said.

"Colonel." Was her heartbeat not unusually quick?

Grant strode toward her, and she could actually feel her heart beating faster. She ordered herself to calm down.

"They hurt you," he said quietly, and reached out to touch her abraded wrist. But he seemed to think better of it, and curled his fingers into a fist, which he lowered with what appeared to be monumental effort.

"I'm fine," Kit said, working to maintain her own control. Yes, she was alone with a man she'd wanted to see for weeks. But there was work to be done, and they both knew it.

"Fouché?" she asked.

"A friend. You can trust him."

"It appears we have a guest."

Kit turned to face the man who appeared on the stairs.

He was as tall as Grant, and while he didn't have Grant's soldierly-broad shoulders, he looked fit and strong, with clear, piercing eyes.

Grant took a step back, gestured to the man. "Raleigh, this is Captain Kit Brightling of the Queen's Own. Kit, please meet Fitzwilliam Amberly, the Duke of Raleigh. Known locally as Fouché."

Her brows lifted. The Duke of Raleigh's reputation was . . . substantial. The eldest of three sons of the former Duke of Raleigh, he'd spent the war in Auevilla—if the gossip sheets were to be believed—carousing, whoring, and generally avoiding his obligations. But he didn't look like a man who'd devoted his life to drink and excess. No, he looked . . . cold. Not empty, like Doucette, who'd seemed to be totally lacking in emotion. But hard, as if all emotion had been pinched somewhere deep below, never allowed to surface.

She wasn't the type to be intimidated, but she could imagine the townspeople might feel differently. Grant and Raleigh were both big men, with careful manners and the gravitas of those who could wield significant power.

"Your Grace," Kit said, affecting a polite bow.

"Your Grace?" Grant repeated. "Why does he get a bow and an honorific? I'm a viscount and received only disdain and mutterings for my aristocratic leanings."

Kit glanced at him, bit back a smile at the glimmer of jealousy in his eyes. "He's a duke. But he doesn't appear to be a wastrel. Or at least not entirely."

Raleigh lifted an imperious brow that Kit imagined was well practiced and quickened the hearts of Beau Monde mamas.

"Your reputation precedes you," he said. "You are, as expected, very frank for a woman without a title." His voice was deep and carried the precision of years of elite education and society training. But she was hardly intimidated by the Beau Monde.

"You're very brave for a man without a ship."

Raleigh watched her in silence, then glanced at Grant. "Maintain hope, Grant. Perhaps you've a thirteenth cousin who'll meet his untimely demise and you, too, can be a duke and subject to these abuses."

Kit was pleased, and a little relieved, to find he had a sense of humor. Seeing Doucette had her comparing everyone now, wary of those who demanded deference.

"You're Fouché?" she asked. "Or pretending to be?"

"Fouché is the name I used when I first arrived here four years ago. It was a lie, but a well-documented one. At the time, I wished to disappear, and so I did."

"Because that was the freedom afforded by power and coin," Kit said. To his credit, Raleigh nodded.

"Later, I was approached by one of Chandler's men to provide information."

"And you agreed despite your desire to disappear?"

"I'm not accustomed to being questioned by sailors."

"I'm not accustomed to being thrown in Gallic gaols and interrogated by Islish viscounts and dukes, so we're both having very unusual days."

His eyes narrowed. "I'm not certain if I like you or not."

"Then it is fortunate I do not answer to you, Your Grace."

He offered a begrudging smile. It seemed sincere but didn't reach his eyes, and surely not his heart. A duke couldn't be single forever; the Beau Monde wouldn't permit it. So gods' luck to the woman dealt this particular hand.

"My loyalties to the Crown were challenged," Raleigh said after a time. "While I may have lived in Gallia, I am still an Islishman. And I was bored by wastreling, as you called it. Gallic officials, of course, knew none of this. They believed I'd left my loyalties behind and employed me to pass along whatever intelligence I received. I've done so, with careful New London coordination. Now they refer suspected acts of espionage to me, which is why you're here."

"That's quite a precarious position," she said, thinking of Jin balancing on one foot on the decking. "Acting as an agent for both the Isles and Gallia."

"It can be," Raleigh agreed, but his smile was chilling. "But we are a very convincing sort."

She looked at Grant. "And you?"

"I'm the protégé," he said.

"Of the drinking, gambling, or wastreling?" Kit asked.

Grant put a hand on his chest, managed a chagrined look. "I'm the dissolute viscount who's turned his estate over to his younger brother's running and come to Raleigh's shelter for wayward Beau Monde. After surveying nearly two hundred miles of coastline."

Raleigh leaned against a tall chair, crossed his arms. "Why are you here?"

"In your home, or in your town?"

"Clever," Raleigh said, with a flash of amusement in his eyes. "Start with the former."

"Cooper and I were arrested for spying. We denied the charges, and Grant was, rather ironically, brought in to scare the truth out of us."

"How did he do?"

"I'm well and thoroughly terrified."

His lips twitched. "And you're in town because?"

"We're searching for the *Fidelity*. And found it anchored at your dock."

Grant looked at Raleigh, smiled. "I told you the Crown Command would recognize it, changes or no."

"So you did," Raleigh said, and looked at Kit with approval. "She's been in port for two days. We sent a messenger to New London, but it won't have arrived yet."

"Gerard?" Kit asked.

"There's been no sighting of him in town, or in villages outside it. It appears the *Fidelity* was sailed with only a skeleton crew."

Kit frowned. "If he's not on Montgraf, and he's not with the *Fidelity*, where is he?" But she understood the truth, disappointing as it was, the moment the words were out.

"The *Fidelity* attracts too much attention," she said. "And it's been here for only two days, but Gerard's been gone for weeks."

"Conclusion?" Raleigh asked.

"He disembarked elsewhere," Kit said. "The *Fidelity* had ample time to sail to some other port, ensure he was settled somewhere else, likely with some of the crew, his personal guards. Then the *Fidelity* sailed on, staying close to shore and out of sight of the blockade. We'd assumed Gerard would be on his flagship, so that's what we've looked for." They'd been wrong, and he'd outsmarted them again.

She cursed vividly, sending Raleigh's brow high.

"You swear rather like a sailor," he said mildly.

She ignored that. "What about the pennants?"

"They were hung by the Resurrectionists," Grant said. "That's the preferred term by Gerard's loyalists. Nationally, they're led by Beaumont and Van Dijk and the rest of the anti-monarchists. Locally, Beauvoir is a supporter."

"Gallia did not blossom under the reinstituted monarchy," Raleigh said. "Some of the nation has been rebuilt, but primarily where the king's aristocratic friends reside. There are more than a few who'd prefer to take their chances again with an emperor when the king has done so little for them."

"We suspect he may have planned to launch his campaign here," Grant continued, "or at least this was one of multiple options."

"And, unfortunately for us, he picked a different option. So where is he?"

"We've people scouring the coast," Raleigh said. "But he's not yet been located."

Kit nodded. "What about Doucette?"

"What about him?" Raleigh asked grimly.

They might have known of the *Fidelity*, but they hadn't known about Doucette. "He's here," she said. "In Auevilla."

"Impossible," Raleigh said matter-of-factly, in a tone that said he was accustomed to deciding facts, not being surprised by them. "He didn't walk away from Contra Costa."

"I saw him myself," Kit said, "wearing the uniform of an imperial guard."

There are different kinds of silence. The pleasant and comforting quiet that might be shared by friends or lovers. The silence of anticipation and waiting, full of tension. And the silence of fury . . . and fear.

"Where?" he asked, that anger seeping through his features.

"Generally about town. We followed him from the dock to a

small park. He picked up something at one building—a red leather portfolio, it appeared. He showed something from it—a map, perhaps—to a man named Sedley he met near a park. Sedley referred to Doucette as a 'marshal.' We slipped away after that."

The duke simply stared at her. She wasn't sure if it was shock, exasperation, or irritation she saw on his face. "You followed La Boucher through town?"

A bit of all three, she concluded, from his tone. "We did."

"You aren't trained for espionage."

"No, we aren't. But that's done little enough for you lot: They know there are two Islish spies in Auevilla."

"Well," Raleigh said casually, "we knew our luck would run thin at some point. I know Sedley. He's a worm of a man, beneath even contempt. He'd done Gerard's bidding during the war, and hopes to find a position within his new cabinet. A map, you say?"

Kit nodded. "You'll also not be pleased to learn Contra Costa has not diminished Doucette's ambition or willingness to manipulate magic. He killed a man at the gaol using only that."

And she told them what she'd seen, and felt unsettled again.

"Blue-green magic, you say?" Raleigh asked.

"It looked not unlike St. Elmo's fire," Kit allowed.

Raleigh frowned. "That's harmless to ships, isn't it?"

"Almost always. The causes aren't entirely known, but it's some sort of atmospheric discharge. Might raise your hair a bit, but doesn't hurt. This was something different. This was the current, or some exterior portion of it. Frankly, I don't know how he did it—drew on the current without killing himself and everyone around him. Pulled it to the surface, somehow, or some residual aether, perhaps."

"Scarring?" Grant asked, gaze dropping to her hands.

"No. I saw no consequence of his actions. Not so much as a singed blade of grass."

And that had her worried more than anything. More than the ban, and Contra Costa, it was the physical consequence—including the scars on her palms—that kept the Aligned from overreaching. Not because they were overly painful, but because they reminded her that the current was *other*, and it always demanded a price.

She squeezed her hands into fists, and Raleigh noticed the movement, his gaze flicking down to her curled fingers.

"Sleight of hand?" Raleigh asked, lifting his gaze again. "Perhaps he was aware he was being watched and wanted you to see it—wanted someone from the Isles to see it."

"I was at a communal window in a gaol cell. He couldn't have known I'd look." She shook her head. "And I'm not Aligned to the land, but even I could feel the vibration. The, I suppose, shudder of power."

"We've a long history of pretending the currents don't exist and then punishing those who tried to make use of them. Contra Costa proved magic is dangerous in untrained hands," Raleigh added, voice quieter now. "We need to learn how to safely utilize it. And I understand the Isles is taking steps."

The queen had admitted to Grant and Kit that the Isles had been secretly investigating how to make more use of magic. Kit didn't care for the idea, but had come to understand the defensive necessity.

"And how will the public react when they learn of those efforts?" she wondered.

"I imagine they'll come to accept it quickly once they learn Doucette is alive and Gerard's given him a promotion."

For a moment, they stood in silence. Captain, colonel, duke. And she wondered if they all considered the same question, so she opted to ask it aloud.

"Could you get close enough to kill him now?"

Assassinating officers wasn't done; that's not how Islish or Continental wars were fought or won. It was foot regiments and ordinary Jacks that did the fighting; officers looked, watched, directed. But if Grant or Raleigh was shocked by the question, neither showed it.

"I would not bother to worry about killing an officer who should be dead already," Raleigh said. "But treaties were signed, and all but the highest of Gerard's officers and soldiers were pardoned in order to permit their reassimilation into Gallic society. Doucette's rank was low enough at Contra Costa to secure that benefit. In the absence of a declaration of war, killing him would violate the queen's prior agreements. And rally more to Gerard's cause.

"But I will include this in my reports, as I'm sure you will. We have allies in town who can keep a watchful eye in the meantime."

Kit nodded. "I know war is a sailor's business, and a soldier's at that. But I was hoping we might avoid it. Save the world from revisiting that terror."

"You've seen Auevilla," Grant said. "They don't appear to want saving."

"No, they appear to want war," Kit agreed. "Was that true in the other places you visited?"

"It depends on the village," Grant said. "Some consider Gerard to be too focused on war and victory, and not enough on caring for the common man. Others think he will finally save the country from the evils of monarchy and make it a financial power."

"Is that why Doucette is here?" Kit asked. "Because the village supports Gerard?"

"Meaning," Raleigh said, "will he—or they—be using this as a base of operations? As the first step toward Saint-Denis?"

"He has support," Kit said. "Doucette is here. He has the *Fidelity*, and he has a river running into Gallia. It's a logical place to begin a march."

"It's possible," Raleigh said. "There certainly are beneficial conditions. It's a wonder, Captain, that you haven't worn a trench right through the *Diana*'s deck."

Kit stopped short at Raleigh's comment and looked around. Without thinking of it, she'd paced to the other end of the room.

"Captain Brightling enjoys a purposeful stride," Grant said.

She made a vague noise of agreement and made herself stop, looked up at a large, gilt-framed painting that hung there. It was a ship, three-masted and proud, tilted against a wave in a brilliantly turbulent sea. The sun hovered at the edge of the horizon, making the water glow from within.

"This is beautiful," Kit said. "The water looks"—she lifted fingertips to the canvas, let them hover above the glimmering crests as if she might feel the sunlight on her fingers—"real," she finished.

"I won it in a game of indigo," Raleigh said, stepping beside her.

"So at least some of the rumors are true."

"Probably more than a few," he acknowledged.

Cragwell appeared in the doorway.

"All is well?" Kit asked.

He nodded briskly. "Midshipman Cooper was delivered to the boat, and they're waiting for the captain just offshore."

"Excellent work, Cragwell. Thank you." Raleigh turned back to Kit. "Your turn, Captain. You'll be taken out as, let's not mince words, a corpse, having succumbed to my rather monumental temper." The words were spoken with absolute flat affect, but Kit had no doubt the man could fire a good anger if the need arose. "You'll be covered by a shroud and taken to the boat in the back of the wagon. If you're stopped, act as if you've been told I was a spy. Give me up in order to save yourselves."

So cold of temperament, Kit thought, but not of heart.

"Why should I follow your orders?" she asked.

Raleigh's smile was thin. "Because, as you so aptly pointed out, I'm the duke." He looked at Grant. "And you won't be going alone."

Grant's eyes fired. "Our work here—"

"Is done," Raleigh finished. "The loyalists now know there are spies in their midst, and it's only a matter of time before they come for us. I want us gone, and our staff secured, before that happens. And I need to report what we've learned."

"As do I," Kit said.

Grant looked at Kit. "It appears I'm to rely on your assistance once again." And the warmth in his eyes had even Raleigh clearing his throat.

"I don't imagine the queen would object," she said, and glanced at the duke. "We can ship you as well, and your staff."

"No need." He pulled a letter from his pocket. "I'll be leaving on horseback shortly, as I've just received a very important missive from the governor about allegations of spies in the area. It is of significant enough import that we must discuss it posthaste."

"And, of course, you'll be leaving the letter behind should anyone have questions."

Raleigh smiled at her. "Naturally."

"And the house staff?" Grant asked.

"They'll be safe," he assured them. "Cragwell isn't the only soldier I employ. If there's danger, they'll ensure the other staff are evacuated and moved to safe houses."

Kit nodded. "Good. That's good."

A maid came into the room with two small pots, a cloth, and a brush.

"Dorcas," Raleigh said, "Kit Brightling, and you know the viscount."

She made a small bow, smiled at Kit. "Would you like to be first, ma'am?"

"First?"

"In the event the gendarmes stop the wagon, we want you to look convincing. This will help with the illusion."

"What is it?" Kit asked, leaning forward to see the brilliant scarlet liquid inside one of the pots.

"Powder in one, and beet juice in the other, mixed with a bit of sugar water to thicken it. It's quite effective, but does stain a bit."

A good thing she hadn't worn her uniform coat.

"Now," Dorcas said, her smile bright and helpful. "Let's bloody you up."

# SIX

Kit's face, neck, and hands were powdered to add a bit of pallor, and then cool liquid was painted across her face and hands, sprinkled across her jacket. Grant got the same treatment, and then they looked at each other.

It was surprisingly convincing, and certainly enough to give the effect they needed—that Fouché had expressed his considerable anger on sailor and soldier.

"Good luck," Grant said, offering Raleigh a hand.

"And to you," Raleigh said, and they shook with aristocratic efficiency. Then the duke turned to Kit.

"Captain. Perhaps we'll meet again under more pleasant circumstances."

"You should return to New London," she said. "You can host a ball and be the talk of the Beau Monde."

"That," he said crisply, "I will not do."

Kit was carried at the shoulders and ankles out to the street. She managed to go limp, but fingers gripped her with such force she imagined she'd see bruises for a week. She was dumped into the back of the wagon. She let her arms and legs fall where they would and kept her eyes closed. After a moment, she felt Grant beside her.

Then muslin was drawn over them, light enough to contour around their bodies and leave little mystery as to the wagon's contents.

The wagon shook, the horses were clucked forward, and they began to move.

Kit opened her eyes beneath the muslin, glanced beside her. Grant did the same, light filtering through muslin casting lacy shadows across his face.

"Hello again," he whispered, in their world of shifting sunlight.

"Hello," she said, and winced as the wagon hit a low spot. "He couldn't have tossed us into the duke's fancy carriage? I assume he has one."

"He probably has several," Grant whispered. "Perhaps we could talk of other things?"

"Such as?"

His smile was wide.

But before he could answer, the wagon jolted. They heard Cragwell's haggard sigh, then: "What's this, then?"

Kit and Grant went very still.

"We've word of spies," someone said in Gallic, in a low and gruff voice.

"I am in the employ of Fouché," Cragwell said. "I know nothing about spies, which is my lord's business. I merely handle the consequences of perfidy, as you are aware." He'd been well trained, and his voice was flat and bored.

"You've already been this way once today." This was a different man, his voice a bit higher.

Cragwell snorted. "Do you think I've control over Fouché's activities? That when he says, 'Go again, boy,' I can tell him, 'No, as I don't find your methods efficient'?" He sighed with great exhaustion.

"He has a point," said High Voice. "It's no business of ours what Fouché does. We don't want his attention on us, aye?"

There was silence for a moment, and Kit poured her energy into willing the men to let them go ahead.

"No," Low Voice said, and Kit's heart sped a bit more. "Beauvoir said to watch carefully for spies. So we'd better look."

"You've got the belly for it?" Cragwell asked. "I've seen them, and Fouché was not gentle or kind. There's quite a bit of, well, blood."

Kit heard the considering pause, swallowed hard. Keep walking, she told them. Just keep walking.

"I've no belly for blood," Low Voice said. "But better someone else's than mine. The marshal's in town, and I've seen what he can do."

"You're right," said High Voice. "We'll have a look."

Footsteps moved toward the wagon's rear. Grant quickly squeezed her hand, then pulled away again.

Kit sucked in a breath, closed her eyes, willed herself to go rigid as the muslin was pulled away and light poured over them both.

They looked in silence for a moment, then High Voice poked Kit's hand with a finger. "The body is cold."

"It's cold outside, you dolt," Low Voice said.

High Voice poked harder. "And a damn shame. She's got a good face and a nice pair of—"

"She's deceased, man. Show a bit of respect." The wagon shifted, probably as Cragwell turned on the bench seat.

"Only recently," Low Voice said, as if the only problem was a bit of unlucky timing. "And ain't this the muscle?" He poked at Grant.

"That's him," Cragwell said, the horses shuffling in their harnesses, ready to move. Which might be the first time Kit had sided with the horses. Her lungs were beginning to burn with need. Pity she didn't have the same ability on land as she did in the water.

"No longer useful when they start working for the enemy."

"To hell with the Isles," Low Voice said. "Long live Rousseau."

"Long live Rousseau," High Voice repeated, but without much enthusiasm.

"You can plainly see they're dead, aye? Show some respect and cover them up. You don't want to traumatize the citizenry, do you?"

Yes, Kit silently agreed. Cover us so we can breathe again.

"'Traumatize the citizenry,'" Low Voice repeated dramatically. "You're a fancy talker for a wagon driver."

"I like to expand my mind," Cragwell said. "If you're done, can we be on our way? Fouché runs a tight schedule, and as you can see, he corrects mistakes with his fists."

"I guess these two got the brunt of that, aye?" Low Voice asked.

"Aye," Cragwell said. "Pitiful thing, too, having to kill a pretty woman. But Fouché doesn't take with spies."

One of the gendarmes huffed but pulled the muslin back over Grant and Kit. She pursed her lips, tried to suck in a breath that moved her body as little as possible.

Another pause, then the sound of a pat on a horse's haunch. "Begone then."

Kit didn't breathe until the wagon began moving again, wheels creaking over the pitted road.

She shifted her gaze to look at Grant and saw his features scrunch, his eyes watering ferociously. Making as little movement as possible, she reached out, squeezed his hand.

He looked at her, wiggled his nose. "The hay," he mouthed, clearly trying to control a physical reaction to it.

She squeezed his hand harder but knew they'd lost when he closed his eyes.

The sneeze was so loud the *Diana* must have heard it. And it was followed by silence—including that of the gendarmes' footsteps.

"*Achoo!*" Cragwell said, then honked loudly, as if cleaning his nose.

Another beat of silence, and then the footsteps grew closer. "What was that sound?"

Grant squeezed his eyes closed.

"My sneeze?" Cragwell asked. "Surely you've heard a sneeze before. Damnable weather. Always makes me sneeze." He honked loudly again, and Kit hoped he'd managed to find a handkerchief.

But the gendarmes moved closer still, each sound speeding Kit's heartbeat. If they were captured now, there'd be no easy outcome. Grant and Raleigh would be confirmed as spies, and all of them punished for it.

Given the information they needed to impart, being captured was absolutely not an option. The Crown Command, the queen, had to be advised about the *Fidelity* and warned about Doucette—not to mention the intelligence Grant and Raleigh had gathered.

She shifted her head to look at Grant, got his minuscule nod as his fingers reached for hers, squeezed.

"Would you like to ride with me?" Cragwell offered. "I need to finish my task and return the wagon."

The gendarmes didn't seem to believe him, despite the impressively chill tone, as their footsteps moved closer still.

"I believe that must be our cue," Grant whispered, his lips near her ear.

"We aren't giving up Raleigh," she said, just as quietly. Not unlike Cooper, she wasn't going to throw someone else into the fire in order to avoid being singed.

"Of course not. But we need to give Cragwell time to make his escape. On three, we're up and we run for the boat."

She'd barely nodded when their "shroud" was ripped away.

"*Three*," Grant called out in Islish, and they scrambled up.

Might as well employ a bit of drama, Kit thought. She jumped to her feet, hands fisted into claws and eyes wide, and screamed at the men in Gallic, "All murderers shall perish!"

The men's faces went pale as death. She thought they might simply fall over, but she didn't wait to find out. She took off at a sprint, Grant in step beside her. A flick of the reins and Cragwell had the wagon moving at a gallop in the other direction.

She didn't know this part of town beyond the minimal sketch Simon had pulled from the ship's store of maps, so she let Grant take the lead and followed him down one narrow street as the gendarmes stomped behind them, blowing whistles and yelling warnings through the town. They turned around a building—the prison, she belatedly realized—and ran into a slender alley between buildings through an inch-deep pile of muck that would require her to burn the boots the moment she returned to the *Diana*.

"There!" The guards were closer now, with more knowledge of the narrow streets than either she or Grant. She'd nearly made it halfway down the alley when a hand gripped her wrist, pulled her into an even narrower slot between buildings. She'd nearly made the instinctual scream when she realized it was Grant who'd taken her hand and was leading her through the alley.

They emerged into a backstreet busy with traders and merchants, carts and horses and people moving back and forth as crates and barrels were bought, sold, shifted.

A man pushed a low cart of wine bottles into the street. Kit swerved around it, made it three steps past, and then turned back and snagged a bottle by the neck.

"*Merci!*" she said, and tossed a coin as she ran on.

The merchant lowered the handles of his cart, began shouting, fist pumping, about the thief. Kit tucked her prize under her arm as they ran toward the shore.

Grant cursed. "Brightling, you are considerable trouble. Was that really necessary?"

"You aren't the first to say so. And I'm not going back without a token for Jin," she said. "I gave him a gold coin. He'll not get better, I imagine."

Calls and whistles erupted behind them as the gendarmes caught up, and they pushed harder, dodging the gawkers who walked the boardwalk, then pitching into the sand.

Running through sand was no easy task, and sailors were rarely afforded the opportunity for long constitutionals. Grant's longer legs gave him an advantage that had her falling behind.

"Stop!" the gendarmes called out in Gallic. "Stop there or we will fire!"

Grant glanced back and she saw the concern in his eyes, imagined powder being rammed down a barrel a dozen yards behind her. "Don't make me carry you!" he called out.

Oh, she would not be carried by a soldier into her own damned jolly boat. Absolutely not.

She thought of the man Doucette had killed, body jerking on the ground, and the fact that only she could relay the details of that story to the Crown Command. If she died, the information would be lost. So she pushed harder.

The jolly boat lay twenty yards ahead, already in the water, Sampson and Cooper at the oars.

*Crack.*

The report of a rifle echoed behind her. Splinters flew out from the boat, and Cooper and Sampson dropped onto the deck.

Grant reached the water first, jogging through the surf to the boat. "Everyone intact?"

Still running, she saw a thumb poke through the hull just above the waterline; then Cooper's and Sampson's faces popped up.

"Fine," they called out together.

Kit hit the water, and her reconnection to the ocean gave her a new surge of energy. Just in time, as the sound of men running behind her grew louder, closer; she refused to look back and kept her eyes on the boat, watched Grant clamber into it. Then his eyes went wide.

"Down!" he called out, and she dropped into the knee-high water, saw the ball shoot past her, leaving behind a slender white wake.

At least it didn't hit the boat. She swam toward it, the damned bottle of wine trying to bob to the surface. But she refused to let it go, not when she'd paid a good coin for it.

She surfaced just beyond the white hull, took the hand Grant offered her, and was pulled over the side. Kit looked back at the beach. They were thirty yards offshore now, their pursuers—Dock Man and half a dozen gendarmes—still on foot. She scanned the horizon as Sampson and Cooper rowed, looking for mast or sail, some indication the chase would continue in the water. But saw nothing.

Two men with rifles continued to reload, but the others looked disinterested in the chase and more interested in the women who bobbed in the water outside their bathing houses, now sodden and staring at the gendarmes whose shots had ruined their fun.

In the other direction, the *Diana* waited a hundred yards away in increasing waves and wind that pushed her closer to shore. Water sloshed through the hole in the jolly boat, pooling in the bottom.

Kit gauged the hole's diameter, then looked at the bottle of wine in her hand. She used her teeth to yank out the cork, then slammed it into the hole in the boat with the back of her fist, pounding a couple of times for good measure.

The fit was perfect.

"Problem solved," she said, then took a well-deserved swig of wine. She'd been right; it wasn't worth the gold coin.

"That's rather magnificent," Grant said, with what sounded like genuine awe in his voice.

"Sailors know a thing or two," she said with a grin. "Let's get the hell back to the boat."

The higher waves made the rowing harder. Kit held the open bottle of wine between her feet and joined the others at the oars, pushing past increasing surf toward the sailors who peered over the *Diana*'s gunwale, waiting to lower the davits.

The jolly boat was hauled up—this time with Grant in it— and they climbed out and into the waiting throng of officers and sailors.

Kit heard the sounds of shock, remembered what she and Grant looked like. "We're all healthy," she said, holding up her hands to ward them off. "This was just color used by a duke's staff to aid our escape from the gendarmes."

Jin's brows shot up. "Bit of a story there."

"Indeed," she said.

"What's this?" asked Mr. Oglejack, the ship's carpenter, flicking the cork-filled hole.

"Rifle shot," Kit said.

He looked it over. "Not a bad repair," he said, offering her a grin. "You want to help holystone the deck next time?"

"I'll pass, Mr. Oglejack, but thank you for the invitation."

Cooper and Sampson all but rolled out of the jolly boat, arms filled with wheels of cheese, long loaves of bread, and more wine.

Kit looked at Cooper, brows raised. "Midshipman. Dare I ask where that came from?"

"It's the duke's doing, sir," Cooper said with a grin. "Sergeant Cragwell insisted."

"How did they manage—" Kit began, but she shook it off. The *how* didn't matter; dukes had their ways.

War was coming, but at least she might mollify Cook. Or

allow herself to be in her cups enough to simply ignore his tantrums. "Here," she said, and thrust the open bottle at them. "Take them all to the galley with my compliments."

Sampson snickered. "He won't believe you traded for them."

Her stare went hard. "Make him believe."

Chuckling, they crossed the deck to the companionway to the deck below.

"I suppose we're obliged to thank the duke"—she slid her gaze to Grant—"as this gift is nothing to *sneeze* about."

"Hilarious," Grant said.

"Colonel," Jin said. "Welcome back aboard."

"Jin, Simon," he said, nodding at both of them. "Lovely to see you again, although the circumstances leave a bit to be desired."

"Given the circumstances," Kit said, "recall that we're in hostile territory."

"You think they'll give chase?" Jin asked.

"There'll be a rather involved story to tell, but the short of it is they believe we're Islish spies, walking away with important information about Gerard's plans. So it's likely. *Tamlin!*" she called out, and waited for the answer from the mast.

"*All clear!*" came the call.

"For now," Kit said. "Let's not give them time to follow." She nodded at Jin.

"Anchors aweigh!" he called out, and sailors ran to the capstan to begin hauling up the chain to raise the heavy anchor.

"Where are we for?" Simon asked.

"Portsea," she said.

"There's more," Jin said. She looked back at him, found him studying her.

She debated telling them, but only for a moment. Because

every sailor on the ship deserved to know the risks they now faced.

"La Boucher is alive," she said, loud enough for the sound to travel the length of the boat. "He was burned at Contra Costa but survived his injuries."

For a moment, it seemed every soul on the *Diana* stopped and looked at her.

Jin just stared at her, eyes wide. "Excuse me?"

"He's in Auevilla," she said, loud enough for all the crew to hear. "I saw him myself. And he has apparently learned how to use his Alignment. And control the current with it."

She squeezed Jin's hand, then looked around the crew. "He is as alive as we are, and I watched him use magic to kill a man. That he can wield the current as a weapon is . . . well, terrifying. It is of great concern to us, to every sailor and soldier in the fleet, and to the queen, to understand what we're facing. We sail for Portsea to report to the Crown Command, and we'll get there as quickly as we can."

Sounds of agreement and shock moved across the deck as sailors prepared to get underway.

"I'm for my cabin," she said. She had a very long report to prepare.

# SEVEN

S he cleaned beets and powder from her face and hands and changed back into her uniform, transferring the bit of ribbon from one lapel to the other. And she gave herself a moment to run the woven fabric through her fingers, wondering at its apparently Gallic origins.

Later, she thought, and smoothed the jacket down again. As was nearly always the case, she'd have to save the personal for later, when she had time and attention for it.

She sat down at her small desk, then began the process of preparing to prepare the report: She sharpened a quill, arranged paper and blotter, opened her bottle of ink, dipped.

"To Her Right and Honorable Majesty, Queen Charlotte," she began, and filled the page with her straight, tidy handwriting, well practiced from the hundreds of log entries and reports she'd penned over the years.

She told the story of their trip into Auevilla, what they'd found at the docks, and whom they'd seen there. Then their following of Doucette, his meeting, their arrest, the horror that had come after, and their rescue by the duke. She referred to him only as Fouché, expecting the queen either knew who he was or could obtain that information from William Chandler, her spymaster. While she intended to get the packet into the queen's hands, theft happened, and she wasn't going to reveal Raleigh's identity in a missive.

When she was done, she sat back, reread. Then penned a near duplicate for the admirals at Portsea; she didn't report to them, but they needed to know what she'd seen, minus the details she preferred to give to the queen.

It took a solid hour before she could blot the pages, fold and seal them, and place them into the portfolio she'd been given for official missives, not entirely unlike the one Doucette had used.

"Finished?"

She nearly jumped at the voice, found Grant standing in her doorway, tailcoat abandoned, sleeves rolled to the elbow, arms crossed. His forearms were rather admirably muscled, she mused, then lifted her brows.

"How long have you been standing here?"

"Long enough," he said, and pushed off, walked into her cabin. He left the door open, which was probably for the best.

Although she didn't especially want it to be for the best. She put the portfolio away, then rose.

"Did you need something?" she asked calmly, although her heart skittered like a frightened rabbit. She didn't care for that, for the wresting of her control. But neither had she liked the weeks that had stretched since she'd seen him. Even if their re-union was awkward and strange. Both of them, she thought, standing at the precipice.

"Jin asked me to relay the anchor is up and the ship is away."

Since Jin would be aware that she'd have felt the ship get underway as the sails were raised, he'd clearly sent Grant down to her for other reasons. On the other hand, Grant rarely did anything other than exactly what he wanted.

"Thank you," she said.

He took another step into the room, then another, until he was so close he needed to look down to see her. He was a tall man, was Rian Grant.

"You're welcome," he said. "It appears we're sailing together again."

"So it does." She felt so damned clumsy, like a sailor new to the mast. But she was no new sailor, and hadn't the weeks they'd been apart been wasted time? So she went with her strength: honesty.

"I'm not sure what to say."

His grin was wide and beautiful and might have had a lesser woman's knees wobbling. "You could say that you missed me, Kit."

She was brave enough, at least, to give him that.

"I missed you," she said, and watched the fire of joy, of pride, come into his eyes. "Entirely too much for my own comfort."

"Good," he said, and looked a bit relieved. "I was beginning to think I was the only one who felt that way. I've been like a boy in knee pants these last weeks."

She cocked her head at him. "Shorter?"

"Minx," he said, and tugged at a lock of her dark hair, then traced its descent to the edge of her chin, where it curled up just a bit at the end. "I've spent nights in abandoned warehouses, in the corners of cathedrals. And one very interesting evening in Pointe Grise in the bed of a beautiful demimondaine."

Her smile fell away. "I beg your—"

"She was away at the time," he explained, grin widening. "And is an informant for the Crown who loaned me the use of her abode while she was traveling. I was quite alone." He inched closer. "And you're beautiful when you're jealous."

"I'm not jealous," she said primly.

He made a vague noise, tipped up her chin with a finger. "Prepare yourself, Captain. I'm going to kiss you now."

Bells began to peal, and Kit instinctively glanced at the clock bolted to the wall. It wasn't time for change of shift.

"*All hands!*" someone called down, and footsteps began to echo through the passageway as sailors ran to their assigned positions on deck.

"Bloody damnable hell," Grant said, and stepped back, putting between them the space he'd have known she needed. His hands were on his hips, and a spark was in his eyes. "It's proving very difficult to seduce you, what with the constant interruptions."

Her eyes gleamed. "Is that what you're doing? Trying to seduce me?"

"Among other things. Do you object?"

"No," she decided, and they headed for the companionway.

⌒

She stepped on deck, Grant behind her, to find the wind had risen further. She looked instinctively across the water, found the waves around them now whitecapped. But there was no other ship in sight. Auevilla was located in a deep crescent of coastal land; it was a slip of shadow behind them. The northern edge of the crescent stood higher and reached farther into the Narrow

Sea, and the cliffs rose high off the starboard stern. But she saw nothing of concern.

"If Cook's already made it through the wine," she said, approaching the helm, "that's none of my concern."

"Ship," Jin said, his expression quite serious, and lifted his gaze to Tamlin. She stood in the mainmast top, hair streaming behind her like a pennant, gaze on the cliffs behind.

"Gallic?"

"I don't know. She just spotted her, asked you to come up. We rang the bells to have the crew in place."

Kit nodded, checked the weight of the sail, considered the wind. It was steady but blowing toward them. Because ships couldn't sail directly into the wind, they'd be forced to tack—sail at an angle—until it shifted. They'd move forward on a diagonal slightly away from their destination, and then tack, or turn, the yards and adjust the sails to move diagonally in the other direction in a zigzagging course. It was the best way to make use of unfriendly winds, but it added miles, and miles added time.

"I'll go up," she said. "Prepare to tack if necessary."

"Aye," Jin said, as she strode toward the mainmast. And heard him ask Grant behind her, "You want to go up, too? The view is beautiful."

"The view," Grant said blandly, "will be water. I can see plenty of that here."

Soldiers, she thought with a grin, and was absurdly glad to have this one on board.

Sailors gave way as she made to the mast, looked up at the ratlines—the grid of netting that kept the mast upright and was used by sailors to go aloft. The mainmast towered nearly 120 feet over the *Diana*'s deck, and the fighting top where Tamlin kept her watch was two-thirds of the way up, just below the spot where the square topsail would be unfurled.

"*Tiva koss*," someone threw out, wishing her luck as she put a boot into the ratlines and began to climb. Shimmying up the mast wasn't an easy job in the best of conditions. The top of the mast moved in a wider arc than the deck of the ship when the waves were high, and climbing in choppy seas could be a mental and physical challenge.

But when she reached the top, she remembered why Tamlin loved it. This was as close to flying as Kit assumed she'd ever be, with the wind in her face and the world streaming beneath and behind them. If ever a woman felt like a god, it was here alone on the mast, surveying creation.

Tamlin, who was shoeless, stood on tiptoe on the narrow platform, where the seas could be watched and enemies could be fired on from above. She waited until Kit stood beside her, then pointed to a spot behind the ship. There, still hidden from the deck by the high cliffs, were the tips of two masts. Tamlin offered the glass she kept tucked in a clever bit of netting. Kit peered through it, which revealed a great deal of sail and Gerard's white and gold flag waving in the wind.

"She won't be able to see us yet," Tamlin said. "There's no one on the mast."

"No," Kit said, lowering the glass. "She won't. But the ship appears to be at full sail. Neither of us has the weather gauge, which is a bit of luck, at least. How long until they do see us?"

"Minutes," Tamlin said.

"Keep an eye," Kit said, gripping the mast hard as a swell had it tipping nearly thirty degrees to starboard. Moments like that always brought her a little closer to the water than she preferred.

When she'd recovered her balance, she climbed down again, straightened her jacket when she reached the deck.

"Gallian vessel off the starboard stern," she called out, and strode back to the helm. "Two masts under full sail. Minutes until they confirm our position."

"You think they'll give chase?"

"That, or they hope to run the blockade."

"If they can't see us now," Grant said, studying the sea with furrowed brow, "how could they be giving chase?"

"Someone in town may have signaled it from the bluff," Simon said. "It's possible they've a shutter telegraph."

"Which is?" Grant asked.

"Mounted boards that can be flipped to show symbols in a certain order," Jin said. "There are typically six shutters in a sign, and the symbols are coded, so they can be used to relay messages to ships at sea."

"That's rather ingenious," Grant said.

"It is when it's not being used against us," Kit muttered. "We are terribly good at spotting boats that ought to be somewhere else. It's a shame they keep showing up."

"Orders, Captain?" Jin asked.

"Gallic brig!" shouted one of the sailors. "Off the starboard stern."

"There she is," Kit murmured. She'd wanted to see what it might do when it spotted them, as that would guide her answer to Jin's question. The timing couldn't have been better.

"Glass," she said, and Jin offered one. She raised it. Two masts, as they'd seen above, both square-rigged like the *Diana*'s.

"Cannons?" Grant asked.

"Gallic brigs of that size typically have eighteen guns," Jin said grimly, and Kit nodded.

"Confirmed," she said. "And a damned lot of canvas." If there was a sail missing from the ship's complement, she couldn't tell. She lowered the glass to the deck, could see the Gallic captain— a woman in Gerard's uniform—surveying the seas through her own glass. The other officers around her wore the same colors.

"Bold," Kit said, offering Jin the glass again. "They bear Gerard's flag and Gerard's uniform on a ship that, at least for now, belongs to the navy of the Gallic monarchy. And given they've apparently little concern for precedent, we need to move out of its path and its range."

They'd been on an easterly heading toward the crescent of land—and now the brig. It was time to turn the ship—which meant turning the wheel and shifting the direction of the horizontal beams that held the sails.

"Bring her to port," Kit said.

Jin stepped forward. "Man the fore-topsail!" he called out, and sailors rushed forward to the foremast to begin the process of shifting sails and steering the *Diana* into the wind and through to the opposite angle.

It took time to turn a hundred-foot ship with thousands of square feet of sails. While Simon made his calculations and Jin issued orders about loosening, shifting, and retightening lines and sails that were relayed by shouts toward the bow, Kit kept an eye on the Gallic ship, watching to see what it would do. The *Diana* had cannons now, but they were useful only if you were in range of the enemy's cannons as well.

Just as the *Diana* finished her tack, the brig began to change its course—and mimic the *Diana*'s.

"Damn," Kit said. "They're following."

She didn't want to engage a damned Gallic ship; they didn't have time for it. They'd have to take the offensive.

She looked at Jin. "Come around hard to starboard, as if we're tacking early. But keep swinging her around, and have the cannons on the starboard side ready to fire."

Some of the sailors nearby had heard the order, and hurrahs followed it. They'd been waiting for an opportunity to use the cannons.

"We'll have to move fast," Jin said, "or we'll expose our flank to their cannons."

"We'll move fast," Kit said. "Have the cannoneers ready." She closed her eyes. That was the signal, not just for Jin, but for the entire crew. They knew what she intended to do.

"Hard to starboard!" Jin called. "On the mainsail! Starboard cannoneers into position!"

She waited until she could feel the hull shift and lines loosen, which allowed the boom to turn, then tighten into position again.

The direction was set, so she'd supply the speed. The current beneath them was steady as a heartbeat. She reached for it, touched it gently as a lover, and could feel the energy flow around her, clean and bright. That was such a change from the darkness of Doucette's magic that she nearly wept from relief. But that must be for later. She waited until the *Diana* nearly quivered with pent-up energy, and for the signal from her crew.

"Ready," Jin said quietly, steadily.

Kit let the current loose. The banked power pushed the ship forward like a spear through the water, the shifted sails first flapping, then filling with wind. Kit opened her eyes, put a hand on the cabinet as the ship heeled into the turn, tilting at an angle that put the starboard side closer to the water.

"Sailing, torn down to its essence, is standing at an angle," Grant called out over the rushing wind and water. "And then standing at a different angle. Yes?"

Simon snorted but covered his mouth at Kit's arch look. "He's not entirely wrong, Captain."

"And there's a reason we don't usually allow soldiers on board."

"Ready the cannons!" Jin shouted, and Sampson and Fahri, a young but bright sailor, rammed in the gunpowder, added the wadding and pricked the powder, then pushed the cannons forward through the gunwale.

"You hit the mast," Kit said, "and there's a gold coin in it."

"I'll take it!" Fahri shouted, and adjusted the cannon's angle.

"Brig preparing to fire!" Tamlin called out, and Kit looked across the water, watched the enemy touch flame to cannon as they sailed toward each other.

"Get down!" Kit said, and sailors ducked as the air concussed, the explosion ringing across the water. The shot was early, struck the *Diana*'s bowsprit. Wood cracked and rigging splintered and flew, dropping down into the water.

"Cut those lines!" Watson said, already running toward the bow. "Dragging the yard will slow us down!"

Trusting her lieutenant to handle that, Kit looked back at Jin, Grant. "You're witnesses. That was no warning shot, and we've been fired on by a Gallic brig in the course of our duties."

Sampson took the slow match offered by Mr. Wells.

"Fire when ready," Kit told him. He and Fahri watched their target, and he set the fire to the touch hole.

The cannon flew backward as the shot flew forward, arcing

high above the water and toward the brig. It struck middeck, sending wood and at least one sailor flying.

"*Tiva koss,*" Kit murmured for the injured man, but she didn't have the luxury of pity. Not when her people were at risk and the brig was still running. It had been a clean hit, but not a disabling one.

"One more shot, Captain?" Fahri asked, looking back at Kit as Mr. Wells swabbed the interior of the cannon with water to douse any remaining embers.

Firing a cannon wasn't the easiest of tasks in harbor, much less at sea on a sharp heel. But they'd done it safely and with some success. And damned if the brig would follow them all the way to Portsea.

"All right," Kit said. "But if you miss, you owe me a gold coin."

Eyes bright, Fahri looked at Sampson, who nodded. "Agreed."

"Bring her around again, Jin," Kit said, and the sails were adjusted, the current touched, the *Diana* making a near circle to move behind the brig, which was slower to maneuver as it dealt with the new hole in the deck. Fahri and Sampson moved to the cannon on the port side, and the preparations were repeated.

"Fire at will," Kit said.

*Boom,* smoke, shot flying across the water. It hit the brig's foremast halfway up, tearing through canvas and rigging. With a *crack,* the top half of the mast toppled, the tangle of sail and wood and rope striking the mainmast as they fell and ripping through the brig's mainsail.

The *Diana* erupted with cheers and applause.

"Your crew is exceptional," Grant said. "And they're going to run you out of coin."

"It is the best problem to have," Kit said. She pulled a coin from her pocket and strode to Fahri, who was presently being embraced and jostled by a very large Sampson.

"Well done," she said, and offered the coin to Fahri. "You'll share it."

"We will," Fahri said, and turned back to her fellow sailors, bit into the coin to prove it was real. More cheers, more applause.

"Straighten her out," Kit told Jin, returning to the helm. "Let's get to Portsea." But she happened to look up, saw the flash of red in the brig's mainmast.

"Sniper!" she called out, ducking as sailors hit the deck. The sniper wasted no time; the *crack* of the rifle filled the air, followed by the bitter scent of gunpowder. Kit waited a heartbeat, then looked up, around. "Report!" she called out.

"No visible damage," Watson called out.

"I believe I need . . . to sit."

Kit looked back. Jin was on his knees, hand clutched at his side, and blood seeping through his fingers, pinging onto the wood planks below.

His eyes closed and he slumped to the deck.

# EIGHT

"Jin!" Kit screamed, and slid to her knees beside him. Fingers shaking, she pulled back his coat, found the mirror stain across his shirt, just above his left hip. She ripped the linen next, revealing the open wound, angry and red and seeping lines of blood.

The sniper had hit her commander.

She looked back at the crew, fury in her gaze. "Take the sniper out," she said, every syllable a new and dangerous threat. "And keep her moving, Watson! They do not get another chance." A tribute to her training, Watson took the helm without question, began shouting orders.

"Allow me," Grant said, and shouldered a rifle, aimed it toward the brig. One second, then two, and gunfire echoed across the water.

Two seconds later, the blot of red dropped from the mast like a stone.

There were tenuous cheers and applause as Grant lowered the weapon, a wisp of smoke curling from the end of the barrel.

"March!" Kit called out. "I need March on deck!"

It took only seconds for March to make her way to the helm and crouch beside Kit. With nimble fingers and quiet, competent speed, she looked over the wound, checked Jin's breathing and the beat of his heart.

"I need to turn him," she said, "and see if the ball is lodged or went through." She leaned up to look at Jin. His eyes were closed, his face a terrifying kind of gray.

"I'll shift him at the hip. You shift him at the ribs," she said, and pointed to the spot where she wanted Kit to help move him.

"I can still hear you," Jin said. "And I can turn myself."

"Excellent," March said, utterly unperturbed. "That will be a great help to all of us."

"Here," Grant said, and offered Jin a bit of thick leather. "Something to bite on, at least until you can take a nip of something warm."

She saw a hint of fear in Jin's eyes, but he pushed it back, nodded, and slipped the leather between his teeth.

Kit met Grant's gaze, gave him a nod of thanks.

"All right," Marsh said. "On three." She counted down, and they shifted Jin onto his side.

His harsh groan clutched painfully at Kit's chest, but she kept her fingers steady, kept Jin turned so March could inspect her patient.

"Figures you'd find a way out of doing your work," Kit said with an exceedingly forced smile, trying to keep the mood light—and ignoring the drumbeat of her heart. It was the universal burden of soldiers and sailors to shoulder the pain of death and gore, and their universal gift to continue fighting.

"Any port in a storm," Jin said, his own (exceedingly forced) smile wiped away when March grunted, nodded at Kit, and they laid him down again.

"It didn't go through," March said. "It needs to come out, and any bit of wadding that might have gone with it. We don't want a fever to set in."

"Bloody hell," Jin said. "If this doesn't kill me, Nanae certainly will."

Nanae was his lovely and thoughtful wife. "I'm not telling her," Kit said. "She scares me."

"She scares me, too," Jin said, and looked at March. "What do we do?"

"You're going to drink a ridiculous amount of any sailor's favorite medicine," March said. "And when you're good and drunk on that rum, I'm going to poke around in your innards and see if I can't find the little blighter. If we're lucky, I will, and I'll sew you up neat and tidy."

"And if we aren't lucky?" Jin asked.

There was a pause. "More rum," March said. "Great, gasping quantities of rum."

Kit hoped they had that much on board. And that it would be enough.

⟨⟩

Grant and Sampson helped move Jin to the officers' mess, as it had the largest table and best lighting on the ship. Cook, to his grouchy credit, had covered the table in linens probably once used to cover the table for fancier captains than Kit, who thought Cook had enough to handle in feeding twenty-four sailors and didn't need to add laundering to the list. March's supplies, so many of them silver and sharp, were placed in a neat leather binding on a chair beside the bottle of wine Kit had brought on board—recorked now—and a bottle of rum.

They carefully put Jin at the edge of the table. As gingerly as they could, the men helped remove his boots, jacket, linen shirt.

"Water and linens," Cook said from the doorway, and Kit moved out of the way as a pot of water and stack of clean fabric were placed beside the tools. He looked at Kit, nodded, his eyes grave. Cook loved to stir trouble, but he was still a sailor.

"And I'll take the clothes," he said, picking up the bundle without argument. Perhaps he was willing to do a bit of laundering after all.

"How can I help?" Kit asked March, as she began to organize her tools.

Wordlessly, she pointed at the bottle of rum. "Liberal application."

Kit uncorked it, winced. She didn't care for rum, preferred even old water to the scouring taste of the cheap tipple the Crown Command provided to sailors. But she knew the necessity here, so she offered the bottle to Jin.

"Have a drink, sailor."

She knew he didn't care for it, either—rarely touched drink at all. That he took a heartening sip, winced, and then took another spoke to the volume of his pain.

He handed the bottle back to her. "Make sure Nanae is taken care of."

Kit managed a snort, corked the bottle again. "You're going to be fine, because March is going to ensure it. And even if you weren't, Nanae is a strong woman." She reached out, squeezed his hand. That statement was as far into vulnerability as she was willing to venture.

"Pardon, Captain," March said, and Kit shifted to the side but kept her grip on Jin's hand. March employed Sampson to help her with her tools. When those were in place, March nodded.

"Very well," she said. "Let's begin."

⟡

It was horrific.

That's all Kit could think after watching March fiddle in Jin's torso, trying to find the bullet. He gripped Kit's hand with bone-bruising strength, and clamped down hard on the leather Grant had provided. Sweat dotted his forehead, and tears streamed from his eyes from a pain Kit couldn't have imagined.

Kit might have seen physicks do worse. There were, after all, any manner of upsetting ways to be injured at sea. Wood splintered, lines abraded, and cannonballs made a weapon of deck and hull; she'd seen onboard surgery for all of them. But never her closest colleague, her confidant. And guilt weighed on her as much as his groans.

Unfortunately, the bullet was tricksy and avoided even March's skilled fingers. The pain eventually sent Jin under, thanks to the gods, so when the blade was called for, he was unaware. That was no less gruesome than the prior effort had been, and blood stained the tablecloth beneath her friend and commander.

Kit didn't let go her iron grip on Jin's hand, even when the plink of blood onto the floor was broken by a *boom* that spilled through the air, the concussion shuddering sea and ship. Instinctively, Kit reached for the current, found nothing amiss.

There were footsteps, and she looked back toward the doorway. Found Grant there, hand braced against the swaying of the ship.

"Captain, you're needed above."

"Watson has the helm," she said, and turned back to Jin.

"And Watson and others have need of you."

"So they sent you to fetch me? I trust they have things in hand."

"They need your leadership."

"*I won't leave him.*" She meant, *I refuse to lose him*, the words an exclamation and a promise.

They'd been friends for too long, and she refused to lose him to musket ball or fever. She wasn't going to tell Nanae that Jin had lost his life under Kit's command. Refused to let his children grow up without their father. And if she stayed here, if she watched over him, if she refused to turn her back, maybe his chance of survival increased. Maybe his odds improved.

"*Captain Brightling,*" Grant said again, his voice hard and brittle as glass. "I order you to return to the deck."

All movement ceased in sheer shock.

With anger now burning at the edges of fear and grief, Kit climbed to her feet, letting go of Jin's hand for the first time in— minutes? Hours? She had no idea. She turned to face Grant, every feature hard and cold.

"I beg your pardon?" she asked, voice low and dangerous. "By what right do you have to give me orders, *Colonel*?"

He looked down his nose at her, and looked every bit the imperious aristocrat. "I am a peer of this country, *Captain*."

Oh, she would have enjoyed wiping the smirk from his face. And what a change, she thought in some vacant part of her mind, from the joy she'd felt at seeing him walk into the room in Auevilla. Perhaps that's why she felt a hollow in her chest, even as she fumed.

"You may be a peer, but that gives you no authority over my ship or its operations."

"Your operations are above," he persisted.

"And Jin is here."

"Jin is one member of your crew. He is being cared for by March; let her do her work. The rest of us are facing war, and there are a dozen more sailors who need your guidance. It's your obligation to care for the rest of them."

His tone had lost its bite but was no less insistent for that.

And as much as it pained and embarrassed her to admit it, she'd seen enough war to understand when leadership was needed. And when she had to leave others behind. She was the captain of the entire ship.

She looked back at Jin, still so pale, and at March, who nodded. "He's my friend, too, Captain."

Without a word, Kit turned, worked studiously not to meet his gaze. "I need a moment," she said, the words chilly enough to frost the air. Then she strode past Grant without a word.

⟜⟝

Kit went into her cabin, scrubbed her hands in the basin until her skin was red and raw. Then dumped the water, splashed more into the basin, and plunged her face into it. It was jarringly cold. Brutally cold. And that helped, somehow. As if the pain was atonement for the sin of his injury.

She pressed her damp face into clean linen and gave herself a minute to feel the fear and panic. Because Grant was right.

She'd needed to be snapped from her trance. She could admit that weakness here, alone. She'd needed to step away from Jin for exactly the reasons Grant had identified. Because Jin was her friend, one of the best of her friends, and she couldn't help him right now. Her crew—every other soul on board the *Diana*—needed her.

Would she have simply stayed belowdecks, holding on to Jin as if she was his anchor, while cannon fire echoed above? For she knew that sound, recognized it for what it was. A shot had been fired. Not close enough to damage the ship, but fired all the same. And the sound of it—deep and low—confirmed it wasn't a small eight-pounder lit as a signal. It was larger, a twenty-four-pounder perhaps, fired as a warning shot. And she'd done nothing.

She tossed the towel aside, now angry at herself for having nearly neglected her duty.

But still furious with Grant, of course. She wouldn't be bullied by a member of the Beau Monde—much less in front of her crew while another was on the table, bleeding from the gut.

Oh, they were going to have words about that.

~⁓⁓

She returned to the deck, found Simon, Tamlin, and Watson at the helm, the last barking orders that were carried down the ship by officers to the sailors at the masts, canvas unfurled to increase their speed. Grant stood near them and watched her—expression blank—as she strode toward them. She ignored him. This wasn't the time for the discussion they needed to have.

"Report," she said, voice hard.

"Captain," Watson said. "We're well clear of damned Gallia, and the brig that shot the commander. But we've other guests."

Without waiting, she handed the glass to Kit. And didn't ask how Jin was, so Grant had given them the report.

"Man-of-war off the starboard bow."

Kit walked forward, with Watson trailing behind her, and followed the gazes of the sailors who'd paused in their work to stare at the shadow on the horizon.

She lifted the glass and made a low whistle.

It was, quite simply, the largest ship she'd ever seen. A four-masted man-of-war, the hull striped in blue and white, and each white strip a separate gun deck. She stopped counting at forty and knew that was an underestimate due to the angle of the ship.

It was easily twice—perhaps thrice?—the size of the *Diana*. Close to three hundred feet from bowsprit to stern, with a great golden figurehead of a buxom woman with flowing hair, holding a mallet in one hand and an oversized needle in the other. Frisia, and particularly its capital of Hofstad, was controlled by merchant Guilds.

Kit swore under her breath, raised the glass to the masts, and found the confirming flag, waving in the wind. "Frisian," she said, lowering the glass again. And even without it, she could still see sailors along the yards, pinpoints of white as they threw off the gaskets to unfurl the sails.

"Warning shot?" she asked without looking back, confident someone would answer her.

"So we assume," Watson said darkly. "Hit the water a hundred feet to starboard."

And still made a mighty roar, Kit thought, and looked up at the *Diana*'s masts, assured herself that the Isles flag—a sea dragon rampant on a field of maroon and saffron—was flying high and plainly visible.

"They're bearing Frisian flags, and fired a shot at an Isles ship," Kit murmured, rather astounded. Whether they'd been signaled by Gallia or the brig, or had simply been hunting in the Narrow Sea, was secondary now.

"They fired on an Isles ship," she said again to no one in particular, her anger building and better directed at Frisia than the viscount. And was heartened by the disdainful mutterings about the man-of-war's temerity.

She walked back to the helm.

"A declaration of war?" Grant asked.

Kit belayed their feud for now; the deck was no place for personal squabbling. "It's an act of aggression, certainly; they cannot be confused about our origin."

"But they could contend they had word of a marauding Islish vessel," Simon explained, "and were helping keep the peace in the Narrow Sea."

"As the Guild ship off Finistère contended," Watson agreed with a nod.

"With Gerard returned to Gallia—wherever in Gallia that might be—it's a moot issue now." She looked at her senior staff in turn. "I wouldn't say this to the crew, but we cannot outrun a ship that large, with that much canvas. And while we could lead them on a glorious chase, we don't have the time to waste on this one any more than we did the last. Not to chase or be chased, when we've a crew member that needs a physick and a sickroom, and admirals that need the information we can provide."

She didn't add that they were severely outgunned, as every Jack could see that for himself. And that's how the chase would almost certainly end.

She moved to the cabinet behind the wheel, looked at the

map Simon had placed across it, the *X* he'd drawn over their current location. They'd been sailing for several hours and had hardly made progress against the headwinds, despite—or because of—the constant tacks. It was a damned inefficient way to fly, but it was the only way they had.

Unless . . .

They waited for her to speak, knowing her well enough to belay their questions until she knew her mind.

"How long to Portsea at our current speed?" she asked.

Simon checked the calculations he'd made in her absence. "Ten hours in good wind at top speed," he said. Much as Kit had predicted. "With poor wind and while tacking? The better part of a day."

Tamlin turned toward the wind, the wisps of red hair that hadn't made it into her long braid swirling around her face. "The wind won't change," she said. "Not now, nor for a day yet. There's a storm in the Northern Sea, and it's altered the winds here. So we'll be heading into the wind the full way."

"We can't fight the man-of-war," Kit said. "Proud as I am of the *Diana*, she can't hold out against that many guns. And we need to get Jin to the physick."

"What are our options?" Grant asked.

"We keep every crew member on deck and shift the sails as quickly as possible at each tack, and we hope the man-of-war isn't efficient with its shot." She looked toward the water, the waves white with foam. "Or we use the current."

"That won't sustain our speed," Simon said. "Not all the way across the Narrow Sea."

"It will if I remain in contact the entire way."

Silence followed that proposition.

"You're proposing to touch the current all the way to the Isles?" Grant asked, his voice carefully neutral.

"Unless anyone has a better idea. We need to move quickly, and to do that, we need to move straight. We run to Portsea and stay out of cannon range."

"Not merely out of cannon range," Simon said. "At a full and record-breaking run."

"The man-of-war will give chase," Grant said.

"Almost certainly," Kit agreed. "But while it's plenty aggressive when we're alone in the drink, with no land in sight, not even the most arrogant of captains would follow us into Portsea. It's too well defended. It would be suicidal—and an undeniable act of war."

"There's nowhere else?" Grant asked.

"There's no closer land other than the channel islands unless we return to Gallia," Watson said, "and Gallia isn't likely to welcome us."

"No, it isn't," Kit agreed. "And the channel islands aren't good enough. We need the Crown Command, and we need its physicks."

Tamlin pushed hair from her eyes. "It will be hard." She had great skill at reducing problems down to their essence.

"Yes," Kit said. "I imagine it will be. Hard on the masts, the hull, the lines, the sails. Difficult for the crew. But it's the best chance we've got."

And that assumed she actually *could* do it without dooming them all. It had taken time for her to learn even to touch the current, to redirect that energy toward the ship. Mistakes were dangerous, and they didn't encourage experimentation.

When she'd been a midshipman, before she'd learned to touch the current, the ship she'd been assigned to had hit the doldrums—the total lack of wind. With the captain's permission, Kit had tried to fill the sails by using the current when the wind stopped blowing. She'd failed. The ship had nearly gone over, and three sailors had been injured, pensioned, because of her mistake.

She'd been cautious since and, with the ban on manipulation, hadn't even tried to stretch her access beyond the quick method she used now. She wasn't sure what effect it might have, or if she was vastly overestimating what she might be able to do.

"And what toll will it take on you?" Tamlin asked. She reached out, took Kit's hands. Very uncharacteristic for a woman who preferred the silence of the topmast to speaking with her fellow officers. Then Tamlin turned them to look at Kit's palms— and the small black scars they bore. But what were a hundred more pinpoints in the constellation if it gave a trusted friend a greater chance of survival?

"I don't know," she said. "And it doesn't matter."

Because she'd already made the decision. There was no better option.

More, it was a kind of opportunity. Doucette was alive, and Gerard had already proven his intent to use magic. The Isles had to better understand how they could use magic, and it would begin with her. If that meant pushing herself to the limit, so be it. This would be a test, she knew. A trial, and possibly one that matched pain and exhaustion against resilience and stamina. If the gods were kind, they'd all survive it.

She'd avoided looking at Grant, expecting she'd see anger in his eyes. But when she girded her bravery enough to check, she found only concern. "This will work," she said.

He nodded. "I know."

She wasn't sure if he believed it or was merely trying to

bolster her confidence. But she found it absurdly comforting and had to look away to keep emotion from filling her eyes.

"Call the all hands," she said, and Watson gave the order.

When they assembled, she looked at them. She was proud of her crew, as always, for their bravery and occasional silliness. But most important, because they followed wherever she deemed it necessary to go.

She pointed toward the man-of-war, now fully rigged. "You can see that four-masted palace for yourselves. The Frisians have quite a bit of gilt to decorate their hulls."

There were murmurs of disgust, of Frisian enmity.

"Jin needs a physick," she began. "March is remarkably skilled, but she doesn't have the tools she needs to give him the best chance to avoid fever. Portsea is our best option, but the wind is against us. The current can make the ship go faster—but I'll need to touch it the entire trip." She waited for the murmured questions, the glances exchanged.

"Won't that hurt, Captain?" Mr. Oglejack asked, brow furrowed.

"I honestly don't know," Kit said. "I've only ever touched the current at intervals. I would not be surprised if it does." She looked at the bosun, Mr. Jones. "I know it will be a challenge for all of us. But do you think she'll bear it?"

No need to specify which "she" Kit meant. His fuzzy eyebrows furrowed, and he tapped his chin. "As long as we've got the sails bent properly, aye. The *Diana*, she loves to fly. Even if she pops a seam, we'll fix it right enough."

"Then make her fly we will," she said. "Lieutenant Watson will have the helm. Mr. Pettigrew will keep us on course. Tamlin will monitor the man-of-war and report continually to the helm.

We will remain at all hands until we arrive in Portsea"—she paused for the predicted groans—"at which time every Jack gets at least a day of shore leave. On my word," she said, and touched her heart. Even if the queen desired she sail again immediately, it would take time to reprovision the ship and repair any damage the trip might cause.

That had the crew cheering.

She gave Simon and Mr. Jones a few minutes to discuss the best angle for the sails to keep the ship from somersaulting through the waves as headwinds battled current. And when they were ready, Kit braced her legs against the deck and waves, faced the wind, and closed her eyes.

It was time to go to work.

The Narrow Sea was deeper and colder here than along the shore. She'd have sworn she could feel the chill against her skin as she reached down for the current. She felt it, very nearly whole, shimmering with power just off the silty seafloor.

She touched it, wrapped it around all of them. And after a moment, felt the *Diana* jump forward through the water, hull and masts groaning from the sudden pressure. She kept her eyes closed against the instinct to look, to check, and focused on maintaining her hold—and her strength.

"She's fine, Captain," Mr. Jones called out, as if anticipating her concern. "Keep her moving. Loosen up that line!" he called out to someone else, footsteps sounding away.

She could feel the mainsail being reefed—pulled up to expose less canvas to the wind, which was against them in any event—

and the shift of the boat in response. If the *Diana* had the current, the thinking seemed to be, it didn't need the sails, or the friction they'd create.

"The frigate?" Watson called out, asking for an update.

"Shifting to follow our course!" was called out by someone amidships. "They think we've caught a wind." There was amusement in her voice.

Behind her, Watson snorted. "They'll figure it out soon enough—probably after their sails are flapping. And . . . there we are," Watson said.

Sails flapped when they lost tension, usually when turning away from the wind, such as in the middle of a tack. But if a captain wasn't careful, the ship wouldn't have enough wind to right itself again and refill the sails. Changing direction when the wind was against you was a very careful dance.

The man-of-war's captain was experienced enough to right the error, and probably to realize the *Diana* wasn't relying on solely wind, but magic.

"They've made it around," Watson said, all amusement gone now. "And they're giving chase."

Kit's hands shook from the energy that moved through her, but she pushed past her instinct to let go or withdraw herself from the sheer volume of magic. She felt the vibration in her bones—not painful, but insistent.

The current ribboned through the water, darting here and there and back again as if exploring the seafloor, or engaged in its own unique dance. She knew it changed position, could often recognize when it was located in a different spot than she'd felt it before. But because she'd never traveled it so continuously, or for so long a period, she'd never felt this waltz. It was more like a living thing than she'd imagined, and she regretted that it had taken her so long to recognize that quality.

That continuity also made the wax and wane of its strength more noticeable. Much like the waves above it, there were crests and troughs in its power, which changed its resonance. She could feel it with such exhilarating detail that she felt, for a moment, she might simply sink into it, become part of its energies. Give herself over to the power so she might fuel some portion of the world.

It would take hours, Kit thought. Hours yet before they put enough distance between them to have the man-of-war turning tail. So she breathed, settled in . . . and fought her own war.

Like every sailor who lived by the watch bell, Kit knew exhaustion. A shift on the masts after only two hours of sleep, repeated throughout a voyage, blurred the lines between sleep and wakefulness. And she understood physical exertion: She'd held lines and wheels against raging winds until her muscles shook, struggled with her crew to raise anchor when storms threatened. But she'd never felt this bone-deep fatigue. Every muscle in her body ached, vibrating from overwork, her brain fuzzy from overconcentration. The day seemed to have been impossibly long, as if tragedy and trauma drew out the experience, ensuring she felt every miserable second. She longed to simply lay her head down on the deck and sleep, and every second was an internal battle.

They'd reached the halfway point, and the frigate still gave chase, apparently intent on either capturing the *Diana* or keeping it running back to Portsea. Or perhaps wondering, as Kit now did, if it was possible to simply exhaust the *Diana*'s ability to use the current to escape them.

She refused to give in to its demand.

The crew sang shanties as they worked to reef or unfurl the sails as the wind required, the rhythms helping them coordinate the pull and release of lines. "I sail for the queen / For saffron, maroon / For cliff and for pasture / Let's away to them soon." But in her exhaustion, the words and rhythm worked their way into Kit's mind, playing an endless loop until she'd hallucinated the queen was swabbing the deck in slops of saffron stripes.

She fought against the literal current, battling to keep herself whole and separate from the magic. Her own creature, her own self.

It was easy to underestimate the sheer volume of magic when one only touched it intermittently. Hours of connection left her with little doubt of its potential; the nation that unlocked it first would win the war—or destroy all others. But that wasn't the only threat. Becoming too close to the magic was equally dangerous. Weren't her hands, after all, proof of the connection between Aligned and current?

She had to open her eyes to keep herself from losing total awareness of her surroundings and simply falling into it, unsure what effect that would have.

The next few hours were a blur, at least until the wind blew harder and the waves rose higher. Orders were shouted above her, around her, to reef sails or lower them, shift the yards this way or that to keep waves from breaching the sides of the boat and pushing her over. That would be deadly under any circumstances, much less a storm at night in tossing seas, where sailors in the water would be virtually invisible even if the ship was righted again.

The rain began at midnight—a hard, straight rain that soaked Kit in seconds. She closed her eyes—she could hardly see through the downpour anyway—and clenched her fists against the chill.

Then Grant was beside her, and a coat of canvas was slipped over her shoulders, over each arm. Grant raised the hood over her head. And then he sat on the deck beside her, slipped his fingers into hers, and gently squeezed.

"I'm still furious," she managed through chattering teeth.

"I was still right," Grant said. But he squeezed her hand again.

She squeezed back with what little strength she had, grateful for the shelter and the warmth. But she had to let her awareness of him fade again to concentrate on the current. And, once the dizziness began, so she could keep what little food she'd had in her belly. That didn't work; she retched over the side of the ship— tears coming from the effort of maintaining her connection— until her body was empty of everything, it seemed, but the magic.

She was its conduit and nothing more. A vessel. Empty and tired, she wanted so badly to cry, to sleep, to scream, and knew she could afford none of those.

Jin could afford none of those.

*Strength*, she prayed, to whatever gods, old or new, might be listening. And it was a promise to Jin, to her sailors, to Grant, that she would hold out until there was nothing left.

Was anything left?

At long last, after she'd stared blindly into darkness for hours, her mind following the current as it ribboned through the water, the rain fell away and the sky began to pinken at the edges.

"Land ahead!" Tamlin called out. "I can see Wihtwara!" That was the island due south of Portsea.

"Jin?" Kit asked, voice hoarse.

"A bit feverish, but he's holding on," Simon said behind her. "You did good, Captain. You did good."

⌒∽⌒

They signaled at Wihtwara for a pilot to lead them into the Crown's quay. Kit waited until she could see the pilot's ship waiting at the harbor's edge.

"I'm—" She had to try twice to manage words. "I'm releasing it," she said, with the last of what remained of her energy.

"All hands, be ready!" Watson called out.

She released her connection and felt the *Diana*'s resounding exhale, the groan of lines and canvas no longer under such powerful tension.

"*Thank you*," she said to the ship, palm on the deck still soft and damp from rain.

The flags that waved over Portsea were the last thing she saw . . . and Grant was there to catch her when she fell.

# NINE

The smell of woodsmoke, the sound of soft whispers. More retching, then a cool cloth on her forehead. Then she was laid in something blissfully soft, and drifted into total darkness.

She slept for a long time. And when her awareness rose again, it was to the call of jackgulls around her.

"Sleeping," she said, and batted them away with a hand. When they continued to sing, she realized they were somewhere beyond her.

"Good to know you're not dead then."

Kit's eyes flashed open, and she turned her head to stare into the face of a woman she'd never seen before.

"Good afternoon, dearie. Glad to see you're awake. The viscount down there asked that I bring you some tea."

She was slightly awake, and very confused. Kit sat up, head pounding like she'd taken a hammer to it, and looked around. She was on a small iron bed beneath an embroidered coverlet, in a small room with a sloped ceiling and lace-covered window.

The woman who'd spoken to her—petite and curvy, with pale skin and pink cheeks—put a tea tray atop a bureau.

"Afternoon?" Kit asked, squinting against the light.

"Aye, just after. You've been asleep since you came into port, poor thing."

"Port," Kit repeated. "Where am I?"

"Well, in the Pig & Pheasant, of course. Best inn in Portsea, if I may be so bold."

Portsea, Kit thought with no little relief. They'd made it. "My ship? My crew?"

The woman put her hands on her hips. "Well, I can't say for certain, but I believe your ship's in the Crown Command's docks there"—she gestured absently toward the window—"and some of your crew are downstairs enjoying a bite and bit of the tipple. We also have the finest tipple in Portsea. If I may be so bold."

She'd plainly already decided to be bold, Kit thought. And if her crew was enjoying food and drink, Jin was out of danger. Kit nodded. "Thank you for the tea."

"You're welcome. Would you like a bit of a cold lunch to go with it? We've some good wurst, or perhaps some cold pork? Milly has a fine hand with turnips."

Nausea was a wave that threatened to overcome her, and Kit held up a hand. "No. No food. I'll just . . . collect myself."

"Of course. Oh!" she said, and pulled a bit of folded paper from her apron pocket. "And this was left for you by the viscount. Tall and nice-looking, if I may be so bold."

"Thank you," Kit said, as the woman offered her the note.

"There's water in the pitcher, and you can ring if you need anything else." The woman made a little curtsy and left Kit alone again.

Kit unfolded the paper, found a confident and tidy scrawl.

*Jin is in the sailors' ward and resting.*
*If I may be so bold. —Grant*

Relief filled her, followed quickly by amusement—he'd also spoken with the innkeeper—and frustration. She was still angry at him.

Kit put aside the note, took an inventory of her body to determine what physical consequences she might have suffered yesterday. She clearly remembered the retching. She was still dizzy, although at least part of that was due to the shift from water to solid land. Her head still pounded, and she ached like she'd been bruised from head to toe. So how to account for Doucette's apparent ability to manipulate the current with impunity? Was he made of sterner stuff than she, or had he figured out some trick to shield him from the misery?

She looked at her hands, expecting to see a new constellation of scars across her palms. If there were more, they weren't enough to blacken her palms completely. She didn't know why—and knew no one to ask.

Carefully, she rose, head still spinning. Watson would have seen to the delivery of her report on Auevilla as soon as they'd docked. She needed to speak to the admirals, update them respecting the chase by the man-of-war.

After she checked on Jin, of course. She appreciated that Grant had taken the time to give her an update—that was one mark in his favor, at least—but she needed to see Jin with her own eyes and assure herself that he was safe. And that Nanae wouldn't be hunting her down.

She found herself in yesterday's pantaloons and shirt, but her trunk was neatly stowed at the end of the bed. She poured water from a pitcher into a white porcelain basin, dunked her head into it until the headache abated slightly. She came up gasping for breath some untold minutes later, hair dripping. The mirror above said her face was paler than usual, the shadows beneath her gray eyes larger. She looked as if she hadn't slept for a week, and had been ill for most of that.

She finished her ablutions, changed into a clean uniform.

When she was tidy, she poured a cup of tea, dumped in enough sugar and milk to make it a pale approximation of the original, and drank it standing until her teeth ached from the sweetness. Then she drank another as sweet as the first.

The sugar seemed to help, at least. After a minute, her hands no longer shook, and the ache in her head was slightly reduced. Never underestimate the power of a good cup of tea, she thought, and doubted the Crown Command could operate without it.

There was a knock at the door. She opened it, expecting to see Watson or Simon. And instead found Grant, hands linked behind his back.

He'd shaved, changed into the somber colors he usually preferred—a dark waistcoat and pantaloons, gleaming boots, and a tailcoat of dark gray. He looked frustratingly handsome, and she was angry with herself that she was relieved to see him—*she was still angry!*—and concerned she didn't look as handsome as he did—*she looked fine enough!*

With those motivations, she gave him the hard stare she usually reserved for sailors who'd utterly failed at their duties—and who rarely stayed long on her ship. Secretly, she hoped she could get in a good rail at Grant, then fall into him. But railing first, perhaps.

"My lord," she said crisply.

He ignored the statement, strode into the room with the confidence of a man who expected to be obeyed. She shut it and turned to face him, preparing for battle.

He stood in silence, tall enough that his head nearly skimmed the rafters, and seemed a giant as he looked down at her. "You look pale."

"Why, thank you," she said flatly. "I feel as if I've been trampled by horses."

He glanced back at the rumpled bed. "It appears you got some sleep, at least. But that's not enough to counter the . . . aftereffects?"

She just shook her head. Then stopped, as that made the nausea rise again. "I assume you helped get me here, so thank you for that." Her tone was still grudging, and she didn't bother tempering it.

"You're welcome." There was concern in his eyes as he peered down at her, but she was still too angry to pity him for that.

She crossed her arms defiantly.

"I can see you need a good steam," Grant said. "You might as well let it out now while we're alone."

She still didn't feel herself, but intended to speak her piece. "You attempted to usurp my authority in front of my crew. And I say *attempted* because—regardless of the title you bear—you have no authority over my ship. Do you have any idea how absolutely infuriating that is?"

"I'm certain it was bloody infuriating," he said. "Perhaps nearly as infuriating as watching you stare at Jin like you're the one who put him there."

The truth in that had her anger flaring. "I did no such thing."

"Liar."

She could barely get out words through clenched teeth. "I should call you out."

"For seeing the truth of it? I don't think so. I know what that pain looks like, Kit, as well as you." He took a step forward, which felt entirely too close in this small room. "Have I told you that I was holding Dunwood's hand when he died?"

She was struck by the change of topic, and it took her a moment to meet him there. "No. You haven't." Her voice was quieter now, as was his.

"His death felt like a failure. It felt personal, even though I was bloody well *not* the man who put him in the prison. And you told me to stuff it."

"I don't believe I've ever told anyone to 'stuff it.'"

"*Just stuff it,*" Grant said, in a high-pitched voice apparently intended to mimic hers. "*And walk right into the sea.*"

She did say the latter, and often. But neither the accurate portrait nor the tone made her smile.

"It's my fault Jin was shot."

Grant's brows lifted. "You fired the rifle? I had no idea you were quite so adept as to shoot a man from sixty yards away and on a ship other than the one you captained."

She walked back to the bed, sat heavily. And because she knew he would understand, she let go of the fear and guilt she'd been holding. "It was my decision to go into Auevilla instead of alerting the fleet. My decision to confront the men at the dock that drew attention to us."

"Or," Grant said, "you did what was necessary to confirm the identity of the ship you believed was the *Fidelity*, rather than wasting the Crown Command's resources chasing a ghost. You confirmed Doucette is alive and, apparently, that Gerard's desire to use magic as a weapon hasn't diminished. You provided necessary information to a key informant of the Crown."

"You or Raleigh?"

Grant's smile was wide and genuine. "Yes. And you got your crew—and one of those informants—safely back on the ship."

"We know war is dangerous. You and I better than most. But it's different when it's a friend."

"Like Dunwood was to me."

She just looked at him, then sighed. "Jin has a wife and children. Two beautiful little girls."

"And the lives of your sailors who don't have immediate family are less valuable?"

"No. Of course not." She paused. "It's my responsibility to direct my crew. It's my responsibility to bear the weight of those decisions, the consequences, whether fair or foul. And that's the bloody worst part of being a captain."

Grant snorted. "To hear Jin talk of it, it's the paperwork you hate the most."

She growled a bit. But she could admit some of the weight had lifted.

"As you've been honest, I will be, too. I know you care for Jin, and I suspected—correctly, I might add—that temper would be the fastest method for pulling you back. I apologize for challenging your decision in front of your sailors."

Kit wasn't sure she was prepared for anyone to believe they knew her so well. Or to be so damnably correct about it. But her anger drained away.

"And I . . . thank you for it."

Grant didn't manage to hide his grin very well. "I can see that admission cost you, so I won't gloat."

"You're gloating right now."

"I won't gloat other than this very small indulgence."

It was her turn to smile, just a little.

"In my years of service," Grant said, "I've found there are two types of officers. Those who command without emotion, who believe casualties are of little concern. And there are those who care deeply for their crews, who acknowledge the miseries of battle."

"And which are more successful?"

"That depends on how you measure success. Those who are emotionless never lose crew they care about, because they care about no crew. Those who have emotions can be overwhelmed by it. The success is finding your way between those paths, because neither leads to happiness, and probably not success in battle."

"That's remarkably wise for a soldier." She knew she was baiting him, and from the glint in his blue eyes as he strode toward her, he knew it, too. Kit swallowed hard, not entirely sure whether she wanted to keep him at arm's length—or pull him against her.

Just as in the duke's town house, desire felt a tangible thing between them, like fog across the Saint James of a morning. He moved like a soldier and viscount, like strength and power united together, and there was no missing the interest in his eyes.

He crouched in front of her. "A mere soldier, am I?"

"Perhaps . . . not so mere," she said quietly, and let herself lift fingers to his face, touch the hard line of his jaw. So much strength, she thought, and didn't realize she'd said the words aloud until his grin spread.

"Indeed," he said, then took her hand, pressed his lips to the beating pulse in her wrist. "And you are no mere sailor, Kit Brightling. And if we are interrupted again, I'm going to simply ignore it."

"Interrupted at wh—"

She didn't have time to finish the words before his mouth found hers. He kissed her hungrily, like a man long denied, but matched against softness, like a man focused solely on her pleasure. She might not have been at her strongest, but there was no battle here. Only joy and comfort.

She met his implicit challenge. Her hands were around his neck, and then in his hair. With a victorious groan, he moved closer, his free hand sliding to her nape, leaving goose bumps in the wake of his fingertips. She had barely a moment to whimper before the kiss became all-consuming, and then—

A brisk knock sounded at the door.

"Do not answer it," Grant murmured, and nipped her bottom lip.

She pulled back, but her smile was as warm as the rest of her. "I believe we discussed your lack of authority over my decision-making, my lord."

With an impressively haggard sigh, Grant rose and moved away, put one hand on his hip while the other rubbed his face.

Kit bit back a smile. "You might just . . ." she began, and pointed toward his hair.

She grinned as she watched him furrow fingers through his brown hair, carefully repairing the swoop she'd mussed while kissing him.

When he was ready, she strode to the door, pulled it open.

Watson stood on the other side, hat in hand—and her eyes lit with curiosity as they moved from Kit to Grant and back again.

"Lieutenant," Kit said. "Good afternoon."

"Captain," Watson said. "Colonel. How are you feeling, sir?"

"I'll stand, Watson."

"Good. The physick asked me to tell you—Jin is awake."

"His fever?"

"Lower, thank the gods."

Kit said a silent *Dastes* to the old gods and a thank-you to the people who'd contributed their luck and prayers. "Thank you, Lieutenant. And for seeing us safely to Portsea."

Much to Kit's surprise, a flush actually pinked Watson's cheeks. "Thank you, Captain. He's at the injured ward if you'd like to visit him."

"I would," Kit said with a nod. Before long, she'd receive orders, but until they came, she'd have time to see to the necessities.

"Then I'll just go . . . downstairs," Watson decided, flicking her gaze to Grant again, and biting back a smile as she left them.

"How long until every sailor in the inn is aware you and I were in this room together, alone and unchaperoned?"

"As long as it takes her to return downstairs," Kit said, and looked back at him. "Are you concerned for your reputation, my lord?"

"Oh, absolutely," he said, then shut the door and kissed her again.

⁓

The Portsea offices of the Crown Command were located in a former customshouse near the dock. There were soldiers and sailors aplenty in the streets, and Kit could see the *Diana*'s mast between buildings, one of the many ships in Portsea for repair, for instructions, for shore leave. The coming weeks would no doubt see many of them, including the *Diana*, depart again, with no certain possibility of return.

They walked to the ward for injured sailors, were directed to a long room with dozens of iron beds. In contrast to many sick rooms she'd seen, the floors were clean, the windows clear and gleaming, the walls and linens crisply white. The room was nearly empty of sailors. Only three in the entire ward, but Kit knew that would change soon enough, too. They saw Jin in the left row of beds and walked toward him.

A woman in gray with a blue apron and short, tidy curls held up a hand. "You may visit with Commander Takamura, but stay behind the line, please." She had an accent of the Western Isle and pointed to the floor, where a line of pretty blue had been painted down the middle of the aisle between the lines of beds.

"Excuse me?" Kit asked.

The woman looked around, then leaned in. "The physick believes illnesses can be spread"—she cleared her throat nervously—"by creatures."

She let that statement fall like a felled oak.

"Creatures," Grant repeated. He looked at himself, then Kit. "I see no creatures other than us."

"Beings so small they cannot be seen," the woman said, then touched the amulet at her neck. "They lurk all about us, and if you get too close to the commander, yours may jump right onto him like wee bugs, and then . . ."

"And then?" Grant prompted.

"Well, I'm not entirely sure. But it would befoul him, so stay yourselves behind the line."

"Small creatures," Kit said again, when she'd left the room, and suddenly felt the need for a shower.

They walked to Jin's bed, staying carefully behind the painted line. He was still paler than usual, but his skin had lost the gray cast. His eyes were closed, chest rising and falling, and she might have thought him enjoying a nap if it wasn't for the location.

"You're thinking very loudly," he said, and opened one eye. "Captain. Grant."

"Jin," Kit said with a smile, and had to fight back hard against the urge to cross the line and embrace him. "Damn, but it's good to hear your voice."

"And good to see you," he said, "if from a strange distance. Did she tell you about the small creatures?"

Kit glanced around to ensure they were alone. "She did. Is the physick a bit . . . touched?"

That had Jin's smile widening. "It makes sense when you hear it from him, at least as far as these things go. Makes me itchy, though."

"Same."

"You look horrible."

She could feel her lip curling. "So I've been told. We had a bit of an adventure yesterday while you were lazing belowdecks. If you ever frighten me like that again—"

"You'll dismiss me from the crew? I doubt it."

"Impertinent to the last."

"Not the last," he said. "Thanks to you. Watson was here earlier and told me what you'd done. I presume that's why you're pale."

She nodded. And a bit achy, and tired, and nauseated, but he didn't need to bear that burden. "It was an experiment for the Isles. And Nanae, as she'd have had my hide if we'd lost you."

"Possibly," he said, and they looked at each other for a moment, refusing to say—in true Islish and Crown Command form—the hundred things they might have said. She opened her mouth to speak, to let go the words she'd been holding in for hours, but his brows knit into an angry furrow.

"If you so much as begin to mutter 'I'm sorry,' I will demand satisfaction."

Since he was right—that's exactly what she'd been planning to say—she simply cleared her throat.

"Life is deadly," he continued, "and our choices all inevitably lead from one to the other."

"That's terribly philosophical. But mostly just terrible."

"Our positions are dangerous," Jin continued, undeterred and dramatic, "and yet we chose them. I'm worth no more or less than any other sailor on the ship—even if you'd be devastated if I was gone."

Kit snorted, the tension relieved again. Was it any wonder she adored him? She didn't have a biological brother, at least as far as she was aware, and Hetta had only adopted girls. But Jin *felt* like a brother, or what she imagined one to be.

Still. There were limits. "I would be devastated," she said, "because replacing senior officers requires an obscene amount of paperwork."

"Which we know you loathe."

"Which."

Jin dropped his gaze to her hands. "Scars?" he asked quietly.

"No more than usual," she said, and showed him. "I think

maintaining the connection doesn't create new scars; it's the first contact that matters. But that's speculation."

"An interesting and useful one." He cocked his head at her. "Although you really do look a bit peaky."

"He's right."

They turned to see a man—tall and thin as a rail—striding briskly toward them. He had a shock of dark hair that rose from a pale face, his eyes inquisitive behind round spectacles.

"The physick," Jin explained. "Bookish."

Kit wasn't certain if that was a warning or a compliment.

"Eston Nelson," the man said when he reached them, and offered each of them a hand.

"Kit Brightling," she said. "And Viscount Rian Grant. Thank you for caring for Commander Takamura. He's well loved by his captain and crew."

"Of course," the man said, stepping across the line to examine his patient. He wore an amulet, and it shifted rather hypnotically as he moved. He put fingers on Jin's wrist, looked absent for a moment, then nodded. Then came the hand to the forehead again, much as Kit had seen March do.

"Improvement, I think," he said, then stepped back and pulled a watch from the pocket of his dark gray waistcoat. He wore no tailcoat, and the sleeves of his shirt were rolled nearly to the elbows. Work wear, Kit thought, in his particular profession.

"How do you feel?" he asked Jin.

"Better."

Nelson nodded, put the pocket watch away, and pulled out a small writing book and pencil. "More broth, more tea," he said, apparently making notes. When that was done, he put the notebook away and turned to Kit again, studied her.

"You're Aligned."

"I am."

He nodded. "As am I. Born at the seashore, and Aligned to that liminal space, or so I believe. Why are you pale?"

"I touched the current nearly all the way across the Narrow Sea." She wasn't sure if he'd know what she meant. There was no common lexicon among those who were Aligned, both because the Alignment was location dependent and so a bit different for everyone, and because the ban on manipulation made the Aligned hesitant to share their experiences. But he nodded sagely.

"You should borrow your rest. You'll feel much better."

Kit blinked at him. "I beg your pardon?"

"Borrow your rest from the current. You've not done that before?"

She just shook her head.

"Well," he said. "It's not often I get to discuss my theories. Assuming you're interested?"

Kit nodded, would have begged him to tell her more. She was that thirsty for knowledge.

"When you touch the current, as you say, you connect yourself to the power. And I presume you redirect that energy to the ship, so you act as the conduit?"

Kit nodded. "Close enough."

"The trick then is to hold back some of the magic for yourself. Not to funnel all to the ship, but to allow just a bit to remain within your body to refresh the blood and organs."

He made it sound so easy, Kit thought ruefully—no harder than sipping a bit of tea for energy.

"Without blowing yourself up, of course."

*There we are*, she thought. That was the wee problem. There was little incentive to try something new when the costs were so high.

"You've done this yourself?" she asked.

"No," he said carefully, "but I've seen it done twice. A young man and woman—twins, you see—born and Aligned to the hill country. They'd learned to use the current to light fires in the family hearth, and kept a bit back for their own comfort. I watched them, and it was very impressive."

Or they'd been warmed by the effort of using the current, Kit thought. Perhaps that was the cost they bore from the activity—much like her scars.

And speaking of which, "Have you ever seen a use of the magic without consequence?" she asked.

He frowned. "Not that I'm aware of. Magic isn't innate to humans, so our bodies aren't naturally inclined to accept it. There's always a scar, a burn, some resulting injury."

Kit understood all three. But what of Doucette? she thought, but didn't ask. That development wasn't hers to share. At least not yet.

"It's a damned shame that we're only just now having these discussions," Nelson said. "The Aligned, I mean. I've always said there should be coordinated instruction, not just teaching a bit here, a bit there."

"I tried to teach sailors how to touch the current." That had been before her promotion to captain, not long after she'd learned the technique herself. "They weren't very receptive. There's a certain . . . commitment that's necessary to put yourself in the hands of such power. Most weren't keen to try it."

He nodded. "Current is a powerful thing, and the ban increases the risk."

"The ban exists for a reason," Grant pointed out.

Nelson nodded. "No argument there, my lord. I think the most important thing is to take the time to listen. To hear what it is, what it would have us do. I'd bet you those at Contra Costa paid little attention to what it asked of us."

"I listen," Kit said dryly. "It doesn't speak Islish."

He chuckled. "No, not in words. But in . . . desire. When you use your technique, does it refuse? Does it fight you? No. It sends you on your way."

That seemed too easy—to presume that because Kit could use the magic, the magic was fine with being used. She'd been at Forstadt, and she'd felt the burned shards of magic that had remained after Gerard's warship experiment. There'd been no acceptance there. Only . . . a hollowness, edged with fury. They said the inferno at Contra Costa occurred because the magic didn't want to be released. Maybe they were wrong. Maybe Doucette had given it freedom, and they'd all seen its true nature.

"You should visit Mathilda," the physick said. "She has a deft hand with amulets and may be able to assist you. She has a small shop on West Street," he explained. "Hardly a cupboard, really, but she knows what she's about."

Kit was one of the rare sailors who didn't wear a trinket on a chain for protection or health or success on a voyage. The closest she'd come was her ribbon, and that was less a charm against some future injury than a reminder of her past.

"She created yours?" Grant asked, gaze shifting to the man's pendant.

"She did. Magic is a complex web," he said. "Perhaps, with enough time and study, we'll understand it all."

# TEN

K it was uncomfortable with the physick's description of an easy current that was pleasant and happy and easy to satisfy, like a small child with a sweet treat.

Added to that, the idea of small, invisible creatures flitting here and there made her itchy and in want of a bath—preferably a complete dousing in boiling water and lye soap, sending any small creatures to meet their maker.

"Why do I feel dirty?" Grant said, when they reached the building's central hall again, and rubbed at his chest with a very discomfited expression.

"You are not the only one." She stopped, looked at him. "Do you believe it? That we're surrounded by little . . . things?"

"I don't know enough to say one way or the other. But I certainly don't *like* it."

"You know what's probably covered in small creatures? Horses."

"I'm absolutely shocked you believe so," Grant said, and sounded not shocked in the least.

They'd just crossed the creaking floor to the door when a man appeared from a doorway on the right. And a familiar man.

William Chandler was the Isles' spymaster. He was a big man, like Grant, with a handsomely rugged face that had seen its share of fists. Kit hadn't expected to see him in Portsea, and there were circles beneath his eyes, lines of worry across his brow. Gerard was leaning hard on all of them.

"Grant, Brightling," he said, offering hearty handshakes to both of them. "Good to see you." He looked at Kit and opened his mouth, but Grant held up a warning hand.

"Don't tell her she looks pale or ill or fatigued. It makes her very cross."

He closed his mouth, made an obvious mental pivot. "How is Commander Takamura?"

"Good man," Grant murmured.

"He's resting comfortably and close to insubordination, as always."

"Good. Let me know if he needs anything."

"I will," Kit said, "and thank you for it."

"Why are you here?" Grant asked him.

"The War Council has been called to plan the Isles' offensive and defensive strategies. The queen asked me to ride down from New London to provide what information I could regarding the movements of Gerard and the Resurrectionists. We're attempting to coordinate across all the ministries. Even Sunderland is here to prepare recommendations."

Sunderland had led the Crown Command's army on the Continent and had personally led the troops that defeated Gerard in Hispania. His strategic skill was undeniable. But so, Kit thought, was his ego.

"And how is that proceeding?" Grant asked, apparently hearing the same undertone.

"As well as one might expect when a handful of skilled, arrogant, and powerful people are thrown into a room together." He rolled his eyes. "They'd like you both to attend them in the morning," Chandler said, and shifted his gaze to Kit. "They'll have reviewed your report by then and may have additional questions. Or orders, presuming the queen is amenable."

Although technically part of the Crown Command, the Queen's Own regiment reported directly to her.

"Who's here for the naval concern?" Kit asked.

"Thornberry, unfortunately, although he's showing a bit of moral improvement. And Perez. You may not have heard she was promoted to commodore for her efforts leading the charge against Gerard's magical warship."

"I hadn't, but well deserved," Kit said with a victorious smile. "About damned time she was given a flotilla."

Kit had been fortunate enough to serve under Captain Perez on the *Ardent* and had been very glad to see the captain's ship come to the *Diana*'s aid against the warship. Kit's induction into the Order of Saint James was due, at least in part, to Perez's assistance.

"Her Highness concurs. And I received your report of Auevilla shortly after you docked. Good work locating the ship—and La Boucher." He said the moniker quietly, as if it were a devil he didn't want to invoke.

"He was rather a surprise," Kit said, then shifted her gaze to Grant. "And not the first of them."

"An interesting coincidence," Chandler agreed with a smile. "Or a bit of fate aligning so you could work together again.

Which work I'm not here to disrupt," he added, which kept Kit from thinking overmuch about "fate" entwining her with Grant.

"I'm also told your trip across the Narrow Sea was exceedingly fast."

"Less than eight hours," Grant said. "Half the time it might have otherwise taken."

"Really," Kit and Chandler said simultaneously. They both looked surprised.

Kit hadn't done the math, but it made sense upon consideration. "I used the current the entire way," she explained. "The wind was against us, and we needed to reach Portsea as soon as possible. It was . . . an experience."

She could see the conclusion in Chandler's eyes—*That must be why she looks like that*—but he managed not to say it aloud.

"We needed the speed," she continued, "to keep Jin alive, and to stay out of cannon range of the Frisian man-of-war that fired on us."

Chandler's eyes changed now, and went cold. No longer a friend discussing another's accomplishments, but an asset of the Isles who'd been set on by an enemy.

"You were fired on by a Frisian man-of war." It wasn't a question, but a statement of fury.

Kit merely nodded.

"That didn't make it into your report."

"The ship appeared after I finished the report. By that time, Jin was injured and haste was essential."

"She was carried unconscious off the deck when we reached Portsea," Grant said, and Kit's gaze snapped to his. She saw the truth in his eyes, the blue of them like stones from some deep chasm in the earth.

"Then I'm doubly glad you're safe," Chandler said. "There's been no formal declaration of war from Frisia; the Isles may take the lead on that point. I'll update the council and the queen regarding your speed and Frisia's involvement. Both will garner plenty of attention."

"If we're to survive what comes next and prevent Gerard from crowning himself again," Kit said, "we must give more attention to Alignment—understanding it and making use of it."

Everyone had a different perspective on the current—what it was, how it operated, how it ought to be used. They wouldn't be able to wield it, much less protect against it, if they couldn't discuss and reach an agreement on the fundamentals.

"Complicated matters," Chandler said, and they all nodded.

Kit was still learning despite years of experience.

"Has there been other news from the Continent?" Kit asked. "Other developments?" Little enough information had trickled through to the *Diana* while she'd been on patrol.

"Not as many as I'd have liked."

"What about Fouché?" Kit asked, thinking it best not to use his real name. She leaned in a bit closer, just in case. "It appeared Doucette had a map, shared it with a man named Sedley. Did Fouché find it?"

"Unfortunately, he did not," Chandler said. "You'll recall he was obliged to leave town shortly after you were deposited at his home," he said, giving Grant a look.

Grant just looked at him. "I wasn't going to leave them in the gaol."

"I know; I know," Chandler said, and ran a hand over his short hair. "I blame the Gallians."

"It's always the best course," Kit agreed. "Fouché made it out safely?"

"He did. He attempted to intercept Sedley on his way out of town, but the 'rat,' to use Fouché's term, had already left the nest. Fouché found nothing in the man's papers."

"*Damn*," Kit muttered. "That map had seemed important, too."

"It's not the only concern," Chandler said. "We ought to have received several more reports by now from those on the Continent, and the silence is concerning."

"Who hasn't reported?" Grant asked.

"In addition to Raleigh, Michaelson and Patrick have reported. It's been several weeks for the others. One, we know, is dead. Cartwright."

"We weren't acquainted," Grant said, "but I'm sorry to hear it all the same. You suspect he was killed?"

"The circumstances of his death were unlikely to be accidental," Chandler said. "Not impossible, but unlikely."

"How did he die?" Kit asked.

"Lightning strike, or so the local physick said. But he died in Hispania during the dry season, and there'd been no storm in the vicinity in weeks."

Kit went cold with fear, and with possibility. It must have shown in her face.

"What?" Chandler asked.

"Lightning, or Doucette?"

That had the color draining from his face. She was having that effect on people this week.

"That's a terrifying question."

"You are not the only one terrified," she said.

"Marcus Dunwood was captured," Grant said. "Cartwright killed, and others haven't been reporting. That's a concerning pattern."

"Also terrifying," Chandler agreed.

A door opened nearby, and a woman in a crisp red uniform peered out, looked around, then beckoned for Chandler.

"It seems I'm needed," he said, and shook their hands again. "In the course of your travels, should you need to assure yourself of someone's alliances, offer '*Ut myrkri, solas.*'"

Kit translated from the old language. "'Of darkness, the light'?"

"Out of darkness, the light," Chandler said.

Kit thought of this morning's dawn, of the light she'd waited so long to see, to finally strike darkness from the *Diana*'s path and reveal Portsea waiting. Out of darkness, the light, she thought again, and wished she'd known the mantra the night before.

"It's a challenge phrase," he continued. "The correct response is '*Ut lyga, firinn.*'"

"Out of lies, truth," Grant concluded, and Chandler nodded.

"Only a select few know it. Should you need to verify if someone has a connection to me, and a loyalty to Her Highness, you can recite the challenge and see if they respond."

The woman called for him again. "I'm sure we'll speak again while you're in town. Where are you staying?"

"The Pig & Pheasant."

"A reputable establishment," Chandler said. "If I may be so bold."

⁓

"We are on the edge," Kit said when Chandler strode away. "Not yet committed. And that is a very dangerous place to be."

"You know what we ought to do about it?"

She was thinking about military strategy when she asked, absently, "What?"

"Food."

She looked up at Grant. "Pardon?"

"We should have a meal. And perhaps ale in great quantities."

"I don't have time for food or ale. I've got to . . ." She trailed off as he looked at her, realizing she had nothing to do until her meeting with the council. There'd be no orders until then, and as much as she might have enjoyed it, staring at Jin would not make him heal faster.

"Well," she said lamely.

"Exactly. You've a few well-deserved hours of rest, and I wager you haven't eaten anything since you boarded the *Diana* yesterday."

He was right. The tea she'd guzzled had helped with her headache, but now that she'd assured herself Jin was safe and her orders had been sorted—or the timing of them, anyway—her hunger returned with a vengeance.

"I've not," she said. "And I could do with a meal." They'd invite more gossip; that didn't concern her overmuch, but she couldn't say the same about him. "But if we go together . . ."

"Then the denizens of Portsea will believe we enjoy each other's company, which is often true."

"Often," she said.

"Unless you're being stubborn."

"I'm simply knowledgeable."

"And impetuous."

"I prefer brave," she added with a smile as they pushed outside.

"I don't suppose you feel the need for a chaperone?"

Kit snorted. "No. I was concerned for your reputation, not

mine. You're a soldier in a sailors' town. You're the one who should worry."

⌒

But she had a task to attend to first. She led him to Portsea's pretty main square, where an enormous anchor had been hoisted upright as a symbol of the city's role as a primary Crown Command port. A border of sea lilies bloomed pale blue and green, and a line of white roses, each blossom big as her outstretched hand, spiraled around a thick obelisk of rough-cut white stone. Atop that a smaller, triangular stone that was roughly the shape of a sail—or the tooth of a shark.

TIVA KOSS had been carved into the stone's front, and offerings had been placed on its top: flowers, shells, feathers, bits of coral and driftwood, sea-smoothed pebbles. A string marked by bits of faded and knotted fabric had been tied around it, and the corners were marked by beeswax candles. It was a memorial—tokens left by friends and family for those who'd died at sea, currency they might use in the world beyond. And it was a kind of shrine—tokens left by sailors for the gods, in hopes their own skies would be fair.

Kit pulled a gold coin from her pocket, placed it on the pedestal. And with her fingers still touching stone and gold, she offered up a silent prayer for those who'd sailed with her before, those who'd sail with her again, and those already lost to the deep.

She stepped back, linked her hands behind her, and gave the monument—and the sailors it stood for—another moment of silence. Then she nodded at Grant.

"All right," she said. "Let's find the tipple."

⤐

They crossed the road, barely missing the steaming pile left behind by the enormous monster that clomped down the lane.

"They leave their waste right in the middle of the road," Kit murmured, "and everyone is fine with it."

"You've quite a grudge."

"Don't be fooled, Grant. They've the grudge against us. And who wouldn't, after being shackled to carriages and made to haul us around for centuries."

"You have a point."

"I often do. Now," she said, "we're to the Whistle & Thistle."

"I presume that's a pub or tavern, and not the name of a lark's den."

"Tavern," Kit confirmed. "Larks aren't nearly so subtle."

"Good. I need a break from the Pig & Pheasant, if I may be so bold."

"I'll give you a gold coin to never say that phrase again," she said, and led them toward the building.

⤐

The Whistle & Thistle, marked by the wooden sign bearing a carved flower above the door, was situated in a plaster and timber building not unlike the ones she'd seen in Auevilla. But unlike those, this building was original Islish—and smelled of hundreds of years of stale beer and woodsmoke. It was also loud and lousy with sailors.

Kit adored it and tried to visit whenever she found herself in Portsea.

The main room was wood, forward to stern, with tables and

tankards and jostling sailors. She and Grant moved through bodies, looking for an empty table. Two young lieutenants in uniform walked toward them, doffing their hats to her as they passed.

Kit found a small one being relieved of its duty by two women in uniform, and they took the benches still warm from their prior occupants. Kit signaled the woman running tankards of ale to and from thirsty patrons.

"They stare at you," Grant said.

"Who stares at whom?" Kit looked around, half expecting to see gendarmes or other rivals.

"The other sailors stare at you as you walk by."

She snorted. "Because I am an officer. As a general rule, sailors believe captains are either their greatest saviors or devils in human form, depending on their prior berths."

"No, Kit. That's not at all why they look at you." His smile was warm and inviting, and food wasn't the only thing she desired in that moment. But basic needs must be met.

"What do they serve here?" He glanced around at the walls, which bore the heads of horned animals no longer attached to their torsos, presumably to their chagrin.

"Mutton, meat pies, and mutton. And you should stay away from the mutton."

"A small but discerning menu," Grant said, as one sailor drew another across a tabletop, threatened him with a fist.

"There's nothing quite as atmospheric as a table in a sailors' grog house," Kit said. The sailors took their fight to the floor, began tussling. "Are soldiers this entertaining?"

"There's some resemblance," Grant said, as ale was deposited on the table, coins exchanged, meat pies ordered. He took a sip. "The ale is . . . strong."

"Sailors," Kit said by way of explanation. "We're used to the drink, so ale's as good as mother's milk." She hadn't been certain if her stomach would allow it, but she found the bite appealing.

She took another sip, watched the sailors wrestle with moves that were of questionable morality but great amusement. And realized she felt almost completely happy. Jin was healing, which gave her relief; Chandler was here, which gave her comfort. And she'd kissed Grant, which put butterflies in her belly, just as her beloved penny novels predicted would happen.

*Almost* completely happy. Because Chandler's news, and the looming threat of war, were weights around them.

"You're tapping your foot," Grant said.

She stopped, unaware she'd been doing it at all. Another habit she'd have to watch.

"Magic," she said generally.

"Ah. Yours, Doucette's, or the physick's?"

He'd come to know her well, and she was slightly unnerved by that. And . . . pleased. "All three, I think. Doucette's magic was so beautiful, Grant. Blue and green mixing together, a fog of dancing color. I'm not explaining it very well; I'm still a bit in awe of it."

"But?" he prompted.

"But then I saw what it could do. I watched the magic snatch at that man—claw at him—and now I think we're right to be hesitant."

Meat pies were placed in front of them, golden and steaming, on thick plates of chipped blue stoneware. They thanked the servant, and Kit waited until the woman had left them again.

Kit put her napkin in her lap. They cut into their meat pies in silence, took bites of steaming, flaky pastry and chunks of beef.

She still wasn't sure she felt well enough for food, but knew her body needed it. So she'd go through the steps.

"It's not a Queenscliffe pie," Grant said, "but it's respectable."

It was more than respectable, Kit thought, although Queenscliffe pies were delicious. It was warm and well spiced, and she began to settle.

"But," she continued, "while I've been working to accept the idea that using magic more than we've done is a necessity, I still have doubts. Gerard and his ilk have no qualms about using it, manipulating it, and unless we're willing to offer up the Continent, we have to be willing to use it, too. But magic is not our friend, Grant. Not to humans, not to the Isles. The physick said we should listen to it, as if we're friends and companions, but I don't think that's right, either." She looked up at him. "And I wonder if it's our enemy."

"No."

She lifted her brows. "You're so certain?"

"How old are you?"

She plucked a flake of pastry from her plate, crunched it. "Old enough that a gentleman wouldn't ask."

"Old enough that you've known of your Alignment for, what, a dozen years?"

"A few more than that," she said. "But close enough."

"Did it ever feel like your enemy?"

Kit opened her mouth, closed it again. "No. It feels like itself."

"I'm not Aligned. But from what I've heard and seen—including the Aligned officers with whom I served in war—magic is not sentient, and it does not pick sides. It simply is—much in the same way that a ship might be."

"The *Diana* will only ever serve right and goodness," Kit muttered.

"I've no doubt of it," Grant said. "But if she was led by a less . . . particular . . . captain—"

"Watch it," Kit warned.

"—she could be used for evil, too. So perhaps the problem isn't the magic and has never been the magic. And what you saw in Auevilla wasn't about the magic."

"It was Doucette. Doing something"—she searched for a word—"untoward with it."

Grant nodded. "He should have suffered for that," he said, and looked about the room as drinks and more than one punch were exchanged. "But you said there were no scars."

"Not that I could see."

Grant swore. "Magic used with impunity. That's the real threat." He turned back to her, put his hands on hers. "I hadn't thought to ask about your scars. And I'm sorry."

"You didn't tell me you carried me from the ship."

His eyes met hers, and for a long time, they simply looked at each other. "You can owe me for that one. And carry me when I need it."

"Deal," she said, and they finished their pies, sipped their ale.

"Your sisters are well?" Grant asked.

"My last letter from Jane said so. I'm hoping there will be more at the inn. How is your brother?"

Grant's brother, Lucien, wasn't unlike Raleigh's version of the Beau Monde, albeit without the funds. But he'd agreed to take responsibility for their family estate, Grant Hall, near the village of Queenscliffe.

"He is . . . adjusting," Grant said, with no little humor. "He prefers mathematics of the gambling variety, and is finding no enjoyment in ledgers and tenancy calculations. But it will be good for him."

"I imagine the Spiveys are glad to have him home." They were Grant's housekeeper and butler and took great pleasure in keeping the estate trim and tidy while the master was away.

"They enjoy having someone to care for—other than Sprout."

Sprout was Grant's little white dog, a small thing with an outsized personality and a great love of its master.

"Captain Brightling!" someone called out.

"Prepare yourself," Kit said, as a bevy of sailors—all of them hers—surrounded the table.

"Watson, Sampson, Simon," she said to the three of them. "You appear to be enjoying your leave."

"Glad we're here, aren't we?" Watson said brightly, and threw an arm around Sampson's shoulders. "And now that the captain's here, I'm sure she'll sport us a round."

It was the tradition, so Kit pulled coins from her pocket, put them on the table. "On me," she said, to the cheers of her crew. Seeing the admission as an invitation, they pulled up chairs.

Grant's lips twitched with amusement as chairs squeaked across wood floors. "We are destined, it seems, for constant interruptions."

Kit lifted her glass. "Every ship is a family. Never by birth, and rarely by choice. But a family all the same."

⁓

"You are a filthy cur and a cheater."

A family, of course, that was occasionally dependent on who won at indigo, a favorite card game of sailors and soldiers alike.

Lieutenant Watson watched, disgust etched in her features, as Sampson slid a pile of coppers across the table to his waiting stack.

Sampson's smile was thin and satisfied. "An expert doesn't need to cheat."

Her sailors were absolutely foxed. She and Grant had partaken of much less ale, but even Kit felt warm and relaxed.

"Sampson," Simon said, "don't make me lock you in the bursar's house again."

"And on that disturbing note," Kit said, rising from the table, "it's time for me to return to the inn. We meet with the War Council tomorrow."

That had a sobering effect on the proceedings but didn't keep Simon from dealing a new hand of cards into the four stacks a game of indigo required.

"We'll be sailing soon?" Watson asked, her voice now grave.

"Soon enough," Kit said. "So enjoy your leave, but do get some sleep." She gave them each a narrowed eye. "And no locking anyone in the bursar's house—or being locked into it," she added for Sampson particularly.

She and Grant walked outside, the sudden vacuum of noise a sharp contrast to the noisy carousing of sailors in port, the air considerably fresher.

"That was quite an experience," Grant said.

She looked up at him, not entirely certain if he was being sincere, or if his Beau Monde sensibilities had been offended by the disreputable chaos. But there was amusement in his face. And as they crossed the road, nearly silent at this dark hour, his fingers just touched hers. It was invitation and caress, and she gave her answer, linking her fingers in his.

He squeezed, stroking his thumb across hers as they returned to the inn, hand in hand.

⁓

A servant girl curtsied as they entered, the inn mostly empty and quiet.

"Mail for you, sir and ma'am," she said, and passed out the letters sent to each of them, following through some undoubtedly circuitous course to end up in Portsea.

Kit took the sealed papers and small parcel and had to work not to tear off the ribbon of the latter while there in the inn's parlor. These were the first letters she'd received since setting sail from New London weeks ago, and she was eager for news from home. But she'd enjoy it more—hearing from Jane and Hetta—if she was relaxed and comfortable, and she knew relaxation and comfort would be rare in the coming weeks. War provided little enough of either.

"Thank you," she said, and looked up at Grant. He could probably see the yearning in her face.

"Go read your letters," he said with a smile, and held up his packet. "I've some of my own. Thank you for a very pleasant evening."

"And to you, Grant."

"I'll see you in the morning."

They parted and she could still feel the tingling of his hand in hers.

⁓

She went back to her bedroom, removed her uniform, and washed her face and hands, and when she'd settled in the small bed with blanket and night shift, she opened the paper parcel.

Inside, she found three new penny novels—two romances and a very Gothic-looking mystery—a pair of rather poorly knitted mittens, a small box, and a letter from her sister Jane.

*My dearest Kit:*

*You've left me again in a House of very loud Girls, and I shall never forgive you—unless you respond to this missive as soon as you receive it and advise me of all the News from the Continent and the Diana. I understand Sunderland will lead a War Council. Of course, I demand you advise me Immediately that you are safe—or as safe as it's possible to be when one is an Adventurous Sea Captain.*

*Are there developments in Artillery? In rifles? I believe I've found an alternative to Powder which is less prone to accidental Explosions and which should be very Useful to the Crown Command—but neither Mrs. Eaves nor Hetta allows me to conduct my experiments in the house. I only charred the single Wall, but they've relegated me to the Potting Shed, which is a Very Unfair result.*

*Hetta receives Letters often, and while she remains as cheerful as Mrs. Eaves will permit, I believe she worries. Astrid worries, too. She'd ordered a new Dress from the Modiste and it may not arrive until after the Appleton ball, which is the talk of the Town, if not of Brightling House. Most of us, I'm Glad to say, have more important things to Mind than the length of hems and the appropriate number of buttons on a glove. Please imagine me rolling my eyes with Great Exhaustion.*

That was easy enough to do. Astrid intended to use her considerable beauty to secure a wealthy husband and comfortable life, and gave little thought to anything else.

*I've enclosed letters from the twins for your amusement.*
*I've also—*

The rest of the words in that sentence were covered by a smear of something brown. Jane's plucky handwriting continued beneath it:

*My dearest Sister, I regret to inform you that our*
*newest addition, dearest Louisa, has snatched one of the*
*Pistachio Nougats I'd intended to send you. And then*
*used one of her chocolate-smeared digits to muss my*
*Paper. She says Hello and be kind to Cook.*

Kit, indefatigable even in the face of maritime danger, nearly squeaked. She opened the small box and found five half-melted, half-squashed pistachio nougats inside. They looked, unfortunately, not entirely unlike the pile she'd encountered in the road.

And it fazed her not at all. "Thanks to the gods," she said, and ate the entire box.

# ELEVEN

She managed to avoid the innkeeper the next morning, and waited for Grant outside the inn for the walk to the Crown Command building. The weather had turned dreary, a cold and gray mist settling over the town. Kit had added her navy wool coat to her usual uniform, the collar raised against the chilly not-quite-rain.

"You look very formidable," Grant said, when he strode from the inn, wearing a similar coat of black wool, "with your sabre and coat billowing behind you. Like a warrior of old."

"If I must be a warrior, may I be a warrior in a tropical clime? No freezing Islish rain."

"Unfortunately, I cannot assist with that," he said. "You look healthier today."

"A solid night's sleep helped." But for the hooting of drunken sailors on the road below, which made for an interesting lullaby.

He gestured toward the road, and they began walking side by side. She suspected they made an interesting pair to watch—both of them with their gleaming back boots, long coats, and purposeful strides.

"Your letters from yesterday were positive?" Grant asked.

"Very. In addition to the business, there was one from Jane and a box of pistachio nougats."

"Which, I presume, are now gone."

"In the sense that the box is empty, yes. But they continue to provide energy and fulfillment."

Grant snorted.

"And your letters?" she asked.

"The price of wheat is very agreeable, and the new draperies in the front parlor at Grant Hall were 'just the thing.'"

"I'm glad to hear it."

Their conversation continued easily, a rather astounding change from their first meeting, which had consisted of little more than sniping and barely veiled insults. It was remarkable, Kit thought, how time could help a body see past her prejudices to the man beneath. Even if he remained rather lordish.

They made their way into the Crown Command building, bustling in the busy morning hours as clerks moved to and fro and ministers and staff made their way to offices for the daily business.

They were met by a clerk, then shown to a room with an enormous table in the middle, presently filled by a map of what Kit presumed showed the Narrow Sea and Gallia.

A woman with light brown skin and dark hair pulled into a knot came toward them, arm extended. "Captain Brightling," she said, and shook her former mentee's hand.

"Commodore," Kit said. "Congratulations on your promotion." She gestured to Grant. "Rian Grant, Viscount Queenscliffe."

"Good to see you again, your lordship."

They shook as well. "'Grant' is fine, Commodore. Or 'Colonel,' if you prefer the military title."

Perez smiled. "I like an aristocrat willing to forgo his family title for a military one."

Other officers stood on the opposite side of the room, brows knit as they considered some strategy or other. Sunderland, Thornberry, and three others Kit didn't know spoke together, and Chandler stood to the side, arms crossed and frowning as he watched them. Grant had once been an observing officer under Sunderland's command. But now he worked for Chandler, and neither of them fit neatly within the group assembled here, or so Kit thought. As a member of the Queen's Own, Kit was arguably just as separate.

"General Sunderland, Captain Thornberry, General Smith, General Watkins, and Minister of War Cargile," Perez said, then introduced Kit and Grant.

"My lord," Sunderland said to Grant, offering a hand. "It's good to see you again."

"General," Grant said, shaking it. "It's good to see you as well."

Sunderland was on the shorter side, with pale, ruddy skin and a crop of wiry red hair cropped short. His uniform was so laden with medals and awards, Kit was half-surprised he didn't collapse under the weight.

"Captain Brightling," he said, offering a small bow. "Your reputation precedes you."

"As does yours, General," Kit said brightly, all smiles. They'd met before, of course, and he'd said the same thing to her. Sunderland was a brilliant strategist, if not much for collaboration.

The rest of the introductions were made, Thornberry the stiffest of the bunch. He had a recent and uncomfortable history with Grant and Kit, due to his being an insufferable prig about the search for Gerard's warship—and about the capabilities of female officers. He made no such comment now, undoubtedly in part because of Perez's promotion.

Cargile, a woman with broad shoulders, pale skin, and cropped hair, began the session.

"You're here," she said, "to assist us as we finalize the Isles' plans for a response to Gerard's escape from Montgraf and aggressions from Gallia and"—she paused, looking at Kit—"apparently from Frisia, given your recent experiences on the Continent and in the water. As a preliminary matter, we've just received word that the queen has formally approved the Isles' participation in a coalition of allies to fight Gerard. Given the Continental blockade is already underway, this Third Coalition—gods save us from a fourth—will also coordinate respecting military activities."

"A formal declaration of war?" Grant asked.

"Not yet." She looked at Kit. "I suspect that will change given Frisia's aggressions toward the *Diana*.

"Now," she continued. "Let's address the details. The first issue is location. Based on the information we've gathered from our connections in Auevilla, including Lord Grant, the informant we know as Fouché, and Captain Brightling's recent report, we believe it is most likely Gerard will launch his ground campaign at Auevilla. There were a number of military vessels in Auevilla, in addition to the *Fidelity*. There were guards patrolling the docks and fear of Islish spies. Their concern suggests a desire for secrecy. And, of course, Doucette is too important an officer to put in a coastal town without reason. From a strategic standpoint, the town has port and river access, which will facilitate troop and supply movement. The Narrow Sea forms a buffer to the Isles, and it's far enough from both Hispania and Aleman to create a buffer should the allies regroup. Which we damned well will."

"Hear, hear!" Perez said.

"Is there any intelligence regarding Gerard's present location?" Kit asked.

"There is not. Given he was not seen at Auevilla either by our spies or by the prisoners with whom Captain Brightling had contact, we believe it most likely Gerard came onshore some miles away." She walked to the map, used a pointed cane to gesture. "Perhaps at Octeville to the west or Pointe Grise to the east. Those options would reduce the risk of his immediate recapture should the *Fidelity* be spotted in port, as it was." Cargile looked at Kit, nodded. "We believe he plans to join the larger force on the road to Saint-Denis, perhaps near Bouvreuil."

Kit surveyed the map, considered. "Has work on the harbor at Octeville continued since the treaty?" The port town was sheltered in the upper end of the tentacular peninsula that reached into the Narrow Sea northwest of Auevilla. The town was well sheltered and blessed with a natural harbor, albeit one not deep enough for the ships Gerard had hoped to anchor there.

"Our informants say no," Chandler offered.

Cargile nodded. "Which suggests Octeville isn't a primary location."

"If they intend to launch from Auevilla," Grant asked, "why did we see no equipment, no fortifications? Shouldn't there have been more soldiers, supply transport, camp women? Some material indication that troops were amassing?"

"Hardly a need for fortifications if the local population supports him," Sunderland said. "He won't be fighting them through to Saint-Denis, and knows it will take time before we discover his whereabouts and he is forced to face us. Certainly, there are villages that remain loyal to the king and will not allow Gerard to move so easily, but he won't take arms until he has to."

"We've been up and down both the northern and southern coasts," Perez said, "and there are no cities with so many markers as Auevilla. Even if the launch there is incomplete—if Gerard will join them farther inland—there's evidence the town will be involved."

"Is there any thought of a naval launch by Gerard?" Kit asked. "We already believe the Guild is building ships for him, and there were several large vessels berthed at Auevilla. Gerard was defeated on the Continent," she pointed out. "Perhaps he intends to try his hand on the water this time."

Cargile seemed to appreciate the question, but shook her head. "Even Gerard, egoist that he is, remembers Barbata."

It was the site of the Isles' greatest Continental naval victory, a rout by Lord Worsley, who had challenged a line of Hispanic ships of the line by, essentially, barreling through the middle of it with his own men-of-war. Barbata had been the end of any aspirations Gerard might have harbored to cross the Narrow Sea and make a claim on the Isles.

At least, during the last war . . .

"We will begin landing troops near Auevilla," Cargile said. "Primarily here, and here." She touched the cane to spots ten miles to the east and west of the town. "While we've small units on the ground in Hispania and Aleman, the bulk will need to sail from the Isles—from here, and from New London and Devonport."

The western edge of the Isles formed a peninsula that tipped into the Western Sea. Devonport was a port city on the southern coast of that peninsula, and another of the Crown Command's major docks.

"How many troops?" Grant asked.

"Ten thousand to start," Cargile said.

Ten thousand Islesians pouring into Gallia hardly seemed a "start" to Kit, but then again, she wasn't a soldier. It did explain the volume of troops in Portsea. The city wasn't preparing just to defend a war—but to launch one.

"The Transport Board has been reestablished by the naval service," Cargile said, nodding at Perez, "and will coordinate with them regarding troop movement and victualing. Lord Duckworth has advertised inside New London and out for merchant ships. But it will take time to make those arrangements. In the meantime, the board has determined to use naval ships to begin the process. Supply ships will follow the same pattern. As with the soldiers, there will be a mix of public and private enterprise."

Perez made no response to that and was probably debating whether she could extricate her ships from that duty. Sailors generally preferred adventure to cargo duty, no matter how valuable the cargo.

Cargile looked at Kit. "Your ship, Captain, will be among those that escort a portion of the troop ships to Auevilla."

That was a slight improvement over actual cargo duty, if not by much. But Kit understood necessity and orders. "When?" she asked.

"We've not enough supplies, troops, nor tonnage on the water to make an efficient supply at this time," Cargile said. "We're hopeful we can begin movements in earnest within the next ten days."

It would be a monumental undertaking, Kit understood, and the logistics would be remarkably complex. But it was still too long.

Grant apparently agreed. "Minister," he said, and all eyes turned to him. "With all respect, that will take much too long. Gerard will have disappeared into the countryside by then. I understand it's becoming more and more difficult to obtain intelligence. If our network has truly been depleted and we don't find him soon, we'll miss our opportunity to do so."

"And what would you propose?"

"Smaller units, deployed immediately to find the armies, track them, and stop them."

"Smaller units," Sunderland said, "will not stand against battalions remassed by Gerard."

Yes, Kit thought, that was rather the point. To prevent the "remassing." But Sunderland plainly knew that, so Grant didn't bother to challenge him again.

"Smaller units will have their place, of course," Sunderland said, and slid his gaze to Chandler, "particularly in intelligence gathering. You were a very good observing officer, Grant. I expect Chandler can make use of your resources again."

"And will do," Chandler said.

Grant merely inclined his head.

"What about magic?" Kit prompted. "La Boucher? How do you plan to deal with them?"

"First," Sunderland said, raising a hand, "let's begin by referring to him by his name. We don't want to frighten the public with tales of La Boucher." He offered the last in an exaggerated Islish accent. "That will not help the public nor the war cause."

Kit's disagreement was core-deep and fundamental; the public needed to know the monster they faced and what he could do. But in this room, within this group, she was merely a sailor. So she nodded.

"As to magic," Cargile said smoothly, "the Defense Ministry has no official position regarding the manipulation of magic as it relates to the Isles, given the international ban remains in place."

"A ban that Gallia has already violated," Kit said.

"Acknowledged. Both ministry and queen were horrified by your description of Doucette's magic, just as we were concerned by the reports of Gerard's activities at Forstadt."

But, Kit thought with growing frustration, that apparently changed nothing. "There are ways to utilize the benefits of the current without manipulating it. We must give our Aligned sailors and soldiers the necessary education and authority to use it when they can. This is too serious a threat to ignore."

"I was at Contra Costa," Watkins said. He was a tall man with dark brown skin and short, dark curls. "I heard the sound, the concussion, and then the cries that followed. It took days to attend the wounded, to bury the dead. And in the meantime, those who'd survived cried out from the field, begging for help. I do not take Alain Doucette lightly, but I also do not lightly take the cost of magic, or the responsibility that using it requires."

"Sir," Kit said with a nod, understanding she'd been reprimanded. "I apologize for the suggestion either the ministry, the War Council, or its individual members did not take the threat seriously." She met Watkins's eyes. "I'll apologize specifically to you, sir."

Watkins nodded, seemed to approve of the quick apology. "Accepted."

Kit shifted her gaze back to Cargile. "May I speak frankly?"

"Do you ever not?"

Given the smile in her eyes, Kit decided that wasn't quite a reprimand, if also not quite a compliment. "I generally prefer frankness, Minister. It's faster."

Cargile nodded. "Go on then."

"Despite his scars, and the pain he must have suffered at Contra Costa, Doucette shows a certain . . . fearlessness in his use of magic. And a rather remarkable skill. I've never seen anyone use magic like that, nor with that level of control, and had no idea it could be done. I was terrified," she added, "down to my bones, and I don't believe it's possible to overestimate the importance of his potential involvement. He is one of Gerard's most trusted men, and his promotion to marshal suggests not only that Gerard trusts Doucette, but that he trusts what Doucette can do—and intends to make magic a central force of his campaign."

"You presently use, and may continue to use, your Alignment in accordance with the rule of Islish law and the orders given to you by the queen," Cargile pointed out. "The same is true for every other person in the service who has an Alignment."

"And if their captains do not approve of the use of magic?" Kit asked, working very hard not to stare at Thornberry.

Cargile clucked her tongue. "Surely, Captain, you do not suggest that the Crown Command simply abandon rank where Alignment is concerned, and allow the odd Aligned seaman to determine the fate of the ship?"

The question was plainly rhetorical, so Kit offered no response. She'd said what needed to be said but understood full well the limitations of her position and her recommendations. That, too, was rank.

"Sir," she said, but it felt a bit like swallowing glass.

"In that case," Cargile said, "I believe we're done for now." She glanced about, got agreeing nods from the other councilors. "Thank you for your time, Captain and Viscount, and you'll receive your next orders forthwith. And gods bless the Isles."

The others quietly repeated the invocation.

"Oh," Cargile said, turning back to Kit. "In case you were not yet aware, Captain, there is to be a ball tonight."

"A ball," she said lamely.

"With the miserably warm punch and the dancing and shoes that pinch," Cargile said.

With Gerard planning to annihilate the Isles? Kit thought with disgust, but only said, "I regret I won't be able to attend."

Sunderland's smile was irritatingly pleasant. "Won't be able to attend a ball? But you're a woman. All women enjoy balls, do they not, Minister?"

Cargile's look was hot enough to singe. "I believe it would be wrong, General, to assume that all women—or anyone else, for that matter—have unified opinions on anything, much less something as controversial as a ball. Nevertheless," she said, and glanced at Kit, "in the event your regrets are made for ethical reasons, recall that we are not yet ready to proceed, as we await the resolution of important logistical matters. It is important for queen and country that a certain . . . unity be shown. And remember, Captain, that there will be plenty of sailors and soldiers in attendance who fear, perhaps rightfully, that this will be their last opportunity for a ball, to dance with a handsome man or pretty girl, to enjoy silly chitchat. Should we deny them their last hurrah?"

Kit opened her mouth to object, closed it again. Her tone was clear enough—and the order within it. "Of course I'll be there, Minister."

"Of course you will," Cargile said, and left the room.

❧

Most of the others followed her out, but Perez stayed behind, waited until she, Kit, Grant, and Chandler were the only ones who remained. Then closed the door.

She seemed to consider her words for a moment, then strode back to them. "I will not go so far as to say that I disagree with my colleagues, but I must admit to reservations."

Her doubt made Kit feel better, validated her concerns.

"Sunderland still enjoys hearing himself speak," Grant murmured.

"He is a very good strategist," Perez said. "But his voice is music to his own ears."

"Is he the one pushing to launch near Auevilla?" Chandler asked, moving a bit closer, as if to keep the words contained.

"He is not the only one, but he is certainly an advocate," Perez said. "He believes the war will be fought between Auevilla and Saint-Denis. I don't disagree that's a possibility, but I think a year without a throne will have made Gerard reconsider his failures. And matching his battalions of troops against ours across a field did not a successful war make. Magic, though . . ." She walked to the map, crossed her arms, gazed down. "Magic could change a battlefield. And he'll have considered that."

"He'll have ruminated on it," Kit said. That had Perez's gaze snapping up.

"Yes," she said, eyes gleaming. "That's it exactly. He'll have ruminated. Contemplated. Considered pensively while staring at a portrait of himself. Because that's the type of man he is."

This was something Kit had always appreciated about Perez. While she was unafraid to give a hard, straight order, she always looked at the totality. At the *context*.

Perez looked at the map in silence for a moment, then looked at Kit again. "Has Doucette ever used magic while he was on a ship? Away from land, I mean."

"Not to my knowledge. But I don't know how far his reach, shall we say, extends. I can stand ashore and feel whether the current is present, in the most general sense, but he's done things I didn't know were possible. So I wouldn't rule out the possibility."

"You're thinking Gerard will use him at sea?" Chandler asked.

"If your most important weapon was mobile," Perez said, "wouldn't you?"

Silence fell heavily as loss was contemplated.

"As Cargile pointed out, captains rule their ships and can allow Alignment to be used in whatever legal manner is available to them. I follow the same rule. Captain Brightling, while I recognize the *Diana* is not technically answerable to the Crown Command, I'd like her to be part of my flotilla—unofficially, of course. You'll find I give great leeway to the safe use of the magical gifts given to the Aligned."

"I so find," Kit said with a grin, "and I'd be honored. I'm sure the queen will have no objection."

"She doesn't." It was Perez's turn to grin now. "I asked her first, of course. Unfortunately, while I agree that haste is absolutely necessary, and our group will be among the first to leave, we've still to wait for that. In the meantime, your assignment."

Kit expected her to pull a packet from her coat, or otherwise produce a sealed dispatch from the queen. But she made no move.

"No paper," Perez said with a smile. "Merely a question. What, Captain, can the *Diana* do for us?"

Kit's smile was wide and wicked.

# TWELVE

I t may have been the best question Kit had ever been asked as a captain. And, oh, but she had thoughts. While Kit didn't think the *Diana* was the right ship to act as escort for troop carriers—bigger ships with more guns were needed to provide that kind of security—her speed and flexibility (and nimble crew, of course) made her an ideal scout. For magic, for Doucette, for signs of enemy activity.

"I'd give you a marque for him particularly," Perez murmured, "but as war hasn't yet been declared, our options are limited."

"Perhaps not for the man," Kit said. "But if an opportunity for a bit of sabotage were to come along?"

"I'm listening," Perez said.

"Watching for trouble is fine and well," Kit said. "But acting on the trouble one finds is much more useful. There may be ships to unmoor. Packets to intercept. It comes to this, Commodore: The gunships will see the troops safe. And the *Diana* will keep the enemy busy."

When the meeting was complete, she and Grant parted ways; he had his own business to attend to, including responding to the communications from his brother and Mrs. Spivey regarding the estate.

After checking again on Jin—still impudent, which was a good sign—Kit took the opportunity to walk through Portsea. The rain had stopped, and while the day was still gray, she wasn't sure when she might have the chance to wander about onshore.

As towns went, it wasn't nearly as pretty as Auevilla. But Auevilla catered to, apparently, hiding Islish aristocrats. Portsea catered to sailors, who were notoriously less particular. And had much less coin.

She turned onto West Street, where the physick had said the amulet maker's stall was located, and found a narrow building stuck between two others like a bookmark between the pages of a large tome. There was a half-circle window above the narrow door, and patterned brickwork inscribed with a symbol: three vertical lines with shorter horizontals together within a circle.

It was a symbol of the old gods, written in their language. Kit didn't know its meaning, but that the building had been marked by old magic piqued her curiosity.

The door was open, so Kit stepped inside. The shop was as short as it was narrow, presumably to make room for the curving metal stairs. The ceiling was a good twenty feet above; the walls had been given over to a collection of goods that certainly weren't from the Isles.

Behind a wooden counter on the far wall—which wasn't really so far considering the size—sat an older woman with pale skin and salt-and-pepper curls piled atop her head. She peered through small spectacles at a book on the wooden counter and didn't look up.

"We've no rum or vice here, sailor. Be on your way."

"I've no need for rum or vice," Kit said. "The symbol over the door. May I ask what it is?"

The woman turned a page of her book. "It's a charm to keep nosy sailors out of my shop."

"Not a very good one then, is it?"

For the first time, the woman looked up. Her eyes were pale blue beneath long, dark brows, and it took only a moment for her to return to her book again. "It's in one of the old languages from the cold lands. A hope for protection."

Since the woman had answered, and hadn't yet kicked Kit out of the shop, she walked to the left-hand wall and looked it over. Woven tapestries with bold patterns and colors, masks that sprouted braided grasses and grinning mouths, brass bells, and strands of amber beads.

"You've a beautiful collection," Kit said, wandering to the left-side wall. "Where are they from?"

"Across the world," the woman said, with enough disinterest that Kit concluded she'd given the same answer a thousand times before to a question she thought was simply inane.

Kit's gaze landed on a sculpted bit of iron, no larger than a man's outstretched hand. It was a sea dragon, sinuous and curving, the body of dark iron and eyes of bright orange-red and full of knowledge. Its mouth had been drawn into a smile that curved impishly, and a front claw held a wreath of small leaves. The piece was so finely rendered the veins on the leaves were visible, each round scale on the dragon's back defined. Kit reached out a finger to test the texture when the shopkeep's voice cut through the quiet.

"No touching," she snapped, and Kit snatched her hand back.

With a loud and thoroughly haggard sigh, the woman bent down a corner of the book's page—heresy, Kit thought—and closed it with a thud. Then she folded her hands, her index fingers ink stained, and lifted her brows. "It appears I'll get no peace while you're in here."

"If you don't want me in here, why is the door open?"

"For the breeze," the woman said after a moment. "Not just a sailor," she concluded, "but a captain of them. Unusual for a woman."

Impatience had already primed Kit's temper. That was enough to set the spark.

"Settle yourself, girl," the woman said. "I meant no offense. You know as well as I that the care of the world is rarely offered to women, much to its detriment."

Kit found the woman's honesty and frankness a bit unusual—but appealing compared to the doublespeak and mincing of her meeting with the Crown Command's high officers.

"You speak your mind," Kit said.

The woman's brows lifted. "Hardly a fault, is it?"

"If it is, it's one I've mastered."

A corner of the woman's mouth lifted. "Your name?"

"Kit Brightling."

"I'm Mathilda," the woman said. "And you've no amulet."

"No. I understand you sell them," Kit said, glancing around again, as unlike the stalls nearer the dock, none were on display.

"*Sell* is a cheap word. I hear what the magic deigns to tell me, and then I Align. Charm to wearer." She tilted her head at Kit. "You're Aligned to the sea, I suspect?"

Kit's stare was flat. "I'm a sailor. Hardly difficult to guess that."

The woman snorted. "The Aligned have no need for guesswork. I was born in the Northlands. There, stone and moor stretch toward the sky. The magic is harder than yours, and I can feel the difference."

"Harder?"

"More rigid," she said with a knowing smile. "And more stationary. It doesn't"—she wiggled her hand—"move about as much as the water does, or so I understand."

"Currents in the water are quite flexible."

The woman nodded. "You're water," she continued. "Your opposite is fire."

"My opposite?"

"The opposite Alignment." Her voice was remarkably patient given her obvious frustration. "The magic you battle, and that battles you."

She thought of Doucette, of his blue-green flame, and the sense she'd had at Auevilla of being actively repelled by him. The possibility their magic had clashed in some deep and fundamental way.

"It's my enemy?" Kit felt as if she was on the cusp of knowledge, grasping at a book that remained just—and frustratingly—out of reach.

"Not always," Mathilda said. "Fire can provoke, and also inspire. Earth and air are your complements. They may offer safe harbors and friendship, or lethargy and temperance."

Tamlin was Aligned to the air, and one of her closest friends. Grant wasn't Aligned at all, but he was undeniably a man of the earth. A soldier, a viscount, a landowner responsible for the lives of his tenants.

"I've not heard of any of this," Kit said.

The woman's expression didn't change. "That you've not heard it hardly means it doesn't exist. Have you been to Akranes?"

"No."

"And yet it exists, in spite of your absence. It's a damnable shame how this country ignores its own history." She linked her hands on the counter, peered at Kit with narrowed eyes. "You've truly had no education regarding your Alignment?"

"No," Kit said, and felt a bit disloyal by the admission. Hetta loved her girls and wanted them to know as much about as many subjects as possible—from languages to fencing. But Hetta wasn't Aligned, and the ban on manipulation kept information limited.

Mathilda looked her over. "You appear to be healthy, well nourished, clean. Your speech is New London gentry. Not quite Beau Monde," she said, head cocked as she considered.

"Certainly not," Kit murmured, Quite Offended now.

"When you have wealth and power," Mathilda continued, "you've no cause to risk your safety or your freedom by engaging in something illegal. But there is knowledge in dark corners and small rooms. There is knowledge at the hearth, at the birthing table, and in despair and want." She met Kit's gaze squarely. "Some do it in order to eat. To sleep. To breathe. Some manipulate the world's magic in order to win dominion over others, like Gerard and his dandies flitting about, tossing the current here and there like a child's toy."

It was Kit's turn to narrow her eyes. "What do you know of Gerard's activities?"

The woman snorted. "You know sailors, girl. They're sieves where information is concerned, and that doesn't include the soldiers. The gods brought magic to the Isles, or told us where to find it, depending how you believe. And yet, because of the errors of fools, we decided dallying with magic is wrong. That manipulating it is a violation of man and earth both, that it risks famine and fire and destruction."

"Contra Costa proved it."

"The error of a fool," she said again. "But I hear tell he's learned to correct that error?"

"At least visibly. It appears he has discovered how to direct the magic—bring it to the surface and control its movement."

"Nonsense."

Kit's brow lifted. "I saw him do it. Watched him kill a man with current he'd deployed."

"I don't doubt what you saw, child. I doubt the mechanism. The current does not *obey* the whims of man. It is not a dog, hoping for praise from its master. It is a force. He cannot move the current. But he can . . . free it. Allow it to move outside its normal boundaries."

This may have been the most valuable conversation Kit had ever had—and one that was needed for the entire admiralty, if not the entire Crown Command itself.

"Is there"—she searched for words—"some sort of manual?"

"A *Cox's Seamanship* of magic?"

Kit leaned forward, avarice in her eyes. "Yes. Exactly."

"No."

"*Blast*," Kit muttered.

"I'm aware of no grimoires, as one does not 'make' magic. One learns how to see the magic that already exists."

"Then how is one supposed to be educated?" Kit asked.

"By learning from those who already know how to see and

hear," Mathilda said with some obvious satisfaction. "As you're doing here. Your Alignment," she continued, reaching behind her for a paper box on a low shelf. "Open sea? Small lake? Burbling stream?"

"I feel the current most strongly in the Narrow Sea."

Mathilda paused as she turned around, then put the box on the countertop. "Well, that's interesting, isn't it? Not many with connections offshore."

Kit had the unsettling sensation that she'd entered a world where she didn't speak the language, didn't understand the customs. But was thrilled at the possibility of *understanding*.

Mathilda lifted the box, began pulling out baubles nestled in the thin paper inside. "A bit of orange coral. Not native to the Narrow Sea, of course, but flexible. Perhaps a bit of dried sea sedum for healing. A bit of silver for reliability, of course."

As Kit watched, Mathilda gathered more items, murmured to herself the entire time.

"Captain."

Kit turned at the voice in the doorway, could hear in Watson's tone that the time for fripperies was over. "Lieutenant."

"I was asked to remind you, by Minister Cargile, that it's time to get ready for the dance."

Kit growled.

Mathilda snorted. "Don't all sailors love the quadrille and waltz?"

"Not the ones staring down the abyss of war," Kit said, and turned back to Mathilda. "Thank you for the information. It was a pleasure meeting you." She made a little bow.

The woman humphed. "I've the information I need. I'll finish this, and send to you when it's complete." And then she named a sum that had Kit goggling.

Kit sighed, pulled coins from her pocket, counted them, dropped them into Mathilda's hand. She smiled, placed them into a chatelaine at her waist.

"And when I receive the amulet, what ought I do with it?"

Mathilda stared at her in silence for a solid ten seconds.

Behind them, Watson cleared her throat. "You'll wear it, Captain."

"I know that much," Kit said. "But need I say a charm, or an invocation, or—"

"The amulet will know what to do," Mathilda said. "That's why they're worth the coin you pay and more." She made a shooing motion. "Now go. And good luck to you, Kit Brightling. May you find the fairest of winds."

⁓

Kit felt a bit off-center, as if the knowledge Mathilda had imparted had mass and weight enough to affect her balance.

And she was both embarrassed and insulted that Cargile had sent a messenger to remind her of the ball. She hadn't made captain by disobeying orders, had she? Fortunately, she kept a dress in her trunk in case some meeting of royalty or admiralty required it.

When she returned to the room, she crouched on the floor beside the trunk and searched through it, but the modest blue-gray silk she'd packed in the bottom was gone. In its place was a paper-wrapped packet tied with a gold ribbon, a note tucked beneath it.

She unfolded it, found Jane's tidy handwriting again.

*My dearest sister:*

*I won't be Satisfied until I've eliminated blue from your Wardrobe. I borrowed these from Astrid, as they'll look much better on you. If they do not, you may direct your Objections to her.*

*All my love, Jane*

Astrid, who was obsessed with the marriage mart and making a smart match, was their most sartorially particular sister. And she'd bet a gold coin that Astrid hadn't voluntarily offered the dress. She probably didn't know it was missing.

This wasn't the first time Jane had tried to remove blue from Kit's wardrobe. The last time, she'd substituted deep red for somber blue. Curious what color had met her approval this time, Kit untied the ribbon and unfolded the paper, revealing soft, dark velvet the color of evergreens in shadow. She unfolded it, revealing short, ruched sleeves, a gold ribbon around the high waist, and a ruched bodice cut so low modesty would flee in terror at the sight. The package included a silk taffeta cape in a slightly paler color with the same gold ribbon at the hem. Kit liked the cape as much as the dress, and took a moment just to rub her thumb across the fabric, watching the shift of light.

"Astrid is going to be livid," Kit said and rose, spread the garments on the small bed, and began to make her preparations.

⌞⌝

It was a challenging thing, squeezing into a corset without a lady's maid, which was precisely why she didn't wear one. Kit rarely had reason to visit a modiste, but at a shipmate's recommendations, she'd found short stays at a shop in London as a young midshipman. They'd quite literally changed her life.

She donned the dress, then brushed her hair and rouged her cheeks with the small pot she'd included in her trunk, and felt suddenly foolish for doing it. She was a captain in the Queen's Own, not a girl making her debut.

There was a knock at the door, too soft to be Grant. She opened it, found a boy of nine or ten with pink cheeks.

"Note," he said, and thrust a bit of folded paper into her hand before running down the hallway again.

Kit closed the door and unfolded it, found a message from Grant—instructions not to wait for him at the inn, and he'd see her at the ball.

Kit set aside the note, threw the cape around her shoulders, and blew out the candle.

While she still thought the affair was a bit ridiculous, she couldn't fault the beauty of a ballroom lit by hundreds of candles and swathed in maroon roses and golden linen. She was announced into the room and moved through the crowd of attendees and their swirling silks and satins, jeweled hair clips, and immaculate gloves.

She curled her fist to hide the small tea stain on the left-hand palm of hers, not that anyone was likely to notice that detail. Most were here less to see than to be seen, to display a new dress or waistcoat, a pretty ribbon or silk slipper.

Yes, it was silly. But Cargile had a point. The lives of soldiers and sailors both were punctuated by war and too often cut short by it. She had no cause to complain that they enjoyed themselves in the interim just because she preferred a grimy tavern to a formal affair.

She looked around, wondering where Grant might be, and wishing there might be some small errand Perez needed done that would require her to spend the next few hours in that grimy tavern.

And then she saw him.

Across the ballroom, a good head taller than most of the others and looking quite . . . dashing. His morning coat was dark gray velvet, his waistcoat white, his trousers black. His hair was perfectly coiffed, his square jaw clean-shaven, his eyes blue as the Southern Sea. She wasn't sure she'd ever seen a man quite as handsome, and she was absolutely positive that she'd never gotten flutters over one before.

"Captain Brightling," he said when he strode through the crowd to reach her.

"My lord."

"You look exceedingly beautiful," he said, and she could feel the blush in her toes. She was a captain, for gods' sake, and had no business with blushing.

"Thank you," she said, and managed a curtsy. Or would have if he hadn't stopped her with a tug of the hand.

"You won't curtsy to me," he said, eyes bright. "We stand as equals."

She stood straight again, met his gaze with hers, knew the statement was another apology for what had happened during Jin's surgery. "Equals," she agreed. "Although you've one more title than me."

He snorted, moved to stand beside her. "So I'm ever-so-slightly superior."

"Viscounts," she said with mock exhaustion, and watched as others moved into the ballroom. Some were officers with spouses; others stepped into the doorway alone, uniforms neatly brushed and eyes bright with excitement.

And realized that some of the eyes were on her—and Grant. Whispers behind fans or folded hands, curiosity in the gazes. Who was that woman standing so near the viscount? Or who was that man standing so near the captain? That wasn't the type of attention she was used to attracting, and she wasn't entirely comfortable with it. Being evaluated on her merits as a Brightling, as a captain? That was part of naval service. But as one of a potential couple? That was . . . different. She'd said she hadn't needed a chaperone, and still didn't. But this wasn't a tavernful of sailors.

"You're glowering, Captain."

She tried to relax her face. "I don't enjoy being forced to attend a party when we're waiting for war and there are thousands of lives in the balance."

"No," he said, "I don't think that's all of it."

She didn't answer but smoothed the front of her dress. And was saved from further discussion when a song began to play. He stepped in front of her, offered his hand.

"Dance with me, Kit."

She nodded, put her gloved hand in his, and strolled through the watching crowd to the space made for dancers. One hand at her waist, and they began to move together across the floor.

It was a strange sensation, to dance with a man in reality after having dreamed of it. She'd imagined it fairly creditably, but for the horror of the ballroom filling with water.

"Captain, a man might feel he doesn't have your entire attention."

"You have a quarter of my attention," she said, without looking at him. "Another quarter is given to my feet, and ensuring I manage these steps appropriately. One quarter is given to the other couples, and ensuring we don't run into them. And one quarter is given to—"

Then she saw them come in—Cargile, Sunderland, and Perez—and their expressions were grim.

"Captain," Grant said, pulling her bodily to the right.

Kit blinked, realized he'd swept her out of the way of two stampeding couples. She took his hand firmly, pulled him out of the array of dancers.

"What is it?" he asked, and she bobbed her head toward the group. She felt his posture change, from viscount to colonel. The straightening of the shoulders, the narrowing of the eyes.

A spoon was dinged against crystal, and the crowd quieted— but for the murmurs of those who'd never seen Sunderland in the flesh, and debated if he lived up to their imaginations.

"I apologize for the interruption," Sunderland said, voice booming across the hall. "But there's news from the Continent."

Even the gawkers went quiet.

His eyes went hard, and she could see the infantryman he'd once been behind the medals and braid. "Ships bearing Gerard's pennants have destroyed two Isles ships in the Narrow Sea. More than one hundred lives lost. There were no survivors."

# THIRTEEN

They were the *Princely* and the *Domination*, one a merchant frigate, the other a brigantine. Destroyed by some combination of eighteen-pounders and, according to the field reports, "a bit of freak lightning."

But Kit knew better. Chandler knew better. And after they'd corralled the War Council, the War Council knew better. Kit and the *Diana*—along with the other troops and ships assembled under Perez's command—would sail at dawn for Auevilla.

She made her way to the Crown Command's dock just before, with the sky still purpled with darkness. Kit would leave Portsea the way she'd come into it—just on the verge of night.

She hadn't slept well. Her mind raced, considering strategies and preparations. And with the increased likelihood of fighting, there were new questions: Did they have enough shot? Enough gunpowder? Enough salve for the inevitable burns, and linens for dressing?

They weren't a ship of the line. But death didn't care for the number of guns on deck; it hunted small ships and large.

The *Diana*, which was a large enough ship, looked miniature when sharing a dock with frigates and four-masted brig-
antines that rose high above her. They were big, Kit thought
as she surveyed them from the dock, but not nearly as spry
as her own. She wouldn't have traded the *Diana*—where she
knew every plank of oak and every sailor from lieutenant to
able seaman by name, even if she was obliged to maintain
a respectful distance from most—for a ship of the line, and
hoped to put off her "promotion" to a larger ship as long as possible.

She made her way on board, thinking the ship looked even
better after only a few days in port. The bowsprit had been replaced, the rigging rerun in the bow. And was the brass in the
binnacle a bit shinier, perhaps? The deck a bit smoother? And
were casks of wine being loaded on board?

"What are they doing to my ship?" she asked no one in particular.

"Fancying her up a bit," Tamlin said. "She gleams now, doesn't
she?"

"Commodore Perez sends her thanks and congratulations for
locating the *Fidelity*," Simon said, stepping up behind Kit.

"Sugar and milk?" Kit asked hopefully.

"A bit of both."

"Well, then. We'll all have cake."

"Unfortunately, there's more." He pointed to the stack of
papers on the steering cupboard.

"*No*," Kit said, her mood deflating.

"Aye, Captain. I'm sorry. They're for documentation of our
arrival and departure in Portsea, provisioning, additional shot
and supplies in the event of battle."

Kit cursed in disgust. "My ship found the *Fidelity*. Found Doucette. And I am *still* damned with paperwork."

"Captain," Simon said, and his quiet tone had her looking up, following his gaze to the dock. She found Jin in uniform and walking toward them, March at his side. But for the slightest hitch in his gait on the side of his wound, he looked the same as he had when he'd boarded in New London.

"What are you doing here?" she asked when he reached them.

His brows lifted. "Last I heard, I was the commander of the *Diana*, and the *Diana* is preparing to set sail. Therefore . . ."

"You're injured."

"I'm standing, and I was cleared by the physick."

She glanced at Simon and Tamlin, and they left her with Jin and March. "No," she said, when only they remained. "You will not risk yourself."

"Only you're allowed to do so?"

"I am the captain of this ship."

"And I have a debt to repay to said captain."

"There is no debt," Kit said. "And you're not healed enough for this."

"Are you saying that because you are my friend, or my captain?"

She stepped up to him. "I'm saying it because I don't want your blood on my hands again."

For a long time, they just looked at each other, a million things unsaid because they were Islish and stubborn and ranked and wearing uniforms.

"It's been three days," Jin said. "I've no fever, I've been stitched on both sides, and the healer has provided several disgusting poultices to be applied daily." He held up a small basket, a bow on the handle and something pungent tucked inside a bit of linen.

"I'll take that," March said brightly, plucking the basket from his hand. She leaned in, sniffed, and quickly turned away, lips pursed. "The odor is absolutely foul. So they'll probably work wonders."

"Do you support this?" Kit asked, gesturing to Jin.

"He'll have delicious scars," March said with a grin. "But aye, Captain. He'll hold up—if he follows my instructions and applies the poultices regularly."

Kit resisted—barely—the urge to poke him in his wound and remind him of his limitations. Having those limitations was no failure, but it was an unfortunate fact, at least for now. On the other hand, there were no sailors to spare to replace Jin while he was gone, and the ship was already leanly staffed. They needed more men, not fewer. And she trusted him as she trusted few others.

Kit watched him. "Half duty. And if you look even the slightest bit pale, you'll go immediately to your quarters."

"Kit—" Jin began, but she held up a hand.

"I am your captain, as you just acknowledged. You serve with the necessary conditions, or you don't serve."

She gave him a moment to be angry—as she'd have felt the same—and was proud when he straightened his shoulders. "Aye, Captain. But I'm eating the chocolates I bought for you."

"All's fair in love and war," Kit said, and squeezed his hand. "Welcome back, Commander."

"Glad to be back, Captain." He looked up at the mainmast. "Let's go hunting, shall we?"

∽

While the dockworkers continued loading the ship, she went down to her quarters, a bit horrified at the possibility she'd find it littered with brass candlesticks and frilly linens and antimacassars. She found none of that, to her great relief. But when she put the stack of papers on her small desk—damn each and every one—and pivoted to return to the deck, she found something new.

Hanging beside the door was a painting—a sleek schooner on a turbulent sea, the water shot through with light. Not the same as the one she'd seen in Raleigh's town house, but a similar style, and a similar appreciation of the sea.

Grant appeared in the doorway, and she gestured to the painting. "Did you do this?"

"Do what?" Grant asked.

"Put this here. It wasn't in my quarters before."

Frowning, he walked in, looked at it. "No," he said after a moment. "Raleigh, I'd presume."

"Is there anything a duke can't do?"

"Apparently not." His voice bordered on petulant now. "Why is he giving you works of art?"

"I've no idea. Perhaps he has a surplus. He is a duke, after all."

Grant muttered something.

Kit glanced back, brows lifted in amusement. "Are you jealous?"

His responsive look was arch. "I'm jealous of a man who can command a token delivered across the Narrow Sea in a matter of days."

"That is rather impressive," Kit agreed, and looked back at the paperwork. "And I'll damned well bet he didn't have to sign his name to a dozen forms to get it done."

"Dukes rarely do."

"It's a beautiful work," Kit said, "and proves that he's safe."

"You needn't worry about Raleigh," Grant said.

"Yes, I'm sure he can protect himself."

"Perhaps I should have said I'd prefer you didn't think about Raleigh."

Kit stopped, looked at him. "What? Why?"

"Because I'd prefer your attention be on me."

She could feel it again, that warmth of his gaze on hers, pushing away the remaining chill of fear and concern. She was beginning to like it. Beginning to rely on it.

And didn't mind that so terribly much.

❧

The provisioning was completed, and by the time the *Diana* was prepared, the tide was fair, the sky was impossibly blue, and the wind straight and strong. And so, with that auspicious start, the *Diana* moved into the Narrow Sea again. There'd be a gunship between her and the troop ships, and she'd wait for them to fall into line before setting sail for Gallia. She moved to the helm. Even now, there was work to be done.

"Call the all hands," she told Jin, and watched as the bell was rung, the order given, and sailors scurried into position. They finished their immediate tasks, then hustled into lines that faced the helm.

"One year ago," she said, "we were relieved of the burden of war. Of the fear and concern. The man who called himself emperor was sent to his prison, where he was to remain while the world tried to right itself. But we find ourselves here again, because some crave glory more than they crave peace. Yesterday, Gallic ships destroyed two Islish vessels. More than one hundred souls lost."

Sailors touched their caps, their hearts, or their amulets, depending on their persuasion.

"Today, the fleet sails for Gallia, to stop the man who wishes to draw us back into fire and smoke and death. Nearly one thousand troops will travel on the ships behind us. We will scout." She thought of what Jin had said. "We will hunt. And we will do what's necessary to keep Gallic eyes away from our soldiers."

There were general sounds of agreement.

"I'm not certain what we'll find today, but there is one thing of which I am certain." She took a step forward, met the gaze of each and every sailor in turn. "We will do what is necessary to save the Isles."

Fists were thrust upward, shouts called.

"We will be quick and expert with cannon and sail alike. We will use magic when we can. And we will be aware— always aware—that those who follow Gerard are prepared to use magic against us. We will trust ourselves and each other, and we will fly."

The shouts were thunderous now, the sailors stomping their feet so enthusiastically, the deck rattled with it.

She moved to the bow of the ship, which swayed silkily beneath her. She'd normally visit the hold, surround herself with water. But she didn't need to descend in order to feel the magic today. It was healthy here, strong and shimmering, with none of the limitations she'd felt to the northeast. She knew it wouldn't last, and she was impatient for the flotilla to arrive so she could touch the current, feel that connection again.

She had a thin splinter of worry that being eager to make that connection was approaching a dangerous line, the kind of line that Doucette had likely crossed some time ago. But her course had been set.

She walked back toward the helm, navy tailcoat blowing in the breeze, and watched Grant watch her as she moved, his eyes warm, and a cocky kind of pride in his smile. She could take that, she decided.

"Map, Mr. Pettigrew," she said, and Simon arranged it atop the cabinet, marked their current location with a coin, smaller coins behind.

"We will sail toward Auevilla," she said. "We plainly know the way."

"Forward and back," Jin agreed. "Although I was unconscious for some of the back."

"It all looks the same," Kit said. "We will sail in formation to approximately here." She marked a spot off the coast. "At this point, we will split. Half the troops will move to the western landing point"—she moved some coins—"and half to the eastern"— she moved the rest of the coins. The eastern point was near the Seine River, which flowed to Saint-Denis. "We'll sail with the eastern group."

Watson and March came to the helm; Watson had a stack of paper and a wee pencil. "Captain, we've double-checked the goods from Portsea and confirmed the manifest. In addition to the food, we've flints, wadding, gunpowder, and an extra supply of goods for our near physick."

"'Near physick'?" Kit asked, smiling at March.

"She may not be officially a ship's physick," Watson said, "but she's close enough for the *Diana*, aye?"

"Aye," Kit said. "And the near physick found everything she might need?"

"Aye, Captain. The Crown Command was generous. Linens, splints, forceps, scalpels, needles, and thread. A newfangled scoop for pulling out shot and"—she paused—"two new bone saws."

"Gods keep us," Grant murmured.

"Thank you for the detail, Lieutenant. Do let us know if you find your kit to be lacking."

"I never need to hear the phrase *bone saw* again in my life," Grant said, when March had gone again.

Simon clapped him on the shoulder. "Better to hope it's never to be used on you, Colonel."

"Ooh, look there!" someone called out near the stern.

Kit turned back, expecting to see one of the transports finally making headway—and caught the sheen of brilliant crimson disappear beneath the water.

"Sea dragon!" came the shout from the top. "Port stern!"

In addition to being a symbol of the Isles—part of the flag and engraved on Kit's sabre—sea dragons were an omen of good luck. They were serpentine in shape, with fins at intervals along their spines and short front and back claws. Their heads were roughly rectangular, with wide eyes that Kit felt always looked thoughtful.

Kit joined the sailors who looked over the port-side gunwale, waiting for the creature to show itself again. After a moment, it did, its sinuous body curving above the surface in an arc, the largest of its shimmering scales big and round as dinner plates. Kit couldn't see the entirety of this particular beast but guessed it was as long as the *Diana* herself.

Every conversation stopped, as if the crew was hypnotized by its undulations. It was a strange and beautiful thing, Kit thought, and wonderful to observe from a safe distance. A single sea dragon was lucky; a horde was a frenzy of movement, teeth, and claws.

"A good omen," Jin said. And Kit hoped he was right.

⌒

It was three more hours before the convoy was fully assembled and moving and the *Diana* could let fly the canvas. The ships loomed behind her, hulks of timber, stuffed with soldiers and noisier than Portsea during shore leave. The *Diana* was a solid half mile ahead, and they still sounded like a hive of rowdy bees.

"Soldiers," Jin murmured, arms crossed as Kit watched them dancing on the deck of the closest transport.

She lowered the glass, glanced at Grant. "Have they no decency?"

Grant just raised his eyebrows. "No less than sailors on shore leave."

That she'd thought the same thing just irritated her.

Fortunately, they all but flew to Gallia—the wind still blew toward the coast, which actually helped them this time. They sailed in formation for hours, biding their time until the signal was made and the squadron split apart. The *Diana* veered east with the others, sailing toward the coast.

The troop ships would make landfall well after dark so they'd be less visible to anyone who might be watching from shore. But that increased other dangers, as the ships had to navigate to shore and the soldiers would have to make their way into Gallia in darkness.

So the *Diana* would provide some needed protection.

"All right, Captain," Simon said. "Don't leave us in suspense.

I know you've a plan in that canny brain of yours. Where are we going? And what shall we do when we get there?" His eyes gleamed with anticipation.

"We're going to make a bit of trouble." She pointed to the cliffs. "There."

"The cliffs?" Jin asked, frowning.

"Ah," Grant said with a sly smile. "I see."

Kit glanced back at him. "Do you?"

"You intend to destroy the shutter telegraph."

"I do," she said with a smile. "I very much do."

They signaled their destination to the lead gunboat in their group, waited for their acknowledgment, then veered farther northeast to the cliffs at the edge of the crescent. There were no other ships in sight this time. No Gallic brigs, no damned Frisian men-of-war.

But the shutter telegraph, once hidden from view by a rise in the land, was plainly visible now as darkness began to descend. It was perhaps twenty feet tall, with two columns and four rows of square boards that hung from wooden rails. There would have been ropes or cranks to flip the boards from one side to the other, and the small building nearby was probably the home of the person who tended it. There'd be others along the coast, so messages could be passed from telegraph to telegraph or—as had probably been the case with the Gallian brig—from someone in town to ships offshore.

Destroying it would give the troop ships more time to land, more time to get away, before the enemy was signaled. Yes, it could be rebuilt, but that would take time, and the troops would have disembarked by then.

The question was how.

She ached to use the ship's eight-pounders again, but the noise would raise alarms. And, if she was being quite honest, the odds of her new cannoneers destroying such a slender target at distance with a single shot—or two or three shots—were slim.

Much to her chagrin, this was not the time for Kit to play at sabotage onshore. But she knew a very capable soldier, so she looked at Grant.

His smile was wide and immediate. "Oh, you don't even need to ask. I absolutely will."

⌒

They waited until the sun was down completely, and the crew was ordered to silence. Only a single lantern on the starboard side that faced the coast was left alight, hung below the gunwale to disguise the size of the ship. Sampson, Watson, and Grant would take the jolly boat to the shore, ascend the cliff on the northern side—which was a low grassy hill, rather than the granite stone on the southern—and take out the telegraph by whatever method they deemed most efficient. They'd have axes borrowed from Mr. Oglethorpe, rifles, a lantern—and a small object that appeared to be a large glass marble, which Kit produced from a velvet bag in her trunk. This was a sparker, a small explosive Jane had designed for Kit's use at sea. They were marvels, and Kit was conservative with her small supply.

While Sampson and Watson loaded the boat, she offered the sparker to Grant.

"Is this a symbolic gift?" he asked with a crooked smile. "Offering me explosives?"

"No, but it is a useful one." She placed it carefully in his hand, pointed to the small depressions on opposite sides. "When you're ready, squeeze here and throw. If you can feel it begin to warm, you should have already thrown it."

He nodded, pulled a handkerchief from his waistcoat, and wrapped it carefully before slipping it into an interior pocket. "I appreciate the token and the gift."

"We're ready, Captain, Colonel," Sampson said behind them.

But Grant didn't break their gaze. "Try to stay out of trouble while I'm gone."

"Try not to get arrested by Gallic authorities."

His grin widened. "If you'll recall, Captain, I'm the one who saved *you* from arrest." He leaned toward her, lips perilously close to her ear. "And if you manage to injure yourself while I'm gone, you'll need saving from me."

She didn't injure herself, except for the muscles she might have strained while stalking the deck. An hour had passed, and then two, with no sign of the jolly boat or its passengers. They'd reached the telegraph—that was certain enough—as the lanterns that illuminated it had been doused some time ago. Unfortunately, that meant Kit could no longer see from the boat whether it was still standing, nor the passage of her crew upon the dark water.

"He'll be fine."

Kit stopped pacing at the helm, looked up at Jin with narrowed eyes. "I have no idea what you mean."

"I meant Grant," Jin said with a wry smile.

"Insubordinate to the last," Simon said.

The oldest member of the crew, Mr. Smythe, shuffled toward

them. "*The lieutenant's spotted the boat!*" he said, in a painfully slow and hoarse manner Kit thought was intended to be a whisper.

She winced at the sound, like rusted nails against tin, but said a *Dastes* and offered up her bit of copper.

⁓

"It was the damned surf," Sampson said, when they'd made their way out of the jolly boat and onto the *Diana*'s deck. He was soaking wet, as were Grant and Watson.

"Some linens, Mr. Wells, if you would," Kit said, and Mr. Wells sprinted toward the companionway. Other sailors began unloading the supplies, which would apparently also need drying.

"We made it in quick as you please," Watson said, wringing water from her hair. "Made it to the telegraph with no one to see it."

"We saw you doused the light," Jin said.

Watson nodded and grinned at Grant, offered him a shoulder bump. "This one here may be a viscount, but he's nearly as good as a sailor."

"High praise," Kit said, shifting her gaze to him. The damp shirt did nothing to hide the muscles beneath, so she focused her eyes—and her attention—on his face.

"Indeed," Grant said. "Took the telegraph out with the axes, and it fell like a tree."

"Made a good bit of racket," Watson agreed with a nod. "But the man in the hut there was so busy singing a tune, he didn't notice a damned thing."

Mr. Wells returned with clean and folded linens, passed them out.

"We ran like he was chasin' us, though," Sampson said, picking up the story. "Made it back to the boat. And then had to make it out of the surf."

"We struggled at it for an hour," Watson said, scrubbing a linen through her hair. "One wave after another—the same that pushed us into shore, now keeping us in again. And they were high, too."

"How'd you manage it?" Kit asked.

"Brightling levels of stubbornness," Grant said, hanging the linen around his shoulders. "We kept the boat straight and paddled like Gerard himself was chasing us."

"Not that he could handle an oar," Sampson said. "Probably never raised one in his life."

"Probably not," Kit said. "Well done on all accounts."

"And what's next?" Jin asked.

"Let's return to the squadron," she said. But she had something else in mind . . .

When the *Diana* made it back around the crescent, the first ship had discharged its crew and supplies, and unloading of the second was underway. They stayed offshore, most of their lights still doused, but for one near the binnacle. On a clear night, they might have used the stars to navigate, but clouds obscured the stars, and with the other ships' lights extinguished, the compass kept them oriented.

The crew stayed quiet, and Tamlin scanned the horizon, but there was no sign of enemy ships.

Kit took the spyglass from the cabinet, raised it, and aimed it toward Auevilla's harbor. And found the *Fidelity* still at the dock, in the same berth where they'd seen it last.

The *Diana* hadn't yet been spotted. What if they crept a bit closer to the harbor, with all quiet and lights doused? And what would happen if they lobbed a couple of Jane's sparkers onto the *Fidelity*'s deck, let the explosion do what the Crown Command hadn't yet been able? Or simply let loose the moorings and anchor, and let tide and sea take the *Fidelity* where it would?

Sailors and soldiers both were superstitious sorts. The loss of Gerard's former flagship by mysterious circumstances, or perhaps suspected sabotage by one of their own, might hurt Gallic morale. Might tempt a few to stay in town, rather than taking a berth on a Gallic warship or, if the War Council was right, joining the march to Saint-Denis.

She lowered the glass, frowned out at the water. The night was clear, the *Diana* would be all but invisible from the shore, and the lights of the town were enough to guide them. Another team could take the jolly boat, get the mission done, and get back.

Kit had nearly convinced herself the risk would be worth it, when she felt the sea shudder. Not physically—not a rogue wave or earthshake—but *magically*. She looked around; no other members of the crew made any obvious reaction. Those on the deck whispered quietly or helped mend sails, waiting for the next spot of action.

So she reached down and found the current flowing normally, or as normally as she'd have expected . . . but for the shudder of something farther away, as if something had slapped the current upstream.

Or *someone* had.

Spyglass in hand, she walked back to the mast, looked up, gave a whistle. Tamlin was on the deck in less than a minute.

"There's something," she said without prompting. She'd braided her hair today into a long queue, and her fingers wound the end of it, over and over, as if nervous.

"There's something," Kit agreed. "Can you tell what?"

She shook her head.

"It felt to me like someone hit the current," Kit said.

"I feel . . . surprise," Tamlin settled on. And Kit reckoned this was one of those times when different Alignments made discussion difficult.

"Is it like what you felt before at Auevilla?" Kit asked. "What Doucette was doing?" He could still be onshore; they hadn't been gone that long.

"No," Tamlin said after a moment. "It's not the same."

Kit wasn't sure if she should be relieved or not. Which was worse—the enemy that terrified you or the one you hadn't yet met?

"Thank you," Kit said with a nod. "Let me know if anything changes."

Tamlin nodded, climbed back up the mast.

Kit walked to Cooper, who stood in her assigned position middeck. She didn't want to embarrass the woman by asking for information that was beyond her Alignment and ken, but Kit needed information.

"I don't suppose you feel anything unusual, Cooper?"

Cooper's brows lifted in surprise. Then she pulled up her sleeve, showed Kit the gooseflesh that pimpled it. "I thought I was imagining it, sir. I can't feel the current from here, but something feels amiss."

"Indeed it does," Kit said, and walked back to the helm where the others waited, if impatiently. "Something is happening in the current. Tamlin and Cooper feel it, too. We don't know if it's Doucette—it feels different than it did at Auevilla. We need to signal the ships."

Simon nodded. "What shall we send them?"

"Magic nearby," Kit said, tucking hair behind her ears as she considered the best and simplest phrasing. "Prepare for incoming."

"Incoming what?" Grant asked.

"Just . . . incoming," Kit said.

And they didn't have long to wait.

# FOURTEEN

Kit positioned the *Diana* between the Isles ships and whatever was happening beyond.

It started with a single light, so far away that it flashed in and out of view with the haze, the motion of the waves, or the swaying of its lantern. Each time it disappeared it seemed an illusion: perhaps only a fishing boat trolling in the darkness, a mail packet, a trick of the mind. But then it would appear again, strong and true—and denial became harder. And harder yet when another appeared, and then another, until dozens of lights were visible, and all were drawing closer to attack. There was no other reason so many ships would move through darkness together.

With each new light, Kit grew calmer. They no longer stood on the edge of war, but at the forefront of it. At the vanguard. There'd be no turning back now.

"How many?" Grant asked.

"At least a dozen," she said. "Perhaps more. They could, as Sunderland thought, be sending troops to Saint-Denis. But I don't think so."

That declaration fell heavily across the deck.

"The ships are Frisian in design," Jin said, lowering his glass, offering it to Kit. "You can just see one in silhouette," he added, and pointed. "The wide planks on the hull, the quarterdeck waist."

"The damned Guild," Grant said.

"The damned Guild," Kit agreed, having confirmed Jin's assessment with her own. "We knew they were building ships for Gerard."

"Yes," Grant said. "But having ships built for your war effort and engaging the Isles—and its vastly superior navy—in battle at sea are two very different things. After Barbata, that would be insane."

"And yet," Kit said, watching the lights grow closer, "the War Council will have to revise its strategies."

"You told them," Grant said quietly. "You told them he might try the sea."

Kit nodded grimly. "His ground war failed the last time. He didn't have the naval strength, so he never made a concerted effort to reach the Isles. Perez was right—he wants to try something different this time. He'll try to take the Isles."

"The Isles will have to rearm the cantonments," Jin said, referring to the string of defensive structures built along the southern Islish coast during the first year of the Continental War. They'd been largely abandoned because Gerard hadn't made more than a superficial naval push toward the Isles.

But that was before.

"Among other defensive strategies," Kit agreed. She crossed to the opposite gunwale and looked back toward the fleet. They'd seen the *Diana*'s signal and were scrambling to move offshore and into deeper water, where they could sail straight and fast if necessary.

"Captain?" Jin asked.

They needed guidance, and she would give it. "The gunships will protect the troop ships," she said. "We don't have enough cannons for that."

But they were swift and nimble. Fleet of foot and canny of mind.

She walked forward, sailors nodding and stepping out of her way as she passed. They were friendly with their captain but knew when she needed space and quiet. Jin and Grant followed quietly behind, with Watson and Simon managing the helm.

She surveyed the line of ships, looked back toward the crescent of land, considered the distance. Then she closed her eyes and reached down, deep, to the current, which seemed colder now that darkness had fallen, and could still feel the shadow in the distance—but not quite so distant this time. If this was Doucette, what was he doing? And was a man Aligned to the land really on board a ship?

She wanted a look. But that was secondary. First was to make more trouble.

"We'll sail around the crescent," Kit said. "We'll hug the shore as close as we dare until we've crept past the outermost ship in the line. And then we'll turn and do what damage we can to the ships on the perimeter."

Grant looked at her, brows lifted. "We're going to outflank them."

Her eyes were hard as ice. "We're going to try our damnedest."

⌒

Kit heard the first echo of cannons behind them and considered the possibility that it would appear the *Diana* was sailing away from trouble. But they were no cowards; they simply had to play to their strengths.

She felt a bit like a child playing a hiding game, creeping around in darkness, hoping no one would see. But no one did see, or at least no one made a move to stop them, and they rounded the crescent safely again. The shutter telegraph remained dark, but there was a light in the watchhouse now.

Cook came on deck, found her at the helm. He wore a pristine apron over his slops, and a few days of facial hair. "Why so much noise?" he asked. "Are we finally fighting to overthrow our monarchical overlords? Be time for that, wouldn't it?"

Kit's smile was thin. "Not as far as I'm aware. You could certainly write to the queen and inquire."

Cook snorted. "I wouldn't get an honest answer, now, would I?"

Of course that would be his objection—not that it would be dangerous to inquire with the queen about plans for her dethroning, but because he didn't trust her to answer truthfully.

"Here," Cook said, and put a tray with a steaming cup on the steering cabinet.

It smelled, she thought, like dirty goat.

She sighed. "What is this?"

"Bit of this and that," Cook said. "It's heartening."

"It smells of dirty stockings."

"That's the nutrition."

Kit narrowed her eyes at him. "Did Mrs. Eaves contact you?"

He put his hands on his hips, looked genuinely surprised by the question. "Your housekeeper? No. Why?" He lowered his head a bit. "Is she in need of educating the uncaring upper class about the harms of service work? Of the bonds of the workingman and -woman and their need to rise up against their oppressors?"

"No," Kit said blandly. "I was thinking more about discussions of spice and flavor."

He made a sound of utter dismissal. "I don't need the fool whims of others to understand flavor, do I?"

In response, Kit merely gestured at the cup.

"It won't taste very good," he admitted. "But it's hearty, and you've a long day ahead. Giving him a damned island kingdom. What did they think would happen?"

"It is a question for the ages."

He humphed. "Be a good captain and drink your dirty stockings. And if you do, the queen offered me a bit of incentive for the early sailing." He picked up a small bit of oilcloth from the tray that had been folded into a kind of packet.

Kit looked at it suspiciously. "What is it?"

"A reward," he said, handing it to her.

She opened it, found a few butter biscuits inside. "Thank you," she said, then closed it again, slipped it into her coat pocket.

"Stay below," she said kindly. "Stay safe."

He snorted. "If they come aboard, they'll find the sharp end of my cleaver."

"No objection," Kit said. "And gods save the queen."

She said it to irritate him, as she knew he much preferred irritation to worry and concern. And when he'd gone below again, she turned back to the line of enemy ships. The *Diana* was close enough now to confirm the mix of Frisian and Gallic vessels, but they gave no indication of having seen the *Diana*, which was perfectly fine by Kit.

She picked a two-masted vessel with the deep quarterdeck of a Frisian ship. "There," she said, gesturing to her quarry. "We move quickly, we take out its masts, and we retreat again. I want space between us and anything with cannons. And watch our stern, as we don't want to be flanked."

"As we've done to them," Grant said.

Kit nodded. "Let's be better than they are."

 ⁓

It was smooth as a Gallic ballet. The darkness and growing smoke helped obscure the *Diana*, and they had the weather gauge, which put them close enough to the Frisian ship to fire a shot before the ship could maneuver away. Fahri and Sampson hit the mainmast on their first and only shot, sending it onto the deck like the felled oak it had been carved from.

"Well done," Kit told her cannoneers, as the *Diana* rushed away again. Fleet of foot. Canny of mind.

Fahri held out her hand, eyes glinting.

Kit just lifted her brows but appreciated the moxie of the request.

"Sir," Fahri said, and pulled her hand back again. "I'll just . . . consider my perfect aim its own reward."

"That would be best," Kit said.

They circled back again, ready to take aim at another vessel, but the smoke was growing heavier with each volley of cannons, which would make it harder to select their targets and get safely away. It also created an eerie light in the darkness as moonlight reflected through the wisps of gray, creating a strange and discomfiting fog.

"Thick as soup," Jin said, squinting into it, as if that ever helped a sailor find a direction.

She was about to say that aloud, when she felt the *thrum* of the hull, as if the *Diana* was a string to be plucked. *Magic.*

"Did you feel that?" she asked to no one in particular, her heart beginning to pound.

"Feel what?" Jin asked. "What did you feel?"

Something that the un-Aligned did not, Kit thought. "Silence the ship," she said, and the order was passed quietly as she strode to the mast. Tamlin was nearly to the deck now, and her eyes seemed huge.

"Yes" was all she said.

Kit nodded, fear and fury and anticipation rising in equal parts. "Be careful," she told Tamlin, who climbed back above.

"Doucette," she whispered, when she returned to the helm. "Be ready," she said, and felt Grant move closer, as if his nearness might protect her.

But could anything protect her, or anyone else on board? That was the part she feared: that no matter the ship's speed or her skills as a sailor, she wouldn't be able to stand against Doucette. That she simply wasn't strong enough.

As if sensing her concern, Grant moved closer still. "Fury," he whispered to her. "Not fear. Fear is for later."

She nodded, grateful beyond measure that he understood.

"Can you use the current to search for him?"

She should have thought of it herself, and reached down. It was there, the pounding of the current, and she followed its course through the sea, listening—feeling—for any change in the tempo, in the strength.

"To the west," she whispered. "And moving closer."

"Kit," Grant said, and she heard the alarm in his tone, opened her eyes.

The smoke had gone to blue and green, swirls of color that she'd seen before.

"Incoming!" she screamed, and reached for the current again, preparing to move the ship from harm's way by whatever means necessary.

The air tingled, and Kit felt that same instinctive sense of disgust that she had in Auevilla. Fire is your opposite, she remembered, and felt the truth of it to her bones.

And then the *crack* of sound. The sky turned to fire, blue and green forks of energy searing the world above them and setting alight everything in their wake. The sails on the foremast caught first, blue and green transmuting to orange flames. Sailors screamed as they were scorched by fire and Doucette somehow—contrary to all she knew about Alignment—worked his land-Aligned magic on the sea.

The lightning crackled and dissipated again, leaving behind its wake of destruction.

"*Fire!*" she screamed, and the sailors who weren't injured began hauling buckets of seawater to douse the flames. "And get March on deck for the injured!"

She rushed to the stern, waiting for the smoke to clear enough that she could see the man who'd done this. She saw him, finally, standing near the bow of a low, wide ship, its two masts pushed back toward the stern. It streamed away from them and toward its next victim.

And she'd done nothing.

Guilt clawed at her but was a luxury she could not afford. She turned back, looked at Jin, whose eyes had gone wide with shock.

"Keep us moving," she said. "Put as much distance as you can between us and that ship."

He blinked. "We're running?"

"No," she said, harder than she ought have. "But we've got

to tend to the damage and care for the injured before we go in again."

And gods help her figure how to do that.

⁓

She had Sampson and Wells assist March with the injured—six sailors, by her count, who'd suffered burns in the attack. They'd doused the sails on the foremast, were pulling away tattered remnants of canvas and tamping out the remaining embers.

"The masts will hold, Captain," said Mr. Oglejack, forehead shining from the salve March had already applied to his scorched skin.

"You're sure?"

"Oh, aye. A bit of char on the forward side, but they're still solid. We'll need new rigging and sails, of course, but Mr. Smythe is already on that."

"Good. And thank you." She pointed to her forehead in the spot where he'd been injured. "You'll keep an eye on that, too."

"Of course," he said, then turned back to his work.

Grant found her then, looked her over. "You're all right?" he asked, and she nodded.

"You?"

He nodded as well. "How did he do this at sea?"

Kit just shook her head. She had no idea; it simply shouldn't have been possible. But while he'd done more than enough damage—scorching men and ship, dangerous though it was—it wasn't the same as killing a man with the power of current alone. Little comfort given the howls of pain from her crew—and the similar howls they could hear echoing through the smoke around them.

Kit wanted to talk to him. Understand his process, what he heard and felt of the magic. Was it different from her? Did it speak differently to him? Or did he simply ignore the sense of violation? But while those questions burned in her heart, they were not her mission now.

The ship jerked, nearly sending her to the deck. But she maintained her balance. "What was that?"

"Sea dragon," Grant said from the gunwale, looking over the side. "Crimson."

"Sea dragon swarm!" Fahri called out, and Kit looked toward the starboard side. The sun was just beginning to rise, and the sea was awash in jewellike colors—crimson, cerulean, turquoise. Not from the breaking dawn, but from the sea dragons that thrashed beneath the surface.

Kit had seen a sea dragon swarm only once before, and she'd nearly lost the dory she'd been rowing in at the time. She'd also heard they could be attracted by magic. There was more than enough of that here.

They rarely attacked humans or boats when swimming alone, which was how most sailors saw them. But in a swarm, they became ferocious. Snapping great ivory teeth at one another as they rolled and spun, so that blood began to spatter the water. A single sea dragon could damage a ship, if inadvertently. A pod like this could destroy it.

"Not always so lucky," she murmured to herself. It was the purpose of war to go into a battle even at the risk that you might not win. She had to figure a way around it. A way to match Doucette's magic with hers. Or at least counter it . . .

Mathilda had said fire was her opposite Alignment. Kit had already proven she could touch the current long enough to cross the Narrow Sea, although it weakened her considerably. Instead of maintaining that connection for a longer distance, could she make the connection itself larger? Large enough to bring the *Diana* within its bubble of protection and repel "opposite" magic? Perhaps? She was still hesitant to push herself where the current was concerned, but wasn't this essentially an extension of the same technique she'd been using for years?

When the *Diana* rocked hard, as if struck by an aftershock of the prior magical blow, and she heard damage reports being relayed from spots around the ship, she knew she had to try.

"Take us around again," Kit said. "He doesn't get another ship or soldier on our watch." She would damned well see to it.

"But, Captain—" Watson said.

"We're going around again," she repeated, in a tone that allowed no debate. She understood the value of input from her officers, but this wasn't the time for that. "I think I can shield the ship."

"Shield it?" Grant asked. "How?"

"There was a woman in Portsea with knowledge of magic; she sold amulets. She said Alignments have their 'opposites.' She said fire was the opposite of my Alignment, and I—I can feel that in a way. I think perhaps my Alignment to the current will repel his, if I can hold the current long enough."

"You can," Grant said, without hesitation.

"So we can get close enough to get off a good shot," Watson said, and Kit nodded.

"I don't have to do anything differently—it's still a touch to the current, albeit one that I'll hold a bit longer, as with the trip to Portsea." She looked at Simon, Watson, Jin. "Are you willing to try this? I'll not send you into that without your agreement."

They looked at one another, and then their captain.

"Sir," Jin said with a determined nod. "Tell us where to go."

⁓

After Kit tossed a coin into the sea, they gave themselves room for a pass on the starboard side, had the powder, shot, and wadding ready. They had to be careful when making the turn—the seas were crowded now with ships, debris, and dragons—but made their way around so Doucette's ship was a point off their port bow.

The wind picked up as the sky lightened, so the *Diana* streamed forward, canvas taut with wind, toward Doucette's ketch.

As they approached, she could see him clearly now. Full uniform, legs braced against the sea. Someone stood nearby—a figure in a long blue cloak, only boots visible below it, the hood raised. Female, Kit thought, with pale skin. And dramatic, given the cloak.

"Stone," Watson said. "I think he's standing on a platform of some kind." She offered Kit the spyglass.

Watson was right—he stood on a slab of umber-colored stone, perhaps two inches thick.

"He's carrying his Alignment with him?" Grant asked.

"Perhaps," Kit said, offering the glass again.

"So we just need to carry you about the Continent in a bathing tub," Grant said.

"I'd be an impressive and intimidating figure, to be sure." She looked at her commander. "Jin, when Fahri and Sampson are ready, call the shot."

"Aye, Captain."

She looked at him, then Grant, nodded at them both, and let her gaze linger on Grant for just a moment.

Kit closed her eyes, blew out a breath, and reached out. The current felt wild as a sea dragon now, as if reacting badly to Doucette's manipulations. She couldn't entirely blame it, and tried to make herself feel as calm and nonthreatening as possible. She touched it, felt it flinch and settle, as if assured she was no threat.

She opened herself to it, let it envelop her, and then the ship. There would be no arrow to loose this time. Only the blanket of current, which she hoped would give them some protection.

She didn't risk opening her eyes but heard the crew murmuring about whatever they saw of her magic. And still kept sailing.

"Ready the cannons," she heard Jin say, as she also felt the rise of Doucette's magic.

"He is preparing," Kit said quietly, to warn whoever might hear her. The magic was, she thought, muffled by her own current, but it was no less repellant.

She felt it strike the ship—her own magic—and would have fallen from the force of it but for the arms that held her upright.

"Fury," Grant said quietly again, just for her. "No fear."

She didn't have the strength to acknowledge him, but poured all she had into maintaining that aether that surrounded the ship. Doucette's magic frizzled along the edges, biting like ants across her skin, but she kept the current flowing.

"It's working," Grant said. "Stay with it, Kit."

"*Fire!*" Jin called out.

Not a warning this time but an order. Then the *boom* of the explosion, the answering *crash* of timber against timber.

She heard the cheers and applause, felt the blow against his magic as their shot was true.

"Direct hit!" Jin called. But she didn't dare open her eyes.

Enraged, Doucette gave a final push, sending power sparking across hers. But water and fire did not mix, and he made no headway.

"I think we're clear of it," Grant said quietly after a moment.

Kit let go of the magic, felt it flow back from ship to current, and opened her eyes. Dizziness had the deck spinning around her, but Grant offered a hand, gave her a moment to settle. Then she looked back at Doucette's ship.

The mainmast was gone. She squeezed Grant's arm.

She found Doucette at the bow, staring at her with those empty eyes, the cloaked person still at his side. She'd won this round, but she knew it would not be their last.

It took a moment for her to gather herself again, to shake off the cast of magic. Instinctively she looked down at her hands again, found no new scars that she could see, and had no idea why that was so . . . and no time to consider it.

A scream drew her attention upward again, then to the gunwale, where the others pointed. Her heart stuttered, immediately thinking of the sniper who'd injured Jin. But there was no human this time.

The mast from Doucette's ketch was in the water, still attached to the vessel by a tangle of lines, and a sea dragon—its scales turquoise and gleaming—had become entangled in the knot. It thrashed, trying to free itself. And each time it pulled, the ketch heeled farther into the sea. Water poured over the gunwales before the crew managed to cut the creature free.

It dove immediately and took the entire mast with it. Either it would figure a way to free itself . . .

Something thumped hard against the *Diana*'s hull, sending sailors to their knees.

. . . or it wouldn't, Kit finished ruefully.

"It's beneath the boat!" someone shouted.

"Not beneath!" Fahri shouted from the stern. "I think the rope's caught in our rudder."

Kit's stomach went to lead. If the rudder was gone, they'd no longer be able to steer the ship with the wheel. They'd be at the mercy of the wind. And the enemy.

She ran toward the stern, looked over at the pitiful creature, eyes wild and wheeling, struggling against the detritus of someone else's fight. It jerked, and the ketch's mast struck the *Diana*'s hull like a hammer. "We have to cut it free."

"Aye," Sampson said as the ship jerked again. "And it's bad luck for a dragon to die near your ship."

It's bad luck for a ship full of sailors to die because their craft was disabled midbattle, Kit thought dryly.

"I'll do it," Grant said, stepping beside her.

She looked back at him, wanted to argue. But her sailors were busy keeping the *Diana* away from Doucette, and she needed someone who could handle himself—and she knew Grant could.

"There's a lot of magic," she said. "And this one's probably injured. Furious, afraid, and strong."

He nodded grimly. "I understand."

"Sampson," she called out, without shifting her gaze. "Help him over the side. And put a rope around him."

"I could go," Sampson said, but Grant shook his head.

"You're stronger than me, and I'll need you up here to pull me back."

"Be careful," she said. "And be fast. The water will be cold, and they dive deep."

"I know it," he said, and looked at her long enough to sear the color of his eyes into her brain. She refused to imagine this was some sort of goodbye, because it wasn't. It was simply work that needed doing.

Sampson pulled a small saw and a thick rope from a storage compartment near the jolly boat. He gave the saw to Grant, tied the rope snugly to a cleat, then made a loop for Grant's waist. Grant put a leg over the gunwale, and they all looked over when the ship jerked and shuddered again. Kit could feel wood grinding against the keel, the vibrations echoing up through the ship.

By the time she looked back at Grant, he was over the side, climbing down the stern handholds to the mess below. The sea dragon, tiring now, made sounds that were half scream and half keening cry. But its teeth were no less sharp.

Grant edged down farther, only a foot away from the whirlpool of debris, and the sea dragon stuck in the middle of it. The stern angled in, so he'd have to push away from the ship—and be dangled above the water by the rope alone.

"All right," Grant said, then looked up at Sampson, tugged the rope. "You've got it?"

"She's secure," Sampson confirmed. And Grant pushed away, spinning once as he worked the saw.

"Bit more!" he called out, and Sampson gave the rope some slack, so Grant hovered near the sea dragon's head—and jerked back a foot when it nipped at the air.

"Steady now," he said to it. "I'm trying to help us both." Then he shifted down, began sawing the ropes that bound the dragon to the ketch's mast.

The concussion of a cannon fired somewhere close filled the

air; startled, the dragon thrashed, body writhing in and out of the water as it struggled. And in its frantic serpentining managed to wrap the tangle of ropes around Grant.

He held to his own rope, muscles straining as the monster tried to roll, each motion pulling at the keel and stern of the *Diana*. The mast became a lever, pushing the ship toward port and terrifyingly close to the waterline. Officers yelled warnings as lines became loose and sailors struggled to maintain their balance.

Grant looked up, met Kit's gaze. "Cut me loose!"

"No!" Kit said, and put a leg over the gunwale. "I can get to you."

The sea dragon tried to swim to port, and the ship listed so far back to starboard, the mast nearly dipped into the water.

She heard footsteps behind her. "Captain, Mr. Jones says we're taking on water below."

"Deal with it!" she demanded, both legs over the gunwale now, her hands on Grant's rope. He bobbed under the water as the dragon pulled, then came up again, spewing water. "Cut me loose," he yelled, "or I'll bring you all down with me! And I'll damned well not have that on my conscience, Kit Brightling!"

Kit stared at him and made her decision.

"Captain!" Sampson said, horror in his voice as Kit aimed her dagger at the rope that bound him to the ship.

Grant watched her, nodded, and, the moment the bond was broken, disappeared beneath the surface.

She didn't pause and she didn't think. She untied her sabre, tossed it onto the deck.

Then tucked the dagger into her belt and dove in after him.

The water was dark and cold and blue—patterned with the morning light shimmering on the surface above her, and just as chaotic. The sea churned with splinters of wood and flashes of color. Fortunately, the sea dragon pod had begun to calm as magic dissipated, but still, a dozen sea dragons did not make for smooth waters.

She searched for turquoise, for the dragon that had dragged Grant down, and it took a solid minute to see a flash of color two dozen feet below her. She dove farther, kicking hard.

The current was vibrant, putting frizzled energy into the water that felt like sparks against her skin. Not unpleasant, but a reminder that however connected she was, this wasn't her domain.

The sea dragon was swimming in circles, still trying to dislodge the weight streaming behind it—which now included Grant. He pulled at the ropes that bound his leg with desperate fingers; she realized he'd lost his saw, probably in the dragon's thrashing.

Kit didn't have time to consider the best way to approach a frantic sea dragon, so she didn't bother. She simply swam as close as she dared. Grant saw her, eyes wide and panic beginning to set in, and held out his hand. She could hold her breath for an unnaturally long time underwater; that seemed an undeniable gift of her Alignment. He couldn't.

She moved closer, reaching out for him—but the dragon darted away, and she turned to see a cannonball surge through the water only a foot in front of her. She nearly cried out with frustration but pushed forward.

It took precious seconds to reach Grant again. This time, she managed to grip his hand, interlacing her fingers with his and squeezing tight enough to bruise.

She'd be damned if she lost him. But he opened his eyes, struggled, looked around, and apparently saw little hope. He pulled away, tearing his fingers from hers. And he pointed up.

"*Go*," he mouthed.

He wanted her to leave him. To abandon him to the deep.

She was instantly, incandescently furious. Hadn't he sat beside her on the deck? Waited with her in the rain while she'd pushed the ship toward Portsea? Held her hand while they'd both been doused with water and magic? And he thought she'd simply let him go.

"*No*," she screamed, but only in her mind. She wouldn't waste her breath on that.

She grabbed him again, swimming now to keep up with the motions of the sea dragon. She pulled out her dagger with her free hand, began to work at the tangle of rope. She managed to cut one loop when the sea dragon, perhaps sensing its bonds loosening, stretched around to look at her, its eyes enormous and black and fringed by dark lashes.

Much to her surprise, Kit found she wasn't afraid. Not of the creature, at least. And since it hadn't attacked, Kit continued to saw at a rope around Grant's ankle as the dragon watched, huffing bubbles through its nose in a movement that seemed like, Kit thought, injured pride at its present circumstances.

I know, she thought in silence, wishing she could communicate with it. It's been a bloody hell of a day.

When it huffed again, she wondered if it *could* hear her. It could plainly sense the magic, so perhaps there was a possibility of connection between them? She felt at home in the water, after all, surrounded by the magic she could only barely access aboard ship, and which was silent on land. She only needed to close her eyes . . .

*No*, she thought, forcing them open again, and gripping her dagger tighter. She'd forgotten the danger of being seduced by the current; but this wasn't her home. She lived above. And would continue to do so, thanks all the same.

She finally freed him from the rope—and dragon from the man—and pushed it away. Grant was free, but they still had to swim up through the debris of battle, and the surface was some thirty feet above them now. She was losing her confidence they'd both manage to survive.

And then she looked at him and saw the bleak acceptance on his face.

Oh, bollocks to that, she thought, finding her fight again. Kit pressed her mouth to his, gave him what little breath remained in her lungs. For a moment, they hung there together in the turbulent water together, her hands on his face.

Then a flash of shimmering turquoise, and the dragon circled them, only a single loop of rope still attached to its front leg. It swam so close Kit might have counted its lashes, and it stared at her with its wide, thoughtful eyes.

And a possibility occurred to her. Not an especially reasonable one, but they weren't in a very reasonable situation. If it worked, it would probably make Grant furious. Which was a bit of a bonus, at least.

Gods save us, she thought. She drew Grant against her body,

and when the dragon passed again, she lunged forward, grabbed one of the spines along its back.

They were jerked forward as the dragon dove, and she could feel the pressure squeezing at her lungs, feel the magic warm and buzzing beneath them as the dragon carried them deeper.

She hoped she hadn't doomed them both.

# FIFTEEN

Kit woke slowly and drowsily from sleep, roused from a dream of dark water by a tickle against her leg.

She opened her eyes, squinted against the light, brilliant compared to the darkness they'd been in, and used a hand to shield her face. It took her two attempts to sit up, to push past the dizziness that wanted to bring her low again.

She found a beach of rock and sand. The ocean and a clear horizon. More tickling.

She blinked, looked down, and squealed at the crab scurrying across her thigh.

"*Absolutely not,*" she said, and swatted it away. It jumped into the sand, then scurried into the sea beyond.

Memories returned, ephemeral as clouds. Dragons and deep water, a hand tightly gripped. And in this reality, both of her hands clenched.

In one, she held a shimmering scale of brilliant turquoise.

She turned her head. In the other, fingers still linked, was Grant's hand. He lay beside her in the sand, eyes closed. Relief nearly had tears rising, but she pushed them mercilessly down. He was breathing, but he'd lost his tailcoat to the water or the monsters in it, and a stripe of red marred the chest of his linen shirt.

Kit cursed, loosed his hand (for the first time in hours?), and pulled at the laces at the top of the shirt to bare the skin beneath. A long, angry welt marred the tan skin. But it wasn't deep, she realized with relief.

"Do you plan to disrobe me here in the sand, Captain?"

She looked down at him, doubly relieved to see the curve at the corners of his lips. His eyes were still closed, but he was awake, alive, and facetious.

"You've a scratch on your chest."

"A weak excuse," he said, and blinked against the watery sunlight. "I hear nothing of town, so I presume we are not back in Auevilla with fine whiskey and a slice of mille-feuille?"

"Island," she said. "No whiskey, no mille-feuille, no sight of the Continent."

"But of course," Grant said dryly.

"How's your leg?"

He wiggled one, then the other. "Fine." He blinked, looked at her. "Did we ride a sea dragon?"

In response, she picked up the scale she'd dropped in the sand, offered it to him. "So it appears."

"Well," he said, taking it and smoothing a thumb over the slick surface. "I thought that had been a fever dream." He squinted up into the sunlight. "Where, precisely?"

"My lord, I have precisely the same amount of information you do." When he handed her the scale again, she tucked it into her pocket and stood up, feeling a bit waterlogged, and took a good look at their surroundings. They were on a long, thin line of dun-colored sand, probably two hundred yards of it, with tall tufts of dark stone and scrubby vegetation at each end. The end closest to them bore a cliff of stone easily fifty feet tall, molded by water and wind into strange columns that made the island seem as much chessboard as terrestrial accident.

She walked to the shore, looked out. There were rocky out-croppings in surf, and it was clear enough to see down to more sand and obtrusions of rock. But there was no solid land in sight. She crouched, put a hand in the water. Cold, but the current was vibrantly strong, which gave her comfort, even if it was little help.

She rose, wiped her hand on her trousers.

"I can't say for certain. But given the water, the temperature, and the sand, I'd wager one of the channel islands." They were a set of islands, islets, and rocks just off the shore of Gallia within the Narrow Sea. They were owned by the Isles, which was some comfort. But they'd apparently landed on a completely unin-habited one, and not within sight of any habituated others.

"Well," Grant said, climbing to his feet. "We're alive, so I suppose that's something."

But how much of something, and for how long? They had no food, no obvious source of water. The sun would be setting soon, and there was a chill in the air. Kit didn't care to be stuck, to be iso-lated, without some manner of moving. She looked back at Grant.

"I believe," Kit said, "you've got your uninterrupted time."

Grant made a sound. "Not precisely the variety I'd had in mind. What should we do?"

She lifted her brows. "Don't you want to lead this particular mission? We're on land, after all."

Grant snorted. "This is hardly land. This is . . . a bare inter-ruption."

"So you assent to my command?"

"Your epaulets are damp."

"So's your hair," Kit said, and tugged at the lock that fell over his forehead. When Grant captured her hand, squeezed it, something warm burned in her chest. And something kindled between them.

"That was stupidly dangerous," he said quietly. "Reckless. Confoundingly stubborn, to dive into a swarm of sea dragons . . ."

"I did what any captain would do."

"No, Kit. I won't let you off quite so easily." His hand still in hers, he watched her for a moment, then brushed hair from her face. "Thank you for saving my life."

"You're welcome," she said. "Thank you for rescuing me from the gaol in Auevilla. My debt is now cleared."

He snorted, and his stomach rumbled.

"Food," Kit said.

"Yes." He looked about. "Should I just call for the servant then?"

"You're a soldier. Can't you hunt?"

"You're a sailor. Can't you fish?"

"Oh," Kit said, and pulled the folded waxed fabric from the pocket of her tailcoat. The biscuits Cook had given her were broken, but they were blissfully dry.

"We can break our fast, at least," she said, and took a piece, then extended it to Grant.

He held up a hand. "You eat them. I suspect you need the energy more."

"We share," Kit said. "I don't plan to drag you around when you drop from hunger."

"I'd hardly drop," he murmured, but took a piece of biscuit, closed his eyes as he savored it. "Oh, that's the best biscuit that's ever existed in the history of mankind."

"And that's why we tolerate Cook," she said. They ate until they reached the last two fragments.

"Now, or save them for later?" Grant asked.

Kit glanced around, considered the likelihood they'd find something edible before they found a ship. Did not find those odds especially comforting.

"Now," she said. "Before they disintegrate completely."

They ate contemplatively, both dampening fingers to pluck the rest of the crumbs from the canvas.

"I'll not lick it clean," Kit said, "as even here on this spit of land I've no doubt Hetta and Mrs. Eaves both would find out about it." Her gaze narrowed as she stared blankly into the distance. "They'd read it in my eyes somehow."

"Or I'd use the information to blackmail you."

"For what?"

"For whatever," he said, with one of those promising smiles that made her knees a bit wobbly.

"Let's take an inventory," he said. "What else do we have that might be useful? I've a knife," Grant said, pulling out a small folded knife from his trouser pocket. "And that's all."

She tapped her jacket, her pockets, found nothing but her ribbon, the dragon scale, and a few coppers. "I've only the biscuits." She looked up at the sky, calculated. "We've a good two hours before sunset, so food may have to wait until tomorrow. We've bigger problems."

"What bigger problems?"

Kit glanced down at the narrow line of sand. "All but the middle strip of sand is wet."

"Yes. Because we're on the ocean."

She rolled her eyes. He employed that sarcastic tone quite a bit more on stranded islands, she decided. "Because the tide is presently low. There's seaweed all the way across the sandbar. And when the tide comes back in, this part of the island will be completely covered."

"So we'll be sleeping in the rocks."

She nodded. "Plus, the sun will be setting soon, and it's only going to get colder. We need to build a fire for ourselves and, to-morrow morning, a signal fire for passing ships. You take the fire," Kit said. "Perhaps there's driftwood or dried seaweed or other bits lying around." She pointed at the higher cliffs, which could be more easily seen offshore. "Up there. And look for water while you're at it. I'll see if there's a dry spot we can make a shelter."

"All right," he said with a nod, and with a final brush of his fingers across her palm, he released her hand. "I'll go up."

Grant nodded, began unbuttoning his waistcoat. Kit was torn between propriety and practicality.

"Fire," she muttered again. "Survival."

"Be careful," Grant said, and she could hear the smile in his voice.

She walked toward the stone wall, then into its dark shadow, the temperature dropping as the sun was hidden. There were notches in the stone here and there where water had worn it down over time, or heat had twisted it as it had grown from the earth. She found a promising nook that wasn't especially deep, but was high and wide enough for the two of them to lie flat. It was situated in a part of the rock that curved gently, which would provide a break from the wind. And it was behind the seaweed-marked high-water line. She knelt down, scooped up a handful of sand, found it cold but dry.

"Not an island paradise," she muttered, thinking of the balmy and breezy oases described in her favorite penny novels. But it was better than freezing.

She began gathering rocks for a fire, arranged them in a circle a few feet from the crevice, and then went exploring. She found a couple of driftwood logs and a tangle of abandoned rope and one side of a wooden crate, dark stenciled letters fading across one board.

She reached down to pick it up, nearly jumped when a lizard skittered away. And wondered how Grant would feel about reptile stew. It probably tasted like most fowl. Most things, come to that, tasted like fowl, which was a strange characteristic, to her mind.

She walked back to their shelter. Grant was already on his knees in front of it, stacking driftwood in the circle she'd made. She added the pieces she'd found, put aside the crate for some later use, and took a seat on a larger rock while he used bits of chipped stone and dry leaves.

"Water in that—well, what used to be a pot."

Nestled into the sand beside her was a crescent of terra-cotta. It held a small amount of liquid that looked surprisingly clean. She carefully picked it up, sniffed it, smelled nothing off-putting.

"It's clean," he said with a smile. The fire caught quickly, and he sat beside her, their bodies just touching. Kit was grateful for the additional warmth—and the physical connection.

"Or as clean as we're likely to get at the moment." He gestured to the ridge behind them. "I found the pottery there, and the water atop the rocks. There are depressions where the rain collected. Rather a miracle the gulls or rooks haven't colonized the rocks and spoiled it."

A bit more luck, she thought, and sipped.

"Drink all of it," he said. "There's more, and I don't much care to drag you around, either."

She did, handed him the empty pottery. "Thank you. It's been quite a day."

He must have heard the worry in her voice. Grant put an arm around her shoulders. She didn't waste the invitation, but curled into him. "I won't promise they're all safe," he said. "No one can do that. But you've a remarkably capable crew, and the Isles' ships had a number of cannons."

She nodded. Hoped he was right. Knew that obsessing would change nothing. But still . . . they were her people.

"Why was he there? Doucette, I mean."

"To wreak havoc?"

"Certainly. But why on a ship? His power must be stronger on land."

"Because Gerard needs him for the attack on the Isles," Grant said. "And his magic is strong enough along the coast, even if he's on a boat, that he can be useful for at least some of the passage."

"All true," Kit said. "But he's a very important man to Gerard—the highest-ranking Aligned soldier that we know of. Gerard puts him on a boat and sends him into what is apparently the first major naval attack by Gallia since the middle of the Continental War. That seems exceptionally risky."

Grant was quiet for a moment. "You're thinking Gerard wants him on the ground in the Isles. You think he has some sort of—what? Magical plan to undertake if he's able to land?"

"I think it's a distinct possibility," Kit said. "Otherwise, you keep your generals on the ground. We needed that damn map."

"It might have been merely plans for Gerard's new town house."

Kit almost objected, then recalled whom they were referring to. It was absolutely within the realm of possibility that the marshal of his army would be responsible for transmitting plans for some château of Gerard's in a fine leather satchel to a waiting compatriot.

"Gold coin says there will be stone lions on the exterior."

Grant snorted. "I'm not naïve enough to take that bet."

"The woman in the cloak—do you know who she was?"

Grant shook his head. "I've never seen her before, at Contra Costa or otherwise. One of Gerard's Resurrectionists, I imagine. Or perhaps one of Doucette's acolytes. She wasn't Aligned, was she?"

"I wasn't close enough to say. She showed no use of magic, at any rate." Silence fell, and she found herself touching her ribbon. Perhaps this was the time to discuss the personal.

"Have you ever been to Saint-Étienne?"

"As a matter of fact, yes. Sunderland had us scout the area before a march. We ended up sleeping in a cathedral crypt."

"No," she said, drawing out the word in horror.

"On my honor," he said. "Fortunately, the inhabitants were not recently deceased, but the bones were still plentiful. One entire wall of them." He looked down at her. "Why do you ask about Saint-Étienne?"

Kit paused, then sat up. She pulled back her lapel, pulled away the fraying ribbon and its small glass-headed pin from her coat, and passed them to Grant.

He looked it over, ran a thumb down the golden embroidery. "It's lovely. Looks old."

"At least as old as me," she said. "It was tied to the basket I was left in. There was a teller of fortunes in Auevilla. She said this was from there."

"And you've no other idea where it came from? Perhaps you're actually a lovely Gallic girl, and not an Islesian after all. You do have a good hand at the language."

Kit snorted. "Hetta Brightling refused to bring up girls who didn't have at least one foreign tongue. And a bit of ribbon available from any decent modiste hardly proves my origin. But that's the only clue I've gotten."

"You were left in the Isles."

She looked up at him, realized he was gazing at her. "What do you mean?"

"I mean, even if the ribbon and its owner came from Gallia, they made it to the Isles." He paused. "I wonder if it is better to not know your origins at all, or to know them and find them foul."

"Your father?" Kit asked, and Grant nodded.

"In fairness, he was tolerable before my mother passed. It was only after she was gone that he . . . wasn't."

"They were a love match?"

"No, actually. They had love, but their marriage was arranged by her parents, what with he a viscount and in possession of an income and several estates."

She goggled. "Several estates? There's more than Grant Hall? And the London town house?"

"Only a small manor in the north now," Grant said.

"So only the *three* estates then," Kit said smartly. "It must be a terrible burden to you and your family."

He looked up at her, a gleam in his eyes. "You're saucy for a woman who's no ship or sabre at present."

"Or three estates," she snickered. "And to your question, perhaps you're asking the wrong one. Maybe the worse thing is to have love, and lose it, and become a broken and bitter man."

"Perhaps," he said, and watched her carefully. Whatever he was thinking, he didn't speak it. But then he shook off the concern. "Perhaps the war will end soon, and you can go to Saint-Étienne."

"Right now, I'd prefer New London. I miss Jane," she said. "And good books and hot baths. And pistachio nougats."

"Pistachio nougats. What sort of sugared abomination is that?"

Even in the darkness, the ire in her expression ought to have been clear. "Do not speak ill of things you do not understand."

Grant's smile was wide. "Lover of sweets, but afraid of horses."

"You've no evidence I fear horses."

He snorted, leaned back on his elbows. "No, only the terror in your eyes when you see them. I recall you walked the entire four miles between Queenscliffe and Grant Hall just to avoid them."

"A mere stroll," she said. And over truly beautiful country. High and green, with sharp gray cliffs where land and sea met and did battle. Whatever horrors the Beau Monde held, the land near Grant Hall was not one of them.

"Pistachio nougats," he said again.

"Don't you have a weakness? A pleasure you can't seem to do without? I recall you have very fine whiskey at Grant Hall."

He turned his face to hers, watched her in the darkness as waves broke along the shore, rhythmic and unceasing. Something comforting in that, Kit thought.

"I didn't particularly enjoy being a continent away from you." He leaned forward and tilted his head, and she swallowed hard.

"What are you doing?" she asked, the words a mere whisper between them.

"I'm going to kiss you again," he said, and his fingers were at her jaw, and her skin felt alive. He leaned toward her, touched his lips to hers—the barest whisper of sensation. She knew he meant to tease, to incite . . . and she didn't mind it. He nipped at her bottom lip, and her eyes flew open. She wasn't inexperienced, but that fleeting bit of pain was new. And she didn't mind that, either. She put a hand on his chest, felt muscle flex beneath his linen shirt, could feel his heart pounding, marveled at the effect she had on him, because it mirrored the effect he had on her.

It shouldn't have been. It shouldn't have worked, the viscount and the sailor, much less alone on an island with no one to see, no one to judge. And no chaperone.

He deepened the kiss, tongue darting against hers. One of his hands dropped to her thigh, then rose to her waist, to just below her breast. He paused there, waited, a silent request for permission, for assent.

"Yes," she said against his mouth, and met his tongue with hers, nearly gasping as his fingers found her breast, and he groaned with pleasure.

"Would that I had a bed," he murmured. "Carved and strong, with pillows of lace and down to lay you down upon."

She pulled back just enough to meet his gaze, ran a thumb across his lips, and looked at his eyes, so brilliantly blue.

Then she pushed him down into the sand, straddled his hips as he laughed beneath her. "Sailors don't need fancy beds, Grant."

"So I see," he said, and put his hands on her hips now, adjusted her against his nearly intimidating arousal. He gripped the hem of her linen shirt, drew it over her head, arched an eyebrow at the half stays.

"Very clever."

"Necessary when you've no maid," she said, and untied the ribbon, revealing herself.

He stared at her for a moment before his hands rose, so slowly, to claim her. And when he did, his fingers soft but firm, teasing but worshipping, her head dropped back.

"Aye," he said, rolling his hips. "That's my beauty."

And when he leaned up, suckled, she nearly saw stars.

"Your pleasure first," he said, and rolled her beneath him. He pulled his shirt over his head, and she saw for the first time the scars that crossed that long, lean torso, and traced a finger across one.

"Sensitive," he said with a smile, and lifted her hand, kissed her palm. Then he released her, levered himself over her, and kissed her thoroughly. There was hunger in the kiss now, bated desire, anticipation for what would come.

He made his way down her body, then stripped away her pantaloons and found her core with deft fingers, with palm. She rocked against his hand, called his name.

"Take your pleasure," he said, the words a growl, and she moved until the fever built, until she fell into the stars.

"Kit," he said, and kissed her forehead, her mouth, as he unbuttoned the placket of his trousers. She managed only to glance down—and she swallowed hard. Now she was *actually* intimidated.

"Stay strong, Captain," he said with pride and amusement. "All will be well." He lowered himself onto her, then into her, his body shaking with need, with the desire to move.

He dropped his forehead against hers, breathing heavily now. "Are you . . . protected?"

"I take herbs," she said, body thrumming with need. "I won't become . . . with child."

Grant nodded, slowly began to move. She wrapped a leg around him, and he slipped his hand between her thighs and began to give her pleasure again.

She could feel it build again, as if it were a wave breaking close to shore, and began to move with him, to match her rhythm to his.

*"Grant."*

"My name," he whispered, voice hoarse with desire. "Say my name."

"Rian," she said on a sob, pleasure breaking again. *"Rian. Rian."*

He moved again, hand on the ground for balance, corded with effort, and, after a moment, groaned his own satisfaction.

He kissed her forehead again and lay in the sand beside her, their breaths equally unsteady. He turned his head to look at her, a lock of hair across his forehead. "No fancy beds."

"Entirely unnecessary," she said with a grin, and rolled onto him again.

# SIXTEEN

They slept together in the cove, her body tucked behind his, curled against him for warmth.

The next morning dawned clear, and with streaks of red at the horizon that bode poorly for sailing weather later in the day, but made a beautiful canvas of morning.

She was alone in the shelter; the fire was already crackling outside above the rhythmic tossing of the waves. She turned onto her side, could see his silhouette against the fire. Was it going to be awkward between them? Would they be self-conscious?

And then she sat straight up. Because something smelled good.

She crawled out, promising herself they'd arrange a better shelter for the night to come—a driftwood platform, perhaps—and stretched out the aches. Smoke was drifting up from the fire in a very pretty column. Kit walked toward the fire, found Grant on his knees beside it, staring at a pile of wet gray atop seaweed, both balanced over the flame on a wide, flat rock.

"Dare I ask?" she said.

"I've obtained breakfast." His grin was wide and boyish, and there was nothing self-conscious in it. She imagined him a child at Grant Hall, thrilled at catching his first clutch of trout.

Her own fears vanished. She sat on a rock, rubbed her hands in front of the fire. "And what is it?" It looked a bit . . . gelatinous.

"A fish . . . of some variety. There are tidepools near the rise. I was picking up driftwood and found this among them. I've cleaned a fish or two in my youth, so I've made a filet."

"How old are you?"

"It's very indecent of you to ask. But I'm eight-and-twenty."

"Ah, yes. You've clearly passed your youth now." She peered at his mane of brown hair. "I see a bit of silvering."

"Liar," he said with a smile, then used a stick to push the fish around.

It seemed to become slightly less gray as it cooked through, which was no small feat. "And the seaweed?"

"A trick Dunwood taught me on the peninsula. The seaweed imparts salt, flavor, and steam, which allows the fish to cook more evenly."

"Very clever."

He slid his gaze her way. "How does a sailor not know that?"

"We travel with kitchens and fire," she said. "And I'm not sure Cook would approve of seaweed-roasted fish." Gods knew Mrs. Eaves wouldn't.

"It won't be much," he said. "But it will be warm, perhaps give us enough fuel to find more. What else shall we do today in our island paradise?"

"Is that what this is?"

He turned his head to face her fully, and looked at her with joy and delight and more than a bit of arousal, Kit thought. He leaned forward, brushing his lips against hers. "Yes," he said, then flicked his tongue against her lips, kissed her long and lavishly.

"We are alone and together, without war or the queen or the Beau Monde. Our only obligation is to survive, and I imagine we are both skilled enough to manage that until we sight a ship. Until then, we have total privacy." His hand found her breast, cupped, and she found herself arching toward him—until her stomach grumbled angrily.

Grant swore. "You need food. Especially if we're to maintain our regimen of . . . exercise."

"Fortunately, we've the fish you found in a tide pool."

"It was a challenging expedition."

∾

They ate the fish, or what there was of it. Grant was unimpressed by its lack of flavor, but Kit found it oddly comforting, and reminiscent of home. Maybe Mrs. Eaves had spent some time on a deserted island.

"We need a signal fire. Up there," she said, pointing to the cliff, "so it can be seen as far away as possible."

Grant sighed.

"What?" Kit asked. "It's our best opportunity to get off this island. Unless our driftwood inventory increases significantly in the next few hours and I suddenly learn how to build a boat. Both of which seem unlikely."

"Unlikely," he agreed, but drew her close, pressed a kiss to her palm. "I rather enjoy having you to myself."

"I've enjoyed being enjoyed," she said with a smile. "But we've war on the horizon and friends in danger."

He grumbled, but nodded. "You're right. And what will you be doing?"

"Second breakfast," she said with a grin. "I'm going swimming."

⟋⟍

Grant had seen her naked, or as much as moonlight would allow. And as a sailor, she'd been bare to the ocean more than a few times. But the thought of swimming naked here made her feel oddly vulnerable. So she pulled off pantaloons and linen shift, but remained in half stays and petticoat. She tied the arms of her shift to make a kind of pouch that would fit around her shoulders. And then she did what she often threatened everyone else with doing.

She walked into the sea.

The water was cool, but warmer than the sand she'd been standing on. She walked until the waves hit her waist, just at the edge of the sand shelf that she could feel with her toes, and dove underwater.

And felt immediately at home. The water was clear here, too cold for exotic corals or the reefs she'd seen in the far Western Sea, but small silver fish darted here and there, and pale crabs scuttled beneath. She could feel the current here; it was close to the surface, pulsing like a heartbeat in a steady, healthy rhythm that made her feel better about magic. She spotted the black, spiny bodies of sea stars, carefully pulled one up by one of it's prickly arms, and placed it into the pouch. She managed two more, and snuck up on a crab that was very unsuccessfully hiding beneath a rock much too small for its size.

She emerged from the water to find the signal fire blazing, sending a column of black smoke into the air, and Grant standing on the beach, hands on his hips and eyes wide as he watched her.

There wasn't much to her ensemble when it was dry; she didn't need to look to know it provided little cover when she walked out of the sea.

"You went swimming," he confirmed, and glanced at the bundle. "And came back with something."

"I used my shift as a basket," Kit said. She walked past the waterline, could feel his eyes on her, then tossed the bundle into the sand, untied it.

"Well," Grant said. "My breakfast feels a bit . . . inadequate . . . by comparison."

"*Cox's Seamanship* is an excellent resource," she said with a grin, and pushed wet hair behind her ears. "Let's cook."

~

They ate their fill of reasonably well-cooked seafood and huddled near the fire again. It was cloudy today, the island cooler without the warming sunlight, and with a chilly breeze that Kit hoped was sending the *Diana* to safety—or to safely find Doucette.

"There are other places we are needed," Kit said, legs stretched in the sand. "But there are worse places to be than here."

She looked up at him and smiled, and his smile was just as grand.

"Marry me," he said.

Kit snorted. "We just ate the only thing that could stand in as vicar."

"I'm quite earnest, Kit. I want you to marry me."

It was the softness in his voice, the gravity of it, that had her looking up. "What?"

His eyes glowed with purpose, and that was enough to trigger her defenses. She didn't want marriage. To be tied down with lace and expectations. "Marry me," he said again, and took her hand, pressed it against his chest. "This isn't some island romance, a bit of tawdry in the midst of war, and I think you know it, too."

What *did* she know? That she was drunk on him and his laughter, on his strong hands and the magic he could work with them. But marriage? Marriage was not for her.

"A great battle of the heart," the fortune-teller in Auevilla had said. Maybe it hadn't all been nonsense.

Grant gave her a half smile. "Am I to have an answer?"

"No," she finally managed, and gently pulled her hand away.

He flinched like she'd slapped him. "I'm sorry?"

"You need a viscountess," she said, bafflement in her voice. How did he not see that fundamental problem? He was a viscount, with land and responsibilities; she had her own, and they were different. Demanding. He needed a viscountess with a pedigree, the ability to run a home, and a proficiency at all manner of domestic activities. Not a sailor with scars and a longing for the sea, who didn't want to live on a country estate, bound to the land. Trapped by the land.

"You'd become a viscountess after the wedding," he said dryly. "That's rather the point."

"Not even the current itself could transform a sea captain into a viscountess, Grant. I know about hardtack and scurvy and sailing points. I'm not going to transform into someone who fancies balls and hiring governesses."

"A rather fascinating collection of activities."

"Not to me." She looked at him for a moment and felt something clench at her heart. "We both know that's not how the Beau Monde operates. How do you think your acquaintances at the Seven Keys would react to your giving your title over to a sailor?"

Grant focused his brilliantly blue eyes on hers, staring so deeply into her, she thought she might be transparent. "I don't think that's the truth. Or not all of it."

"Are you calling me a liar?"

He just lifted his brows.

When anger burned away her sadness, Kit was glad he hadn't been consoling. "Watch yourself, Grant. I've called soldiers out for less."

"You'd call me out after last night? After we were together? After I was inside you?" There was nothing of desire in his eyes or his tone now. Just anger and insult.

Kit made a sound of frustration. "You're making too much of this. There's risk to my reputation here," she said, waving a hand around them, "even if I gave a damn for such things, which you know I don't. We have obligations, Grant, that take us far from the Isles. We'll have those obligations as long as the war lasts, and maybe beyond. And there's much of the world that I haven't seen."

Wouldn't see, if she had to give up her commission, her ship, for a life in a home on a windswept hill. For taffeta and silk and gardens and nurseries. She felt a clutch of panic. And when she looked at his face, and saw the hardness return to his eyes, for a moment he was the same viscount she'd met in the throne room in New London—haughty and arrogant, with little patience for a woman he believed ran errands for the queen along the Islish coast.

"I'm made to be a sea captain. I don't want that to change." Not now. And maybe not ever.

He breathed deeply and stood up, putting space between them. Then he looked down at her, and his eyes were hard as flint. "I've asked you for marriage, and you've declined. I'll not beg a woman for her hand."

She could find no words to comfort either one of them. "I'm sorry" was all she could think to say.

And that made it somehow worse.

‿◦

Their interlude was apparently over, as he hardly spoke to her for the rest of the day, and the signal fire brought no salvation.

She felt empty, unspeakably lonely, and her chest ached with something she refused to call longing. That only infuriated her more. She'd been telling the truth. She didn't want to give up the *Diana* or her crew. She didn't want to trade the sea for Grant Hall, even if it was beautiful and its caretakers, Mr. and Mrs. Spivey, were charming and helpful.

But Grant had been right, at least a bit. She was afraid. If she kept moving, if she kept sailing and seeing and exploring, she might discover who she was. Who was she to give herself to a viscount? A stranger with no history, no connections.

There were still coppers in her pocket, so she pulled one out, kissed it, then tossed it into the sea.

"We need off this godsforsaken island," she murmured. "If I've any luck left—and I can calculate my debts as well as anyone—we could use it now."

‿◦

They slept in the cove again, but with distance between them now.

It was dark out, the fire faded to embers, when she felt the jerk of movement before his groan of grief and pain, and was afraid he'd been shot or bitten or succumbed to dyspepsia from the damned spiny stars. It was just dawn, the light milky, and

Grant lay between her and the outcropping's edge, his face turned away. And his body shuddered.

She put a hand on his shoulder, squeezed. "Grant. Wake up."

He shuddered again.

His eyes were wide and staring, as if tracking some enemy that she couldn't see.

A nightmare, she realized, and rued that she hadn't thought of it sooner. He'd seen horrors during the war, and she'd seen the wide-eyed look on his face at Finistère after she'd lobbed a small bomb into the courtyard of a pirate fortress. Even beyond physical injuries, war left long shadows on the mind and soul.

"It's all right," she said softly, calmly. "It's just me and you, and we're safe. There's no fight here."

His breath shuddered in, out, and the pained sound made her own chest ache. She wanted to touch him, but he'd drawn a line between them yesterday; while she didn't understand it, she respected him enough not to cross it.

Another shudder, and she'd reached her own limit. He needed someone, and she was the only person available at present. If he was angry at the violation, so be it. They'd deal with that, too.

She put her hand on his, and his fingers linked, squeezed.

"You're safe," she said again, and brushed damp hair from his forehead. "There's no battle here."

He curled against her, so she stroked his back until his breathing slowed, softened, and he fell asleep again.

~⁓

He was gone when dawn broke. She was cold and damp and hungry—and now anger was an added insult. She found him by the fire, sat down a few feet away.

"Are you all right?"

"I'm fine." His tone was clipped but perfectly pleasant.

"You had a nightmare."

"No, I didn't."

"You did. It was, I think, war related."

He looked away, brow furrowed as he blinked, as if trying to recall the darker hours. "Is that why I . . ." He trailed off, apparently discomfited by the admission he'd needed the nearness of her.

"Slept heavily," she said. "I thought you might be tired when you woke."

He looked at her for a moment. "I'm fine. And I've lit the signal fire. So we'll wait."

～

Since he was apparently in no mood to talk, she let him have the quiet. So they waited in horrible, awkward silence, all the worse compared to the joy they'd taken in each other the day before.

Fortunately, Kit's coppers did the work. It took less than three hours, after two days of waiting, for a barquentine to appear on the horizon. It was long and sleek, with a bowsprit that stuck out like a narwal's tusk. Easily a third longer than the *Diana*, with two square-rigged masts. This boat was built for speed and bore no colors showing its allegiance.

"Do you recognize it?"

They were the first words Grant had spoken to her in hours. Gone was the lightheartedness that had buoyed her mood around the fire. He'd closed whatever door had been opened there, and his guard was up again. His voice was hard, cold.

"No," Kit said, ignoring that because they had to. "A privateer, most likely. I was hoping for an Isles vessel, or the *Diana* if our luck was superior. But I suppose even an enemy ship is better than starvation."

Another hour of waiting—while the ship moved closer and, Kit imagined, its crew debated whether Kit and Grant might be worth the trouble of a rescue—and then a boat was lowered, rowed out, maneuvered deftly through the waves, until Kit could see the rather grubby appearance of the crew. Four in all: two appearing male, and two female. And given their slightly grimy appearance—

"Pirates," Grant concluded. "Excellent. We could fight them."

"We could," Kit said. "Presuming rocks and sticks are a match against swords and muskets. But even if we managed to best them, to what result? Either the ship attacks us, or it continues on its way. In either case, we end up here." Not to mention the possibility of chasing pirates in circles around the island was more a comedic farce than a viable escape plan.

For a moment, Grant didn't answer. Kit wasn't sure if that was because he wasn't convinced or was simply still angry.

"We survive," Kit said. "One bit at a time. We make it off the island, we figure out how to get back to the *Diana*, one way or the other." That hadn't been one of Hetta's official Self-Sufficiency Principles, but it was a theme of her advice.

The women jumped from the boat when they reached knee-level water, used thick ropes to pull it toward the shore. The men stayed in the boat, pulled pistols from their belts, and looked appropriately menacing for pirates.

"I'm Rian Grant," he said. "Viscount Queenscliffe. We're in need of assistance."

"We know who you are," the smallest woman said, pulling a cutlass from the burgundy scarf tied at her hips. "We were at Finistère."

252 | CHLOE NEILL

Given Kit had lobbed several bombs on Finistère, that would probably not help them overmuch.

"My apologies for not recognizing you," Grant said, and would have attempted a bow, had the tip of the cutlass not dropped menacingly. "Or not," he said, and gave Kit a look nearly as pointed as the sword.

"Wrists," the other woman said.

Kit sighed but held them out. "We're hardly going to commandeer the boat," she muttered, as one of the others pulled rough hemp around her hands. "Where else would we go?"

By way of response, the hemp was pulled tighter, burning across her skin.

"Not especially talkative, I see." She was shoved to her knees with a sharp elbow in her back, barely missed knocking her head against the plank that crossed the boat, serving as a seat.

She growled but managed to turn, shift to sit against the curved hull. As much instinct as practice, she reached down to the current, was relieved by the strong pulse of magic, powerful as a heartbeat.

Grant, wrists tied, was pushed down into the opposite end of the boat. Little enough chance of collusion now, she thought, regardless of tied hands. He didn't so much as glance her way from his spot near the stern, with the pirates between them. Still hurt, given the hard set of his eyes and the miserable set of his shoulders.

They'd survive. But at what cost?

❧

The crew was silent as they rowed back to the ship, the jolly boat rising and falling ominously as they now pushed against the waves that had carried them ashore.

Kit took the opportunity to look over the sailors, with their sunbaked skin and clothes that needed a good and hearty wash. Mrs. Eaves would have enjoyed correcting their "deficiencies." And why, Kit wondered, were pirates always depicted as so dashing and, well, clean in penny novels? Had the authors never actually met a damned pirate?

"A damned fiction," she cursed, and earned an arch look from the woman closest to her. Kit managed a wan smile. "Just thinking about literature."

The woman snorted. "You think we don't read because we're pirates? We enjoy a good story just like anyone else, aye?"

"I like a good bit of socioeconomic satire myself," the man at the stern oar said, then spat exuberantly over the side of the boat.

Kit, standing very corrected, closed her mouth.

⌒

Since their hands were still tied, they were hauled bodily aboard, Kit's shoulders yanked so hard, she thought they might wobble in their sockets. The ship was in better shape than Kit would have expected. The wood sanded and oil-rubbed, the masts and rigging tarred, the brass gleaming. The figurehead, she'd seen during the trip aboard, was a great golden bird, wings spread as if holding up the bowsprit. The ship had a deep waist, with short curving stairs leading from the quarterdeck to the fore and poop decks.

They were pushed down a set of stairs into a large room. It took a moment for her eyes to adjust, and then she found dark wood, candle smoke, and heavy velvets. It smelled of herbs and musky oils, not entirely unpleasantly.

A man sat at a long table, worn black boots crossed on the scarred tabletop. He glanced back at them, dark eyes gleaming.

"Well, well, well," he said. "If it isn't the woman who lobbed a bomb at me."

Bloody hell, Kit thought. It wasn't just a ship of pirates. They'd been rescued by a damned pirate king.

# SEVENTEEN

H is given name was Donal, last name unknown, at least to Kit.

And she had, in fact, thrown a bomb at him. But only because, despite the pretty looks, he was a pirate king. One of the pirate kings known as the Five who'd captured an Isles spy and held him in the dank island fortress he and his compatriots called home.

He was a handsome man, with golden skin and dark hair, and brown eyes beneath dark brows. A divoted chin and wide mouth, and a musical lilt in his voice that Kit pegged to the Western Isle.

"Better than starvation," Grant murmured. "Is it, really?"

"I should have left you on the island."

"The queen would be most displeased. And you'd be overwrought with grief."

That he'd made a quip eased her heart, even considering the circumstances. That she couldn't imagine marriage didn't mean she couldn't imagine Grant.

"Well, well, well," Donal said. "Look who's darkened my door again. Captain Brightling," he said, then shifted his gaze to Grant. "And Viscount Queenscliffe." He linked his fingers together across his chest, watched them with obvious amusement. "Welcome aboard the *Phoenix*."

That explained the figurehead, Kit thought.

"Soldier and sailor," Donal continued, "together again, just as at Finistère. And the repairs are coming along quite well, thank you for asking."

"It's a pirate fortress," Kit said dryly. "Where you were holding an Isles citizen captive. A citizen who later succumbed to his injuries."

Donal's expression darkened then, and Kit saw what looked like regret in his eyes. For a moment he actually looked crestfallen, as if he'd cared about Dunwood or his disposition. But that sentiment was wiped away quickly enough.

"Fools who get caught," he said, "deserve what comes to them."

Grant bolted forward—or tried to—but the pirates held him firm. "Bastard," he spat out.

"I am many things, but not that. My old man was certain of it. And now that I have you here together, what should I do with you?"

"We are officers of the Isles," Kit said. "We'll thank you for the rescue but demand our freedom, as is proper. If you'll deposit us at the nearest village or allied ship, we'll request the queen compensate you accordingly."

He watched her with faint amusement. "No, I don't believe I will, Captain. You see, I had a very interesting conversation with the crew of the Frisian brig we rescued from the rocks off Finistère."

The brig that had fired on the *Diana* after their escape from Finistère, which the *Diana*—with Kit and the current at the helm—had managed to lead into rocky shoals. The Guild had officially denied the brig had been one of its ships; Kit knew that was nonsense.

Donal kicked his legs off the table. "The crew was rescued, I'm sure you'll be glad to hear."

"They fired on my ship."

"They say they merely wanted a conversation. Would sailors exaggerate?" The pirates around him chortled in amusement. "The crew suggested the *Diana*'s captain had a very . . . *potent* Alignment. You've some aptitude, it appears."

Kit didn't respond to that; she wasn't going to antagonize him, but nor was she going to give him any more personal information than necessary.

"And as you're now in my custody, I plan to take advantage of your skills."

"Piracy and impressment are banned by Isles law."

His smile was thin. "We aren't in the Isles. And I'm not a pirate at present." He pulled a folded bit of foolscap from his jacket. "Letter of marque," he said, but didn't offer it for her examination. "I've a right, particularly in a time of war, to do what's necessary to capture enemy resources."

"How did a pirate king obtain a letter of marque?" Grant asked.

"In his actual name," Kit guessed. "Something of the Western Isle. And given the speed with which he obtained it, I'd guess his wealth and title helped."

Donal looked none too pleased with Kit's deduction.

"Don't worry," she said. "I don't know your position. But I

know a member of the Beau Monde when I see one. The sense of entitlement that most of your lot tend to carry."

That she'd added the *most*, Kit thought, was the only reason Grant hadn't actually growled.

Donal, careful man that he was, shook off the insult. "How did you end up in the drink? Or on the island."

"We fought in the Battle of Auevilla," Kit said.

"That was a very nasty business. The Isles lost two ships, I hear."

Kit's heart thudded wildly against her chest, driven by fear. "The *Diana*?"

He glanced back. "That was your pretty little schooner?"

She objected to *little*, but nodded.

"Survived, I'm told, due to a bit of clever sailing. No hands lost. Other than you."

She allowed herself a moment to close her eyes, to say the *Dastes* for Jin and the others. The sea dragon, the island, and whatever happened here were worth it.

"They believe we're lost," Grant said, as if the realization had just struck him. "Of course they would."

"They know I'm a good swimmer," Kit said. "They might have held out hope." But that hope would be thin and brittle and might have broken completely in the days that had passed without their return.

"Good?" Donal asked. "You, somehow, survived the first conflict of the new war and a swarm of sea dragons, or so I'm told? It would take more than 'good' to clear that."

She didn't answer.

"Have you eaten?"

Kit opened her mouth, instinctively ready to bite back, but saw there was actual concern in his eyes. "Not recently."

He looked at the blond woman, who nodded, then left the room. Donal said nothing but watched them over the rim of a glass half filled with amber liquid. No, Kit thought. He *studied* them, as if he might uncover their weaknesses by careful review alone.

Kit just met his gaze coolly, found it interesting that a pirate king took the trouble to evaluate anyone, rather than relying on force and will. Donal was a careful man, and she'd be careful of that.

Moments later, the woman came back with a tray. Two tin plates and two tin cups, which were put in front of them on the table without ceremony.

Kit's stomach growled audibly.

"You're welcome," Donal said, then looked at the woman again. "Untie them, please."

She did, and Kit's shoulders sang with the release. She rolled them, checked her wrists. Chafed and raw, but she'd manage. Grant's looked worse; his bonds had apparently been tighter. But if they pained him, he didn't show it.

The food—potatoes, a bit of roasted meat, and thick slices of tropical fruits Kit had only seen in Continental markets—smelled delicious. But they were both experienced enough to look at the food with longing, but make no move toward actually ingesting it.

Rolling his eyes, Donal leaned forward and plucked a slice of fruit—white with black dots—from the table and bit in.

"Eat," Donal said. "I need you focused."

"For what?" Grant asked.

Donal chewed, swallowed. "For the negotiation, of course."

~ ∽

They ate the meal, which was surprisingly tasty for a glorified pirate ship, letter of marque or no. When a sailor obligingly removed the plates, Kit looked at Donal.

"Thank you," she forced herself to say.

"You're welcome. Claude makes a decent horse stew."

Kit felt her gorge rise.

"But that was only a bit of old goat," Donal said, amusement in his eyes.

It always was, Kit thought, and reminded herself that her belly was full and she was someone else's guest—even if he was a damned pirate. She'd add the threat of horse stew to the pile of emotional turmoil that would need dealing with later.

"And now that you've been rescued and resuscitated, we can move to matters of business."

"What do you want?" Kit asked.

"You," Donal said, leaning an elbow on the table and propping his head on his spread fingers. "Or, rather, your very unique talents."

"Careful," Grant muttered, the word a dangerous growl. Kit forced herself to not look at him.

Donal's brows lifted, but he ignored the warning. "Your Alignment," he told Kit.

Her brows lifted. "What Alignment?"

"Come now," he said, and sat up, linked his hands on the tabletop. "The gun brig you managed to ground in the archipelago. The Frisians watched your ship dart to and fro, Captain, and believed it not entirely natural."

Damn Frisians, Kit thought. "And if I am Aligned?"

"I have a hold full of wine that needs to make its way to Frisia."

"There's a blockade."

"Exactly," Donal said. "I need to go around the blockade. In addition to your magic, you are a captain in the Queen's Own, if my information is correct—and that position rarely comes without knowledge and skill. You assist me in avoiding the blockade and reaching Frisia, and you can walk away in Hofstad or we'll transport you to the nearest allied port."

"And if I decline those options?" Kit prompted. Given the aggression of the man-of-war, she had little interest in being dropped into the Frisian capital and home of its all-powerful Guild.

The remaining wryness in his smile faded away, leaving behind the mercenary. "We'll drop your viscount in the water right now. Could he survive without you?"

Kit cursed silently, swallowed hard, but kept the emotions off her face—the fear that he wouldn't survive alone this far from shore, and satisfaction at the possibility he'd get the dunking he needed. And she refused to look at Grant.

Both options were poor. One slightly less so than the other. But she knew how to negotiate.

She put her foot on Grant's under the table, pressed, willing him to understand that she needed to take the lead. "You think we'll help you after what you did to Dunwood?"

Donal stiffened. "This is neither the time nor the place for that discussion."

Kit watched him for a moment. "I want confirmation you're being earnest about the cargo." She understood the necessity of compromise, but not if it might harm the Isles or Crown Command in the long term.

His expression went dark. "We aren't running weapons."

"Then you'll have no problem proving it."

His jaw worked, but he nodded. A woman came into the room. And she looked familiar.

No scarves or cards, but Kit had no doubt she was the fortune-teller from Auevilla. And apparently a pirate. Why was she on Donal's ship?

The woman's stride hitched as she recognized Kit, but her eyes stayed cool. And she gave Kit the tiniest shake of the head— as if a warning not to reveal her identity.

All right, Kit thought. She could play along for now. There were plenty of nooks on a ship this size to allow for a private conversation. And plenty of time to change course if it came to that.

"Bonjour," the woman said with a nod.

"Captain Brightling," Donal said, gesturing to them, "and Rian Grant, Viscount Queenscliffe. This is Jean-Baptiste."

"Jean-Baptiste?" Grant asked.

"My father wished for a son," she said. "I was a disappointment from the first."

"Jean, show the soldier into the hold. He wishes to inspect our stowage."

"And he comes back in the same condition as he goes down," Kit added.

"Another insult," Donal said. "Given I've been nothing but hospitable in the meantime."

Kit glanced at Grant, nodded.

"Stay alert," he whispered, and followed a sailor toward a companionway.

~⁓

They stood in tense silence for the ten minutes it took Grant to make it back to the room.

Donal spent the time sipping from his wineglass, watching Kit over the rim. She spent the time surveying the room, looking for clues to his identity. His past was no business of hers, but if it provided leverage to help her and Grant off the ship, she'd happily use it. But she found nothing personal on the table, on the walls. It was amply provisioned with gold and weapons and mirrors and statuettes, all probably treasure pillaged by his crew.

"Wine," Grant confirmed, looking at Kit. "Silk. Cinnamon."

She saw no lie in his eyes, nor any particular concern. Other than the general concern that they'd been taken captive by pirates. Which was entirely logical.

Donal spread his hands. "Are you satisfied, Captain?"

"No," she said. "But I don't see that we have much of a choice. So I'll help you slip past the blockade, and you'll release us. I have one more demand."

Donal's lips twitched. "Which is?"

"We'll want baths."

She was fairly certain she heard Grant snort.

Donal just stared at her. "Baths."

"We've spent a lot of time in the sea over the last few days. I feel a bit . . . brined."

With a considering smile, he nodded. "Then baths you shall have. Our bearing?"

"Toward Frisia," she said. "It's not information that will get you past the fleet, but me."

Donal watched her for a moment, then stepped closer, flipped a dagger into his hand, held it in front of her. "I may have been someone else once upon a time. But I am now one of the Five, and if you lie to me, I'll lose no sleep over tossing you both into the deep."

❧

To his credit, Donal upheld his end of the bargain. Kettle after kettle of steaming water was poured into the narrow copper tub in a corner of Donal's rather grand cabin. There was a wall of gilt windows across the stern, half of them filled with colored glass, an enormous wooden bed against one wall, and half a dozen additional pieces of furniture, all of it elaborately carved, bedecked with heavy velvets, or covered in gleaming gold. It was . . . a bit much.

Donal appeared in the doorway, glanced at Kit and Grant, who were being watched by guards.

"I suppose even pirates can bathe," Kit said, and gestured at the tub. "But you couldn't move this out of your quarters?"

"Privateer," he said, as if it mattered much to her. "As I know you're well acquainted with the limitations of space on sailing ships, I won't respond to the other."

"So respond to this," Kit said, turning toward him and crossing her arms. The bath could wait a bit. "Dunwood. I want the truth. All of it, or our deal is off."

Donal snorted. "Or, what? You'll go willingly into the drink?"

Kit just watched him. "I believe I've proven my prowess at that."

She stepped toward him. "You and I both know how ships operate, Donal. The dark times. The quiet times. This wouldn't be the first time I've escaped a hold. But barring that, if you're not honest, instead of keeping you from the blockade, I'll lead you toward it."

"Then you'll die."

"We are sailor and soldier," Kit said, gaze steady on his. "We are made to die for the Isles. And you appear to be missing the larger picture."

"Which is?"

"Dunwood was an important man. A beloved and loyal man, and a colleague of the viscount."

Donal slid him a glance and couldn't have missed the loathing in Grant's eyes. "Is that a threat?"

"Would you like it to be?"

Kit held out a hand to stop Grant's advance. "I remember our discussion on Finistère," she said. "You said Dunwood had been delivered to you, and you had plans for him."

Donal's expression went sour again. "Damn, but you're stubborn."

Grant murmured his agreement.

Donal huffed, turned for the door. After shooing the guards out, he closed it, muttering about troublesome women. And then he walked to a sideboard, poured liquid into a short glass, downed it. And offered none to his guests.

"A privateer brought him to the island. One of my colleagues believed it was too dangerous to let Dunwood live. I paid to keep him alive."

That, at least, was consistent with what Dunwood had told them.

Kit surmised the colleague was one of the Five but, given the vagaries under which they operated, wondered if the Five were solely a thing of myth. Perhaps pirate kings came and went; "the Five" certainly bore more cachet than "a Few Pirate Kings" or "Five Pirate Kings, More or Less."

"And what had you planned to do with him?" Grant asked.

"Give him to the Frisians," Donal said. "They planned to ransom him back to the Isles, which was fine by me. My interest is in goods and gold. I wanted no part of murder or kidnapping."

"If that's true," Grant said, and his tone made it clear he doubted it, "why did you fight us for his release?"

"You invaded and blew up my home." He had a point. But then his smile went sly. "I don't suppose you've any more of those beautiful explosives?"

"Not on my person, no," Kit said.

"A disappointment."

"You didn't sail after us," Grant continued.

"The gun brig had already given chase, and I didn't feel especially moved to chase down an Isles ship. I may not be Aligned, Captain, but I can read the signs as well as anyone. Gerard does the world no favors, and the Isles stands against him."

They watched him in silence for a moment.

"You'd already gotten the money," Kit surmised.

Donal nodded. "And that."

"He was a good man," Grant said finally, voice heavy and low. "And he is dead because of your greed and the greed of your colleagues."

For a very long time, Donal and Grant looked at each other. And Kit saw, just for an instant, guilt and regret flash in Donal's eyes. "I don't disagree," Donal said. His accent was a bit softer in those words, as if he'd pulled back a corner of the cloak that usually draped him. "But what's done is done."

A pity, Kit thought, that he'd chosen this course. A man with power and wealth could do better than running silks for the rich.

Kit cleared her throat. "Now that we've finished our business, perhaps a bit of privacy for the bath?"

Donal gestured toward the door. "Mr. Viscount Colonel, after you."

"Actually, I'd like to speak with Mr. Viscount Colonel before he goes."

Donal watched them for a moment. "Five minutes," Donal said, gesturing for the others to leave. They did, but kept the door open.

He'd wandered to the bed, ran fingers along the ornately carved wood. "Now I wonder if he stole the ship from woodcarving gnomes. Or maybe Alemanians. They enjoy woodcarving."

"There is a lot of . . . everything," Kit agreed.

He came back to her, stepping so close she could feel the warmth of him. His voice was lower now, quieter, and she knew the conversation was turning to Donal. "Do you believe him?"

"That he paid to keep Dunwood alive? I do. And I fancy you've seen enough pirates in your time to recognize, as I do, that this ship runs differently than most. Little good it did Dunwood in the end." Many a pirate wouldn't have bothered with food or baths or making deals. They'd have demanded, and violence would have been the only other option.

Grant nodded. "Whether he's mannerly doesn't excuse him, nor does the possibility that he's nicer than his colleagues. He still bears responsibility for what became of Marcus."

"I agree," Kit said. "He positions himself as one of the Five for the benefits it accords him. Some of the blame weighs with him, too."

"And you're sure about the deal?" he asked.

"For the bath? Yes. They're delightful," Kit said. "You'll enjoy yours, I suspect." Since she'd done him the service of demanding baths for both of them.

He growled, and she looked at him, saw concern joining the anger in his eyes. "Negotiating with the pirate, knowing what we know of him?"

Yes, she'd made a deal with the metaphorical devil, but she was captive on his ship in enemy territory, and she had others to think about. "Was Donal wrong? Could you make it to land? Survive in the water on your own?"

He ran a hand through his hair, looked like a dangerous Beau Monde rake while doing it, and made her a little more angry. "Probably not," he admitted. "You said you'd escaped from worse."

"I've escaped," she said. "Whether it was worse is debatable."

"Then you're a very good actress," he said, and she didn't think that was a compliment.

"My job is to protect the Isles, protect my sailors. At present, that includes you, and tossing you to another horde of sea dragons would not be an especially good show of leadership.

"We survived Auevilla," she continued. "We survived the Narrow Sea. We were rescued, if by nominal villains, and the *Diana* survived with no hands lost. We're going to keep doing what we can, and perhaps our luck will hold."

"And the blockade?"

"We've learned my skills with the current are . . . broader . . .

than I thought. Speed is the best way to get him past Isles ships without loss of life. And I'll lose no sleep over Frisians having a bit more cinnamon and silk, little though they need them." She cleared her throat. "If we're to survive this, we need to be able to work together."

His eyes fired. "Do we?"

"You're angry I won't agree to give up my ship to play hostess in Queenscliffe."

"No, Captain, I'm angry that the best you can think of me— the most you can think of me—is that I'd want you to give up anything."

She looked at the ceiling, prayed for patience. "A woman cannot be a viscountess if—"

"No," he said, turning on her. "*Cannot* does not matter here. A viscountess—*my* viscountess—will follow her mind and her heart."

She held out her palms, dotted with the small dark scars. And there was pleading in her eyes. "What viscountess has these?"

"Need I show you my own scars?" he asked, voice heavy with challenge. "Need I prove to you my unworthiness of my own title?" His anger and frustration seemed to sharpen the air as if it was something tangible.

"You aren't unworthy. You were born into it. I'm a sailor, Grant."

"You could be whatever you wished, Kit, were your stubbornness not interfering with your eyesight."

"I don't know what I'm supposed to be."

She hadn't meant to say it. Hadn't known she wanted to say it. And maybe because of that, the words came out in a rush, like water through a sieve.

He stared at her. "What?"

"I have no roots," she said, "or don't know what they are. I don't know who my parents are. I assume I've got two of them, considering the biology. But I don't know them—that part of my life is missing." She swallowed hard. "That part of me is missing. And viscounts don't just marry foundlings. It isn't done."

She'd expected sympathy but instead saw anger in his eyes. "Did you not just stand in a room of privateers—one of few women in the room, I might add—and negotiate for a hot bath?"

"That's different. I know my way among privateers. The Beau Monde is different. Don't viscounts deserve more? Aren't they to marry gentlemen's daughters?"

"You fight for our country. How can that be worth less than a gentleman's daughter?" He looked at her for a moment, narrowed his gaze. "If it was anyone but you, would you begrudge me?"

"What?"

"If I'd asked for Astrid's hand, would you begrudge her the union because she is a foundling? Reject her entrée into polite society? Give her the cut direct?"

Oh, Kit would begrudge it. But not for the reasons he'd identified. "No. Of course not."

"Then you're a coward. Because if it's not principle, it's cowardice."

Her eyes flashed. "Don't you dare call me a coward because I'm concerned about your reputation. Do you want to receive the cut direct? Do you know what it's like to be judged by your . . ." She trailed off, realizing he did know.

"My family?" he finished, voice quieter now. "Yes. Of course I do."

Kit sighed. As if a jouster spotting a weakness in the armor, he moved closer.

"Who might your parents be that you think I would turn you away—or would allow anyone else to do so? Tradespeople? Cobblers? Larks? Or, gods forbid, soldiers?"

Arranged just so, it sounded quite inane.

"You're a snob," he concluded.

That had her ire up. "Excuse me?"

"Thinking you're too special and mysterious to join our ranks."

"I'm neither mysterious nor special. I'm—"

"You are Kit Brightling of the Queen's Own," he said, cutting her off. "Don't ever forget that." He was quiet for a moment, and they both watched steam rising from the surface of the tub. Grant gestured to the tub. "Of all the things you might have asked for, and you opted for a bath."

She swallowed hard. "I doubt he has pistachio nougats or penny novels on board, so it seemed like the best substitute." They stood quietly for a moment, and she realized Donal had given them more than five minutes. "I feel like there's something I ought to say."

Grant looked at her expectantly. "Do let me know if you figure it out." Then slammed the door.

# EIGHTEEN

K it worked to ignore the anger, and the hollow in the pit of her stomach.

She'd focus on the bath, she decided. There was oil in the water, green droplets that gave off the heady scent of evergreen trees, the crispness of snowcapped mountains. She might smell like a Western lord when she climbed out but decided it would be well worth the risk. She disrobed, folding her clothes neatly beside the tub in the event she needed to grab them quickly. And then sucked in a breath, dipped a toe into the water.

It was deliciously hot, so she stepped inside and eased her way down, fingers clenching the copper edges as her body adjusted to the temperature. She hadn't been this warm since she'd left New London; being a sailor for the Isles meant facing, more often than not, wind and drizzle and the constant chill created by the mix of them.

She sat down, closed her eyes, and rested her arms on the sides. She wasn't sure even the queen's order could have summoned her out of the warmth.

She exhaled and, finally alone, offered herself the opportunity for a good cry. But she wasn't the weeping kind. Kit was nothing if not practical. She didn't forbid others their sobbing, but she didn't usually see the point in it. Tears solved no problems; action did. But she'd earned a good, melancholic soak today.

She hadn't expected a proposal of marriage—hadn't needed a proposal. Unlike the older of her sisters, she'd had no season in New London; sailors almost never did. And she was no lark, but she'd decided many years ago that the life of a sailor was too short to waste. She wasn't greatly experienced, but there'd been a few men here and there. She'd demanded precisely *none* of them propose, and she had no regrets. Marriage was a phantom that might lurk in some future she'd never really imagined, and didn't want.

But there went the damned viscount, making her an offer.

And she'd said no, and the look in his eyes when she'd done so. Gods be, she'd remember it forever. The shock—he was a viscount, hardly accustomed to rejection—and the hurt.

She punched a fist in the bath, which did nothing, of course, but splash water on the floor.

"Honor be damned," she said. She rejected completely the notion that a man and woman somehow lost their honor merely by enjoying each other, as if honor was something cast aside like an unwanted cravat.

She didn't want to hurt him. He'd become important to her, which wasn't something she could say of many people. But the woman he needed was a woman she couldn't be. It simply couldn't be helped, the difference in what they wanted.

But still . . . After so many weeks of wondering about him, the idea of his being absent from her life seemed wrong in ways that left a strange and unfamiliar hollow in her chest.

"Bloody hell," she murmured, before sucking in a breath and dunking herself entirely beneath the water. It filled her ears, blocking out sound, and gave her the slightly unnerving experience of floating in water while floating on water, she and the tub gently bobbing together while the sea bobbed beneath and around them.

She emerged, pushed her hair from her eyes, then the water from her hair, then let her head drop to the back of the tub. And found her problems hadn't, unfortunately, dissolved in the bathwater, oiled and scented though it was. Grant was angry, and she was on an unfamiliar ship, had given a promise to betray her fleet. Or to sneak past it, anyway.

There was a pounding at the door. No sinking past that. Kit sunk lower, covered her breasts with her hands.

"This room is occupied," she called out. "Go very far away." To ensure she was understood, she said the former in perfect Gallic, the latter in very loud Islish.

Not loud enough, she judged, when the door opened despite the warning.

Jean came in.

Kit nearly sat up straight before recalling where she was—and how very naked—as water sloshed onto the floor over the tub's sides. She sunk down again. "You don't follow directions very well."

"You aren't my captain," Jean said simply, and closed the door. "I've brought you some clean clothes and a hammock. You'll find space for the latter in the officers' mess. Two doors down, port side." She put a pile of dun-colored fabric on a chest near the bath. Then she turned back to Kit. "There are matters of which we should speak."

"I'd be happy to speak with you at a more mutually convenient time. This is the first hot bath I've had in weeks. I'm not getting out."

"You don't have to." Apparently undisturbed, she pulled a chair from Donal's table, took a seat.

"Do make yourself comfortable," Kit said, closing her eyes and leaning her head on the back of the tub. She wasn't so modest, after years in the Crown Command, that she was going to let this opportunity slip out of her grasp like so much soap. "We're bosom companions."

"We've bosoms," Jean agreed, "but we aren't companions."

"I was being sarcastic."

"I'm aware. I preferred to clarify."

Kit opened an eye, looked at her. And for the first time, saw something concerning in her eyes. But decided she'd let this play out a bit. Let the woman tell her own story. "What do you want, fortune-teller? You're very bad at that, by the by."

Jean snorted. "I'm as good as I need to be."

"For what purpose?"

"Whatever may be needed."

Kit watched her for a moment, considered. "*Ut myrkri, solas,*" she said. That was the challenge phrase Chandler had given her, the one she could use to determine if someone was an asset for the spymaster. Given her travels, Jean seemed like a good candidate.

"*Ut lyga, firinn,*" Jean said, reciting Chandler's response.

"You're one of Chandler's," Kit said.

"We share mutually beneficial information."

Kit sunk down again. "That's why you were outside that building in Auevilla—the one Doucette went into. You were monitoring?"

"I was. It's owned by the regimental captain and used to pass messages."

Kit knew it. She tapped fingers on the rim of the tub. "Doucette obtained a packet from there."

"So I saw. We've friends who will do what they can to take a peek."

"Friends other than 'Fouché'?"

Jean's stare went considering. "You met with Fouché?"

"The gendarmes believed my midshipman and I were spies," Kit said, and told her the rest of the story.

"You were very busy in Auevilla."

"Not by choice," she said. "And Fouché is safe. He was preparing to secure the staff and leave the town when we left it. He got out safely."

"Good," she said, with obvious relief.

Kit cocked her head at Jean. "You and he . . . ?"

"What? No." She snorted. "I've no interest in a duke or the lifestyle that marrying him would require."

Kit's relief was nearly as soothing as the bathwater. "I understand completely."

Jean crossed one leg over the other. "It can't be a wholly comfortable life, despite the money. Being forced to wear gowns and gloves. Eating their strange delicacies. Being subject to the whims of those who imagine they're better than you because of who they know. No, thank you."

Kit rarely said no to a decent delicacy. But she wasn't in a position to argue about aristocratic expectations, all things considered, so she changed the subject. At least in a sense. "Does Grant know you?"

"Not that I'm aware of," Jean said. "Spies knowing each other is generally considered poor practice. Your viscount is one of Chandler's?"

"He's not my viscount," Kit said. "But he's mostly one of Chandler's. Donal lets you come and go? He's not suspicious when you leave the crew?"

"He knows I trade in information. Occasionally, he gets some of it. That suits him well enough. He's a good man," she added.

"He's a pirate," Kit said. This was not the bathing experience she'd hoped for.

"He's a privateer."

"You can dress it up however you'd like, but he's a literal pirate king. And he's responsible, at least partly, for the death of a good man."

Jean's expression didn't change. "You mean Dunwood."

"He told you."

"He's mentioned the man in passing—and his regrets. But more, this ship is small enough for word to travel. You spoke of him and were overheard."

So, no privacy aboard the *Phoenix*. Good to know.

"He's a good man," Jean said again, with less patience this time. "He rescued you and the viscount, gave you food, gave you a bath."

Kit put her elbows on the tub's edges, linked her fingers, and studied Jean-Baptiste. "He's titled, or a son of someone titled, from the Western Isle, who has apparently turned his back on that life and the Isles, and instead turned to thievery, kidnapping, and murder." She lifted a finger. "And extortion. He is a criminal who acts in direct contravention to the needs of the Isles."

"Things are rarely so simple."

"Except when they are. Why are you here? And what's Donal hiding?"

Eyes narrowed, Jean watched Kit for a moment. "Nothing of note. And my experiences with members of the Crown Command haven't been positive, so it is difficult for me to trust you with the secrets of others."

"I'm not one of Chandler's people," Kit said. "And I don't need to know others' personal secrets. I have few of my own to offer in trade."

"A foundling," Jean said. "Raised by Hetta Brightling, Aligned to the sea. Involved in a bit of a row with a very handsome viscount."

"There's no row," Kit said, and didn't like feeling defensive.

"My father was a Guild member," Jean said. "And I was thirteen when he tried to marry me off to a lecher in exchange for better trade routes. If I wasn't a boy, he said, he'd get his money's worth some other way."

"I'm sorry," Kit said, and meant it. She knew how fortunate she was, as a foundling and otherwise, to have found a mother in Hetta Brightling. She'd had no thought but for empowering the girls to do not just what they could, but what they *might*. Kit had taken that lesson to heart; that's why she was one of the youngest captains in the Crown Command, woman or no.

Jean nodded. "As was I. And bound and determined that future would not be wedlock to a man older than my own father. So I left. I made mistakes," she said. "I thought bravery would be enough to get me a position on the docks. But I didn't know capstan from cleat, and I was small and female. You may be aware that we don't make competent sailors," Jean said, voice dry as old teak.

"So I've heard," Kit said in the same tone.

"But I was desperate, as my father had sent men to find his investment, so I hired onto a sloop. Fortunately for me, being a greenhorn, I inadvertently climbed aboard . . . the wrong ship. And it was Donal's. He let me stay, taught me what I needed to know. Saved my life three times, including allowing me to stay aboard."

Kit cocked her head. There was more here, she thought. More to this particular tale that was hiding in that pause before "the wrong ship."

"What was the other ship?" Kit asked.

Jean waited a beat. "The *Mary Margaret*."

"Damn," Kit murmured. "John Read's ship." Or Red Jack, as he'd been known, for the blood he spilled while ravaging the Narrow and Western Seas. He'd been the most violent of pirates born of the Saxon Isles, and hunted for years. He'd been killed by his own crew, or so the story was told, his body tossed to the sea dragons.

"Aye," Jean said.

"How did you end up working for Chandler?"

"I had information about an Islish aristocrat who sent money abroad for Gerard's final campaigns. In addition to that atrocity, he had a predilection for hurting women in his employ." Her smile was thin, and there was nothing of joy in it. "That information made its way to Chandler. The aristocrat is still rotting in prison, and Chandler ensured a portion of his estate was redistributed to the women he injured. That assured my loyalty."

"It would mine as well," Kit said.

Jean hopped down from the chair. She crossed her arms, gave Kit a cool, considering stare. "Some of us run away from the past.

Some of us run toward the future. I think it matters less which we choose than that we're honest about our paths."

"I appreciate honesty," Kit said, but kept her gaze on Jean. "And?"

"And . . . Donal did me a service. I consider him an asset under my protection. So if and when I'm forced to stand between you, I wanted you to understand why."

"All right," Kit said after a moment, and she did. Hadn't she touched the current across the entire Narrow Sea to save her favorite thief? Faced sea dragons to save Grant? They were, for better or occasionally worse, her other family. A person who lacked in that department had to make their own. Jean had made her own way, moved beyond the world she'd been born into, and made her own family in the meantime. She couldn't fault Jean for taking care of them.

"As long as you remember," Kit said, "that one good deed doesn't make a hero. I made a deal with your captain, and I'll stand by my word. He'd better do the same."

⁓

She was clean and mostly dry when she donned the clothes left for her: slim trousers and a blousy shirt, both in linen made soft by wear and washing. She pulled on her boots, picked up the bundle of her discarded clothes, and opened the door.

Donal leaned against the opposite wall, arms crossed. "As you've delayed my work for nearly an hour, I hope you found that refreshing."

"I did, thanks for asking."

"You and the soldier are . . . ?" Donal asked, and there was little mistaking the interest that lay beneath the question.

Kit's stare remained flat. "Being held against our will?"

Donal's smile widened, his dark eyes going somehow drowsy, seductive. He moved a step closer, propped an arm on the door. "If that's your only involvement, perhaps you'd be amenable to . . ."

He took her hand, pressed it against his chest. It was admirably firm, and that was all the approval she could muster. Kit suspected his charms were enough to tempt many women into being "amenable." But she wasn't one of them.

"Release my hand," she said, in the mildest of tones, "or I will break yours off and feed it to the sea dragons."

He did, but his grin only widened. "You are a woman of fire."

"I'm captain of the *Diana*. I am an officer of the queen. And I've no interest in children who hunt for coins while others fight."

This time, his eyes flashed. "We're delivering supplies."

"You're delivering smuggled liquor and silk," she corrected, then held up a hand. "And I don't care what you intend to deliver. We made the deal necessary to get us off the ship, and I will hold to it. But that's it. If you want my admiration, use your brains and your wealth and your ship for something more than padding your pockets.

"And thanks for the bath," she added as she strolled down the corridor, because she wasn't totally without manners.

⁓

Kit shook out the hammock—she didn't need fleas added to her current list of concerns—and hung it in the officer's mess. And undoubtedly crawling things she decided not to dwell on. Every ship had rats; only some of them walked on four legs.

The bell signaled the change of watch and Grant's entry,

hammock in hand, hair damp from his own bath, one dark lock falling over his forehead. He wore quite fitted pantaloons with his boots and a linen shirt. No waistcoat, no frock coat, as Donal and his crew had apparently dispensed with those. What remained of the ensemble left little to the imagination, from the curve of strong thighs to the skin visible in the V of the linen.

He looked, she realized, like a damned pirate. And a damnably convincing one.

One who'd refused her, she reminded herself, because she refused to give up her ship. So she schooled her features.

"Do you know how to hang your hammock?" she asked matter-of-factly.

"I believe I can manage." He did so, making decent knots before testing its strength. Then he turned back to her. "I saw you speaking with Donal."

"Well, it's his ship, after all."

"It appeared to be an intimate conversation."

She couldn't help herself. "Then it would hardly be any business of yours, would it? You've made it clear my physical activities don't interest you, Grant."

"As you will damned well remember," he said, stepping closer, "my name is Rian." His voice was a low growl, and the shiver it sent through her was decidedly not magic related.

She didn't want to shiver from a single word, or be so affected by his nearness. But that was the way of their world at present. She was somewhat mollified that the frustration in his eyes echoed her unsatisfied arousal.

"I have no interest in him." Or anyone but you, she quietly amended.

He watched her for a moment, gaze skimming from her own

ensemble, which was missing nearly as much as his. "You are a torment."

"You torment us both and for no need," she said quietly. "We could—"

"There *is* a need," he insisted. "I will not. I have my pride, and my honor. I'll not ruin a woman's reputation, sailor or no, for my own pleasure."

Her anger lit again. "My reputation is mine to manage."

"Very well then. I'm not interested in less than all of you."

She stared at him.

"I've made an offer, and you've declined. If you wish to change our terms, you'll have to come to me."

"Then I suppose we're done here." She swung into the hammock, settled herself. Heard rope creak as Grant did the same beneath her, with considerably less finesse and a lot more cursing.

Soldiers, she thought with a curse, but then recalled the island, his nightmare. And silently wished him undisturbed sleep.

⁓

She managed four hours of it before the bell signaled the change of watch, and sailors moved around her, climbing out of their own hammocks to get to work, pulling them down from the rafters for stowage abovedecks while they worked. Their murmurs were low and concerned, and Kit could hear the patter of rain on the decking above her.

Grant, she noted, was already gone.

She swung out of the hammock and left it hanging, then pulled on her uniform jacket, flipped up the collar, and made her way through the dark and to the companionway.

On deck, the air had chilled and the wind had shifted,

blowing hard from the northwest. The ship, big and steady as she was, was swaying now, and the waves were white—and disconcertingly large. Rain hit the deck hard and struck her hood with a noisy *pat-pat-pat* that seemed to echo in her ears. Gods, but she could use her good wool topcoat.

She crossed her arms over her chest, tucking her hands into the tailcoat, and joined Donal at the helm, handling the ornate, gilded wheel himself. He stood with Jean and other members of his crew and looked every bit the dashing pirate—black hair and brown duster blowing.

"It's blowing fresh," she called out over the beat of rain and wind.

"Wind picked up an hour ago," he said, body braced as he worked to maintain control over the wheel. "Rain just started, and we're damnably shorthanded."

Kit had wondered about that, as there hadn't been nearly as many crew on a ship this size as she'd expected. She'd simply assumed pirate ships ran lean; the fewer the sailors, the greater the individual profits.

"The viscount is already at work," Jean said, gesturing to the port gunwale, where he helped to haul in a line; the mainsail had been struck, given the increased wind. She'd have done the same on the *Diana*.

"How can I help?" she asked.

Donal's brows lifted. "I'd not have expected a fancy captain of the Queen's Own to assist the rabble."

"I already agreed to assist you," she pointed out, "in exchange for a bath and freedom. If we don't make it through the weather, I won't be able to collect."

"Death is a cold bastard," he agreed. Then he opened his mouth to make a suggestion, when a *crack* issued across the sky.

Lightning and Doucette were the first things she considered—and then she looked up. One of the ropes of the fore-topgallant—the highest sail on the forward mast—had snapped. The sail was flapping, and the poor bastard who'd been on the yard was twisted in rope and hanging by an ankle. While two more sailors rushed to help him, the sail flapped uselessly despite the increasing rain.

Instincts firing, she'd started to run forward when Donal grabbed her arm. She looked back, eyes narrowed against the action and the falling rain.

"Don't do anything stupid," he said, but there was fear in his eyes. "A man's luck doesn't always hold."

She wasn't sure if he meant her luck, his, or the sailor's on the yard. But what little respect she had for the man diminished. She wrenched her arm loose.

"Your sailors are caring for the man," she said. "I'm for the sail. The yard is down, but it needs to be furled. We don't need any more canvas aloft in wind like this. Do you have staysails or storm sails?"

"I don't know."

She stared at him. *How didn't he know?* "Have someone check. We need at least one hanging if you want to keep the ship upright."

Donal gave an order, sent a sailor to a storage area.

"Have your men on the lines for the topsail," she told him. Before he could argue, she strode forward, slipping past the few sailors on deck to reef the sails still hanging from the masts. She passed Grant, but he didn't seem to notice, likely because she still had her hood up. At least he couldn't also give her a lecture about danger.

"For gods' sake," she murmured, shielding her eyes to get a look at the foremast before climbing up. "A sailor's going to face dangers. That's the damned point." Satisfied she knew the proper holds, she began to climb. She reached the yard where the sailor had nearly been righted, one leg still hanging at a bad angle, still caught in the line, but his torso was upon the yard.

"Do you need help?" she called out. If the two sailors who turned to her—one man and one woman—were surprised to see her, they didn't show it. And their eyes were reassuringly steady. Sailors, Kit thought with relief. Real and true sailors.

"No!" the woman called out. "We've got Fredrick, but we need to secure the sail."

Kit nodded, looked up again, and kept climbing.

The *Phoenix* hit a trough, sending the ship and the mast tipping toward port, and she gripped the mast with arms and legs to keep from falling into the drink. After a moment, and a promise to offer a gold coin when she returned to the deck, the *Phoenix* righted again.

"*Dastes,*" she said, swallowed down the fear, and kept climbing. She reached the yard and the flapping canvas, found a lone sailor on the port side, eyes wide and arms clenched around wood.

A greenhorn, she thought, and not without sympathy.

"What's your name?" she called out.

He looked at her blankly. "What?"

"Your name, sailor." She used her most captainly tone, as they didn't have time for squabbles about authority.

"Blakely, sir."

He couldn't have been more than fifteen. But she'd seen

sailors younger than him on the mast. "Blakely, you're to do exactly as I tell you, yes?"

He swallowed hard, nodded.

"Good man." She made herself smile. "Shit duty, isn't it? Being on the mast in weather like this."

"It's not what I expected."

Life rarely was, she thought. She tested the footrope, found it solid, and moved out. And then began to give the orders.

It took twice as long as it ought have, and she wasn't sure she'd ever been so soaked through, but once the man was free, and with the help of sailors on the lines below, she and Blakely managed to get the topgallant furled.

She jumped down to the deck, stayed crouched for a moment, so relieved was she to feel something flat and solid beneath her feet.

She rose again to find Grant standing in front of her. He'd no jacket, and he was soaked to the bone, which left very little of his body to the imagination—which a few of the sailors nearby had clearly noticed.

She tried not to recall that she needed no imagination for that.

"What the hell were you doing up there?"

She was tired and sad and sick to death of being questioned. Did no one trust her or her instincts, honed after so many years at sea?

"I was doing what needed to be done, as I always do. And you've made clear that's no business of yours."

He let her go but was swearing as he walked away. He could

curse at her as long as he wished; the words would have as little effect on her obligations as they did on the storm itself.

The ship dipped into a wave again; the bow struck the wall of water, sending a surge across the bow. Grant grabbed Kit by the waist, pulled them both against the mast, held tight, as water—achingly cold—poured over them. His body was rigid behind hers, his arms banded like steel around the mast. Kit could hardly breathe but knew well the force of water, and the likelihood it would have swept her overboard. He'd done her a service.

The bow of the ship rose again, the water washing down the deck and through the scuppers. And yet he remained for a long moment . . . until he finally stepped back, cold air filling the space between them.

She glanced back, found his gaze on hers. "Thank you," she managed.

He said nothing, but turned away.

Lightning flashed, illuminating the world—and Kit realized that their sadness, and Donal's weaknesses as a sailor, were not their only concern.

They'd been sailing along the coast, farther in than they might have, in order, Kit presumed, to avoid the blockade. But the wind had pushed them closer—and was still pushing. And the cliffs of what Kit guessed was the Alemanian coast—hard and jagged and eroded by wind and water into daggers of stone—were entirely too close.

"Damn," she muttered, and ran back through the ship to the helm, Grant at her heels. Donal and Jean were both at the wheel now, struggling to keep the ship on course. They had, at least, managed to get the staysail sheeted home.

"We have to get away from the cliffs!" she called out, the

wind louder now, and whistling through the jagged, pitted rocks like a *bean sí* of the old world.

A sailor ran toward them. "Sir, there's a foot of water in the hold. We're pumping, but it's getting deeper."

Donal cursed in the Western language; Kit thought it sounded rather like music but assumed the words were different enough. "I knew I shouldn't have taken this boat last week."

Kit went absolutely still, and the rising anger was like a welcome fire. "*Last week?* What do you mean, *last week?*"

"It's a very long tale," Donal said, and swung the wheel toward starboard. "Suffice it to say, its previous captain owed me a debt and I collected. It just happens he was . . . unaware of the collection."

"You're sailing a massive ship you hardly know, without enough crew, to smuggle goods to Frisia during a bloody war?"

"This is when you tell him to walk into the sea," Grant murmured behind her.

They were saved from her outburst—or Donal's—when a horrid grinding sound echoed from somewhere below, along with the groaning of wood pushed past its limits.

They might not actually survive this, Kit thought, and that just made her furious.

Donal made to leave the helm, when Kit stepped in front of him. "Where are you going?"

"To check what that was!"

"*Vas tiva es?*" she muttered in the old language. Roughly translated, it asked, "What have the gods done now?" It was the quintessential question of a sailor in a very tight spot.

"You'll stay on the damned helm and in control of this ship," she said, then pointed to Jean. "Check the hold. If anyone's working with the cargo, take them with you to assist with the pumping, and have the carpenter work on repairing whatever that was, at least to get us through the night."

Jean looked relieved by the order—by the direction—but still looked at Donal for confirmation.

"Go," he said, and struggled to hold the wheel by himself.

"You," Kit said, pointing at another sailor. "Help your captain with the wheel."

"And what are you going to do?" Donal asked. Apparently acknowledging their survival was at stake, there was no more petulance in his voice.

She breathed out through pursed lips. "I'm going to touch the current. And you'll do exactly as I say."

He nodded. "And it won't hurt my crew? Or the ship?"

"Using me was your idea," she reminded him. "The deal you requested."

He swore, pushed wet hair from his eyes. "Fine." She could see his temper flare again, but he controlled it. "What's the worst that could happen?"

"I might drive the ship into the rocks. Apurpose."

A rather stunned silence followed that statement. And she was amused, probably more than she should have been, at the fact that she'd managed to stun a pirate king.

"But I probably won't," she said, then looked at Grant. "I can give us speed; I'll need you to be my eyes again."

He looked back at the cliffs, visible now without the shocks of lightning. "Stay away from those."

"That's very helpful. Do more of that." She looked at Donal. "You'll want to hold on."

His expression was defiant.

"They all make that mistake the first time," she murmured, and closed her eyes, reached down through the many layers of wood and tar—and silk and wine—to the water below. The water was shallow, the current deep and vibrant, as if energized by the action of wave on rock. She felt no hiccup signaling Doucette's magic, and the Forstadt gaps were nearly gone now. The current had nearly healed, which was a substantial relief.

"Northwest," Grant said, body close but not touching. She wasn't actually sure what would happen if she was touching someone else while she touched the current, and didn't much want to find out. "We need to go hard northwest."

She nodded, eyes still closed, and followed the current as it arced through the surf, then cut sharply out and into the waves. The wind was against them again, but as she'd seen on the way to Portsea, that could be managed with care.

"Trim the braces," she said, as there were still sails flying despite her warning. But she could use that, and worked the angles in her head, hoping Donal was listening. "As if heaving to."

He made no comment, but there were footsteps around her, calls to man the lines. "Nearly ready," she said, as she felt the ship shudder as the yards were rotated, repositioning the canvas at an angle.

"Ready," she said, and touched the current beyond the shoals, where it turned straight for the Isles. She nearly gasped at the flow of power, its flavor somehow different along this stretch of coast, and let it envelop her and the ship. She kept her inner sight trained on the current, even as she braced her legs against another rise and fall of ship on wave.

They would be an arrow, she thought, coursing straight and true, and she let the power go. The lambent energy that she'd stored pushed the ship forward with a jolt. She opened her eyes just in time to see Donal hit the deck on his knees.

"Well," Grant said, watching him fall. "That actually makes me feel better about doing that my first time."

It took a moment for current and inertia to meet, to fight, and then the *Phoenix* was gliding through the water. The ride was no more smooth here—the ship was pushing through waves that struck the bow, water thundering across the deck. But they were moving away from shoreline and shoal, just as she'd intended.

Hands still on the wheel, Donal climbed to his feet again. Sailors moved forward, surrounding Kit and Grant. And all amusement was gone as they stared down Kit with shock and awe and not a small amount of fear.

Most wouldn't have felt the touch of current before, and that Kit had positioned them toward safety wasn't enough to overcome their ingrained suspicion of the activity.

Grant shifted closer.

"Feeling protective?" she murmured.

"Merely positioning myself to throw you in front if they attack."

"Very chivalrous."

They watched Donal watch her, unsure if their captain meant to upbraid or attack. Then he looked up at the canvas, full and taut against the wind, and slipped through the sailors to the port side. He looked into the water, then he turned back to look at Kit.

"Bloody hell," he said with a widening smile. "That's brilliant."

# NINETEEN

A s the other sailors eased back, Donal strode toward her, eyes bright as emeralds. "How did you do it?"

"I touched the current."

"'Touched'?" he asked, shaking his head. "What does that mean?"

"It means I don't manipulate the power. I only . . . step into it, and bring the ship with me." And use your precious barquentine like an arrow, Kit thought, but was wise enough to keep that to herself.

"This is how the *Diana* moves so quickly."

"The *Diana* is a solid ship with an excellent crew. That's why she's fast."

"Mm-hmm," Donal said noncommittally. "And my goals have now changed. You need to become a privateer."

Grant's snort was neither delicate nor subtle. "Good luck with that."

"Meaning?" Kit asked.

"Meaning she isn't one to break rules." Grant looked at her through slitted eyes. "Even the ridiculous ones."

"I'm a sailor," she protested. "I've broken my share of rules. But becoming a privateer won't be one of them."

⁓

The storm eventually fell to rain, then to mist, and the seas fell with it. Donal kept insisting she should change her livelihood, so Kit disappeared below, moving through the hold for a few moments of dark and quiet—although the scurry of rats told her she wasn't entirely alone.

She considered, for just a moment, trying to "borrow her rest," as the Portsea physick had suggested. Taking just a bit of the current to buoy her own strength. But it was a dangerous enough idea at the best of times, much less when she was on a strange ship and . . . *emotionally compromised* seemed the best way to put it.

By the time the bell was rung for dinner, Kit was famished. A sailor passed along that Donal had invited them to join him in his personal dining room, the same place they'd eaten the night of their arrival.

Two cooks came into the room and distributed the meals, beginning with Donal, of course. A silver dish was placed in front of her, loaded with small round potatoes and an enormous wedge of roasted bird with crackling brown skin. It wasn't the same meat they'd had last night, but it smelled better. Rather amazing, actually.

Kit sighed lustily and felt Grant's gaze on her.

"How has an Islish woman never had a roasted bird?"

"I've had roasted bird," Kit said. "Cook makes a fine one, but there's been none on this trip. And at home, we have Mrs. Eaves. The only fowl served at Brightling House is slightly gray and a bit rubbery. I think she boils it."

"I suppose she also refused you sugar? Little wonder you're obsessed with pistachio nougats."

*Obsession*, she thought, was a strong word. But she didn't think it worth the argument given the amazing smells rising from her platter. When all were served and Donal had given a nod, Kit plucked fork and knife and carefully split through the bird, took a bite. And closed her eyes.

"It appears," she said after a moment, "that Mrs. Eaves tosses the good bits to the cats."

When their plates were clean, Donal offered port. While she was no friend of Donal's, she wouldn't say no to wine. Grant's expression said he felt similarly. Donal selected a bottle from a stash in a cupboard, brought it to the table. The room was warm, Kit's belly full, and the sea gently rolling following its earlier tantrum.

"Your woman has great moxie," Donal said, handing a glass to Kit.

The look Grant gave Kit was heavy with meaning, and she had to force herself not to look away. "She's not my woman," he said mildly.

"And she doesn't enjoy being spoken about as if she's not in the room," Kit said, and sipped. The port was delicious, probably smuggled from some wee Gallic village. "Why don't you go home?" she asked him.

Donal took a seat, looked at her as he swirled the liquid in his glass. "Because there's nothing that awaits me there."

296 | CHLOE NEILL

"No estate?" Kit asked, and gestured at Grant. "This one has three."

"Money was never the issue," Donal said. "Responsibility was."

"Do you know the Duke of Raleigh?" They were two of a pair; and based on the current census, the Isles had a significant problem with recalcitrant aristocrats.

"The gambler?" Donal asked. "Only by reputation."

Kit snorted. "He's not nearly as much of a reprobate as you might imagine."

"Oh? You and the duke are friends, aye?" He was looking at Grant, but Kit knew the question was intended for her—and the irritation for both of them.

"No," Kit said. "I hardly know him. But I'm told his reputation is at least moderately exaggerated. And while we're discussing notorious men, what do you know of Alain Doucette?"

He went still at the name, as if the words themselves were a curse that might damn all of them.

"I know he's alive," Donal said, "because he somehow crawled out of the hell he created in Hispania."

Kit recognized the conviction in his voice, because she and Grant had shared it. "You fought in the Continental War," she guessed.

There was another hint of his identity. Not that it mattered; she wouldn't use his name against him. But the more she knew, the better she could predict his behaviors. And the sooner she could get herself and Grant off this damned ship.

Donal's expression shuttered, as if his eyes alone might give away his secrets.

"I was at Contra Costa." They looked at Grant. He stood

against the wall, arms crossed and glass in one hand, gazing through the window toward the moon-tipped sea. Candlelight shifted beautifully across his face, as if sketching a poem there. "And I've faced him on the sea."

Donal made the connection. "Doucette was at Auevilla."

Kit nodded. "His magic called the dragon swarm."

"So he was the reason you were in the drink."

"One of the reasons," Kit said. She swallowed hard against the lurching fear, and the desire to look at Grant, to have that comfort. She didn't want to share that intimacy here, or that vulnerability. Their linked fingers . . .

"I've fought him before" was all Donal would admit.

"At sea?" Kit asked.

"On the peninsula. Why do you ask about him?"

Kit took a moment to consider what information she could trust Donal with. And went with her instinct, which said Doucette was their common enemy. "Because he is, excepting Gerard, the most dangerous man to the Isles right now. His Alignment is stronger than anything I've seen, and he'll use his gift to Gerard's benefit, regardless of the cost." She told him what they'd seen at Auevilla, in and out of the water. "Every allied sailor and soldier is in danger until he's dead or captured."

"He was near Sarnia."

Sarnia was a small island just off the Gallic peninsula near Octeville.

"Was?" Kit asked. "How long ago?"

"Two days ago? Three?"

*While we were on the island,* Kit thought, damning the time already wasted.

"We didn't see him directly," Donal said. "We stopped to

visit with some old and beloved friends." Smuggling, she presumed, from the smile on his face. "Our . . . friends had been onshore and had seen him in town. He made a show of demonstrating his skills against a prisoner being held there."

Just as in Auevilla, Kit thought. Small bites to satisfy bloodlust, or a useful way to frighten coastal villages into supporting Gerard?

"Were there troops in Sarnia?" Grant asked. "Ships? Fortifications?"

"None that were mentioned to me. And I think they would have been. We may not be uniformed, but we care when cannons might be hurled in our direction from a coastal fort. I've another crew member who may have more information." He looked at the footman who waited by the door, nodded. Apparently understanding the cue, he slipped into the corridor.

Barely a minute had passed before a young man joined them. He couldn't have been more than seventeen and still bore the awkwardness of a boy. He pulled off his hat, nodded at Donal.

"Sir," he said, with a slight Gallic accent.

"Mr. Ernault," Donal introduced him. "Captain Brightling here would like to know about La Boucher."

The boy's eyes went hard as obsidian, and all sense of young innocence dropped away. She'd seen similar transformations before—usually in children forced into adult responsibilities before their time. Her youngest sister, Louisa, was one of them. She'd joined the family only a few months ago after stowing away on the *Diana*. While still a child, there was gravity in her eyes.

"He is a son of a bitch," the boy said. Much to Kit's surprise, Donal reached out, put a hand on the boy's shoulder, squeezed.

"Correct," Donal said. "Captain Brightling is attempting to

locate him," he added, apparently having guessed Kit's motivation. "Tell us what you know."

"I know he is a son of a bitch," the boy said again. "I was born near there, watched the village burn. Lost four members of my family in the fire."

"I'm very sorry," Kit said.

The boy nodded, worked to firm up his chin.

"I've been told he healed from his injuries somewhere else."

"In Tolosa," he said. "A village perhaps a day's walk away."

Kit frowned. "Did he have friends there? Family?"

"No," Ernault said. "Those who remained alive in Contra Costa refused to help him. Ignored his demands for help. They knew what he had done, had heard the screams. They had pulled their own children and sisters and brothers from the fire."

Kit glanced at Grant, just to assure herself that he was managing in the face of such details. He looked a bit pale, but his eyes were sharp. He glanced at her, inclined his head slightly, confirming he was managing. She felt a wave of relief. At least he hadn't shut her out there.

She looked back at Ernault. "When did he leave Tolosa?" She didn't know what tracing his movements would do, what that might tell her. But it seemed important to ask.

"He did not leave. He was taken."

"Taken," Grant said. "By whom?"

"Officers," Ernault said. "All in fine dress, or so the story goes. A year ago, perhaps?"

"A year ago," Kit murmured, eyes downcast as she considered. "After Gerard was imprisoned."

"Perhaps when plans were being made," Donal said.

"He's been back to Contra Costa."

Kit looked back at Ernault. "What?"

"I have received letters from my family; he has been seen in Contra Costa within the last several months." His tone was fury bridled by leather gone thin and worn. "At least twice, both near the—the spot where the fire occurred."

"Why?" Kit finally asked.

"I do not know. I would say he has perhaps offered his regrets to those killed. But I do not think he is that kind of man."

"No," Kit said. "I don't, either." She thought of the prisoners at Auevilla, what they'd heard of Doucette's exploits. "They say he has been searching for something related to his magic. Do you know what that might be?"

The boy shook his head.

Donal looked at Kit, who nodded. They'd done what they could here.

"Thank you, Ernault," she said, and offered her hand. "Your information is greatly appreciated."

The boy stared at her for a moment, then her hand, before finally gripping hers, shaking. Then looked at his captain for orders.

"You're dismissed," Donal said. "Thank you."

She needed to think. And to think, she needed to move. "I'm going to get some air," she said, rising, and held up a hand to keep them in their seats. Then she left them before either could volunteer to accompany her.

❧

She made her way to the deck, nodding at the sailors she passed. The wind was cold and bracing, and steady enough that the sails were reefed. The sailors on watch talked quietly at their stations as they waited for conditions to change, a ship to be spotted, or an order to loose the sails or take them in.

A brilliant crimson sunset gave way to indigo and stars, a billion pinpricks in the dark blanket of the sky. Shooting stars pulsed overhead with glittering trails, which looked, Kit thought, like castoffs from the current—bright and powerful, if only temporary.

She crossed to a quiet bit of gunwale near the mainmast, looked out toward the Northern Sea. The sky was clear, the moon nearly full, only a sliver gone from its silvered edge. Its light rode upon the inky water like it had been painted there, and each wave sent it scattering again.

"Return to the sea," Hetta had once told her. "Always return to the water."

And so she had, time and again, until the tightness in her chest was gone and she could breathe again. Not as good as simply tossing her troubles overboard like so many notes in bottles, but at least it might help her deal with them. She hoped it would help clear her mind. Or, as silly as it sounded, her heart.

This time, it didn't work. She was still conflicted, still frustrated, wanting so badly to be off this damned ship. Sailing, she understood well, wasn't made for an impatient soul, and sailors didn't always have a chance to fly across the water.

So she paced from one end of the ship and back again. And when she returned to the gunwale, she found Grant smiling at her, eyes bright and dark hair falling over his forehead. Kit had no doubt he knew exactly how attractive he was, exactly how good he looked.

"What?" she asked.

"You're pacing again. You appear to be . . . frustrated."

"I'm not *frustrated*," she threw back, and could hear the petulance in her voice. "I'm perturbed about being on this ship and wondering where Doucette is and worrying about my crew."

"Perhaps perturbed," he said, unfazed, "but it's got nothing to do with this ship, love." With an arrogant smile, he turned, walked toward the companionway.

"Into the sea, Grant," she muttered. "You can walk right into the sea."

"I could," she heard him say. "But you'd swim after me."

# TWENTY

The next day, the third of their unintentional voyage on the damned *Phoenix*, the fog was thick as milk tea, and almost the same color. And it drove Kit very nearly mad.

Sailors may have feared fire, but they loathed fog. It took their control, their visibility, their foresight. Many a ship had misjudged a coastline or failed to see an enemy until it was too late, and timbers were dashed by rock or shot.

There was a little wind, but it did nothing to ease the miasma, and they'd furled the sails as a precaution against yesterday's troubles. Otherwise, there was nothing to do but wait.

Kit stood at the gunwale, peering into the fog as if the narrowing of her eyes might be enough to disperse it and give them a clear view of their surroundings.

Grant joined her.

"I feel like we're being watched," Kit said without prelude.

He looked at her for a moment, then nodded. "All right," he said. "Where?"

His unwavering confidence in her was another little twist in her heart.

"Port bow," she said. "I thought I saw something, and then I thought I heard something. And then I wondered if I was merely seeing small creatures."

He snorted. "I'm still fairly certain that's nonsense. But where ships are concerned, I trust you implicitly."

He stood by her in silence, and she thought it might be the first time they'd done so without squabbling since they'd stepped foot on this ship. Would that he'd never made that proposal.

"There," she said, the word a whisper, at the flash of light.

"I saw it," Grant said.

He followed her back to Donal, who leaned against the railing that overlooked the quarterdeck. "There's a ship off the port bow," she said.

He stood up straight. "Origin?"

"I've no idea. I only saw the light."

Bells began to ring, a cacophony of sound.

"Report!" Donal yelled out, as sailors rushed to and from positions on the deck.

"Frisian ship off the port bow!" someone called out. "Fully rigged and headed toward us."

At least three masts, Kit translated, each of them bearing columns of square sails.

"As I said," Kit murmured, but Donal's face had gone hard.

"You're certain it's Frisian?" he asked the sailor who came running toward him.

"Aye, sir. It's not a blockade ship, but one of the Frisians. And it's a big ship, sir."

He swore. "Prepare the cannons, have the weapons at the ready."

"Aye." As the sailor saluted and ran back to give the order, Donal immediately turned for the companionway that led below.

Kit followed him back to his quarters. "Why are we preparing to fire? You've seen what I can do. I can get the *Phoenix* out of range."

"First, because I'm a pirate. We rather like firing on ships. And second, because we have no choice."

Kit looked back at him. "Why? Why is there no choice?"

He belted on a sabre with a complicated basket hilt and stuck a pistol into his belt. "Because we're wanted in Frisia."

Kit could all but feel her blood boil. "You asked me to help you run an Isles blockade to smuggle goods into Frisia, where you're also wanted?"

Donal grinned. "I didn't say it would be easy, did I? And remember—if I hadn't come for you and your viscount, you'd still be sleeping in the sand and praying for fish."

"You're despicable."

He looked back at her, fire in his eyes. This, Kit thought, was the pirate—arrogant, violent, and determined to have his way, and damn anyone in the way.

"I am," he agreed, leaning close. "And don't forget that."

She waited until he was gone before staring daggers at his back. She'd have thrown one if she'd had one handy. She could forgive many sins, but not dishonor.

"He's on deck?"

Grant stepped into the doorway with his vast overabundance of honor.

"Yes," she said. "Just." She pushed her hair behind her ears.

"What has he done?"

"He's wanted in Frisia."

He closed his eyes for a moment, muttered a curse. "Is there a bounty?"

"I don't know. But that's why he wants to engage them." She stalked to one end of the room and then back again. She might as well pace her way across the damned Northern Sea, she thought.

"Well," Grant said, "that and the piracy."

Kit growled. "Running from an Isles ship is one thing—there's no harm there. It's not entirely honest, but giving over wine and silk to the Isles isn't going to help our position in the war. But engaging Frisia? Even assuming they don't have magic, and this ship and her crew are skilled enough, it's still death. Still destruction. And we could avoid it completely!"

"And it's beyond your agreement with him."

"It bloody well is," she said.

Grant moved inside the room, closed the door. Brows lifted, Kit watched as he walked closer, and pushed back against the desire that would only scorch them both.

"So what's next?" Grant asked. "They've broken the agreement, so we break ours?"

"And, what, just swim to shore?"

"You're Aligned, Kit." He moved a step closer. "You're learning more every day what that means, and what it will allow you to do. You are the captain of any ship you board."

She just looked at him. He met her gaze squarely, a dare in his eyes.

"I should return to the deck," she said, and pushed past him to the corridor. And felt like a coward for doing it.

She found them preparing muskets and cannons on deck. And when she saw Donal grinning with amusement, she realized he was no longer angry at the possibility of being caught or boarded—but entertained by the possibility of obtaining a Frisian ship as a prize.

"Bloody damned pirates," she muttered.

"Chin up, Captain," Grant said, and strode past her to the helm. "You're going to engage the Frisians?" he asked Donal curtly.

"Of course we are," Donal said, then looked up at him. "Are you going to help us or hinder us?"

"These wouldn't be the first Frisians I've killed. But I see no point in engaging the ship. Why take the risk?"

"Because risk is rather the point."

They could hear it now, the sounds of the ship growing closer—sailors yelling in Frisian as sails were shifted, sheeted home. The fog shifted as the wind picked up, revealing small images of hull and canvas. Even from those morsels, it was clear she was a very, very big ship.

"Straight ahead!" someone on the *Phoenix* shouted. "Hard to starboard!"

The *Phoenix* heeled as she was turned, and barely missed striking the Frisian vessel head-on. They skimmed past each other, barely ten yards between them. The Frisians were in uniform—green and tan—and loading cannons as the *Phoenix* worked to put space between the ships.

"Incoming!" came the answering call from the *Phoenix* as the explosion struck the air.

Kit closed her eyes and touched the current just enough to have the cannonball hit the water past the *Phoenix*'s stern.

"A miss!" a *Phoenix* sailor called out. "They missed us!"

"You're cheating," Donal told her, then went to the cannons on the quarterdeck to check the preparations.

"I feel very dishonorable," Kit said dryly, as the *Phoenix* ran ahead, buoyed by the wind at her back, while the Frisian ship struggled to tack.

"Deservedly so," Grant said, just as facetiously. "What with keeping that shot from tearing across their bow."

"Bring her around!" Donal said. "I want a shot at them!"

She didn't speak Frisian, but she imagined the cracking commands from their ship's captain amounted to much the same.

The remnants of the fog dissipated as they came round again, prepared for a volley of shots as the ships passed each other once more.

"I revise my prior comment," Grant said. "Sailing isn't merely standing at an angle, but circling around and around."

"Right as always, my lord."

He snorted at the title.

"*Ready!*" Donal called out, and Kit touched the current.

"If you would," she said to Grant quietly, eyes closed.

"*Aim!*"

"Nearly there," Grant said.

"*Fire!*"

"Now, perhaps," Grant said mildly, as dual explosions concussed the air.

Kit released her touch, and the *Phoenix* flew forward. The Frisian ship's shot missed completely. Because of its new momentum, the *Phoenix*'s shot only skimmed the Frisian ship's stern, throwing splinters off the gunwale.

Donal rose from his crouch on the quarterdeck, looked back at her with a glower.

"I believe you've made him cross," Grant said.

"New ship!"

Kit looked to the sea. Having a bit of fun with Frisians and someone else's ship—and keeping them out of harm's way in the process—was one thing. But staring down two was a different matter.

Donal used the spyglass someone offered him, then turned to the helm, glowered at Kit. He took the stairs at a run, stared her down. "You reneged on your bargain. You've led us to an Isles warship."

"What? I've done no such thing. I've 'led' you nowhere and, if you'll recall, I saved your bloody boat in a storm. I also offered to get you past the damned Frisian ship."

Donal just made a noise of disgust. "And right into the arms of the blockade."

"Insult her honor again," Grant said, "and I imagine she'll skewer you through. And I might take a shot when she's done."

Grant's voice was hard as granite.

"If she led us—"

"*She wouldn't*," Grant said, in an aristocratic tone that allowed no defense, no argument. "I suspect you know better by now."

"See for yourself," Donal said, and thrust the looking glass at her.

Kit peered through the glass. Then put it down, blinked,

raised it again. And grinned wildly. "It's not the blockade. It's the *Diana*!"

The Frisian ship didn't much care; the sight of the Isles' flag was apparently enough, as it immediately trimmed the sails and turned back toward Frisia.

"Why are all my sailors wearing blue caps?" she asked, lowering the glass a final time. "No matter. We need to signal them." She glanced at Grant. "How's your semaphore?"

He grinned back at her. "Exceedingly nonexistent."

"Then this will be very entertaining."

They either signaled "Kit aboard" or "angry cat." Either, she figured, would be enough to get Jin's attention, and was. The *Diana* streamed toward them, and Kit could hear the shouts of excitement from the crew.

Donal, for his part, glowered. "We haven't made it to Frisia."

"No, we haven't. But given you reneged on your bargain, I have no need to stay." She looked at him. "Come with us. You could help us fight Gerard in this very formidable ship."

"We cannot," he said. "We don't all have the luxury of reaching for what we desire, Kit."

If he thought she had that luxury, he was sorely mistaken, and she had to work not to look at Grant. But that was no matter. So she looked at Jean.

"No," Jean said with a mirthless smile. "That life is not for me."

"So you'd rather be under the thumb of Gerard and Frisia?" She knew that was hardly the truth, but also knew Jean needed to keep up the appearance of being Donal's sailor.

"I'm under no man's thumb," she said. "I make my own decisions, and lining up a ship so we can have our turn at the cannons shall not be one of them."

"Seconded," Donal said, "to the extent I'm allowed to have a say in the running of my own damn ship."

"Apologies, Captain," Jean said, but with no contrition in her voice.

"In that case, we'll take our leave."

"Shall we lower a boat?" Donal asked dryly, with obviously no intention to do so.

"No," Kit said, glancing up at the *Phoenix*'s rigging. "We'll go the fun way. *On the line!*" she called out, then jumped onto the gunwale—four inches of railing—and loosed one of the mainmast lines.

She grabbed it with both hands, pushed off, and swung over the ten-foot breach across the roiling water below.

Sampson waited on the other side and extended a hand to her. Kit grabbed it, caught her balance on the *Diana*'s gunwale, and glanced back at Grant.

"Be ready!" she told him, and shoved the rope back.

She could hear him cursing across the gap and bit back a smile. He was owed a bit of frustration, she thought.

She jumped down to the deck to give Grant room, then turned back to Sampson, found his grin was fierce, his hand still clenched around hers. She half expected him to pump it in a hearty shake. "Welcome back, Captain."

"Thank you, Sampson. It's good to be home." She heard the whoosh of air as Grant flew out behind her, but before she could turn was ensconced by her commander.

"It's good to see you again," Jin said, arms like steel bands around her.

"You'll see me collapse in a moment if you squeeze any harder."

He let her go, and this time did shake her hand. The traditions of the Isles were difficult to break. "Thank all the gods. Do you have any idea how much damnable paperwork I've had to do?"

"Of course that's the only reason I was missed."

"And your tea is better than ours," Cooper said helpfully. "Welcome back, Captain."

"Thank you," Kit said.

Simon stepped forward, a clean uniform jacket folded neatly over one arm. "Captain," he said, and extended his arm.

The sun was warm, and she didn't especially need the coat for warmth, and knew it would look strange over the clothes she'd borrowed from Jean-Baptiste. But she needed the coat for comfort and for authority, so she transferred the ribbon from one to the other, pulled it on, and immediately felt more like herself.

"What should we do with them?" he asked.

Kit looked at Grant, got his nod. "Let them go. They have their own business to attend to. And they did save our lives." Perhaps through extortion, Kit thought, but few privateers would have stopped.

She turned to Jin. "Perhaps the most important question, other than how you came to be here, is why everyone is wearing a cap."

"Tamlin has taken up knitting."

She looked at Tamlin. "You've taken up knitting." She repeated the words as if they made no sense to her, because they made no sense to her.

"My mother had shipped a bit of wool and needles. She has

concerns about my domestic skills. I took them into the tops with me; I don't have to look while I do it."

"There are just . . . so many," Kit said.

"I was nervous while you were gone." Tamlin looked at Jin with warmth. "You made a very good captain. But you're not really *the* captain."

"I understand," Jin said kindly.

Now that she was closer, she could see some of the caps slumped a bit, and others were a bit lopsided. But no sailor had taken them off, and a few looked as if they'd seen some things between their making and Kit's return.

"And how did you come to be here?" Kit asked.

"We've been searching for you since you left. Tamlin sensed a bit of your magic near the Alemanian coast, and we've been following it."

"There was a very large storm," Kit said. "And a very handsome captain who wasn't aware if his vessel carried staysails."

Jin cocked his head. "Are we certain it was his vessel?"

"It was *recently* his vessel," Kit said. "Very stolen. What about you? The battle?"

"No casualties," Jin said, "and the burn injuries are healing nicely, thanks to March." He grimaced. "Well, we don't know about the dragon."

"The dragon was fine," Kit said. "We freed it beneath the water, washed up on one of the channel islands. Then we were rescued by the pirate king. And how was your week?"

"We helped push back the Gallic ships, ensured the rest of the troops were taken safely to Auevilla, although what good they'll do now we don't know."

"Does he intend to fight the war fully at sea?" Kit asked.

"Yet to be determined," Jin said. "At least partially at sea. Although they'll find that more difficult with three lost ships."

"Good," Kit said. "We heard Doucette survived."

"He did," Jin said, "and we've a new assignment."

"Oh?" Kit said, and had a feeling she knew what it was.

"Find Alain Doucette, and bring him in. Whether he's breathing at the time is entirely up to us."

❧

They met in the officers' mess. Simon spread a map across the table that showed the position of major Isles activity and the available information regarding Doucette's locations.

"Now that you've finished your run of piracy," Simon said, adjusting his glasses and giving her a warm smile, which she'd truly missed, "we can move back to the business of war."

"Technically, it was privateering," she said.

"It's all at the expense of the common man," Cook called out from the kitchen.

Gods, but she'd missed her ship. Even the irritating bits.

"His last known location," Jin said, ignoring the outburst as they all did and pointing to a spot in the Bay of Vizcaya, the curve of water nestled between the rounded coasts of Gallia and Hispania. "Known," he continued, "because he sunk a frigate."

"Bloody bastard," Kit said. "Which?"

"The *Formidable*. Forty-two hands lost. Eighty-four survivors."

"Captain Thornton?" Kit asked.

"Below now, with the ship."

"*Tiva koss*," she murmured, the phrase repeated around the table.

"Donal said he'd been spotted in Sarnia." She traced a finger between Auevilla, Sarnia, and the bay, along the other two locations where he'd been sighted. "He's sailing south along the coast."

"Yes," Jin said.

Kit looked at Grant, who met her gaze, nodded. "I think he's going back to Contra Costa."

"It was his greatest victory," Grant said, and they all looked at him. "He managed something no man has ever done before, and he survived it. Perhaps he wishes to revisit that moment."

Kit nodded. "That may play a part. But I think it may be even simpler. When I'm in the water, the magic is . . . it—it's *welcoming*," she settled on, thinking it was difficult to describe this without sounding addled. "It gives a sense of peace, of comfort. Of home.

"Doucette does not appear to be a happy man," she continued. "He was not helped by others after his injuries at Contra Costa. He was taken back into Gerard's army by force, it appears. Perhaps he's looking for that peace, that comfort. And thinks Contra Costa—the place it all began for him—is where he'll find it. So we'll go south," she said. "And when we reach Hispania, we'll see what we find."

❧

She found, of course, ample paperwork on her small desk, along with a pretty box. Surprised, she opened it, pulled away the paper. And found nestled inside, in more paper, a necklace on a bit of thin gold chain. As Mathilda had promised, there was a bit of red coral, bits of dried greenery, and silver.

She pulled the dragon's scale from the pocket of her other coat, then sat down at her desk, used a bit of needle to press a hole into the edge. She added it to the collection and pulled it over her head.

She was moderately disappointed not to feel some shift inside her, some transition to a phase in her life in which she *understood* magic in a new way, and could wield it accordingly. It didn't feel uncomfortable, certainly. It didn't really feel like . . . anything.

"What's this?" Grant walked into her cabin—because gods forbid she have privacy on her own ship—and lifted the necklace from her uniform, used fingertips to flip through the charms.

"An amulet," she said, and felt a bit silly saying that aloud. "I'm—I'm not entirely sure what it's intended to do. Mathilda said the amulet 'would know.'"

"Hmm," he said noncommittally, and let the necklace go again. "That's the one you bought in Portsea."

It was only then she recalled they'd talked about it on the island. They'd left it only a few days ago, but it seemed like a world and a million years away. The loss of his camaraderie was potent and made her wish, not for the first time, that things were different. That *they* were different. That they could change the rules.

"Yes," she said.

She looked up at Grant, found him studying her. And saw something in his eyes she couldn't name. Something that disappeared before she could study it in return. Instead, she returned to the something she needed to ask him.

"Are you all right sailing toward Contra Costa?"

He paused for a moment. "It's not ideal. You cannot dwell on the horrors of war. Otherwise, you'd think of nothing else. But Contra Costa was . . . different. It was a surprise. The mechanism,

I mean. The devastation and death were on a scale no one had seen before. It's not a weapon, not really. But it was as if there'd been one. A terrible weapon of remarkable power. It was beautiful."

"So I've heard."

She could see in his face that he was surprised she hadn't recoiled in horror. "The blue-green fire."

Grant nodded, ran a hand through his hair. "So many images of the war were permanently recorded in my mind. And they revisit me. Not often, and rarely, unless I'm exhausted or overly concerned about something. The flames are one. The victims are the other. So, no, it is not ideal," he said again. "But needs must."

"Needs must," Kit said, and felt a stab of guilt that she'd caused, or contributed to, his concern.

"We can find you another ship," she said. "Every member of the crew would help you get aboard it, and none would judge you for the act."

His laugh was mirthless. "*I'd* judge me for the act. Even if not cowardice, it would feel remarkably akin to it."

She nodded and told Grant about the mistake she'd made before as a midshipman, when she'd nearly sunk an Isles ship.

"Did you trust your captain?" he asked.

"It was Perez," Kit said. "Of course I did."

He nodded. "She would have understood the risks, believed it was worth it, and let you proceed. There is nothing under the sky that does not carry risk, Kit. Nothing," he added, and Kit had a sense he wasn't speaking of magic any longer.

Kit walked to her windows, looked outside at the sea, glassy and calm now. "As captain, I take risks. But not all of them. I didn't try to touch the current again for another year."

"But you did try."

"I practiced on a jolly boat pulled behind whatever ship I was on."

"How many times did you end up in the drink?"

"All but the last," she said, and looked back at him. "Perhaps, if I'd done better that first time, or hadn't been so afraid of hurting someone afterward, I might have learned more techniques. I might be as advanced as Doucette. We'd have captured him in the first battle, and that chapter of the war would be closed. But I didn't, so you'll be sailing toward a place that hurts you." She looked back at him. "I'm sorry for that."

He moved toward her, reached out a hand to touch her, but dropped it again. "You owe me no apologies, Kit. Not for being true to who and what you are. As for the magic, Contra Costa scared the Isles, as it should have. But it should have driven them to do more. That's an oversight the queen is trying to remedy. But she may not have time."

*She may not have time.*

Kit sat with those words for a long, quiet time, thinking about what she could and couldn't do with magic. And what the Isles needed from her, and from every other Aligned soldier and sailor on the islands. She rubbed the dragon scale as she considered, thought of Mathilda and what teaching she'd gotten there, and thought of Doucette. She thought of the damage he might cause, and the risks they'd all have to take. Being able to use the current as a shield had worked, which was its own miracle. But that wasn't enough to capture Doucette, much less to win a war.

Because they had days of sailing yet, she settled herself with the pile of dispatches and began to leaf through them. And was nearly ecstatic when a knock sounded at the door sometime later.

She pushed the papers aside, linked her fingers on the table. "Come."

Jin opened the door, came inside, and closed the door quickly. "Why did you say no?"

Kit blinked. "I'm sorry?"

He came to the table, folded his arms, and gave her a very cross expression. "Why did you reject Grant?"

She actually felt her cheeks warm, which just ignited her anger. "I didn't reject Grant. I merely declined his offer of marriage."

After a moment of staring, Jin pulled out a chair, sat down. "Why would you have done that?"

"He spoke to you about it?"

"He was joyful when he left the ship. He was not joyful when he returned. I asked him the reason. He said you rejected him."

She wasn't comfortable with that word—*rejection*.

"What's wrong with a bit of romance without commitments?"

"What's wrong is it's simply not done."

"Women in service 'wasn't done' a generation ago," she countered. "And men have leave to court whomever they wish without the bounds of marriage. Why aren't women entitled to that option?"

"Because it's not done," Jin said again, crossing one long leg over the other. "At least, not in polite society. Men can have mistresses. Women can have . . . schnauzers."

"I don't want a schnauzer." But she thought of Sprout, Grant's little white terrier, who'd trotted after him at Grant Hall like a tiny soldier, and that made her a little sad.

"What do you want?"

"Not marriage."

His lips thinned. "Because marriage is so bad?"

"Because I'd have to change. I'd have to be someone else."

Jin just stared at her, and the pity in the look made her squirm a bit. "Have you considered the possibility that Grant accepts who and what you are?"

"He may. But the Beau Monde? The weight of societal expectations? Surely relationships have foundered under less."

"So your concern is the man—a viscount, I might add—cannot stand up for himself, or would not stand up for you?"

Put like that, it sounded . . . unreasonable.

Cook stepped into the doorway with a biscuit tin in hand. "Welcome back," he said with a sneer, dropping the tin on the table with a *thud* before turning on his heel and walking out again.

Kit lifted the tin top. Found four pale butter biscuits. Or so Kit guessed they'd been, as they were crushed into angry little pieces.

"He's angry, too?" she asked, and felt her cheeks heat. "Does anyone on the ship not know? It's been"—she checked the wall clock—"three bloody hours."

Jin snorted. "A quarter hour would have been enough time for news like this to travel. And, yes, Cook's angry, too. About Grant, and Louisa."

Kit lifted her eyes skyward, asked the old gods for patience. "I'm still not going to allow a nine-year-old girl—much less one now guarded by Hetta Brightling—to work on a warship."

Sighing, she plucked a largish crumb from the tin and crunched into it. "Would you have ever believed you'd offer me romantic advice?"

He snorted. "Yes."

"What?" There was no little insult in her voice. "You believed no such thing."

"Your interest in Kingsley, may he find no comfort in damnation, indicated you'd be amenable to a man, should the right man come along. Grant is the right man."

She made a disdainful sound, mostly because she wasn't entirely comfortable with the certainty in his tone. "Grant is a man. That's all I can agree to at present."

"Amenable," Jin continued, unperturbed, "to a man who was your equal. A man of integrity and honor and strength—to deal with your stubbornness."

"I'm hardly the more stubborn between us."

"You're proving my point."

His long, dark hair was braided at the crown today, and he absently twirled a lock of it, as he often did when he was consternated. Which wasn't terribly often. Kit guiltily realized there was more concern in his eyes than could be attributed to her romantic concerns.

She leaned forward. "What else is wrong?"

Jin sighed. "The crew is . . . uneasy."

"About me and Grant?" She put a little horror into her voice, and it had his lips curling, just as she'd intended.

"Well, that, too. He's handsome enough, they say, and probably has ample funds to keep you in pretty gowns."

"In pretty gowns. That's quite a recommendation," Kit said.

"Women have been known to enjoy gowns."

"And I'm occasionally one of those women. But it's hardly a valid basis for marriage." She waved it away. "Regardless, that's not what the crew is uneasy about."

"No," Jin said. "They're nervous about facing Doucette. They have concerns we'll be outmatched by a power that we barely understand and cannot equal. They don't question you or your abilities," he added. "But they thought they lost you at Auevilla. That type of fear is difficult to overcome."

Kit didn't like this. Didn't want her crew worrying—that was her job, her responsibility. To lead them to danger and through it, and assure them they'd survive—or would make an honorable show of it for gods and country.

She knew exactly how they felt, because she felt the same. Outmatched by Doucette's skill, and bound by rules to which he didn't subscribe—morality, honor, responsibility.

"Thank you for your honesty," she said. "It's on my mind as well."

"As to Grant," Jin said, and she scowled at him. But his smile was wide. "Do you remember the first night we stepped on board the *Diana*?"

She blinked at him. "Of course. You hated it."

"I did. I thought it was a wee bit of junk beneath you—and me, of course—and better suited to packet work. Not even a single cannon aboard. But the Crown Command was adamant it was the best ship for you, new captain that you were."

"And young, and female," Kit said, recalling the disdain of the departing captain, an older man greatly offended that his ship—which he'd hardly cared for—was being delivered into the hands of a girl. "He was insistent the *Diana* needed a man's hand on the wheel, as no woman had ever sailed her before."

"The Crown Command was right," he said, and put a hand against the hull, smoothed it lovingly. "And he was wrong. She is a good ship. If occasionally an ornery one."

"Is this tale leading to some point?"

"You and the *Diana* rose to meet each other. She is, in many ways, your match. In Grant, you've met another. And it would do you not a bit of good, Captain, to pass up that opportunity just because it's not been done before. Someone always must be first."

# TWENTY-ONE

Two days passed, and the sailing was smooth and uneventful. They passed two Islish blockade ships, made the appropriate signals. If Gerard intended to keep pushing toward the Isles, either he'd taken a break after Auevilla, or the fighting had moved farther from the Gallic coast.

On the third day, just as they passed the border between Gallia and Hispania, they found a terrible clue.

Timbers. Rigging. Bodies.

A field of debris spread over nearly a mile, and it told a miserable tale. A ship burned to the water, bearing an Islish flag. It was a trail leading toward the man who'd put them there, and the ship that had carried him to and from the atrocity. The current was another marker, still bearing the scar of whatever he'd done to cause this much fire and death so far from shore.

So they would follow these markers, and they would find Doucette and put an end to the misery he created.

For the first time, Kit touched her amulet for comfort, for

consideration, then tossed a coin into the sea. By one method or another, she'd need the gods' help.

〜

Five hours later, as the sun rose to midday, Tamlin spotted the ship. It was the same ketch in which Doucette had sailed before, albeit repaired since their last confrontation, and likely because of the stone platform they'd mounted there. It would have required extra bracing and wouldn't be easily moved from one ship to another.

"Do we need a rousing speech?" Kit asked, trying to keep the crew's mood up.

"I love a good rousing myself," Watson said with a grin. "But I don't believe they need encouraging, Captain."

Kit followed her gaze to the bow, where the eldest member of the crew, Mr. Smythe, was using Mr. Wells to explain how to slice a Gallic soldier from bow to stern.

"Mr. Smythe," she called out. "Please stop mock-fileting Mr. Wells."

"Aye, Captain," he grumbled, and let the man go, but not without obvious disappointment.

"If I had a coin for each time we asked him to be less violent," Kit said, "I'd be neck-deep in pistachio nougats."

Watson made a sound of disgust that had Kit looking over. "Problem, Lieutenant?"

"Sir, I respect you a great deal. It's just—isn't that a square of white tar with little mealy bits in it?"

Jin and Simon took large steps backward, as if putting space between combatants about to come to blows.

"If I was a lesser woman, I'd call you out."

"It's the best of all sweets," Watson said dryly. "I was plainly incorrect in my assertions otherwise."

"Apology accepted," she said. "And best you call all hands, Jin."

He frowned but did so, and the sailors gathered round.

"Today, we will face down La Boucher, a man who has shown himself willing to slaughter. To kill without honor. To kill without cause. And to use whatever power he wishes to do so. Alain Doucette is called the Butcher because he is bound by no conscience. We've all seen what he can do."

"Does he outmatch us, Captain?"

The question was asked by young Mr. Wells, and she knew there were plenty of captains—including some she'd served under—who might have punished the inquiry, or become enraged by it. But Jin had already told her of their fears, and she'd rather address them head-on. So while Cooper chucked the boy on the shoulder—as was appropriate—Kit met his gaze.

"Marshal Doucette has skills that we do not understand. Yet. And we are learning each day, as our awareness and attitude shift, how to make use of the current. Without unnecessary risks," she said, trying very hard not to look at Grant. "Without harming those we purport to protect. I do not know what we will find today. But I give you my word that I will do my best to protect you from whatever he brings. And to capture him, and see him in prison, or in hell, where he belongs."

When shouts of approval rang out, she turned back to the officers at the helm.

"Watson, you'll take the helm with Mr. Pettigrew. Jin, you'll monitor the cannons. Give them as many shots as they can take."

"Aye, Captain," Jin said with a frown, "but why are you giving us these orders now?"

"Because I'm going in the water."

They went silent.

"In the water," Jin repeated, as if the words made no sense.

She slid her gaze to Grant. "Although it's been suggested I could be more use fighting from a bucket of water on deck, that's not the most practical idea in a rolling ship. I think it's time to see what else the current can do. Not by manipulation," she said, and thought of Nelson and Mathilda, "but by listening and hearing what it desires to do. What freedoms it requests, and perhaps granting it what freedom I can. I need to be in the water to try that."

"You're going to try something new," Grant said. She looked at him, nodded, and couldn't quite read what lay behind his eyes.

"*Try* being the key," she admitted. "It's important for the Isles, for the queen, for the war effort, that risks be undertaken. That attempts be made. And I need to be in the sea to do it." Not just because it would be the most efficacious method, but because she hoped she might shield her sailors—and Grant—from whatever might happen there.

There was silence for a good long minute, and the looks on her officers' faces told her they understood that terrible math.

Grant spoke first. "Aye, Captain," he said, meeting her gaze. "How can we help?"

She just stared at him.

Of all of them, she'd expected his objection to be the loudest. For him to proclaim that her plan was too dangerous, too risky. That she should stay on board, guarded by the rest of them, while they faced down danger.

He looked at her—not as a bauble to be placed in a cabinet,

to be held back and protected—but as a trusted friend and colleague. As someone he respected. As someone with whom he'd confronted demons, and would again.

Maybe it wouldn't be seclusion in Queenscliffe and warm punch at mandatory balls. Maybe it would just be . . . a partnership.

But she put that away. "Let's get ready," she said.

⤜⤏

They stayed in the ship's wake, sufficiently behind to allow cannons to be readied, and Kit to prepare her plan. She left her coat and sabre in her quarters but kept boots and dagger . . . and her amulet.

She lifted the charms, looked them over again. "You know more about this than me," she said quietly. "Any assistance you can provide would be appreciated."

But if it was intended to respond, it said nothing. And Kit began to wonder if she'd been bamboozled.

There was a knock at her cabin door, and Kit was glad she'd thought to close it before talking to inanimate objects. She opened it, found Cooper in the doorway. "We're ready above, Captain."

Kit nodded. "Thank you, Midshipman. Let's finish this."

"Honored to be part of it, sir."

Kit snorted. "Generally best to wait until *after* the battle to express your appreciation, Cooper."

"Noted, sir," Cooper said. But that didn't wipe away her grin.

On deck, they'd gathered buckets of water and had provisions in the jolly boat in the event they needed to search for Kit. But once she was off the ship, she knew she'd have to rescue herself. The sea was much too large.

"Wait until we're in range," Kit told Jin. "I'll touch the

current until his first volley of magic is done. Even he would need time to replenish after that."

"And then you swim," Jin said.

"And then I swim."

"And after that?" Jin asked.

She was still considering the details, but she knew that if she told them even that much, they'd try to dissuade her. She didn't have time for an argument, and she wanted them focused on the *Diana*, not its captain.

She reached out, squeezed his arm. "I have an objectively reasonable plan with a very high possibility of success."

His mouth narrowed to a line. "You're a very bad liar."

"Nonsense," she said. "Pishposh."

"Captain," Watson called out. "They've seen us. They're beginning maneuvers."

"All hands," Kit said. "Be fleet, be canny." She looked at each of her senior officers, then gave herself a bit of space.

She closed her eyes, reached out . . . and felt Doucette's manipulation immediately.

"Down!" she warned them, and enveloped the boat just as the current he'd cast in their direction struck. She could hear sizzling of current against current, land against sea, and felt the shake of every timber in the *Diana*'s hull. She apologized to the current, for what little good that did, for setting it against its brother. But she kept her hand on the power until she felt Doucette's diminish again.

She let the current go with a *Dastes* for its trouble, then opened her eyes, watched Mr. Smythe stamp out a spark near the bow. But that was the only obvious damage. So it was time for what came next.

Grant took her hand, squeezed it hard, but made no objection. And she could see what it cost him. "Be good," he said. "Be careful."

"Always," Kit said, and dove into the water.

The water was brilliantly clear here, and deliciously warm. The southern edges of the Narrow Sea were a wonderful change from the frigid temperatures farther north. It was also much easier to see in the water now, before it was littered with the scraps of human war—or sea dragons—and that might make her task a bit easier.

She turned toward Doucette's ship and considered her plan: If she could envelop the current around a ship, to propel it, then why not herself?

Grant had been right—life, much less war, required risk. It all depended on how much. True, she'd once cracked a dory in half when she'd given it too much current for the small vessel to bear. She was smaller than a ship, certainly. But she touched the current with some frequency now, and other than the scars—and nausea from her trip from Auevilla—it hadn't torn her apart.

She steeled her nerves and reached down for the current, leaving her eyes open given there were fewer distractions in the water—and could feel it thrumming below, its pulse slower than before Doucette had touched it. She extended her hand, let it flow around her. And as she did, she felt something warm against her chest.

She looked down, afraid she might have been shot, and found the amulet floating. But not just that—it was vibrating, as if it, too, could feel the current. The warmth wasn't uncomfortable; to the contrary, there was something rather comforting about it—like the touch of a hand. It was . . . familiar.

The amulet had the same Alignment as she did, Kit realized. She wasn't sure what luck or skill or craft had allowed Mathilda to manage that, but she didn't mind the sensation that she wasn't facing the current alone. Wasn't fighting alone.

*It would help her.* Kit wasn't sure how she knew that. But here—in the water—she was absolutely certain. So it was time to begin.

She narrowed her gaze on a spot in the water ten yards from Doucette's ship. Let the current gather, spill from the boundaries that usually contained it, and surround her in its—if she was honest, prickly—embrace.

She did not force it to move. She did not demand it follow her orders.

Just as she had with the *Diana*, she simply let it go.

And she flew. Just as she'd planned—and just like the *Diana*—she sliced through the water like an arrow, propelled by the current she'd released. If she'd been above the surface, she'd have screamed with joy. No horse could move this quickly, she bet.

But this wasn't a lark. The current's power had weight, and it pushed against her skin in every direction, as if it might collapse and run right through her. The amulet vibrated harder now, so hot, the water seemed to boil around it. She thought of the dory she'd cracked and wondered if that would have been her right now, but for the strange collection that hung about her neck.

She had questions for Mathilda. And suspected she owed the woman a large debt of gratitude.

Doucette's ship grew closer and closer still, and Kit had some concern she'd drawn too much current and it would propel her right into the oak like a human torpedo.

Kit extended her arms, grimaced at the pressure against her limbs, but managed to slow to a stop just beyond the hull of Doucette's ship.

But the current hadn't yet exhausted itself. It struck the hull, pushing the ship with enough force that Kit could feel the shudder of oak, hear the groan of it. And all that power—all that displaced water—bounced against the hull and reflected back again, sending her tumbling backward through the water, ocean and sky blending into a disoriented haze.

Her head was spinning now, her body aching from the power she'd taken on, the excess not absorbed by the amulet. Added to it, she was running out of air. Her Alignment allowed her leeway underwater, but she still had to breathe, and could feel the tightening in her lungs.

She was nearly out of time, and she'd be damned if she died alone down here.

Focus, she silently demanded, and shook her head to clear the growing fog. She righted herself again, then turned until she faced Doucette's boat.

One more shot, she promised—herself, the current, and the amulet—and knew it would be her last, and best, chance to win this battle.

She'd nearly struck Doucette's ship in the flow of the current— and the excess she'd released had struck the boat with some force. Why couldn't she use the water as a weapon? If water could move ships and ships' captains, why not move itself?

So she set her sights on the hull of Doucette's ship, the planks just above the keel.

She touched the current, let it gather and grow around her, let it flow into the water where it would. The amulet was nearly hot now, vibrating furiously from the power, as if funneling some of it away from Kit.

She let the current go and let the water fly.

It hit the side of the hull with a deep rumble of sound, as if the ship was groaning with pain.

For a moment there was nothing, and Kit feared she'd used the last of her energy for naught.

But then a muffled *crack* sounded through the water . . . and a foot-wide section of the hull simply disintegrated, oak and tar disappearing as water rushed into the hole she'd created.

The pull was strong, and she had to push aching muscles to get away from the stream. She wanted so badly to rest, to close her eyes and sleep. To open her mouth and breathe deeply.

She pinched her cheek sharply, hoping the pain would keep her conscious. *She had orders.* She couldn't leave this fight until she was satisfied Doucette was in the *Diana*'s brig—or no longer breathing.

She found the handholds in the hull, began to climb up the side of the ship, and when she broke the surface, gasped for air. "*Dastes*," she said, and kept climbing.

And as she climbed, she realized there were no new scars on her palms, nor any other injuries that she could feel, despite having been ensconced in magic. She surmised she had the amulet to thank for that.

The *Diana* fired, the cannoneers unaware their captain was attempting to board Doucette's ship. She covered her head with a bent arm, felt the ship shudder around her and the sprinkle of debris from the explosion.

She reached the gunwale and saw only chaos. There were few sailors on the ship; they'd either gone below to try to staunch the rising water, or they'd taken boats to escape. Soaked through, the amulet still and cool again, she strode toward the bow, and there found Doucette.

He lay on the deck, his back against the raised glass of the forecastle, a splinter extending nearly a foot from his chest.

She might have taken the ship, but the *Diana* had taken Doucette.

He looked up at her, blinked. "You are the one who stopped my fire." His voice carried a heavy Gallic accent, and it was hoarse, as if fire and smoke had scraped it raw.

"The current did the work; I just gave the current the opportunity."

He snorted. "We control the current, not the opposite. We are gods. Not in myth, but reality."

"If you're a god, why do you bow to Rousseau? Why aren't you the emperor? And why are you lying on this deck, your blood seeping into the wood?"

She heard the order from the *Diana* to cease fire; they'd seen her on deck. Then she heard members of her crew board the ship but kept her gaze and attention on the man at her feet.

"We are not gods," she said, when he didn't answer. "We bow to its whims, and not the reverse." She crouched in front of him. Death was near; she could see and smell it. But she'd have what information she could. "How do you avoid the consequences?"

His mouth formed a thin line. "There is always a consequence," he said, and pulled up his shirt. His abdomen was so thin, it was nearly concave. And it was crossed by dark veins that beat like monsters beneath his skin.

"*Vas tiva es?*" she murmured, and stumbled backward.

"Yes," Doucette said. "Now you can see the price that will be paid. By flesh or by blood, there is no way to avoid it. The world, the current, takes what it will. And leaves us to die alone. So we ought to take what we can, when we can." He turned his gaze to hers, offered a hard laugh. "You are on the precipice of something monumental, and you hardly know it."

Was this the cost of manipulating the current? The penalty the human body must bear? And what the amulet had really protected her from?

Doucette coughed until blood stained the deck, drawing her attention again. She would not lose him without getting the information she needed. "Where is the map?"

"What map?"

"The map you had at Auevilla—the map in the red leather portfolio. The map you showed to Monsieur Sedley. Where is it now?"

He looked momentarily startled that she knew of it, but then his smile grew again. "You will get no help from me." One final cough, and the light faded from his eyes.

"And you'll get none from me," she said. "Everything on this ship, including the map, now belongs to Her Majesty Queen Charlotte."

The cloaked woman pulled her sabre, silk flowing like water around her.

Kit's sabre was on the *Diana*, but she had her dagger. She pulled it from its sheath, circled the woman.

She moved forward with purpose, cloak flying, and no question about her intention. The sabre was aimed at Kit's heart. Kit used her dagger arm to deflect. But the sabre's tip grazed her forearm, sending hot pain across her skin.

Kit spun and came up hard, slicing against the woman's boot

and into tender skin beneath. The sabre flashed again and Kit jumped back, kicking upward as she moved.

That had the hood of the woman's cloak flying back, revealing her face.

And Kit stared into the face of a woman who looked like her. Not exactly the same—her chin was rounder, her nose a bit longer. But she had the same dark hair, marked by decorative braids of silver, and her eyes—wide and gray—were the same. And the bow of her lips matched Kit's nearly exactly. She could have been a sister.

She might have been a sister.

Kit's hands shook. "Who are you?"

The woman's expression went cold and unreadable. "My name is unimportant. He was only one, as am I. There are many more of us, and you cannot stop the Resurrection."

With a burst of speed, as if to punctuate the statement, she jumped onto the gunwale, then propelled herself into the water.

"Wait!" Kit said, and ran to the gunwale, gripping it with white knuckles as she searched for the woman. But the woman had disappeared beneath the waves.

Kit could take that fight, she thought, and prepared to go over the rail. But she found an arm on hers, gripping tightly.

She looked back, found Grant shaking his head. "You're bleeding," he said, and gestured to the cut on her other arm. "Even if you weren't exhausted, you'll call the dragons and whatever else lurks in the deep. You can't fight every monster yourself."

She was furious that he was right, and furious the woman had disappeared. She stared at the water for what felt like an hour, looking for some sign the woman had reappeared, had taken a breath. But she saw nothing.

Either the woman hadn't survived the deep, or she could hold her breath as long as Kit.

"She looked like me," Kit said after a moment.

"I know," Grant said. "But she wasn't you."

*You are on the precipice of something monumental.*

❧

The remaining Gallic sailors were taken as prisoners of war, and then the ship was quickly searched for contraband, munitions, and, of course, wine. With no one to pump the ship, it wouldn't remain afloat for long.

Kit searched Doucette's quarters personally. She found she needed the quiet, needed the space to think. To brood. To wonder at the girl who'd looked like her, who'd been willing to kill her on sight, and who'd then disappeared into the drink.

The room was bare as a gaol cell. Hammock, small desk. Nothing else. She found no map, no plans for the invasion of the Isles, no hint of what might come next, and no study of how Doucette managed to use magic so skillfully. Although the decay that had spread across his chest was probably explanation enough.

The ship was beginning to list, so she walked toward the door, but as she did, she spotted a bit of white near a plank in the wall. She walked to it, cocked her head, and wiggled the board. It was loose, so she pulled it away. The paper, a scrap of something torn, fluttered to the ground.

She picked it up, found a sketch in dark ink. Thirteen circles, or circular objects, drawn in a rough ring to make a larger circle. None were perfect, and there were gaps between them. But Kit had seen this shape before. She knew what it was.

A henge. A magical circle from the time of the old gods, used to calculate or communicate or otherwise structure the lives of the peoples who believed in them. Or, perhaps, used for some purpose no one had imagined.

Something related to Alignment?

She flipped over the paper, found nothing on the back. Found no other paper in the room but this one small piece, with its one small drawing. She didn't know why it was in Doucette's room, and the only ones who could tell her were dead or gone.

That was one more mystery she'd have to solve.

There were celebrations in the officers' mess, and Kit gave them the evening for their fun.

She made her way to her cabin and felt suddenly nervous. There were things she needed to say to Grant. Things that made her palms sweat.

"Did you find the map?"

She nearly jumped at his voice in the doorway.

"Not as such," she said, when her heart had slowed. "If there was a map, it wasn't there. But I did find this."

She offered him the bit of vellum.

"A henge?" he asked, glancing up at her.

"That would be my guess. Magic in the landscape and all that. Perhaps it meant something to Doucette, given his Alignment."

Grant nodded, offered the paper back. Kit put it in the portfolio on her desk, then turned back to him.

She nodded. "There are things—"

"I need to—"

They both began talking at once, then stumbled over the

pardons. Before Kit could speak again, Grant walked to the door, closed it, locked it, then came back to her. And there was misery in his eyes.

"Seeing you go into the water nearly killed me."

She just looked at him. "You said nothing."

"Because you needed me to say nothing. You needed me to support your position. So I did." He dropped his forehead to hers. "I want you, Kit. At my side, in my bed. And the wanting doesn't stop, despite the force of my will—or the fact that I'm a viscount. Irony, that."

She said nothing, as she wasn't sure what she ought to say, or what he needed to hear.

"So I'll withdraw my demand."

She went very still. "You'll . . . withdraw it?"

He took her hand, placed it against his chest. His heart, beating hard and strong, was an instant comfort. "Assuming you'll still have me, I will take as much as you're willing to give. No wedding, if that's not what you want. If that's not what you need."

That, for some absurd reason, was all she'd needed to hear. His support on the deck had been more than enough, more than she probably deserved given the things they'd said to each other. And that he was willing to let her be who she was—even if who she was wasn't a viscountess—was the most important thing.

"Just . . . come back to me."

"No," she said.

"No?" He looked absolutely baffled, and very insulted, and a little hurt. But there was a story she needed to tell yet.

"I slept in the window seat. At Grant Hall," she added lamely, as if he might be confused by the number of places she'd slept in window seats.

He watched her for a moment. "I know. Did you think Mrs. Spivey wouldn't tell me?"

Kit opened her mouth, closed it again. She hadn't thought of it at all, frankly.

"She was concerned you hadn't slept well," Grant said kindly, "and worried the room wasn't to your liking. I described to her your berth in the *Diana* and told her we had, as observing officers, been trained to sleep with our backs to a surface—boulder, wall, sandbank—that would provide us protection from enemies behind. It was one less vulnerability for us to concern ourselves with."

And yet, he'd not only allowed her to sleep behind him on the island, but had encouraged it. Because he trusted her. Because he *understood* her.

He smiled now. "I also told her you'd almost certainly let me know if you found your quarters lacking."

Kit snorted. "I'm not sure anyone could find that much silk and down and sunlight and art 'lacking.'"

The look he gave her was dry as the sand at Auevilla. "And yet," he said, with no little irony in his voice, "the point is, how you sleep is not a deficiency. Unless, of course, you think a soldier with nightmares of war is less of a man because of it?"

Her stare was flat. "Of course not."

"Well, then." He watched her carefully.

"I couldn't sleep a single night in that big bed in that big house. I don't know if it's something I could accustom myself to." She tucked a lock of hair behind her ear. "Do you think it's really possible?" she asked finally. "To be a different kind of viscountess?"

There was a light in his eyes, as if he saw victory on the horizon. "I think, Kit, that you have the courage and will to be whatever kind of viscountess you deem possible. I don't want you because you could become Viscountess Queenscliffe, but because Viscountess Queenscliffe could become you. My viscountess will not kowtow to the expectations of society, whatever those expectations may be. She will be loyal to herself, her family, her friends. Her crew. And if the Beau Monde doesn't like it, then damn the Beau Monde."

The words, the warmth in his eyes, put a warm glow in her belly. The kind a sailor could carry with her and use when times were cold and dark.

She cleared her throat, as this was the nervy bit. "In that case, I suppose I'd like you to withdraw your withdrawal."

The room went absolutely silent. So quiet, in fact, that Kit could hear her heart pounding against her chest. Since he said nothing, but just stared at her, she continued. "And I suppose I'm open to a betrothal. A very long betrothal."

He paused. "Is that the best offer I'm going to get?"

"Yes."

He looked down at her, hands linked behind his back. She had the decided sensation of being inspected by the viscount. Which would be an excellent penny-novel title. "You're quite certain."

"Yes, Rian."

His eyes glittered like fire. "You called me 'Rian.'"

"This seemed like an appropriate occasion."

He embraced her then. "Sometimes, Kit, circumstances bring us low. Sometimes, circumstances give us the opportunity to fly. I will never bring you low. And I will always help you fly."

"Give up your horses."

"No," he said. "Impertinent minx." He tugged her hair. "Let's go get drunk on very good Gallic wine."

"Very well," she said, in crisp aristocratic tones. "Maybe there are biscuits, too."

## ONE

Vampires were made, not born.

All except one.

All except me.

I was the daughter of vampires, born because magic and fate twisted together. I'd spent nineteen years in Chicago. Tonight, I stood nearly four hundred feet above Paris, several thousand miles away from the Windy City and the Houses in which most of its vampires lived.

Around me, visitors on the second level of the Eiffel Tower sipped champagne and snapped shots of the city. I closed my eyes against the warm, balmy breeze that carried the faint scent of flowers.

"Elisa, you cannot tell Paris goodbye with your eyes closed."

"I'm not saying goodbye," I said. "Because I'm coming back."

I opened my eyes, smiled at the vampire who appeared at my side with two plastic cones of champagne. Seraphine had golden skin and dark hair, and her hazel eyes shone with amusement.

"To Paris," I said, and tapped my cone against hers.

It had been four years since I'd last stepped foot in Chicago. Tomorrow, I'd go home again and visit the city and spend time with family and friends.

For twenty years, there'd been peace in Chicago among humans and sups, largely because of efforts by my parents—Ethan Sullivan and Merit, the Master and Sentinel, respectively, of Cadogan House. They'd worked to find a lasting peace, and had been so successful that Chicago had become a model for other communities around the world.

That's why Seri and I were going back. The city's four vampire Houses were hosting peace talks for vampires from Western Europe, where Houses had been warring since the governing council—the Greenwich Presidium—dissolved before I was born. And vampires' relations with the other supernaturals in Europe weren't any better. Chicago would serve as neutral territory where the Houses' issues could be discussed and a new system of government could be hammered out.

"You look . . . What is the word? Wistful?" Seri smiled. "And you haven't even left yet."

"I'm building up my immunity," I said, and sipped the champagne.

"You love Chicago."

"It's a great city. But I was . . . a different person in Chicago. I like who I am here."

Paris wasn't always peaceful. But it had given me the time

and distance to develop the control I'd needed over the monster that lived inside me. Because I wasn't just a vampire. . . .

Seri bumped her shoulder against mine supportively. "You will be the same person there as you are here. Miles change only location. They do not change a person's heart. A person's character."

I hoped that was true. But Seri didn't know the whole of it. She didn't know about the half-formed power that lurked beneath my skin, reveled in its anger. She didn't know about the magic that had grown stronger as I'd grown older, until it beat like a second heartbeat inside me.

Sunlight and aspen could kill me—but the monster could bury me in its rage.

I'd spent the past four years attending École Dumas, Europe's only university for supernaturals. I was one of a handful of vampires in residence. Most humans weren't changed into vampires until they were older; the change would give them immortality, but they'd be stuck at the age at which they'd been changed. No one wanted to be thirteen for eternity.

I hadn't been changed at all, but born a vampire—the one and only vampire created that way. Immortal, or so we assumed, but still for the moment aging.

The university was affiliated with Paris's Maison Dumas, one of Europe's most prestigious vampire Houses, where I'd lived for the past four years. I'd had a little culture shock at first, but I'd come to love the House and appreciate its logical approach to problem solving. If Cadogan was Gryffindor, all bravery and guts, Dumas was Ravenclaw, all intellect and cleverness. I liked being clever, and I liked clever people, so we were a good fit.

I'd had four years of training to develop the three components of vampire strength: physical, psychic, and strategic. I graduated a few months ago with a sociology degree—emphasis in sup-human relations—and now I was repaying my training the same way French vampires did, with a year of mandatory armed service for the House. It was a chance to see what I was made of, and to spend another year in the city I'd come to love.

I was three months into my service. Escorting delegates from Maison Dumas to Chicago for the peace talks was part of my work.

"How many suitcases are you bringing?"

I glanced at Seri with amusement. "Why? How many are you bringing?"

"Four." Seri did not travel lightly.

"We'll only be in Chicago for four days."

"I have diplomatic responsibilities, Elisa."

I sipped my champagne. "That's what French vampires say when they pack too much. I have a capsule wardrobe."

"And that is what American vampires say when they do not pack enough. You also have diplomatic responsibilities."

"I have responsibilities to the House. That's different."

"Ah," she said, smiling at me over the rim of her drink. "But which one?"

"*Maison Dumas*," I said, in an accent that was pretty close to perfect. "I'm not going to Chicago on behalf of Cadogan House. It's just a bonus."

"I look forward to meeting your parents. And I'm sure they'll be glad to see you."

"I'll be glad to see them, too. It's just—I've changed a lot in the last few years. Since the last time I went home."

They'd visited Paris twice since I'd been gone, and we'd had fun walking through the city, seeing the sights. But I still felt like I'd been holding myself back from them. Maybe I always had.

"It's not about you or Cadogan or Chicago," I'd told my father, when we'd stood outside the private terminal at O'Hare, in front of the jet that would take me across the world. I'd been struggling to make him understand. "It's about figuring out who I am."

In Chicago, I was the child of Ethan and Merit. And it had been hard to feel like anything more than a reflection of my parents and my birth, which made me a curiosity for plenty of sups outside Cadogan House who treated me like a prize. And the possibility I might be able to bear children made me, at least for some, a prize to be captured.

I'd wanted to be something more, something different . . . Something that was just me.

"You couldn't fail us by living your life the way you want," my father had said. "It's your life to live, and you will make your own choices. You always have."

He'd tipped my chin up with the crook of his finger, forcing me to meet his gaze.

"There are some decisions that we make, and some that are made for us. Sometimes you accept the path that's offered to you, and you live that path—that life—with grace. And sometimes you push forward, and you chart your own path. That decision is yours. It's always been yours.

"I don't want you to go, because I'm selfish. Because you are my child." His eyes had burned fiercely, emeralds on fire. "But if this is your path, you must take it. Whatever happens out there, you always have a home here."

He'd kissed my forehead, then embraced me hard. "*Test your wings,*" he'd quietly said. A suggestion. A request. A hope. *"And fly."*

I had flown. And I'd read and walked and learned and trained, just like everyone else.

In Paris, I'd been just another vampire. And the anonymity, the freedom, had been exhilarating.

"We all carry expectations," Seri said quietly, her eyes suddenly clouded. "Sometimes our own, sometimes others'. Both can be heavy."

Seri came from what the European Houses called "good blood." She'd been made by a Master vampire with power, with money, with an old name, and with plenty of cachet—and that mattered to French vampires. Seri had been the last vampire he'd made before his death, and those of his name were expected to be aristocrats and socialites. Unlike in the US, French vampires selected their own Houses. She'd picked Maison Dumas instead of Maison Bourdillon, the House of her Master. That hadn't made her many friends among Bourdillon's progeny, who decided she was wasting her legacy.

"Are you excited to see Chicago?" I asked her.

"I am excited to see the city," she said, "if not optimistic about what will come of the talks. Consider Calais."

The most recent attack had taken place in Calais a week ago. Vampires from Paris's Maison Solignac had attacked Maison Saint-Germaine because they believed they weren't getting a big enough cut of the city port's profits. In the process, four vampires and two humans had been killed.

The European Houses had lived together peacefully, at least by human standards, for hundreds of years. But after the GP's dissolution, all bets were off. There was power to be had, and vampires found that irresistible.

More than a dozen delegates from France, including Seri and Marion, the Master of Maison Dumas, would participate in the talks. Marion and Seri would be accompanied by nearly a dozen staff, including Marion's bodyguard, Seri's assistant, Odette, and me.

"Yeah," I said. "I don't know how successful it will be, either. But refusing to talk certainly isn't doing much good."

Seri nodded and drank the last of her champagne as two guards passed us—one human, one vampire—and silenced the chatter. They wore black fatigues and berets, and looked suspiciously at everyone they passed. Part of the joint task force created by the Paris Police Prefecture to keep the city safe.

The vampire's eyes shifted to me, then Seri. He acknowledged us, scanned the rest of the crowd, and kept walking, katana belted at his waist.

Vampires in the US and Western Europe used the long and slightly curved Japanese swords, which were sharp and deadly as fangs, but with a much longer reach.

Sorcerers had magic. Shifters had their animal forms. Vampires had katanas.

"There's Javí," Seraphine whispered, and watched as they kept moving, then disappeared around the corner. Javí was a Dumas vampire doing his year of service.

These weren't the only guards at the Eiffel Tower. Humans and vampires alike stood at the edge of the crowd below, wearing body armor and weapons and trying to keep safe the tourists and residents enjoying a warm night in the Champ de Mars.

We turned back to the rail, looked over the city. So much white stone, so many slate roofs, so many people enjoying the warm night. But the specter of violence, of fear, hung over it. And that was hard to shake. No city was perfect, not when people lived in it.

"Let us take a photo," Seri said, clearly trying to lift the mood. She put an arm around me, then pulled out her screen and angled the narrow strip of glass and silicon for a perfect shot.

"To Paris!" she said, and we smiled.

The moment recorded, she checked the time before putting the device away again. "We should get back. The Auto will arrive in a few hours." She slipped an arm through mine. "This will be an adventure, and we will be optimists. And I look forward to pizza and Chicago dogs and . . . *Comment dites-on 'milk shake de gateau'?*"

"Cake shake," I said with a smile. "You and my mother are going to get along just fine."

We'd only just turned to head toward the elevator when screams sliced through the air, followed by a wave of nervous, fearful magic that rolled up from the ground.

We looked back and over the rail.

Even from this height, they were visible. Five vampires in gleaming red leather running through the green space with katanas in one hand and small weapons in the other.

Not knives; there was no gleam from the flashing lights on the Tower.

What was shaped like a knife, but held no metal, and would turn a vampire to dust?

Humans had been wrong about vampires and crosses, but they'd been absolutely right about stakes. An aspen stake through the heart was a guaranteed way to put the "mortal" in "immortal."

I didn't know which House the vampires were from. I was too high to see their faces, and the gleaming red leather didn't give anything away. Leather was a vampire favorite, and French vampire Houses appreciated fashion as much as the French fashion houses did.

But their intent was clear enough. They ran through the crowd, weapons drawn, and took aim at everyone in their path. Screams, sharp and terrified, filled the air. I watched one person fall, another dive to the ground to avoid the strike, a third try unsuccessfully to fight back against the vampire's increased strength.

Paris was under attack. My stomach clenched with nerves and anger.

I wanted to help. I was stronger and faster than most humans, and trained as well as any vampire from Maison Dumas would have been. But there were rules. There were roles and responsibilities. The Paris police, the task force members, were supposed to respond to events. I was just a civilian, and only a temporary one at that. I worked for Dumas, and should have been focused on getting Seri safely back to Maison Dumas.

But the screams . . .

The guards who'd walked past minutes before ran back to the rail beside us and stared at the scene below in horror. And neither of them made a move toward the ground. It took only a second to guess why.

"Can you jump?" I asked Javí, the vampire.

He looked at me, eyes wide. *"Quoi?"*

I had to remember where I was, shook my head, tried again. *"Pouvez-vous sauter?"*

*"Non."* Javí looked down. *"Non. Trop haut."*

Too high. Most vampires could jump higher and farther than humans, and we could jump down from heights that would easily kill humans. But the trick required training, which I'd learned the hard way—believing I could fly from the widow's walk atop Cadogan House. I'd broken my arm, but vampires healed quickly, so that hadn't been much of a deterrent. My mother had taught me the rest.

Javí couldn't jump, so he'd have to wait for the elevator or take the hundreds of stairs down to ground level.

But I didn't have to wait.

I squeezed Seri's hand, told Javí to take care of her, and hoped he'd obey.

Before anyone could argue, or I could think better of it, I slid the katana from his scabbard, climbed onto the railing, and walked into space.

~⌒~

I descended through rushing darkness. A human might have had a few seconds of free fall before the deadly landing. But for a vampire, it was less a fall than a long and lazy step. Maybe we compressed space; maybe we elongated time. I didn't understand the physics, but I loved the sensation. It was as close to flying as I was likely to get.

The first level of the Eiffel Tower was wider than the second, so I had to jump down to the first level—causing more than a few humans to scream—before making it to the soft grass below. I landed in a crouch, katana firmly in hand.

My fangs descended, the predator preparing to battle. While I couldn't see it, I knew my eyes had silvered, as they did when vampires experienced strong emotions. It was a reminder—to humans, to prey, to enemies—that the vampire wasn't human, but something altogether different. Something altogether more dangerous.

Two humans were dead a few feet away, their eyes open and staring, blood spilling onto the grass from the lacerations at their necks. The vampires who'd murdered them hadn't even bothered to bite, to drink. This attack wasn't about need. It was about hatred.

I was allowed only a moment of shocked horror—of seeing how quickly two lives had been snuffed out—before the scent of blood blossomed in the air again, unfurling like the petals of a crimson poppy.

I looked back.

A vampire kneeled over a human woman. She was in her early twenties, with pale skin, blond hair, and terror in her eyes. The vampire was even paler, blood pumping through indigo veins just below the surface. His hair was short and ice blond, his eyes silver. And the knife he held above the woman's chest was covered with someone else's blood.

Anger rose, hot and intense, and I could feel the monster stir inside, awakened by the sheer power of the emotion. But I was still in Paris. And here, I was in control. I shoved it back down, refused to let it surface.

"*Arrêtez!*" I yelled out, and, to emphasize the order, held my borrowed katana in front of me, the silver blade reflecting the lights from the Eiffel Tower.

The vampire growled, lip curled to reveal a pair of needle-sharp fangs, hatred burning in his eyes. I didn't recognize him, and I doubted he recognized me beyond the fact that I was a vampire not from his House—and that made me an enemy.

He rose, stepping away from the human as if she were nothing more than a bit of trash he'd left behind. His knuckles around the stake were bone white, tensed and ready.

Released from his clutches, the human took one look at my silvered eyes and screamed, then began to scramble away from us. She'd survive—if I could lure him away from her.

The vampire slapped my katana away with one hand, drove the stake toward me with the other.

I might have been young for a vampire, but I was well trained. I moved back, putting us both clear of the human, and kicked. I made contact with his hand, sent the stake spinning through the air. He found his footing and picked up the stake. Undeterred, he moved toward me. This time, he kicked. I blocked it, but the force of the blow sent pain rippling through my arm.

He thrust the stake toward me like a fencer with a foil.

The movement sent light glimmering against the gold on his right hand. A signet ring, crowned by a star ruby—and the symbol of Maison Saint-Germaine.

I doubted it was a coincidence Saint-Germaine vampires were attacking the ultimate symbol of Paris only a few nights after they'd been attacked by a Paris House. While I understood why they'd want revenge, terrorizing and murdering humans wasn't the way to do it. It wasn't fair to make our issues their problems.

I darted back to avoid the stake, then sliced down with the katana when he advanced again.

"You should have stayed in Calais," I said in French, and got no response but a gleam in his eyes. He spun to avoid that move, but I managed to nick his arm. Blood scented the air, and my stomach clenched with sudden hunger and need. But ignoring that hunger was one of the first lessons my parents had taught me. There was a time and a place to drink, and this wasn't it.

I swept out a leg, which had him hopping backward, then rotated into a kick that sent him to his knees. He grabbed my legs, shifting his weight so we both fell forward onto the grass. The katana rolled from my grasp.

My head rapped against the ground, and it took a moment to realize that he'd climbed over me and grabbed the stake. He raised it, his eyes flashing in the brilliantly colored lights that reflected across the grass from the shining monument behind us.

I looked at that stake—thought of what it could do and was almost certainly about to do to me—and my mind went absolutely blank. I could see him, hear the blood rushing in my ears, and didn't have the foggiest idea what I was supposed to do, like the adrenaline had forced a hiccup in my brain.

Fortunately, beyond fear, and beneath it, was instinct. And I didn't need to think of what would bring a man down. He may have been immortal, and he may have been a vampire. Didn't matter. This move didn't discriminate.

I kicked him in the groin.

He groaned, hunched over, and fell over on the grass, body curled over his manhood.

"Asshole," I muttered, chest heaving as I climbed to my feet and kicked him over, then added a kick to the back of his ribs to encourage him, politely, to stay there.

Two guards ran over, looked at me, then him.

"Elisa Sullivan," I said. "Maison Dumas." Most vampires who weren't Masters used only their first name. I'd gotten an exception since it wasn't practical for a kid to have just one name.

They nodded, confiscated the stake, and went about the business of handcuffing the vampire. I picked up the katana, wiped the blade against my pant leg, and dared a look at the field around me.

Two of the other Saint-Germaine vampires were alive, both on their knees, hands behind their heads. I didn't see the others, and unless they'd run away, which seemed unlikely, they'd probably been taken down by the Paris police or Eiffel Tower guards. Fallen into cones of ash due to a deadly encounter with aspen.

Humans swarmed at the periphery of the park, where Paris police worked to set up a barrier.

Some of the humans who'd survived the attack were helping the wounded. Others stood with wide eyes, shaking with shock and fear. And more yet had pulled out their screens to capture video of the fight. The entire world was probably watching, whether they wanted to see or not.

I found Seri standing at the edge of the park, her eyes silver, her expression fierce and angry. She wasn't a fighter, but she knew injustice when she saw it.

I walked toward her, my right hip aching a bit from hitting the ground, and figured I'd passed my first field test.

I suddenly wasn't so sad to be leaving Paris.

**Chloe Neill** is the *New York Times* and *USA Today* bestselling author of the Captain Kit Brightling, Heirs of Chicagoland, Chicagoland Vampires, Devil's Isle, and Dark Elite novels. She was born and raised in the South but now makes her home in the Midwest, where she lives with her gamer husband and their bosses/dogs, Baxter and Scout. Chloe is a voracious reader and obsessive Maker of Things; the crafting rotation currently involves baking and quilting. She believes she is exceedingly witty; her husband has been known to disagree.

## CONNECT ONLINE

ChloeNeill.com
 AuthorChloeNeill
 ChloeNeill

Ready to find
your next great read?

Let us help.

**Visit prh.com/nextread**

Penguin
Random
House